THE LAST MIDWIFE

KAREN LAWRENCE

exodus
— BOOKS —

THE LAST MIDWIFE

For all the midwives, especially those who taught me, supported me, worked, laughed, and cried with me.

You are all warriors.

'For in any society, the way a woman gives birth and the kind of care given to her and the baby points as sharply as an arrowhead to the key values in the culture.'
    - Sheila Kitzinger, Women as Mothers,

'The king of Egypt said to the Hebrew midwives ... when you act as midwives to the Hebrew women, and see them on the birthstool, if it is a boy, kill him; but if it is a girl, she shall live.' But the midwives feared God; they did not do as the king of Egypt commanded them, but they let the boys live. ... So God dealt well with the midwives; and the people multiplied and became very strong.'
    - The Book of Exodus, Chapter 1: 15-20

PROLOGUE

JOIN OUR TEAM

Deliver London's Future: Join Our Team at the Genesis Centre

re you an ambitious and hard-working nurse with a passion for obstetrics? We are recruiting dedicated staff at all levels to join our dynamic team.

The Genesis Centre

The Genesis Centre is London's newest fully-sustainable Women's Health Hub. We pride ourselves on delivering exceptional care . Our state-of-the-art unit is equipped with the latest technology, and our expert staff are committed to the highest standards in future-oriented healthcare.

What We Offer

- Comprehensive Training: Our training programmes

are designed to enhance your skills and ensure you
stay at the forefront of obstetric nursing.

- Health Worker Visas for International Candidates:
  We celebrate diversity and can help you arrange
  your visa via our smooth and seamless onboarding
  pathway.
- Accommodation: We provide comfortable and
  convenient accommodation to make your transition
  smooth and hassle-free.
- Generous Salary: Enjoy a competitive salary that
  reflects your expertise and dedication.
- Golden Hello: Generous joining bonus to help you
  feel at home right away.
- Rapid Promotion Opportunities: For the right
  candidates, we offer fast-tracked career
  advancement, so you can grow and progress within
  our organisation.

What We Are Looking For

- Ambition: A drive to excel and a commitment to
  continuous professional development.
- Hard Work: A strong work ethic and the ability to
  thrive in a fast-paced environment.
- Willingness to Learn: An openness to new
  knowledge and techniques in the ever-evolving field
  of obstetrics.

How to Apply

If you are ready to take the next step in your career and join our
prestigious team dedicated to delivering new opportunities, we

want to hear from you. Send your CV and cover letter to recruitment@genesis.MPH.uk.

Join The Genesis Centre and help set new standards in obstetric care. We look forward to welcoming you aboard!

PART I

1

A GOOD NURSE

'So what's it like in London? I'm so jealous! Can you really buy anything in the shops? Have you seen the Defender's Palace? Do you get to eat meat every week?'

'*Lente, lente,* slow down Gemma. I can't tell you everything at once. It's - well, it's fantastic. You can have meat most days if you want, and everything is so big and bright.'

'Like Palermo?'

'Even busier, but you feel safer. The roads are wide, and it's all very clean - no rubbish in the streets, no graffiti. The skyscrapers shine in the sun. Most of the buildings are new, and the people are rich; they wear lovely clothes, and talk slow and low, like this: *Good morning. How are you today?*' Chiara does her best imitation of an English accent, and Gemma giggles.

'What's the tastiest thing you've eaten?'

Where to begin? How can she explain the shops bursting with melons, strawberries, and foods she's never heard of - more than she ever dreamed of?

'It's all delicious - I'll send you some English treats. Chocolate?'

'Ah *grazie,* I can't wait!' Gemma's thin cheeks turn pink; you can almost hear her salivate. 'You're so lucky, Chia. Hey, let me see your room? Do you have air-con?'

'Take a look.' Chiara scans the little bedroom with the screen of her phone. 'It's in a tower called Francis Galton - I guess that must be an English saint? Lots of nurses live here. I've got my bathroom, and there's a kitchen down the hall. I don't think you need air-con in England - it's freezing outside and raining all the time.' She's had to buy a thick coat and one of those English woolly hats just to survive the walk from the nurses' accommodation to the Genesis Centre.

'Your own bathroom - like in a hotel? And friends? Do you have parties? It's so boring here I've started talking to myself.' Gemma's features take on that pinched, unhappy look.

'I don't have time for parties.' No time for anything except work, study and sleep.

'But there's loads of people, right? And bars and nightclubs? Have you bought any new clothes yet? Can you get me some jeans, real American ones?'

'I'll try, but there isn't much time to go shopping, and I don't get paid till the end of the month. And I promised Mamma I'd send her money for the roof first.'

'Please Chiara!' Gemma makes the puppy face she knows her big sister can't resist.

'Sì, okay. As soon as I can, I'll send you some Levis. But I'm not here to shop. I'm here to work.'

'Yeah, I know. Mamma's still telling everyone how proud she is of her brilliant daughter in London. She was showing Padre Antonio the picture of you in your uniform after Mass last Sunday. Again.' Gemma rolls her eyes.

'Dear Mamma! But I've got to make sure they keep me on. I'm still on probation, don't forget.'

'You'll be fine. You were good at looking after the old people, weren't you? They made you that big cake when you left, and some of the old ladies cried - I saw them.'

'Yes, but it's different here, with babies.' You're not even supposed to call them babies, for a start, but she won't tell Gemma that. It would take too long to explain.

'You'll still be great. And it wasn't your fault about Nonna.' Gemma nods decisively, but Chiara squeezes her lips together; no point going over all that again.

'Have you cuddled lots of cute babies?' Gemma returns to a safer subject. 'Have you actually seen one being born yet? Was it gross?'

'No, not gross. It's lovely seeing them come out all pink and wriggling and alive. Like a miracle, but the doctors do most of it, of course, and I have to concentrate to make sure I get my bit right. I do all the checks and enter everything onto the computer. There's more to being a good nurse than cuddling babies.'

Graphs, timings, observations, efficiency. You've all got the potential to be excellent nurses, Sister Miller told them on the induction day. Don't disappoint me or yourself.

'You're so lucky, Chiara.'

'*Sì.* So how's college?'

Gemma grimaces.

'Boring. It takes hours on the bus every day, and the teachers are useless.'

'Well, if you work hard -.'

'Yeah, yeah, work hard, get qualifications and *tutto è perfetto!*' Gemma's pretty mouth twists into a sneer. 'It's perfect for you, Chiara; you're the clever one. What's the point in college when you live in a dump like this? If Mamma would let me go to Napoli, I could get a job right now. This place is finished - just empty houses and old people waiting to die. The Ferrantes moved out last week, so I'm literally the only teenager left in the village.'

'Armando and Maria? Did they find work? Where did they go?'

'The usual - Napoli and beyond. Maria has a cousin or something in Germany. Why don't we have any rich relatives abroad?'

'Well you do now!' Chiara taps her own chest. 'A big sister in London! Not rich exactly, but I'm working on it.'

'Yeah, I guess, but it's so unfair - you having fun in England while I'm stuck here in this hole.'

Gemma pouts childishly, and Chiara sighs.

'Gemma - you know I'd have brought you with me if I could. And maybe one day, if -.'

'Yeah, if I work hard and pass all my exams and then study for another hundred million years. Besides Mamma got me trapped here; she says I'm all she's got left. I'll never have a fancy room like yours.'

'It's not that fancy,' Chiara says, needled, 'and it's not all fun here either.' She glances up at the clock. Less than an hour until she has to be on the ward again. She takes a big gulp of her coffee.

'Hey, what's that on your arm - the red thing? Did you get a new sports watch? It's flashing.'

'Is it?' As Chiara tilts her wrist to look at the screen on her Femband, her cooling coffee cascades down her front. '*O dio mio!* This was my last clean uniform. I'll have to iron yesterday's and hope Sister doesn't notice. Sorry, Gia, but I've got to go.'

Chiara is already unbuttoning her dress. She needs to get this into cold water straight away and pray it doesn't stain. So stupid!

'Call me again soon, hey?' The corners of Gemma's mouth wobble. 'I miss you.'

'I miss you too. I'll call as soon as I can.'

Chiara hangs up. She checks her Femband again, but it was only a reminder to record when her period starts. That's another thing she hasn't explained to Gemma yet - the whole Femband system. Another day, perhaps.

She runs water into the basin, shoves in the coffee-drenched dress, and digs through her laundry basket for the least grubby alternative. A good nurse is always smart, clean and well-turned out. She plugs in the iron to heat up while she showers. She'll eat an energy bar on the way to work. A good nurse is never late.

A LULLABY CASE

'You coming out with us tonight, Chiara?' The plump nurse speaks through a mouthful of cereal. Chiara shakes her head.

'I need to study.' There's another test next week, something about neonatal assessment. She hasn't even read the material yet.

'Give yourself a break, sweetheart. All work and no play? You won't last five minutes in this place without some down-time. It's two-for-one cocktails on Thursdays at the *Starlet*, plus there'll be medical students. Thought you said your boyfriend back in Italy had dumped you? The lads like a filly - taste of danger.'

She cocks an eyebrow at Chiara, who blushes scarlet like her wristband. The numbers on its screen indicate that her ten-minute break is almost over.

'Maybe next time.' Chiara gets up and replaces her book into her locker. 'I need to go. I have to take the next lady to Theatre and she was very nervous earlier.'

'Bay Four? Twitchy little incubator with the blonde hubby? Good luck with that one, sweetie. Rather you than me.' The plump nurse turns her attention back to her breakfast.

Chiara's shoes squeak on the shiny floor as she hurries to Bay Four. Her next mamma-to-be is called Katie, but Chiara's not supposed to call her that. It's too familiar, Sister says. Katie had a lot of questions when she arrived on Deliveries this morning. Now she is pacing the narrow space beside the bed, her hands clasped across the mound of her belly. The blue band that pregnant women wear looks too tight on her swollen wrist. Her husband, who does indeed have strikingly fair hair, sits bolt upright in the chair.

Chiara places a hand on Katie's shoulder, guides her back to the bed, and sits down beside her. Of course it's scary, having your first baby. Back home in Sicily, on the geriatric ward, Chiara used to sit for hours with the confused old ladies, brushing their thin hair and listening to their broken fragments of stories. So much of nursing is about making people feel cared for. But everything seems so rushed here.

'Don't worry, Mrs Harris,' Chiara says. That's what she's supposed to call her, Mrs Harris, or 'the incubator'. 'You will be fine, you and your little baby - sorry, neonate. The Genesis Centre is the best hospital in London - everyone says so. Our doctors do lots of deliveries every day. I will come with you to Theatre, and I'll be there the whole time to watch over you. You and your baby are safe, I promise you.'

A tear spills out of Katie's eye and rolls down her cheek. She looks as if she needs a hug but it's against infection control.

'I'm your nurse, Katie,' Chiara says. Sister Miller might be watching through the cameras, but surely she can't hear what everyone's saying? 'I'm here to look after you. Soon we'll be together in recovery, and I'll be helping you feed your baby. We'll dress her in that beautiful rosebud sleepsuit you chose for her. And you have a name, yes? Bella? And it's Italian - *piccola Bella*. You'll be a wonderful mamma, Katie, I know it.'

Katie wipes her eyes.

'Thank you, nurse. You're so kind. I'm so lucky to have you looking after me.'

Chiara completes the pre-Theatre checklist. Anti-sickness meds, shave, catheter, anti-embolism stockings. It's getting easier already. And she's here, after all the form-filling, and the tests, and the interviews, working in the newest hospital, in the richest, safest city in Europe. Sometimes she has to pinch her cheeks to be sure she isn't dreaming.

'KNIFE TO SKIN,' announces the scrub nurse.

The lights glare white overhead. After the skin comes yellow fat, then fascia, then muscle. The surgeon opens Katie like a parcel, layer by layer, looking for the treasure inside. Little wafts of smoke spiral upwards as he cauterises the blood vessels. It smells like barbecued meat. The suction slurps and guzzles as the collection vessel begins to fill with body fluids. Now he's pushing those big curves of stainless steel deep into the wound and pulling, pulling her apart. It takes a lot of force. More than you might expect.

Chiara's scalp itches, up there on the right, under her theatre cap. Can't scratch it. Mustn't touch anything. She's sterile. A twitch and wriggle of the nose will have to do. She pulled her hair up too tight in the rush to get ready this morning. Maybe she should cut it shorter; it would be easier for work. But Nonna always loved Chiara's long hair. *'Like Santa Rosalia,'* she used to say

'Nurse? Is everything all right?'

Katie's top half is hidden behind the blue screen shielding her from the sight of her own insides. Her voice sounds shaky. Chiara can't see her face; she has to stand here with the sterile cot behind the surgeon, ready to take the baby.

'Is everything all right?' Katie asks again. No one answers. The scrub nurse is busy with her trays of scalpels and forceps. The surgeon isn't speaking. The anaesthetist seems preoccupied with his infusion pumps and gases. Katie's husband is beside her, but he's speechless - probably as anxious as his wife.

Smiling as wide as she can behind her mask and goggles, Chiara steps around the screen. No one shouts; perhaps no one noticed her move from her position. Katie raises her head off her pillow and reaches out her hand. Chiara keeps her gloved hands raised in front of her chest. Sterile.

'Don't worry,' she says. 'Little Bella is almost here.'

The scrub nurse directs a frown at Chiara, before passing the surgeon more swabs. Chiara hurries back to her spot beside the cot. It won't be much longer. But where is the paediatrician? He should be here by now. Just as she's staring to worry, a young man wearing scrubs decorated with cartoon animals comes rushing through the double doors. He pulls on a mask and a pair of gloves and comes to stand beside Chiara.

'Sorry,' he says, after a quick flick through Katie's notes. 'I was held up on Butterfly Ward, talking with a two-year-old.' He speaks with a soft Hispanic accent. Floppy hair spills out around the sides of his Theatre cap. 'I am Salvador,' he tells her. 'One of the baby doctors. You are new here, I think?' His face is friendly - at least what she can see of it'.

Chiara,' she whispers.

'Chiara,' he repeats, saying her name the way they say it at home. '*Italiana?*'

'*Sì*. I was a nurse in Sicily. I arrived in London three weeks ago.'

'First time here? Are you settling in okay?' He checks the equipment Chiara has laid out on the resuscitation trolley. Hopefully she's got everything correct.

'It's all very new,' she begins. But her words are obliterated by a loud gurgle of fluid like bathwater going down the plughole. The surgeon has incised the uterus and cut open the amniotic sac. They'll need the cot in a moment.

'Relax,' Salvador says. 'You're doing fine.' Wisps of black beard curl around the edges of his mask. He has bright blue eyes and he's looking straight at her. Chiara's face flushes. She wants to hide it but she mustn't touch anything, so she focuses on the dials on the medical gas cylinders.

'Very new,' she repeats. 'Thank you. There's a lot to learn.'

He nods sympathetically.

'So many protocols, hey? It was the same for me at first.'

'Oh yes - .' She's about to tell him what happened last week, when she forgot to shave the woman - sorry, incubator - and the obstetrician was annoyed, but another voice cuts in:

'You. New nurse. Did you hear me, or are you too busy with your boyfriend over there? The cot for the neonate, if you don't mind.'

Chiara feels her blush deepen. She grabs the sterile cot and wheels it to the side of the operating couch.

'Sorry,' she says.'

The surgeon lifts a wet and bloody infant from Katie's abdomen, wipes it with a large swab, and places it into the cot. The baby is small and purple, like a doll drowned in beetroot juice. A tiny girl. Bella. Usually they kick and wriggle as they come out, but this one isn't moving. She's not crying either.

Chiara hurries over to the resuscitation trolley with her precious load. The heater is on, and the towels are warm. Probably this little one needs a good rub, a bit of stimulation to get her breathing, like the doctor did last week when a baby came out flat. *'Flat'* - that's what they call it. Bella lies still under the lights. Salvador picks her up, looks at her, then puts her down again. She is floppy, limbs dangling. Chiara's stomach feels empty, as if she has dropped down several floors in a lift. The clock ticks on the wall.

'She is not breathing, no?'

But Salvador knows this; he is the expert, the baby doctor. The baby's chest is motionless. Her purple colour is deepening to a dusky blue. But it will be okay. Chiara did that training course last week: *Basic Newborn Resuscitation.* You have to use the mask, get a good seal over the baby's mouth and nose, then give it five long slow breaths to inflate the lungs. Usually that's enough to get them started. If not you repeat the breaths, and do chest compressions, and ...

Why isn't he doing it?

Salvador inspects the baby. He looks at her hands and feet. He opens her eyelids, measures her head, turns her over and runs his finger down her spine. He listens to her chest with a stethoscope. He seems to be moving in slow motion, like someone underwater. How long has it been now? Surely Salvador knows what to do? Chiara's heart is racing, racing.

'Salvador,' she hears her voice squeak. 'The baby is not breathing. Why are you not helping her? The mask? No?'

Salvador reaches for the mask and bag. Chiara can't decipher the look on his face. He squeezes a little air into the baby's lungs. Once, twice. The infant wriggles a little, twitches, but doesn't cry. Salvador stops, looks at the baby's hands again, lowers his head.

What's wrong?

'Is my baby all right?' Katie calls from across the room. Nobody answers. The silence hangs like fog on a river. The baby twitches again and opens her mouth, gasping like a landed fish.

Chiara reaches for the mask, ready to elbow Salvador out of the way. Even if they shout at her, she has to. She's done all the training after all. But he grabs her wrist and yanks it back. His grip hurts.

'No,' he says. 'No, Chiara. We can't.' His voice is a sharp hiss.

'What? Why? We need to be quick. Baby needs help to breathe.'

'No,' he repeats, shaking his head. 'God, I hate these cases.'

'What cases? What do you mean? Let me do it.' She tries to twist free but he's too strong.

'Shh!' Salvador puts a finger to his lips. 'Don't make it worse for them. This is a lullaby case; I'm certain this time.' He screws up his eyes. 'We have to do our job; be decisive, my consultant says.' His voice drops to a whispered torrent of swear words in Spanish and English. Chiara feels sick.

Katie calls again, 'Is my baby all right?' You can hear the panic in her voice.

Salvador releases Chiara's wrist and shows her the baby's hands. His own hands are trembling.

'Look, she's got a sixth finger on both hands. And she's small - two thousand, three hundred grammes. Her head is small too and her ears are low-set. It might be a rare syndrome, something the antenatal screening missed. I can't take the risk.'

'What risk? Look, she's moving her legs.'

'My God. Be quiet and help me, Chiara. Listen: if we resus a defective neonate there'll be a shitstorm, and we'll get the blame, me and you, Chiara. We could both lose our jobs, or worse. Is that what you want?' Salvador's whisper is frantic.

Chiara blinks. The mask and bag lie beside the baby, easily within her reach.

'Shouldn't the parents decide?' she falters.

'No. You don't understand. It's not up to them.'

And she doesn't, not really. She knows about the Population Mandate, of course - how couples have to get a licence, have to be married and prove they've got enough income before they're allowed to incubate. And then, once the baby's here, the mother gets Sealed, to protect the planet and give everyone a future. The slogans emblazon the sides of the trams and shine out from signboards on street corners:

'Every Child Counts.'

'Small Families, Bright Futures.'

Baby Bella is a dark, cyanotic indigo. Her little body shudders.

'Do we have a decision? I can't stand here all day.' The surgeon looks at Salvador, eyebrows raised.

'Yes, sir. Sorry for the delay, sir. I wanted to be sure. It's a Type Two - Lullaby Case. Maternal sterilisation not required.' Salvador's voice cracks; he sounds like a little boy forced to grow up too fast.

The surgeon nods and turns back to his work. The scrub nurse passes him sutures. The anaesthetist says something to Katie and her husband. Chiara doesn't catch his words. There was a dog once, on the street in Palermo; Chiara saw it run over by a lorry, its back completely crushed. Its howl of agony comes back to her now. Chiara did not know a woman could make such a sound.

'No. My baby. Perhaps there is a mistake. Do something, please. Help her. My baby. My baby!'

Chiara's skin turns to ice. She promised. She said she would look after Katie and her baby, she would keep them both safe. She wants to run to Katie's side. She wants to seize the baby, breathe air into her mouth, save her.

But there are so many rules in the hospital. The Theatre staff all look calm, professional, slightly bored even, as if they've seen this all before. And she hasn't done that reading yet, on neonatal assessment. She's got such a lot to learn.

What would a good nurse do?

Chiara tries to step forward but it's like one of those nightmares when your legs turn soggy like polenta, and you want to run but you're paralysed.

So she stands and watches as Salvador places his right hand over the baby's face. He pinches her nose closed with his finger and thumb. He stops her mouth. The baby's legs are still moving.

'Chiara, please, could you draw up some potassium chloride? Three mils should be enough. My hands -.'

Salvador raises his left hand for her to see: it's shaking uncontrollably. He jerks his head towards a tray of implements. There's a tiny cannula set, some needles and syringes, and two glass vials containing a clear liquid. Familiar equipment; a simple nursing task. A good nurse does as she is told. Perhaps this is a medication to help the baby, Chiara tells herself, even as she knows it is not.

Katie's cries cut off; the anaesthetist has put her to sleep. Chiara breaks the end off the first vial, but she isn't quick enough and a shard of glass pierces her finger. It smarts, sharp as a bite, but she takes no notice. She finds a syringe, inserts the needle into the vial, and draws up the dose. Then the second vial. Three millilitres, just as he asked. As she passes the drug to Salvador she sees blood running from her cut finger down to her wrist. She watches it trickle as he injects the potassium into the baby's vein.

Chiara shuts her eyes and breathes in and out three times. The cold has got deep inside her now. When she looks again, the baby is still. Her naked body is a dark mottled purple, her mouth open and unmoving. Salvador is listening with his stethoscope.

He listens for a long time. Then he stops, folds up the stethoscope and replaces it into the pocket of his scrubs. He writes something in the notes, then wraps the infant in a white towel so that only her face is showing. She looks as if she is sleeping.

Salvador is saying something about calling the mortuary. About speaking to the parents. But Chiara can only see the baby. Her eyes are wide open - clear blue like the sea in Sicily.

'Dolce bambina,' whispers Chiara. Then she closes the baby's eyes with the tip of her index finger. The sting from her cut tells her this is really happening.

3

A GIFT AND A SURPRISE

She'll tell him tonight. It's the perfect occasion.

'Over here, my love.' Martin's hand is on Rava's waist as the maitre d' leads the way to their table. It's a good one, near the window; Martin must have requested it specially.

Some of the diners glance up as they pass, noticing the elegant young couple, wondering if they've seen them somewhere before, on TV perhaps? Rava smiles graciously. This sort of attention used to make her nervous, but she's used to it now.

The maitre d' gives a little bow as he pulls out her chair, asking if Madam will be quite comfortable here? He would hate her to be in a draught.

'It's perfect,' Rava tells him. The restaurant is deliciously warm, so there's no danger of goosebumps on her exposed skin. And it's true, this dress is on the revealing side, but it's Martin's favourite. The sea-green silk is exactly right for her colouring, and, as Martin likes to say, what's the point of having a fabulous figure if you can't show it off?

Always the gentleman, Martin waits until she's settled before sitting down himself.

'D'you like it?' he asks, gesturing around the room. 'I've been wanting to bring you here for ages.'

'I love it.' And she does. She loves the deep carpets, snowy tablecloths, and twinkling chandeliers. She loves admiring their reflections in the big, gilt-framed mirrors, which multiply the clientele among flurries of orchids and gladioli. 'But I love you more.' She blows him a little kiss across the table. 'Happy anniversary, Martin.'

'Happy anniversary, my darling.'

The evening unfolds delightfully. The food is exquisite: an *amuse-bouche* of sherried scallops, followed by pate de foie gras, Devon crab, monkfish, Scottish beef Wellington, all accompanied by wines selected by the restaurant's award-winning sommelier. The helpings are small, but Rava tastes only a mouthful or two of each course, and scarcely sips at the wine. She needs to look after her waistline. Although soon that won't matter so much.

Martin is attentive, asking her opinion of the food, the wine, the paintings on the wall. When she shivers ever so slightly, he leaps up to drape his jacket around her shoulders as if she's some fragile Victorian consumptive. He points out an elderly couple sitting in a corner. The man has an immense pot belly, and the woman must be over sixty, with white, undyed hair.

'We'll never let ourselves go like that, will we?'

'Don't be silly, darling. If I ever look like that, you can march me straight off to the nearest Peaceful Rest centre.' Aunt Nasreem has white hair, but it's different in Scotland, and besides, she's very religious. Martin and Rava grin at one another, and he reaches across to caress her shoulder.

'You'll always be beautiful, my love.'

'You're not so bad yourself!'

TOO FULL FOR DESSERT, they sit over coffee and petit fours as the candle on their table burns low. Martin's smooth features are more alluring than ever in the soft lighting; he could have been a male model, she likes to joke. Rava's about to suggest they call for the car when the maitre d' comes over carrying two glasses of champagne.

'Let's drink to us. Five perfect years!' He raises his glass.

'To us,' she echoes. 'Thank you, darling. The day you married me was the best day of my life.'

'The best day? Have things gone downhill since then?' He widens his eyes in mock horror.

'No, silly.' She taps him lightly on the cheek. 'I just mean everything changed for me when I met you. I never dreamed I could live like this.'

Rava pictures her old life: the terraced house in Aberdeen, the hijab, all the rules and restrictions. She escaped all that when Martin appeared like a prince in a fairy tale.

'Everything changed for me too,' Martin says, 'when I fell in love with you.' He sounds serious now. 'Right, time for your present. Close your eyes and open your hands.'

Rava holds out her palms and he places something small into the centre.

'Can I look?'

'Of course.'

She opens her eyes, and it's a box, with the lid open. An enormous diamond sparkles in a bed of blue velvet.

'It's beautiful.' She clasps a hand to her mouth. Can it be real? She's never seen such a huge stone. She wants to ask what it cost - old habits die hard, when you've grown up poor - but she knows she mustn't. 'Thank you. It's - oh, you've made me cry.'

As soon as she's wiped the tears from her eyes - thank God for waterproof mascara! - he takes the ring from its box and slips it onto the fourth finger on her right hand. It fits perfectly;

he must have had it sized, because her hands are tiny, like a child's.

'Five carats - mined, not lab-grown. I wanted to give you something special. Thank you for marrying me, my darling.'

The diamond catches the light from the chandeliers, dazzlingly bright. He's given her jewellery before: a heavy gold necklace, her diamond earrings, real pearls, and some things he said belonged to his mother, but this out-classes them all. Things must be going well for him at the Ministry.

She kisses him on the cheek, her lipstick leaving a shadowy print. 'You're so good to me, Martin. I'm sorry, but I didn't get you anything. Except, well, I do have a surprise for you. Not a gift exactly, but I hope you're going to be pleased.' She hesitates. Maybe he's guessed already? Maybe she won't have to say.

But he only looks at her, handsome as ever, brows creased in expectation.

'Well, what is it? Tell me; I can't wait.'

She's rehearsed this moment so many times in her head, imagining his response, his delight, and the lovemaking after. But now she feels shy - embarrassed, almost.

'Okay, well, I think - I'm going to have to change my Femband.'

She looks for his smile, and there it is. He nods approvingly.

'Ah Rava, I married a wise woman! The costs of incubating keep going up, and it would be a massive hit to our lifestyle. I've always said it's your choice, but there are so many advantages to getting Sealed. More and more married women are choosing it; I see the statistics every month.' He pats her on the hand.

'No, Martin, you don't understand.'

But he keeps talking.

'It's okay, my love, don't worry. Yes, part of me would have liked a son to carry on the family name and all that old fixed-mindset stuff. But it's your body, and I respect your choices. A Sealed woman controls her own destiny, as they say! You'll be able to get promoted at work, get the recognition you deserve, and we could put the Sealing award towards a special holiday if you like?'

He squeezes her fingers, but she pulls the hand away.

'Listen, Martin. I didn't mean a gold band. I'm sorry, I should've been clearer. What I meant to say was, well, I think I'm already incubating. A blue band, I meant.'

Martin freezes as if someone has pressed pause, then blinks several times. He reaches for his drink and takes a long swallow. He doesn't speak.

'I was shocked too at first, when I realised. But then I thought, we've been married for five years, and you'll be getting promoted soon, and we love each other so much. Perhaps this is the perfect time.'

Please say yes, Martin. Please be happy about this.

He tugs at his collar as if it's too tight and wipes his mouth with his napkin. His right eyebrow twitches, almost imperceptibly.

'Have you done a test?' he asks. 'How did this happen?'

'Yes, it was positive.' She's done three tests, to be certain, and for the thrill of seeing that double blue line again. 'I guess I forgot to take a pill. I had the implant removed, remember, because of the bleeding? We talked about that.' It was her choice, he said, her body.

He's silent again, for too long. Rava shivers.

'I thought you'd be pleased,' she says, tears welling again.

He downs the rest of his champagne.

'I'm sorry, Rava. It's a shock, that's all. We always said we'd plan this together, didn't we?'

'Yes, and I'm sorry. It just happened - an accident.' Surely he can't suspect her of engineering this?

'It's a big decision, and I have to think about my position. I'm not the only candidate for the Junior Minister role. I have to set an example.'

'I know, darling, and I'm so proud of you. But we'd be within our rights, wouldn't we? I thought the Defender wants suitable families to generate. Don't you think we're suitable?'

Finally, he smiles.

'More than suitable, my treasure! Perfect! If it was down to me, I reckon we should qualify to have two offspring to propagate our excellent genes. But it's not that simple, is it? Too many irresponsible breeders, and only one planet.' He shrugs. 'Let's go home and sleep on it. It's late. We can discuss this at the weekend.' He picks up his phone to call Daniel, his driver.

TO THE WAITER, THE MAITRE D', and the other diners, the young couple leaving the restaurant appear as happy and glamorous as ever. One or two of the more observant even spot the gigantic new diamond glittering on the woman's right hand. Only Rava notices that Martin no longer rests his hand on her waist. In the dark, leathery interior of the Mercedes, they sit side by side in silence, each lost in their own thoughts.

4

SISTER MILLER

Sister Miller's door is closed. Chiara peeps through the little window to see Sister engrossed in something on her computer, her fingers busy at the keyboard. Chiara taps twice on the glass, but Sister carries on typing as if she hasn't heard.

Should she come back later? It's tempting to tiptoe away, but she might not find the courage again. Clutching her envelope in sweaty fingers, Chiara knocks again, louder this time.

'Come in.' Chiara enters and shuts the door behind her. Sister finishes whatever she is typing before swivelling her chair. She removes her spectacles and scans the bank of screens on the wall displaying the camera feeds from the patients' rooms. Only then does she focus on Chiara.

'Ah, Nurse Santori, I've been meaning to speak to you. Sit down.' She indicates the hard chair in the corner. 'So, how are you settling in?' Sister adds with a thin smile.

'Well, that's why I came to see you, Sister. Something happened last week, and I can't stop thinking about it and I don't think I can do this job anymore. Although it's a wonderful opportunity and I'm very grateful.'

'I see. And what's that in your hand?'

'My resignation letter. I'm sorry, Sister. But maybe if there's another role? I used to work in geriatrics back home. My family are relying on me - there's not much work in Sicily.'

She holds out the envelope. She was up all last night, and the night before, trying out different versions. In the end she wrote only two lines. She has no idea what she's going to tell Mamma.

But Sister Miller doesn't take the letter.

'This is a women's health institution. We don't have much call for geriatric care in this country since the rollout of Peaceful Rest. I think you and I need to talk, Nurse. There are things you haven't understood.'

Chiara's mouth is dry as sand. She forces herself to meet Sister's gaze.

'I can't do this job.'

Sister shakes her head without displacing a single blonde hair from her immaculate bun.

'My dear girl,' she says. 'Put that envelope back in your pocket. Now, how long have you been at the Genesis Centre?'

'Nearly four weeks, Sister.' Chiara's voice comes out in a high-pitched squeak.

'Four weeks.' There's a mole above Sister's right cheekbone, and it wobbles up and down as she laughs. 'Four weeks, my dear, is scarcely enough to find your feet, is it now? You're one of the Italian nurses, aren't you?' Chiara nods. 'And, let me guess, you've been feeling homesick? Missing your family?'

'Yes I am, but that isn't why -'

'Well of course you are, Nurse Santori. It's only natural that you feel a little lost right now. Whom have you left at home? Is your mother alive? A boyfriend maybe?' She chuckles again. Her lips are painted a pinky shade of orange, and her teeth are even and small.

Chiara doesn't have a boyfriend. But she aches for Mamma's *pasta con le sarde*, and the cats lying in the shade, and little Gemma begging her to come out and play. She can still hear the voices of the fishermen, and smell the scent of oregano and lemons. All memories from her childhood, dried up and gone now, but more real than ever at this distance. Those first few nights in London, she cried herself to sleep remembering, listening to the electric trams buzzing outside her window, missing the steady wash of the waves on the beach.

But that isn't why she's here in Sister's office.

'No Sister. It's hard to be away from home, but there's something else.'

Sister raises her neatly-plucked eyebrows.

'Really? So what's been upsetting you?'

Chiara swallows.

'It was last Thursday. I was assisting at a birth, in Theatre. And the baby wasn't - and the paediatrician - he - .' Chiara bites her lip; she promised herself she wouldn't cry in front of Sister. 'He -,' she tries again.

But Sister Miller raises a hand like a stop sign.

'All right, Nurse. It's good to see you appreciate the seriousness of the incident. I know precisely what happened. The Harris stillbirth was shockingly badly handled. I'd have spoken to you sooner, my dear, if I wasn't so busy fending off a formal complaint. The young doctor's the main one to blame, I realise that. You're too inexperienced to know what you're doing, or at least that's what I told the Committee. Don't worry, I believe in sticking up for my nurses.' Sister taps her pen on the desktop.

'Oh Sister, I knew it was wrong. That poor little baby was trying to breathe, and the doctor, Salvador, he squeezed her nose shut, and covered her mouth, and - I keep seeing it, all the time. He told me we had to kill her, but I knew it was wrong, but I panicked.'

Chiara covers her face with her hands to hide her tears. He was a rogue doctor, a Frankenstein, a Hannibal Lecter. How could she have been so stupid?

Sister Miller sighs and passes Chiara a box of tissues.

'You have a great deal to learn, Nurse Santori, but I believe in being patient. Let's start from the beginning. Have you read the legal and procedural manual?'

'I've mostly been concentrating on the clinical learning. There's been so much -.' A sob escapes her.

Another, deeper sigh from Sister.

'You're aware that we have a progressive population policy in England, and especially London?'

Chiara nods.

'At present, each couple may generate one live offspring, provided certain conditions are met.'

Chiara nods again.

'After the dreadful environmental disasters of recent years, this is how we ensure decent living conditions for our citizens, such as you have been enjoying here in London. You appreciate this?'

'Yes,' says Chiara, blowing her nose.

'So naturally couples want to ensure that their child is born fit and healthy. And here at the Genesis Centre we make a guarantee: if a foetus is, tragically, stillborn, the couple are offered another incubation licence, free of charge, plus a substantial discount on their next round of treatment. Obviously we provide a comprehensive programme of prenatal screening to minimise the occurrence of these sad cases. But sometimes they still happen. Do you understand?'

Chiara frowns.

'Yes, sometimes babies die before birth; I understand that. But this one was kicking - I saw her.'

'No.' Sister raises her stop-sign hand again. 'You saw no

such thing. Defective neonates are not born alive at the Genesis Centre. That would be a breach of our promise to our valued clients. The Harris case was a stillbirth. We call it a Lullaby birth, which sounds kinder, don't you think? Still heartbreaking, of course.' Sister assumes a sorrowful expression.

'But -.'

'No buts, Nurse. I am well aware of the dithering and the chit-chat that occurred between you and the paediatrician, causing enormous distress to the poor incubator. I should add that Theatre staff witnessed you, a probationer, drawing up a lethal substance. Only doctors and senior nurse practitioners who have undergone specialist training are permitted to administer these medications. As you would know, Nurse Santori, had you completed the required reading.'

The room begins to spin. Chiara grips the sides of her chair.

'But, Salvador only needed the injection because the baby was trying to breathe. It wasn't dead, not until -.' Chiara's throat tightens. It's too hot in this office. Sister's perfume is sickly-sweet, like lilies in stagnant water.

'I'm not going to repeat myself, Nurse. I'm sorry you experienced this so early on, but we expect our recruits to cope with a steep learning curve. I have gone to considerable trouble to reassure our Governance Committee that you deserve a second chance. I know how much this employment means to you foreign girls.'

Enough to eat every day. My room, where the roof doesn't leak. Money to send home for Gemma's future. A career, and maybe, one day, a family of my own. You have no idea, Sister, how much it means.

But Chiara's barely slept since last Thursday. Every time she closes her eyes she sees little Bella gasping for air.

'No, I'm sorry Sister, it's no good. Please -.' She holds out the letter again.

Sister Miller takes it, rips it in two without opening it, and drops the pieces into the bin under her desk.

'Okay, I'm going to have to spell this out for you. If, as you seem to be implying, that foetus was born alive, injecting it with potassium chloride would be a criminal offence. I would have to call the police. Is that what you want?'

'No Sister!' Chiara's throat feels blocked; she thinks she might choke.

'It goes without saying you would forfeit your nursing registration.'

'But I can't afford that. My family is relying on me.'

The narrow office quivers, and Chiara fixes her eyes on her shoes. The black leather spreads and widens as if she could fall into it. She clutches her cheeks, but the tears are coming again.

'Come on now, no need to cry.' Sister gets up and embraces Chiara in a stifling hug.

'I understand, my dear.' Her breath is moist in Chiara's ear. 'That first Lullaby case often comes as a shock. I look after my staff, so long as they're loyal to the Centre. Provided we understand one another, I think we can treat this unhappy incident as a learning opportunity and leave it in the past. How does that sound?'

Chiara sniffs.

'There, there, come here.' Sister Miller grabs a handful of tissues and wipes Chiara's face as if she were a child. 'Blow, dear!'

Chiara blows her nose.

'You poor overseas girls have so much to learn, but I believe you have the makings of an excellent nurse, Miss Santori. We wouldn't have taken you on otherwise. It just takes a while to get used to a modern approach. You'll be fine next time.'

Next time? She can't; she just can't.

'Please, Sister, that mother, she was screaming. I'm so scared it might happen again.'

'Incubator,' Sister reminds her with a frown. 'We don't call them mothers until the neonates are signed off to go home, do we? For obvious reasons.'

Sister returns to her desk, her kitten-heels tap-tapping on the floor. 'I'll tell you what, Nurse. I'll move you for now. You can work on Serenity Ward while you catch up with your training. No deliveries there; just happy postpartum clients and healthy neonates. How does that sound?'

'Oh yes, thank you Sister. I'm sure Serenity Ward will be wonderful. I'm very grateful for another chance.' At least she won't have to disappoint Mamma.

'Good, I'm glad we've got that straight.' Sister's golden Femband flashes. 'Right, I'm already late for a crucial meeting, but before you go, Nurse, there's just one more thing. Sit!'

Chiara had stood up to leave. She resumes her perch on the edge of the chair. Sister picks up a pen from her desk and begins to roll it between her finger and thumb.

'Have you read your contract, Nurse Santori?'

'I - I think so.' It was a long legal document in English, more than eighty pages. She glanced over it once, back home, before running out to join the party Mamma threw to celebrate Chiara's new job. Mamma borrowed sugar, eggs, and margarine from their neighbours - enough to bake a cake. She lit lanterns and invited everyone - not that there's more than a handful of villagers left now, since the industrial trawlers emptied the sea of fish and the tourist flights were banned. They all drank home-made wine, and sang, and even danced a little. Chiara was off to England to make their fortunes.

'So you know about the conditions, then? For repaying our costs if you resign?' Sister's voice is cool. Didn't someone on the induction day say something about a repayment clause? Chiara's stomach tightens, and the taste of bile rises in her throat. She didn't pay much attention back then; she was too busy marvelling at the giant skyscrapers.

'What conditions?' Chiara's knees loosen. Sister sighs.

'So many of you girls don't read the contract properly. It costs the hospital a great deal of money to recruit and train overseas staff. And then there's the very generous initial payment you receive to help you with travel costs, your first month's rent, uniforms, and so on. That's why we sign you up for a minimum three-year term. If you leave within the first year you have to repay two years' salary towards our costs, plus that initial sign-on sum. Should you resign, you would be liable for the full amount immediately. Is that clear, Nurse Santori?'

The caretaker at Chiara's school used to trap rats in a wire cage. Chiara remembers watching a rat circling frantically in his narrow confinement, eyes popping, desperate for a way out. She thinks she understands how he felt.

'Yes, Sister.'

'You're not the first new nurse to come in here waving a resignation letter. We always manage to sort things out. And it gets easier. You'll soon get used to it; everyone does.' Sister Miller stretches her lips into a smile and smooths her black-and-grey striped skirt. 'Now, if you don't mind, I am very busy.' She scribbles something on a piece of paper and hands it to Chiara. 'Take this note to the nurse in charge of Serenity and tell her I sent you.'

Sister turns her chair back towards her computer screen. As Chiara puts the note into her pocket, her fingers brush against Nonna's old rosary beads she keeps with her for good luck, and the tiniest spark of courage flares inside her.

'Sister Miller,' she asks. 'I was wondering, does anyone ever give birth here the natural way? Not by C-section, I mean?'

Sister flinches as if Chiara has used a disgusting swear word. Her cheeks flush. She picks up her pen and presses the point into the palm of her left hand.

'Have you ever seen a woman bleed to death? Because, trust me, Nurse, you don't want to. So-called natural birth is incredibly dangerous. In the past, women used to suffer for days.' She shudders. 'I trained under the old system, and I don't ever want my staff to see some of the things I had to see. Barbaric! Besides, why put the poor incubator through a second surgery for her sterilisation? Where's your compassion? You've got a great deal to learn, Nurse. A very great deal.'

5

OUR BABY

Rava and Martin sit at the breakfast bar in their white oak kitchen. Rain pours like rivers down the windows. Sometimes you can see all the way to Hackney and the Essex marshes beyond, but this morning the landscape disappears into a smudge of green and grey.

Martin has finished his croissant and is onto his second cup of coffee. Louis sits at his feet, licking his velvety jowls as he waits for the next morsel of boiled chicken.

'I know I spoil him. But you're such a cutie, aren't you, Louis-wooey?'

The dog snaffles up the treat with a happy growl. Martin pats his head.

'We both do,' says Rava. 'He's our baby -.' She stops. Neither of them has mentioned that subject since the anniversary dinner on Wednesday. They've both been so busy with work, and Martin's reaction - well it wasn't exactly what she'd hoped for. Several times she's wondered whether she should order the Fresh Start pills and have done with it. After all, this wasn't how they planned it, and everyone says a planned child is a happy child.

'Okay,' Martin says. 'Let's talk. Basket, Louis.' Louis gives him a long look before accepting another piece of chicken and padding off to his bed. 'I've been thinking. Did a few calculations.' Martin drains his coffee cup and reaches for his laptop.

'Of course it's expensive,' Rava begins. 'And you've been working so hard, and I'm sorry Martin, I know we said we'd do the sex-selection IVF. But when I skipped my period I got so excited, and I wanted to surprise you. So silly!' She combs her fingers through her hair, loosening the slight tangle at the back.

'It's not silly, my love. You did surprise me, that's all. But I want you to be happy.'

'And I am happy.' She caresses his arm, careful not to scratch him with her new nails. The big diamond glitters. Martin's such a loving husband. So why this nagging ache for a baby? Isn't their life complete?

'I want what's best for both of us.'

'Yes, Martin.'

'And my promotion's not a done deal - nowhere near. I'll need to pull out all the stops at work this year, and if you incubate now, that'll mean more pressure on both of us. Come and look at the numbers.'

'Okay.' Rava presses her lips together before moving her stool closer to Martin's so she can see the screen on his laptop.

Martin shows her page after page of spreadsheets. He talks about income streams and interest rates, school fees, projected housing costs, and healthcare insurance, as well as the staggering incubation licence and hospital charges. When she sees his totals she gasps.

'But that can't be right? No one could have a child, if it costs that much.'

Martin taps the screen.

'This is Government policy. You watch the news, Rava, don't you? The country's still not under control: those riots in the camps on the South Downs, the crime figures, the price of food.

We've abandoned twelve million acres since the first inundations. Twelve million - and maybe more this spring, if more sea walls breach. And the wildfires - Ashford won't be rebuilt for years, if ever.'

'I guess you're right.' Her shoulders slump. 'But - with your role at the Ministry - can't you get special terms, for the licence at least?' Her voice drops to a whisper.

Martin's eyes widen.

'Rava! How can you suggest such a thing? I'm a Secretary of State - elected to serve the people; I have to be above reproach.'

She hangs her head.

'Sorry, Martin, I shouldn't have-.'

'No, you most certainly shouldn't.' He puffs out his chest, indignant.

'I'm sorry. Will things ever get better, d'you think?'

'That's what we're all working for. If everyone acts responsibly, we can thrive, like the Defender says. She's a truly wise woman - if only everyone would listen.'

Rava tries to make herself small. Martin's so ethical, always putting the planet first. But suddenly she has to get up and go to the window, fighting down an enormous lump in her throat. She stands there, staring out but not seeing, making herself take long breaths. She's nearly got herself under control, when he comes up behind her.

'Rava, my darling.' He smoothes the hair from her face. 'I can't bear to see you unhappy. Tell me how you really feel.'

So with his solid body to lean on and his lips soft on her neck, she speaks:

'I didn't use to mind. I didn't want a baby when I was younger. I didn't want to end up like Aunt Nasreem, always cooking and doing laundry, wearing herself out. But since last year, when I had that breast cancer scare, I can't stop thinking about it. It's like there's something inside me that wants a baby, so very badly, and I know this isn't how we planned it, but when it happened by accident, I thought, I couldn't help wondering, maybe this was meant to be? It's ridiculous. I'm sorry.'

He kisses the crown of her head.

'It's all right, my love. I understand. It's your hormones making you feel this way. You've been so patient, and it's a sacrifice, isn't it? A son would be a dream come true for me too.' He pauses. 'Look at me, sweetheart.'

He turns her gently to face him, and she gazes into his pale, steady eyes.

'This has to be your choice, Rava. If you really want to incubate now, you have my support. Alternatively, we could let this one go, and review it again in a year or two. Or you could get your golden band straight away. There's no rush, my darling - take your time.'

'Oh, Martin.' She clings to him, pressing her cheek to his chest. 'I know it's selfish, and we should think about population control, and consider the planet, but, if we could afford a baby now, it would make me so happy. And this one, well, it's sort of already here, isn't it?' The size of a raspberry, the website said, with ears and eyelids beginning to form.

'No pressure, okay? Incubating isn't easy on women, physically or mentally, so you mustn't feel any compulsion - no outdated moral imperatives. You're too precious to me. But if it's what you want, we'll make it work, okay?'

'Oh thank you, Martin, thank you!' She dissolves into his arms, her tears soaking into his shirt. She hadn't realised, until now, how much she wanted this.

HE MAKES them both fresh coffees, and they cuddle up on the sofa while Louis snores in his bed.

'The Genesis Centre,' Martin declares. 'I won't have you go anywhere else. The Kensington Women's isn't bad, but nowhere compares to the Genesis. It's state-of-the-art, with guaranteed outcomes. Cost billions to set up.'

Thank God for a husband who works for the Ministry of Population and Health. Martin's an expert on London hospitals; he was involved in the project to build the Genesis Centre. Rava curls her toes into the Persian rug.

'Can we afford that, Martin, where all the celebrities go?' Rava's seen the adverts, with beautiful bedrooms, fabulous food, and A-list couples with their gorgeous babies.

'We'll find a way. I might need to call in a few favours - all above board, obviously. Henry, the Centre Director, and I go right back. And the Chief Surgeon owes me one. We might even be able to leverage this for PR. How d'you fancy featuring in the Genesis Centre's next advertising campaign, my love?' He caresses her fingers.

'Me?' She pictures herself with flowers in her hair, a lace wrap enfolding her and her cherubic newborn. 'Would they want to use me?'

'I don't see why not. You're prettier than all those actresses and models.'

She giggles, and he starts kissing her throat as she nestles into him, tasting his smoky cologne. They'll need to go shopping - buy things for the baby's nursery. A traditional theme, with a touch of urban chic. White, perhaps, or natural oak? Emma at work went for swags and frills, but that's not Rava's style. She prefers -.

'Edward,' Martin says. 'What d'you reckon? I've always liked it - traditional and English. We could pick an Arabic middle name if you like, to reflect your heritage?' His hand works its way up her thigh.

'Mmmm, that feels nice. Maybe.' The name sounds stiff and old-fashioned to her, but it's his baby too, and he's being so understanding. 'I guess. Edward.' She tries it out. 'And, for a little girl?'

'A little girl?' His hand stops moving. 'What d'you mean?'

'If our baby's a girl. Do you have any favourite girl's names?'

'Er - no.' He laughs awkwardly. 'No, we're not having a girl, are we? We agreed. Our baby will be a boy.' He says this as if it's obvious.

'What? When did we agree?' A moment later it dawns on her. 'Well yes, before, when we were going to do IVF. But this is different now, isn't it?'

He removes his arm from her shoulder.

'No, sweetheart, we still have a choice. If this conception turns out to be female, we'll start again and go down the IVF route. It's the best way to deal with an accident, and you'll still get your baby, don't worry. It'll just take a little bit longer.'

Rava rubs her eyes, trying to get things straight. Louis whines in his sleep and shifts his position.

'I didn't think that was legal - termination for the wrong gender? I'm eight weeks already, Martin, nearly nine. I'm not sure that I want -.'

'Well, technically, yes, you're right; that's the letter of the law. The Defender's not in favour of discrimination. But in practice most people want boys, I'm afraid. It's a fact of life. It's not that I don't value women, or respect them. I'm a passionate advocate for women's health. Why d'you think we built the Genesis Centre and reformed the Femband policy? In an ideal world, with unlimited resources, I'd love to have a son and a daughter, but we have to be realistic. The way things are these days - the world's very hard on women, don't you think? A boy has more opportunities.'

'Yes, but if we did have a girl, we'd still love her, wouldn't we?'

'Of course we would. Of course, in an ideal world. Don't worry, my love, you can leave all the legal stuff to me. It won't be a problem at the Genesis Centre; there are always ways to smooth things over. Everything will be fine. Now then -.'

He reaches for her again, as if the subject is settled.

'Come here. It's the weekend, so let's make the most of it.' He lowers his face to her breasts, his hand resumes its journey up her thigh, and she feels herself respond, more than half-willingly. He's so good at this, generous and attentive. And he's probably right - everything will work out fine.

6

SERENITY WARD

Chiara can't understand why they call it *Serenity*; her days on the postnatal ward are anything but serene. She dispenses medications, checks wound dressings, completes the spreadsheets for the four-hourly observations, on what feels like an endless treadmill, till her head aches and the patients' call bells seem to be ringing inside her brain.

The woman - sorry, incubator - in room six rings incessantly. Her iron tablets are five minutes late. She's worried her drip might be falling out. She needs help doing her hair. Like most mothers here, she's used to having people do things for her. The toiletries beside her bed are brands Chiara could never afford.

In Sicily, at the care home, Chiara had time to chat with the residents, admiring pictures of their grandchildren - all gone abroad now - and listening to their stories of the old days when fish and fresh food were plentiful. No one at the Genesis Centre has time to talk about anything much. The nurses are focused on the next drugs round, IV drips and catheters, and keeping up with all the checks and tests. Visitors aren't allowed, except fathers for a short time each afternoon. Recovering incubators need a lot of rest, Sister says, and grandmothers and other female relatives get over-excited and disturb the routines. Besides, it's unwise to let them get attached too soon, before the neonates are signed off for discharge.

Chiara wants to help the new mothers, but many sleep through the day, pacified by regular doses of lorazepam and tramadol. Some are reluctant to touch their own babies without endless reassurance. They have won the childbearing lottery but don't know what to do with their prize.

'Am I doing it right?' asks a pretty woman with flawless make-up, as she pokes a bottle into the corner of her wailing infant's mouth. 'Is he choking?' Her face is screwed up in worry, and she relaxes only when Chiara takes the tiny boy from her. 'I'm the first of my friendship group to incubate,' the mother says. 'I did six online courses, and we've hired a nanny, but I'm still not sure we've bought all the right equipment. What if he gets sick after he's discharged?'

'There's a class every afternoon in the education room,' Chiara tells her. This is a small lounge at one end of the ward where parents are given lectures about childcare law, developmental check-ups, tests, and immunisations. Not exactly a cure for anxiety, but the nurses have to make sure the women attend.

'Would you like to cuddle him?' Chiara asks when the little boy finishes his feed. 'Shall I show you how to change his nappy?' She holds him out, the security band blinking on his wrist, but the mother shakes her head.

'Can you take him to the nursery? He'll be safer with the professionals.' She fans her face. 'Not again! I'm having hot flushes - it's the sterilisation, isn't it? Can you check when my next painkillers are due?' So Chiara wheels the cot back down the corridor to the hot room where rows of neonates sleep watched over by green-uniformed nursery nurses.

Room twenty has been quiet all morning, so when that bell

buzzes, Chiara hurries to answer. The blinds are tightly closed and the mother sits in twilight, holding her infant daughter as if she is made of glass. The woman blushes scarlet as she whispers:

'Would it be all right if I tried to feed her myself? You know - from my chest? Is that safe?'

'Of course. Here, hold her nice and close.' Chiara remembers Mamma breastfeeding Gemma. These days Italian women sell their milk; it ends up here, defrosted and fed in bottles to the London newborns. But this woman unbuttons her nightdress with shaky fingers, and the baby opens her pink mouth wide. 'That's it, now relax and let her suck. She knows what to do.' It takes two or three attempts, Chiara offering all the encouraging words she knows, but after a few minutes the sucking settles into a steady rhythm.

The mother strokes her child's head in wide-eyed wonder.

'I'm doing it,' she murmurs, smiling beatifically. Chiara sits at the mother's side, ignoring the buzzing of the bells and telling the mother what a great job she's doing, when someone bursts into the room without knocking. It's one of the senior nurses.

'Been looking everywhere for you, Clara,' she says. 'Two of your clients need their antibiotics, and room six is complaining about her wound. I haven't got time to do your work as well as -.' She breaks off, her mouth falling open, and points at the mother in the bed. 'Wait a moment, don't tell me - is that incubator chestfeeding? What meds is she on? It's dangerous with tramadol, don't you know that, Clara? And anyway, the neonates all gotta have their test feeds and weighings done before discharge. How can we measure how much she's had? Have to start again from scratch now. Lord, you foreign girls crack me up.'

The nurse slaps a hand to her forehead as the mother hastily re-fastens her nightdress, her face puce, her baby screaming in protest at the abrupt end to her feed. 'You'd better get this one her lorazepam,' the senior nurse adds. 'Settle her down. I won't tell Sister this time, all right Clara?'

Chiara hurries away to fetch the tranquillisers, tears stinging behind her eyelids. Will she ever get it right?

BY THREE O'CLOCK, Chiara's feet ache and her vision is fuzzy. She plods like a robot from room to room, calculating the hours and minutes to the end of her shift. Too long. There's no thermometer in room nine so she goes to look in the room where the babies have their health checks. Pulling open the door, she almost falls into the arms of someone carrying a big stack of patient notes.

'*Scusa.* Sorry.' she says. Then she recognises the pastel scrubs with the cartoon print. It's him. She stumbles backwards, her face burning. She thought maybe he'd been fired. Him. The one who made her do it. Words scramble in her mind, a jumble of English and Italian, but all that comes out is:

'*Mamma Mia! È te.* It's you!'

He lowers his pile of folders and stares at her, knitting his eyebrows.

'Er - hi. Chiara, isn't it?' He hesitates. 'So - how're you doing? Were you okay the other day, after - you know? I meant to speak to you, but you disappeared.' He gives her a wary half-smile. She ought to march off and find a thermometer somewhere else, but she hesitates a split section too long. 'Chiara,' he asks again, 'Are you okay?'

Something cracks inside her, like the first splits in a dam about to burst. How dare he? She steps up, forcing him to back into the empty room.

'*Zitto!* No, not okay.' She jabs her finger at his face, still coming at him. 'How can you say okay? You make me do something terrible, made me part of your lies. I saw with my own eyes - that baby was not stillborn - no! She was trying to breathe, trying to live. And you call yourself a doctor? Now they trap me here; I will go to prison, they say, if I tell the truth. It is you who be in prison. You have made me something I never wanted to be. It is horrible what you made me do.'

She takes a shuddering breath, and he stands there, mouth open. She waits. He's going to give her some line about hospital policy, laws, and the greater good. He'll tell her she doesn't understand, that she doesn't belong here. She should keep quiet and be grateful. Her head hurts with it all.

'Well?' she says, when he still doesn't speak. 'How can you live with yourself, murderer?'

He's backed right into the corner now. He dumps his files and leans on the desk with both hands, those silly, floppy curls tumbling around his face.

'You're right, Chiara.' She has to move closer to catch his words. 'I am everything you say, and worse. None of this is okay. None of it. I've been searching for a way out, but it's like a spider's web: you get more and more tangled.' He rubs at his forehead. 'My consultant's a powerful man; you don't want to upset him. I've been applying for transfers, but nothing's come through, and, in the meantime, I am trying to do what I can, to help.' He straightens up and looks at her. 'It's more complicated than you think.'

'Really?' Chiara raises an eyebrow.

'I do my best, try to overlook things when I can, make exceptions. And sometimes I help people find other ways.' He trails off, and she looks at him through narrowed eyes, silent until he adds, 'But you're right: basically I'm shit-scared.'

Me too, Chiara thinks. Me too. She squeezes her fists. She's been blaming Salvador for doing his job at the hospital, but she's still working here, isn't she? She thought she had principles, things she'd never do, but she didn't even try to save that poor baby. She tries to focus on the floor: grey tiles, very clean.

A bell rings. Room six again, most likely. Chiara grabs the thermometer from its holder on the wall.

'I'm running late,' she says.

'Wait,' he says, glancing to left and right. 'Meet me after work, and I'll tell you more. It's not safe to talk here.' He grabs a paper towel from the dispenser, writes something on it, and hands it to her. 'Make sure you're not followed.'

Her eyes widen.

'Haven't you got me into enough trouble?'

'Fair enough,' he says. 'But I'll be there if you change your mind.'

7

A PLAN AND A SCAN

'I'm worried about Toby. He's got the Health Secretary eating out of his hand.' Martin rubs his neck as if it's aching and re-fills his glass.

'What's happened? I'm sure it will all be fine, you're so hard-working.' Rava leans in to listen, patting her husband's hand. Martin's always been a worrier.

'Thanks, sweetheart. I hope so, but Toby's very ambitious. He thinks he's got the Junior Minister post sewn up, with his Peaceful Rest expansion project and his friends in high places. All very well for the jolly Oxbridge contingent, isn't it?' Martin's right eyebrow jumps. He went to a state school, then onto university in London, where he did brilliantly. He ought to be proud of his achievements, but that's not enough, he always says, to get on in Government. It's all about who you know and where you came from.

'Nepotism rules, as ever.' Martin takes a big swallow of wine. 'But I'm going to give Toby a run for his money this time. I have to, don't I, with our son and heir on the way?' He pats Rava's stomach. 'I think I've got an idea, how to get in the spot-

light, and make a difference too. Midwives.' He drains his glass
and sets it down with a flourish.

'Midwives?' The word sounds old-fashioned, but Rava
thinks she's heard it somewhere before. Back in Scotland,
maybe? 'What do you mean, Martin?'

'Well -.' He leans back in his chair. 'A midwife is a primitive
kind of obstetric nurse, with no proper training or supervision.
Dangerous amateurs.' He tuts. 'They all had their licences
removed years ago, after a series of scandals - stillbirths, brain-
damaged infants, that sort of thing. The younger ones were
retrained in modern systems, and maternity care's one hundred
percent safer now, I'm glad to say.'

'Thank God! They sound scary.' Martin nods.

'Their removal was long overdue. But unfortunately the
Safe Futures policy has resulted in some resurgence. One of the
unintended consequences. Very worrying.' His eyebrow
twitches again. 'The police should've got on top of the problem,
but there've been very few arrests. I'm getting grief because
sterilisation figures in East Sector are down for the third month
running, and all because the midwives encourage the great
unwashed to breed. But I'm going to snuff out the old witches -
every last one of them!'

'Oh that's awful, Martin.' Rava pictures a toothless hag
cackling over a baby; her hand flies protectively to her belly.

'I'm sorry, darling - I need to remember you're in a delicate
condition. Trust me, you'll n ever see a midwife in the Genesis
Centre, or any London hospital.' He gets up and switches on
the espresso machine, raising his voice above the whirr of its
motor.

'No, the point is, Rava, this is how I'm going to get my
promotion. I'm heading up a new initiative to reduce unregistered births. It's a key role; a chance to demonstrate how the
Defender's policies are still making London safer. And it's going
to put Toby's euthanasia gig in the shade. I've got one or two

contacts I can leverage, plus, – let's just say I understand how these people think. Whereas Toby, that privileged half-wit, doesn't have a clue.'

'Wow, that's amazing, Martin.' He's so clever, he's bound to get the promotion.

Martin yawns.

'It's been a long day. Let's leave the clearing-up till the morning.' He places his dinner plate on the kitchen floor and makes a lip-smacking sound for Louis to come and eat up the leftovers. They turn on the TV and settle in front of a show about luxury homes. It's one of Rava's favourites, but this evening she struggles to keep her eyes open, nodding sleepily through a blur of designer kitchens, home cinemas and glamorous walk-in wardrobes. The baby's still only the size of a kumquat, but it's already draining her energy.

'URP, URP, URP'. Rava wakes with a start to see Louis standing in the middle of the living room with his chest low to the ground, his small body heaving. As Martin leaps to his feet, the French bulldog opens his mouth and ejects a yellow mound of vomit onto the carpet.

'Oh, poor Louis,' Rava murmurs, but Martin is beside himself.

'Oh my God, Louis! What's the matter?' He scoops up his pet in his arms while Rava goes for kitchen paper to clean up the mess. 'What's wrong, Louis? Have you eaten something bad?' Louis's only reply is to throw up again all over Martin's shirt. 'He's sick, Rava. What's he had? Was there something in that dinner? Did you watch him properly when you took him for his walk? Quick, where's my phone. I need to call the vet.' Martin's eyebrow judders.

Louis wriggles free and returns to the carpet, sniffing at his regurgitated food with interest, while Martin dials the vet's emergency number. Louis looks lively enough to Rava, who saw plenty of stray dogs on the streets of Aberdeen, but Martin won't be reassured.

'Vomiting can be serious in dogs, and Frenchies have a lot of health issues. He's a delicate pedigree breed. Were there onions in that gravy?' Martin glares at Rava before picking up Louis again and inspecting his mouth, his ears, his round, intelligent eyes. The phone rings and rings. 'This is meant to be an emergency line, for goodness' sake. What if? - Ah hello! Hello. Yes, my dog is very unwell.'

Rava scrapes up the smelly heap from the carpet, while Martin describes Louis's symptoms to the vet. She's been feeling nauseous herself these past few weeks, and the stink makes her gag, but Martin doesn't notice; he's too intent on the dog. It's nearly midnight by the time the vet has been and gone, diagnosing mild gastroenteritis and prescribing a bland diet. Rava collapses gratefully into bed, leaving Martin to spend the night on the sofa, 'keeping a proper eye on my poor baby.'

'Can I see?'

The sonographer purses her lips.

'Everything looks normal so far,' she says. Her probe presses deep into Rava's full-to-bursting bladder. She clicks buttons on the machine. 'Just taking a few measurements.'

'Can you show me?' Rava asks again when the clicking stops. 'I'd like to see my baby.'

The sonographer is focused on her screen, but Rava senses her frown.

'We don't recommend it, not at this gestation. Emotional attachment can make things difficult later on if any problems emerge.' Her tone is cool and professional. The probe digs in hard.

'But it's my baby. Just a quick look, please?' Rava's cousin in Aberdeen had a fuzzy black-and-white picture of her pregnancy scan; she shared it on social media. The rules are different in London, but surely looking at the screen can't hurt?

The sonographer is a woman in her fifties with close-cropped, iron grey hair. For the first time, she looks at Rava's face.

'Your husband couldn't come today?'

'No, he's busy with work. He asked me to tell him all about it. Please can you let me see?'

The sonographer shrugs.

'Well, if you're sure. But don't say I didn't warn you.' She gets up, crosses to the door, and locks it. Then she turns her screen towards Rava.

'There it is.'

Rava looks. At first it's all a blur, but then the sonographer rolls the probe around, and she sees a small creature squirming in a black space. It's got a big, domed head, a belly, and tiny arms and legs, hands and feet. And it's moving.

'Here's the spine.' The sonographer rolls the probe, and Rava follows a bright line along the curve of the baby's back. 'Here are the bones in the arms and legs, and there's the umbilical cord. Fingers here, look, and the ribcage. And that's the heart beating.' A softer note has crept into the sonographer's voice. The baby's face has a gentle, curved profile with a big forehead, a nose, and a chin. Rava stares hard, fixing it all in her memory.

'Can you see the baby's sex on this scan?' The question comes out before she can stop herself. She wants to know, and she doesn't.

The sonographer gives an amused grunt.

'If I had a pound for each time someone asked me that! Yes,

and no.' She slides the probe again. Rava's desperate to pee.
'They call it the nub theory. The external genitals aren't fully
developed yet, but the angle of the tubercle gives us a pretty
good idea. The blood test's more reliable, though. Are you
having the full DNA work-up?'

'Yes, my husband ordered that.'

'Good. That will tell you everything. They'll take your blood
in clinic, and results take about a week.' Rava nods. 'So this is
just an indication, okay? About ninety percent accurate, they
say, although it depends on baby being helpful and opening its
legs. Come on, little one.' She dollops another blob of gel onto
Rava's stomach. 'Oh, you're a wriggler, aren't you!' The baby
rotates, moving like an underwater swimmer. Its face looks
right up at Rava.

'Ah, here we are. It's quite tricky to see at this gestation, but I
think - yes, I'd say this is a little girl. Ah, that's a bit clearer now.
If it was a boy, there should be a little nub pointing upwards,
but I've got a good view, and it looks flat, so, yes, female.'

'Oh!' cries Rava, louder than she intended.

'Sorry, is that bad news? I can't be certain, though; you need
to wait for the blood test.'

'Yes. Thank you. Can I go to the toilet now?' It's not just her
bladder; she's afraid she's going to throw up. She's too hot and
too cold all at once.

'Are you all right, Mrs Robson? You've gone very pale. Are
you feeling faint?'

'I'm all right.' She pushes herself up to sitting, but the
nausea makes her dizzy and she has to close her eyes.

'Slow down. Take some deep breaths.'

Rava does as she's told, and the sickness begins to ease.

'I'm sorry,' she says as soon as she can speak. 'It was a bit of
a shock. My husband -.'

Someone taps on the door of the room. The sonographer
swivels the screen sharply back, out of Rava's view.

'Almost finished,' she calls. Then she speaks rapidly to Rava: 'Take no notice of what I said; it has zero clinical value. And there'll be nothing in your notes to indicate you saw the screen. In case you or your husband might be thinking of making a complaint.' She's using her professional voice again.

'I'm not going to complain,' Rava assures her. But the sonographer is typing rapidly.

'You can use this to wipe off the gel,' she says, passing over a handful of blue paper towels. Rava cleans herself, dresses, and goes to the toilet to empty her bladder. She is halfway down the corridor before she realises that she is crying.

8

CUCINA PICCOLA

C hiara's shift is supposed to finish at 8.00 pm, but the night shift nurse arrives late. Again. It's gone 8.30 by the time Chiara escapes. She tries not to look at her refection in the mirrored walls of the lift: a dead-eyed woman with slumped shoulders and dull skin. Her head throbs. All she wants is to eat something and then sleep, preferably for a long time.

The vast, high-ceilinged Atrium is quiet, with the coffee shop closed and shuttered. Chiara's footsteps echo on the marble floor. She's famished; lunch break was an eternity ago. Those eggs in the fridge are way past their use-by date and she can't face cooking anything more elaborate. Breakfast cereal again then, if the milk hasn't turned sour.

As she walks down the steps to the Plaza, her phone buzzes. She pulls it out of her coat pocket - only a low battery alert for her Femband - and finds herself holding a crumpled piece of tissue which she must have shoved in there earlier. She's about to toss it into a bin when she notices handwriting on it in black biro. Best be careful; they had a whole lecture about patient confidentiality with horror stories about nurses accidentally taking home patient details. Sometimes you need to jot down a blood pressure or a neonatal jaundice reading on a scrap of paper before you can get to the computer. But if you forget to shred it and someone finds the paper and traces back to you, the penalty is instant dismissal.

So Chiara smooths out the tissue and reads it under a streetlight.

Cucina Piccola, 38 Gabriel Lane. I'll be there until 10.00pm. S.

She glances at her Femband: 08.48. Why did she keep Salvador's note anyway? He roped her into that awful lullaby thing and nearly got her fired. She ought to go straight home and flush this down the toilet.

A waft of something tasty floats from one of the restaurants bordering the Plaza, and Chiara's stomach groans. Cucina Piccola sounds like some sort of cafe. On a hungry impulse, she keys the name into her phone, and up pops the website for an Italian trattoria with a menu that makes her salivate. *Fettuccine Aglio, Olio e Peperoncino. Tortelloni al Burro e Salvia. Spaghetti al Tonno.* She mouths the delicious phrases under her breath. It's only a few hundred metres away, on her way back to the nurses' accommodation, just down that little side street.

She carries on walking, still undecided, but when she gets to the turning, she peers down the narrow alleyway. Halfway down on the left, she spots the name glowing above a lighted window: *Cucina Piccola*. It looks so inviting - Italian food, somewhere warm to sit down, and an evening away from her reproachful laptop full of training courses. Her empty insides clench and rumble. She rounds the corner.

SALVADOR'S RIGHT at the back, his head bowed over his phone. He doesn't look up until she's standing almost beside him. When he sees her, he smiles.

'You came. I was starting to wonder.' He gestures at his nearly empty beer glass.

'I'm only here because I'm starving. I had to stay late, and there's nothing to eat in my room.'

'You've come to the right place then. Sit down.' He pulls out a chair. 'The pasta's to die for, and they have real cheese, and decent olive oil. I thought it might remind you - .'

'Of home.' She completes his sentence. 'Perhaps. It's not easy being so far from my family, but there isn't much of the old life left there since they banned tourism and collectivised the farms. This -,' she casts around at the red-and-white chequered tablecloths, the candles in Chianti bottles, the photographs on the walls of plump, happy families - 'this is all a fantasy now.'

'Yes, but why not enjoy it for an hour or two?'

She shrugs, too hungry to argue.

'Okay, but I'm not here to talk about work.' She sits, and he passes her a menu.

'Fine by me! Some wine - *rosso, bianco?*'

'No, I have to be up early.' She's only met this man twice before, and in appalling circumstances. She must stay on her guard, eat fast, and leave soon.

THE TORTELLONI IS EXCELLENT. Chiara mops up the last of the buttery sauce with a hunk of bread and wishes she could afford a dessert. The little restaurant is cosy, the candlelight soothing, and they're tucked away in a corner. Even without alcohol, she can feel her defences softening. Salvador chats harmlessly about music and his favourite TV shows. They joke together about the crazy unreality of TV hospital dramas. He says he likes football, and Chiara tells him she used to play for a girls' team at school.

'Does the hospital have a women's team?' she asks. Maybe it would help her make friends once she's got the worst of the studying out of the way.

But he glances down at her wrist and then looks away.

'Only for gold bands, I'm afraid. There's a lot of discrimination in this country, as you must have noticed.' He tugs at his hair, pulling it low across his forehead. 'Would you like some ice cream?'

'No thanks. Yes - I'm still getting used to it - all the things I can and can't do with a red Femband. I can get promoted one grade, but that's all. And somebody said there are rules about housing?'

'Yes.' He fidgets again with his hair. 'I don't like it, Chiara. In Spain, things are more relaxed but we are poor - like in Italy. A Filly -.' He grimaces. 'Sorry - horrible word! As a single, fertile woman in London, you get only one room or a studio apartment. You are dangerous - that's why it's a red band. With more space, you might get ideas about breeding and make a fuss. To get a larger home, for a senior job, and to go to many places - theatres, nice gyms, luxury restaurants - you have to be married, or sterilised. Preferably both.' He spreads his hands wide. They are broad hands, with very clean fingernails. He wears a sports watch but no rings.

'Well, I don't want -.' Chiara hesitates. This is a very intimate conversation to be having with a virtual stranger. She was going to say she's not ready to get sterilised yet; she's still young, and who knows? But she stops herself just in time. 'What about the black bands?' she asks as the heat rises to her face. Most of the cleaners at the Centre wear them, and women working in shops and on the trams.'

'It took me a while to work it out too. The black Fembands are for women with jobs in the city, but who don't have a permit to live here. Mollies, people call them. They travel in from outside - the camps, or condemned housing, or miles and miles out in the wastelands.'

'Camps? And are they fertile, or married, or what?'

He shrugs.

'I don't think anyone gives a shit. At least, not until recently. It's the Wild West out there; a different world from our glorious Defender's London.' He makes a mock bow. 'Gangs, Mafia types mostly run the show outside the protected cities. For a long time it suited the Government to ignore them, but they're starting to get too powerful.'

Chiara's skin prickles.

'*Mafiosi*, like in Sicily? To upset them must be very dangerous.'

'Sure. And the population's rising, they say, in the unsupported zones. They never expected that; everyone thought the stubborn old grannies and undesirables would give up and die off of their own accord. But instead, the age profile's getting younger.'

'Sorry - I don't understand.' Chiara wrinkles her forehead. 'I thought the English countryside was evacuated after the flooding crisis? We learned about it in school.'

'*Total Urbanisation*,' they called it, to keep people safe and give nature a chance to recover. Some people think Italy should do the same, but the Government's never been stable enough to implement it.

Salvador nods slowly.

'Yeah, that's what they told me too. I thought I was coming to the promised land, streets paved with gold, and all that. But it's not so simple.' He picks up the menu. 'Look, I'm getting a gelato. Are you sure you don't want one? I'll pay.'

'Just a coffee, thanks.' But she returns his smile. He has kind eyes, she thinks.

———

BETWEEN SPOONFULS of chocolate and vanilla ice cream, Salvador speaks in a low voice. There's only one other couple in the restaurant now, over near the door, and this place is okay, Salvador says. He knows the people who run it. Despite this, he keeps throwing glances towards the door and over his shoulder.

'It's true that life's comfortable here,' Salvador says. 'London's the envy of half the world. And things have been fairly stable for almost thirty years, since the first Defender took control.'

Before I was born, Chiara thinks. When Mamma was young, and Papà was still alive.

'After the first big inundations, when the sea walls breached, the Defender negotiated massive foreign investment, from China, I think. Most of the money went to London. New flood-proof buildings, new trams to replace the Underground, new Thames barriers, and embankments, and the whole drainage canal system. A safe city for grateful citizens.' His mouth twists.

'Well it is impressive. I've never seen anywhere like this. In Palermo and Napoli people starve to death in the streets.'

'In Madrid too. And yes, London and the other protected cities in England have food, and housing, hospitals, and schools. Luxuries, even. Security. Why did we come, you and I?' He scoops up more gelato as if to emphasise his point.

'I'm not here for myself,' she protests. 'I'm sending money home for my sister and my mother.'

'Me too,' he assures her. 'So, anyway, years back, all the

people whose homes were flooded got free re-settlement in the cities. The Government didn't repair the seawalls, because it was pointless, they said, with the climate changing so fast. They could never protect everyone over such a vast area, and besides, private cars and old-style farming were too harmful for the environment. Some groups questioned it at first, but then there were more floods on the south coast, and the wildfires that destroyed Reading and Doncaster sealed the deal.'

'So terrible.' Chiara has seen the pictures. Whole streets and districts reduced to ash. 'A lot of children died, didn't they?'

'Yes. There was a school they couldn't evacuate in time.' He lays down his spoon and leans in towards her. 'Some people said the fires were deliberate, started by Government agents. And the sea wall breaches too.'

Chiara gasps.

'That can't be true. No one would do such a thing.'

Salvador shrugs.

'Who knows? Anyway, the dissenters were soon silenced. The Defender did a good job. People felt safer, richer, happier even. They cracked right down on urban crime. The Government ramped up artificial food production and signed a load of import deals so agricultural land could be left to go wild. People who stayed in the countryside had to live off the land or starve. Then they brought in the population laws - *Safe Futures*,' as they call it now - to prevent overcrowding.'

'Didn't people complain about only being allowed one child?' Chiara's Nonna had six children - scattered across Europe now; Mamma had two.

'How many babies do most women have in Sicily these days?' Salvador spreads his hands.

'In the villages? That's only old people now. In the cities - it's true, most women choose not to have children. It's too expensive, and there's no childcare, and none of their friends are getting pregnant.'

'You see?' He raises an eyebrow. 'Most people were fine with the one-child policy. Combine it with Peaceful Rest to deal with the pesky demographics, and everyone's a winner. Contentment all round.' He scrapes the last traces of gelato from his dish. 'There were just a couple of problems, which no one was too worried about at first.'

'What were they?'

'Well, certain groups -.'

The street door opens, and Salvador stops in mid-sentence. He watches as a man enters the restaurant and goes to sit at the bar. Chiara checks her Femband: nearly 11.00 pm. She hadn't planned to stay this late.

'Listen, Chiara.' Salvador drops his voice to a whisper. 'Things are changing. Some people, some groups, have been more resilient than anyone expected, and the Government's getting rattled. And the ways the policies get implemented - well, you saw, the other day.' He frowns and rubs at his cheek. 'If you're not happy - if you want to help - there's a network, Chiara.'

He pauses and studies her face, watching for her reaction.

'A network? What do you mean?'

'Shhh!' He presses a finger to his lips. His forehead is almost touching hers.

'There are people working in secret helping women have babies. Women who can't pay, or don't qualify, or don't want to be part of the system. Women in desperate circumstances. Some of us at the Genesis Centre do what we can to help - information, medications, that sort of thing. Do you understand?'

Chiara flinches. Her headache, which had gone away, is back, thundering inside her skull.

'But, isn't that against the law?'

'Of course.' His eyes look for hers, but she won't meet his gaze.

'Who are these people helping the pregnant women? Are they in the hospital?'

'No. Midwives mostly. In their homes, or other places.'

'Midwives? You mean, wise women? *Levatrices del villagio*? Not proper nurses. But that's not safe, not professional.' Nonna gave birth at home, in her cottage, but that was in the old days, before modern healthcare. 'Why are you telling me this?'

'You'd be surprised how qualified the midwives are.' Salvador speaks so fast, Chiara is struggling to catch his words. 'They've got decades of experience. They used to work in the hospitals, but there was a whole series of scandals - babies dying, mistakes made, that sort of thing - and the midwives got the blame. It was - convenient.'

He pauses, waiting for Chiara's response. There's a tight feeling in her gut.

'Is the mafia involved?' The thought makes her feel sick.

'I don't know. They're very independent, these old midwives, but they need help, especially now. And I thought, from your face in Theatre the other day - there's something about you, Chiara. Kindness. You have a good heart, and I couldn't help wondering whether you might be interested?'

He waits. She says nothing.

'But maybe I was wrong?' His hopeful expression fades.

Chiara swallows. The man at the bar is looking straight at them. This could be a trap, a test of her loyalty to the Genesis Centre and the Ministry of Population and Health. And even if not - no. No way. She'd be out of her mind. Mamma and Gemma are relying on her.

She pushes back her chair and stands up.

'It's been nice - thank you - but I don't know why you told me all this. I'm sorry, but I'm not that sort of person. I'm here to work in the hospital, that's all. I've got a family at home, and a career, and I've worked very hard to get this far.'

She fumbles in her purse, finds a banknote, and places it on the table. Too much, but she needs to get out of here.

'Okay.' Salvador tries to hand back the money, but she turns away. He offers to walk her home, but she refuses.

'All right,' he says at last. 'Go carefully, and stay on the well-lit roads, and please, just forget we had this conversation.'

'Sure, that's all I want,' is her parting shot. 'Let's forget we ever saw each other.'

9

EVERYTHING SHE NEEDS

Rava opens the package. Inside is everything she needs: pregnancy test, painkillers, instructions, and the tablets. One big tablet and four little ones. Just like last time.

She's only done this once before, and that was almost twenty years ago, when she was a scared teenager, but it feels like yesterday. It was all a mistake - she'd never meant things to go so far. Her boyfriend was three years older, and he seemed so mature, and she'd wanted to please him. Such a fool she'd been back then.

Now though, she knows this is the sensible thing to do. She's the mature adult now. It wouldn't be fair on Martin to continue this pregnancy, and he promised they can try again. In a year or two, he said. It'll be okay.

She reads the instructions. It's quite simple: take the first tablet today, and the others twenty-four to forty-eight hours later. There'll be pain - she remembers that from last time - and bleeding. It was more blood than she'd expected. A lot more.

THERE WAS ONLY one bathroom in the terraced house in Aberdeen, and after a while Aunt Nasreem started banging on the door, asking why Rava was taking so long and whether she was all right in there. In the end, Rava put on three pads and went out, telling Aunt Nasreem she was fine. She was going to college to study.

The toilets at college were unisex, and there were boys hanging about by the washbasins, laughing and joking. She locked herself in the cubicle; the door didn't reach to the floor, and there was a stink of un-flushed faeces. She sat down, covered her ears with her hands, closed her eyes, and bit down on her tongue so she wouldn't make any sound.

She doesn't remember how long it took. Eventually the boys went away, and the lights went out, and she was alone in the darkness. At some point, the alert on her phone sounded: time for evening prayers, and she almost began to prepare herself. But of course it was pointless. She was impure, unclean in every way.

She never meant to look at what came out, but in the end she couldn't help herself; she had to know. She shone the light from her phone into the toilet bowl. It was all a mess, clots, indistinct, and she isn't sure now what she saw and what she imagined, but she's never been able to get it out of her mind. Even now, the smell of a dirty toilet can bring it back.

When she finally got home, Aunt Nasreem was waiting. She scolded her for being late and asked if she'd been with that no-good unbelieving boyfriend again.

'No, we split up,' Rava told her, before making her way upstairs to the bedroom she shared with her cousin. She lay awake all that night, and the night after, but she doesn't think Aunt Nasreem ever guessed what she'd done.

THIS TIME WILL BE different - of course it will. She's got nothing to hide; women do this every day. She's being responsible, putting the planet first and respecting her husband's wishes. It's not right to have a child before you're both ready. Both parents have to want it.

Rava goes to the kitchen and fills a glass with water. She'll take the first pill now, tell Martin tonight, and phone into work tomorrow to say she needs a Fresh Start break. You get a whole week off, no questions asked, only a form to self-certify afterwards. Some people complain women take advantage, claiming two or three 'extra holidays' in a year instead of getting sterilised. But the Defender is adamant: 'Women's health, women's choices,' she says. No one is forced to claim a gold band before she's ready.

The instructions are simple, with reassuring hand-drawn pictures. The pregnancy test is for afterwards; no need to check now. It was only four days ago she had the scan, and saw the baby - no, the foetus, or is it still an embryo? Rava's not sure. Anyway, she knows she's pregnant, because there it was, wriggling around in there, with fingers, and toes, and a face.

A wave of nausea catches her off guard. All the more reason to do this, she tells herself firmly. But she wishes she hadn't asked to see the screen; she should have listened to the sonographer's warnings. The baby had a heartbeat. It was moving. No, stop this. She's only making it harder for herself.

Rava's own heart thumps painfully in her chest. She wipes sweat from her forehead and gulps down most of the water, leaving the pill on the table. Maybe she should tell Martin first; he's always so understanding, and he wants what's best for her. He'll help her get through this; no need to do it on her own like last time. And it's not as if she's religious anymore. God must hate her now.

IT WAS ALL VERY WELL for Aunt Nasreem; she grew up in a different world. She was married at sixteen, had four children, and never, ever omitted her prayers. She came to Aberdeen to look after Rava and her father, her Baba, after Rava's mother died, may Allah have mercy on her. Aunt Nasreem meant well; she scrubbed, and cooked, and mended from morning till night. But she had fixed ideas about how the world should be and how everyone should behave.

Rava did her best, studied hard, dressed modestly. She truly wanted to please Baba and Allah and be a good Muslim girl. The boyfriend was an aberration. No one had ever looked at her that way before, and she thought she was in love. By the time she realised she was pregnant, he had already dumped her for one of her friends. All she wanted afterwards was to forget the whole thing.

No one warned her about the dreams, the nightmares that still come, now and then, and catch her off guard. No one warned her that something would change inside her. She felt like an outsider; someone who didn't belong. Soon she was making excuses to miss family prayers: her period had started early, she had a late class at college and would pray there instead. She could never look Baba in the face after telling such lies.

She became convinced Nasreem hated her. They argued about silly things: whether Rava was wearing too much make-up; the thickness of her socks; what time she got up in the morning. 'Stop treating me like a child,' she would yell at the plump, interfering old woman. 'You're not my mother, anyway!' By the time Rava turned eighteen, the sound of Nasreem's voice set her teeth on edge.

Baba started talking about marriage to a second-cousin who lived in Edinburgh:

'The young man comes from a good family. They will look after you well, although I will miss you very much.' He showed

Rava photographs of a smartly dressed boy with good teeth and a neatly trimmed beard, and she considered the possibility. She would escape Aunt Nasreem's constant nagging, and Edinburgh was a beautiful city, everyone said. But something stood in her way. She wasn't the right sort of person to get married. The potential husband wouldn't like her. She was untidy, too thin, too angry. Something was fake about her, as if she were made of plastic like a mannequin in a shop window.

Baba cried when Rava told him she was going to London. She found a job at a bank, very junior, but it paid just enough to cover the rent on a shared room. A few years before, his tears would have broken her heart, but now she felt numb. She said she would visit often, but that was another lie. In twenty years, she's only been back three or four times.

RAVA'S STOMACH PITCHES, and bile rises in her throat. She drank too much water too fast - so stupid! Clutching a hand to her mouth, she runs for the bathroom, falls to her knees and vomits into the toilet. Once she's coughed up the last dregs, she washes her face. Her throat burns.

That's the second time today. If she takes the pill now, she might just throw it straight up again. Then she'd have to send off for another kit, and she's already ten weeks, nearly eleven - running out of time to do this at home.

She'll do it tomorrow, when she's feeling better, and she'll tell Martin first. That's only fair. It's his baby too, after all, and it's not her fault she's a girl, poor little thing.

Tomorrow. Rava closes the box, re-seals it, and puts it back in the drawer. She'll do it tomorrow.

10

EXTRA SHIFTS

'You didn't call last night. I was waiting.' Gemma's face fills the phone screen. She looks annoyed.

'Sorry Gia. I was working late.' She forgot, but Chiara's not about to admit that to her sister. All these extra shifts, trying to save money, to buy herself more options. She barely has the time to wash herself or eat, let alone phone home. 'What's your news?'

'*La solita solfa!* Nothing ever changes around here. Old Signor Guiseppe had a stroke and got taken off to hospital. I doubt he'll be coming back; this place is a mausoleum.'

'Oh, poor Guiseppe!' Nonna always had a soft spot for him, and he was kind when Papà died. 'Is Mamma okay? How's college?'

Gemma yawns.

'Don't ask. Yeah, Mamma's fine. I think she's finally getting the message; she's put the cottage up for sale - not that it's worth much, of course. Who'd want an ancient heap of stones in this scrapyard?'

A hole opens up deep in Chiara's stomach. Gemma scarcely remembers the village as it used to be: the feast days with wine and dancing; the harbour busy with fishing boats; the throngs of holiday makers. It's true there's no work anymore; everyone's moving to the cities. But if Mamma and Gemma sell up and leave the village, her family won't belong anywhere. She'll be homeless.

'Don't make that face, Chia. I can't wait! In Napoli, I can get a life at last. Or maybe we'll go to Roma. It's all right for you in London, but there's nothing for me in Sicily, is there?'

'I guess not.' Chiara's voice is flat. Maybe the cottage won't sell. Maybe Mamma will change her mind. 'But how will you and Mamma afford to live in Napoli? Some districts are very dangerous, and the Mafia controls all the jobs.'

Gemma shrugs.

'It'll work out. You're sending money, aren't you? This is my big chance to escape. What's the point of college when there's no work? In the city -'. Her eyes shining, Gemma chatters on about shops, and theatres, and meeting the right people, while Chiara pictures crumbling buildings, hollow-eyed prostitutes, and narrow streets piled high with rubbish. She spent a year in Napoli, as part of her nursing training; it's no paradise.

'Anyway, what've you been up to, *sorella mia*?' Gemma changes the subject, perhaps noticing Chiara's lack of enthusiasm. 'How many babies have you delivered this week?'

'I don't actually deliver them; the doctors do that. And I'm mostly working with the postnatal incubators, and sometimes the antenatals.'

'The whats?' Gemma blinks.

'Sorry, I mean the new mammas and the pregnant ones. We have weird names for everything here.'

'Okay. It must be fun though, living in the coolest city on earth. You're so lucky. Have you got a boyfriend yet? A gorgeous doctor maybe?'

'No, no, I'm far too busy working.' Chiara shakes her head rapidly. 'But I'm very lucky to be here.' She stretches her lips into a smile. 'Look, I'm sorry, Gemma, but can I call you again tomorrow, or at the weekend? I'm exhausted right now. Love you, Gia.' She hangs up before Gemma can protest, her smile crumpling like a used tissue.

———

CHIARA WAKES at 6.00 am sharp the next morning. Get up, shower, strap on wristband, press uniform, eat cereal that tastes of cardboard. Then it's time to walk to work, dodging the street cleaners' trucks and ignoring the calls and whistles of builders and security guards. The scarlet Femband, which is supposed to be visible at all times when she's out and about, attracts endless unwelcome male attention.

Chiara speeds up her pace. Gemma's just a kid. She thinks her sister came to London on some sort of extended holiday and that obstetric nursing is like playing with dolls. It's not meant to be fun, not a game. It's work, that's all - hard, professional work, but decently paid, and with prospects, compared to Sicily at least.

As for the boyfriend thing, it's true what she told Gemma: she doesn't have time. Some of the nurses boast about how many men they've had - a different one almost every night, it seems - but Chiara supposes she must be old-fashioned, because that isn't what she wants. Mamma was just eighteen when she married Papà; she says she knew straight away he was the one for her. Chiara doesn't think she'll ever find a love like that.

On the plus side, she's getting used to the Genesis Centre. She's learned a lot. Last week there was another intake of scared, wide-eyed new nurses, and Chiara realised she knows a lot more than they do. She's not a raw newbie anymore.

She's working out how to get the job done on time. Sometimes now she's the first to grab the drug trolley and make her rounds dispensing pills and injections. She no longer stops to chat with the incubators or engage with their endless questions.

'I'll send the healthcare assistant in shortly,' she says. 'Now swallow your medication. It'll help.' And she's away and on to the next one. You have to get round quickly, and without mistakes, or you'll have Sister on your back. But Sister's mostly left her in peace this past week or two, so maybe she's doing something right at last.

She's much quicker at taking bloods. She can insert a cannula in two minutes, even in patients with near-invisible veins. Prepping a woman - no, incubator - for Theatre is easy now. Clothes off, jewellery off, stockings on, medications, shave, catheter, Theatre gown, and cap - all packaged up and ready to go. She's learning to deal with the relatives too: the anxious grandmothers constantly phoning, and the husbands who want to linger after visiting hours.

'One quick kiss,' she tells them, 'and then you have to leave. Your wife needs her rest.' Officially these rules are for infection control, but you can't get everything done with relatives scattering their belongings and emotions all over the ward. *It's for your patients' safety,'* Sister likes to remind them. *'An efficient ward is a safe ward.'*

This morning starts okay. Chiara picks up a coffee on her way through the splendid Atrium, with its marble frieze running around the walls. She admires the carvings of placid mothers, plump-cheeked babies, and muscular fathers, interspersed with pomegranates and ears of wheat. The scale and grandeur remind her of a great cathedral, but with all the colours drained out. Above the entrance to the lifts, gold lettering declares the Centre's motto: *'Delivering Sustainable Futures.'*

She's inside the lift, waiting for the doors to close, when a man with dark, floppy hair dashes inside: Salvador. He grins at Chiara, his blue eyes bright.

'Hi, how's it going?'

'All right, thanks.' She fixes her gaze on the floor, determined to avoid conversation. She's minimised contact with Salvador since that evening at the Italian restaurant, but there's nowhere to hide in this mirrored box. The lift seems to take forever to reach the forty-sixth floor; she can feel him looking at her the entire way up.

On the ward, she recovers her composure before taking handover from the night staff. Determined not to let thoughts of Salvador distract her, she gets her drug round done in record time. By 09.48 her allotted incubators - she nearly always remembers now not to call them mothers - are all settled in their rooms, watching TV or sleeping. Their neonates are lined up tidily in the nursery, antibiotics administered.

She's updating her notes when an alarm shrieks. It's the high-pitched one that means a baby is in the wrong place. Chiara presses save on the computer and rushes to see what's happening.

A woman - not one of Chiara's patients, thank God! - is wandering the corridors with a baby in her arms, its security wristband flashing. She's trying to cover the infant's ears against the howl of the siren.

'What are you doing out of your room with that neonate?' The words fly out of Chiara's mouth.

The woman freezes, her face turning scarlet.

'But it's my baby,' she says, 'I couldn't get him to sleep. He kept crying, so I thought a little walk might help him settle. I wasn't going to take him anywhere.' She hangs her head like a child caught out in a crime.

'No.' Chiara takes the infant from her. 'You can't take the neonate out of the room. It's not safe, and besides, he's not signed off to go home yet. It's not allowed - you know that.' She has to raise her voice over the wail of the alarm. The woman looks blank. Chiara calls over her shoulder. 'Can someone go to the office and switch that off, please? It's just an incubator wandering. I'll sort it.'

The siren dies; Chiara's ears are still ringing. The baby is screaming almost as loud as the alarm.

'I'm sorry - I didn't realise.' The incubator looks shocked and tearful.

'Take this one to the nursery.' Chiara passes the infant to a healthcare assistant. 'And check when he's due for his medication, please. Now, let's get you back to your room.'

Chiara takes the incubator by the arm and walks her back to where she belongs: a little white cell with soft bedding, room service, and gentle music on tap.

'Lorazepam, I think, and maybe something to help you sleep, how does that sound? I'll find your named nurse to check your drug chart. We'll keep the neonate in the nursery, so you can get some rest.'

The woman nods gratefully.

'I'm sorry.' she says again. 'So silly of me. Obviously, I don't know anything about babies or being a mum. I'm probably going to mess it all up, aren't I? My husband was right when he said we're not ready.' She is weeping freely now.

'Calm down,' Chiara says. She passes the patient some tissues. 'You'll feel better when you've had some sleep. Hop into bed now.' She pulls back the covers and smooths the sheet, and the woman climbs obediently in.

Once she's given the medication and got the incubator properly settled, Chiara leaves the room. Sister Miller is standing right outside in the corridor, every blonde hair in place.

'Come to my office,' Sister says. Her voice sounds sweet, but that means nothing. Chiara's palms start to sweat. What's she done wrong this time? Is there a stain on her uniform? Has someone made a complaint?

'Take a seat.' Sister pats the soft armchair. Not the hard chair in the corner today. 'Don't look so worried, dear. Well, now.' She steeples her fingers. 'I've been hearing some reports about your work, Nurse Santori.'

Sister Miller leans forward. Here it comes. Not a drug error - please don't let it be a drug error. Maybe it was that discharge form she got wrong? But Sister is still smiling.

'Relax, Nurse; it's good news - you are making progress. I've received positive feedback from several members of staff. All these extra shifts you've been taking on are making a difference. Experience counts for a great deal, you see.' Chiara's mouth has dropped open. She closes it, and Sister chuckles. 'See - I notice your efforts. I said you'd soon settle in, didn't I? I was very impressed just now by the way you dealt with that hysterical incubator. You were calm and professional. Well done.'

'Thank you, Sister.' Chiara's worked hard for this. She supposes she ought to be pleased.

'I can see you are going to be an excellent nurse, Miss Santori. Management material, perhaps. Have you considered going for your golden Femband? Then we could look at the fast track. I'm sure your family at home would be very proud.' Sister beams, showing all her neat little teeth.

'Thank you. I - I'll think about it, Sister.'

'No need to decide straight away. Now, I'd better let you go. Go for your break, Nurse, and take an extra ten minutes - you've earned it.'

11

IT'S BACK

'Are you all right, Rava? You look a bit peaky.'

Rava picks up her untouched coffee, smells it, and puts it down again. She's gone right off all the things she used to enjoy.

'I'm fine,' she says. 'Just need a bit of fresh air'

She grabs her phone and gets up from her desk, ignoring her colleague Jess's puzzled glance. The bank maintains its offices at a constant, air-conditioned 21 degrees Celsius: the research-based temperature for productive work. But beads of sweat are breaking out on Rava's forehead - that bagel she ate for breakfast was a mistake. She dashes for the toilet, holding her nose against bad smells, and locks herself in.

Rava's always tried to avoid public toilets; even the ones at work sometimes stink. But now she seems to spend her life in them, either throwing up, or thinking about throwing up, or trying to decide what to do. She still hasn't told Martin about the baby. The moment never seems quite right. How can she tell him she's let him down and conceived a girl?

Another wave of nausea grips her. Rava grips the sides of the toilet seat, gagging and doing her best to take deep breaths. She can't take much more of this - it's ridiculous she's let it go on this long. She'll take the pills at the weekend; no need for work to know. There's no shame in it, of course, but she'd rather keep it private.

HER PHONE RINGS on the way back to her desk. She glances at the screen: Aunt Nasreem. One of the cousins' birthdays, maybe, or heavy hints about another loan? It's expensive living in London; Nasreem has no idea, she thinks they're made of money. Rava would like to ignore the call, but her aunt has an annoying habit of ringing repeatedly until she gets an answer. Best get it over with.

'Auntie, I'm at work. Can you call later if it's important?'

'Rava, is that you? I'm sorry, Rava.' There's something wrong with Auntie's voice. She sounds older, shaky. 'I'm sorry, but it's bad news. Your Baba, Rava. Are you sitting down?'

Rava puts out a hand and finds the window. Floor-to-ceiling plate glass, hard and cool. Thirty-seven floors down, miniature people go about their ordinary lives.

'Are you still there, Rava? Abdullah went to the doctor - I've been trying for months to persuade him. I knew something was wrong. And it's back. It's come back, Rava.'

The floor tilts under Rava's feet. She should sit down, like Auntie said, but there's no chair nearby. Her stomach plummets, like a stone falling all those hundreds of feet to the ground below. She knows what 'come back' means. Baba had prostate cancer three years ago. That was the last time she went home, just in case.

But he got treatment and got better. '*Cancer clear,*' the doctors said, thank God. And Rava got on with her London life. '*Good old Baba, he's tough as leather,*' everyone said.

'Back,' she echoes, sinking to the floor and sitting with her back against the window.

'It's bad this time - in his bladder and his bones. The doctor said -.' Nasreem's voice cracks. 'He said a year, maybe eighteen months.' Aunt Nasreem sniffs, and Rava pictures her in the little, old-fashioned kitchen, wiping her eyes on the sleeve of her black abaya. 'He wants to speak to you, but if you're too busy?'

'No, no - put him on.'

In the office, people walk past, carrying files, talking and laughing, but it's all a blur. Baba is her Daddy; he always loved her. He couldn't help being depressed after Mama died.

'Oh my sweetness,' he says, 'Please don't worry, I'm fine. You know how Nasreem likes to fuss. You're far too busy with your husband and your important work at the bank to bother about an old man. The doctors have wonderful medicines, inshallah - if God wills. Let us submit to Allah; in submission we find our peace.'

Rava holds the phone tight to her ear, taking in her dear Baba's voice, his familiar accent rising and falling, his reminders to be a good wife, to trust God. We are all under the eyes of Allah.

'I'll come and see you, Baba,' she tells him. Why has she wasted all these years, not visiting, barely speaking? 'I'll come as soon as I can.' She'll have to get time off work, ask Martin, get a permit to fly to Scotland, but she'll find a way.

'There's no hurry,' he says. 'You have your own life, your own husband to care for now. It would be a great blessing to see you, my sweetness, but I know it is not easy to get here.'

'Of course I'll come,' she says.

'My life is almost complete, *inshallah*. I have been greatly blessed: a beautiful daughter, a son-in-law who provides so well -.' Baba pauses and sighs. 'I have very few regrets - it is wrong to regret. Allah asks us only to submit; his way is best.'

Baba falls silent, and Rava knows with a cold weight of shame what a disappointment she's been to him. His only child, married to an infidel, hundreds of miles from home, and scarcely a visit in all these years. She hasn't even managed to give him -.

'I must let you go,' Baba says. 'Don't worry, my daughter; it is the will of Allah. I have no pain.'

He's about to hang up, but it's no good, she has to say something. She has to tell him.

'Wait, Baba - I have some news for you too.'

'Yes, my sweetness?

'It's good news, Baba. I - I'm expecting a baby.'

Baba falls silent. A passing colleague pauses and gives her a curious look, but she doesn't care. Has the line cut off? Has Baba not heard her, not understood?

'Did you hear me, Baba? I'm having a baby - a little girl, I think. A granddaughter for you. I'm nearly twelve weeks now.' She holds her breath.

'Praise be to God!' he exclaims. 'Praise be. In my old age he grants me this joy! Allah has answered my prayers. Oh my daughter, what a blessing! Your husband must be so happy, so proud. God is good, God is good. Your Auntie will be so excited. When will the child be born?'

'In September,' she tells him.

'If God wills,' he adds. 'Oh Rava, you have given me a reason to keep living. If God wills, I will see my grandchild before I die and give her my blessing. You make me so proud, my dearest Rava - so very proud.'

12

EXPECTANCY

Chiara sits on a bench in the Plaza outside the Genesis Centre. She's got ten minutes before her shift, and the weather is a little warmer today. It's still chilly compared with home, but the spring sunshine is pleasant on her skin and birdsong drifts above the traffic noise.

She's thinking about what Sister Miller said: that she could go for fast-track promotion. That her family would be proud. She could help Mamma buy a new home in the village, or properly update the cottage. Or, if they insist on moving to Napoli, Mamma and Gemma would at least be able to rent an apartment in a decent district. Gemma could go to a good university too. And they would be proud of her; they are already. The only problem is, there are so many things she isn't telling them.

Every day she takes babies from their mothers to be fed with breast milk purchased from poor women in faraway countries. She makes her patients take powerful sedatives to ensure they comply with the rules. If they're good, and pass all the tests, she rewards them with a golden wristband and a baby to take home. Even worse, some babies disappear from the ward, and Chiara hasn't worked yet worked out what happens to them. The parents are usually told their child has an infection and needs a stay in Neonatal, but Chiara's not sure that's the whole story.

When she phones home, she talks about the glossy shops and lush parks, the food, and the lofty buildings. She hasn't mentioned the advertisements for Peaceful Rest with pictures of cheery elderly people extolling the virtues of euthanasia. *'I'm choosing dignity,'* they say. *'I'm choosing for the next generation.' 'I'm choosing for our planet.'* They grin at you from hoardings, and the sides of trams, and screens in hospital waiting rooms.

Chiara can't bring herself to tell her family she has to enter data about her monthly cycles on a Government website and report for an obligatory contraception review every six months. Of course, if she gets herself sterilised - *Sealed,* as they call it - she'll be released from all that. You can see the attraction.

Perhaps she should do it. She used to think she wanted children one day, but that seems increasingly unrealistic. She doesn't even have a boyfriend. And she's getting used to the job, toughening up, just like Sister Miller said she would. She's less emotional, calmer, more able to distance herself from the patients. Before long, the Genesis Centre methods will be second nature. She might even become a Sister herself one day.

Is this why she came to England? Would Mamma be proud? Would Nonna?

Nonna was a nurse once, years and years ago. She looked after cancer patients, and, later, children in a hospice. You'd think it would be depressing, but Nonna loved to reminisce about her nursing days.

'I would play with the little ones and make them laugh,' she told Chiara. 'Laughter is the best medicine - laughter, prayer, and kindness. You will be a wonderful nurse one day, Chiara, because you have a kind heart.' Then Nonna would hold out her arms and Chiara would run into them. Nonna was soft, and she smelled of home-made rosemary soap. She told wonderful stories about dragons, and mermaids, and saints. Santa Agatha, Santa Rosalia, and the Holy Virgin were like dear old friends to her.

Deep in her coat pocket, Chiara's still carrying Nonna's rosary beads. She's not sure whether she believes anymore. Mamma still goes to Mass every Sunday, and Chiara always went with her, until Nonna died. Since then she hasn't been back, except for the funeral.

Everyone said it wasn't Chiara's fault, but that's not true. Nonna was sick, and old, and alone. Mamma was working nights in the canning factory and it was Chiara's job to check on Nonna, but instead she went out with her friends after work. They spent the evening laughing and drinking in a bar, and when Chiara got back, much too late, Nonna was cold. Chiara found her sprawled open-mouthed in her chair.

They said she'd had a stroke; that she didn't suffer. But she died neglected and alone. Chiara was supposed to make her dinner. She was supposed to make sure Nonna took her tablets and got safely to bed, but she didn't. She forgot. She was too busy out enjoying herself. So much for being a wonderful nurse; she couldn't even take care of her own beloved Nonna.

The red band vibrates on Chiara's wrist: *New message.* When she checks her phone, it's as if the system has read her thoughts:

'*Special incentive this month. All unimpregnated women under thirty choosing sterilisation this April will receive a luxury two-day spa package at HeavenScent Sanctum in Regent's Park. Unwind in style with two treatments of your choice, afternoon tea with fizz, and a three-course dinner. Celebrate your Sealing and embrace the benefits. Book your golden future now.*'

CHIARA'S WORKING IN EXPECTANCY: the antenatal clinic on the forty-fifth floor. Sister Miller said a stint here would enhance her experience. The work is an endless repetition of tests and checks: taking bloods, completing forms, and scheduling scans and appointments. It's dull, but less exhausting than Serenity.

Couples sit in the elegantly furnished waiting area, paging through glossy magazines or looking at their mobile devices. The women wear long dresses in pastel shades; most of the husbands are in tailored suits or designer-branded chinos and polo shirts. Everyone looks like everyone else.

Chiara calls out the next name from her list. A pretty, petite woman gets to her feet. She has glossy hair and immaculate make-up. She's alone, which is slightly unusual, and she's clutching tightly onto her Gucci handbag.

'This way.'

The woman follows Chiara into the examination room and sits in the chair, her spine rigid.

'What happens today?' she asks.

'Oh, it's all routine,' Chiara begins. 'We test your urine, and blood pressure, draw bloods for screening, check your medical history. Did you bring a urine sample?'

The woman unzips her bag and fumbles inside. As she hands over the plastic bottle, her hand shakes so badly she almost drops it.

'Are you all right?' Chiara asks. 'Are you scared of needles?' The needle-phobic patients are hard work.

'No, it's not that.' The woman speaks very quietly. She twists her wedding ring round and round on her finger. Chiara waits.

'I'm a little nervous,' the woman confides at last. 'I have some questions about the tests. You test the DNA today, is that right? Find out the baby's sex?'

'That's right.' Chiara's getting used to questions like this. 'Gender, and other things too. Down Syndrome, other defects, probabilities of certain diseases in later life.' She hands the woman a leaflet: *Information to Help You Choose.* 'If you want to select the gender you'll have to talk to one of the doctors. And they'll want to speak to with your husband too.'

You're not allowed to write anything in the notes about sex selection because it's illegal once the embryo has implanted, but quite a few patients ask. In practice, when a foetus is the wrong gender - virtually always female - a doctor comes up with a medical reason for ending the pregnancy and this is what goes in the records. There are running jokes at the Genesis Centre about the ratio of baby boys to girls - another thing Chiara hasn't told Mamma.

But the woman shakes her head.

'Do I have to have this test?'

'I think so.' No one's asked her this before. 'I think it's a condition of the incubation licence.' Chiara makes a mental note to review her reading on this topic. The laws are mind-numbingly complicated. '

'Okay.' The woman starts fiddling with her wedding ring again. 'And how do I get the results? Is it a letter? An email?'

'An email, I think - to you and your husband. It comes from a private diagnostics company. Are you feeling all right?'

The woman has turned very pale. Chiara offers her water.

'No thank you - I'm fine. It's just that - I want to surprise my husband, you see. Is there any way you can send the email just to me, so I can tell him myself?'

The woman won't meet Chiara's gaze. She's dry-washing her hands in her lap, and Chiara's suddenly certain there's more to this than she's letting on.

'Well, your details are on the computer, you see. Your's and your husband's. The testing company gets them when I upload the blood form.'

'Could you change the details? Please?'

'I'm sorry,' Chiara begins, but the woman reaches across and touches her arm.

'Please,' she repeats. 'You see, I think my baby's a girl - that's what they said at the scan - but my husband wants a boy. I'm sure with a little more time, when the baby's bigger, he will change his mind. I know he will love our baby. It's just that this all feels so rushed. If the DNA results come to me first, I can tell him when we're both ready.'

Chiara bites her lip. She could get into trouble for this. If the husband finds out and complains, she'll probably lose her job. The woman gazes up at her with wide, pleading eyes.

'Hmm. Let's do your observations.' Chiara glances at the clock. She mustn't draw attention by being slow to process her patient. Once she's recorded the woman's blood pressure - slightly high - and dipped her urine, Chiara draws blood for the screening tests. The woman has tiny veins, so she selects the finest needle, being as gentle as she can.

'Thank you, you're very kind,' the woman says when the test tubes are filled. Chiara flushes. Kind? The word stings like acid on a wound.

'You have a kind heart,' Nonna used to say.

'There's something about you: kindness,' Salvador said.

Ever since she was a little girl, bandaging her dolls and looking after stray kittens, Chiara's wanted to be a nurse. A real nurse, who helps people when they're hurting, not a hospital drone who obeys without question, turning a blind eye for the sake of efficiency and a quiet life.

Nonna used to help feed the kittens, saving milk for them from her ration and ignoring Mamma's scolding about the waste. Chiara cried when Mamma got angry, but Nonna hugged her tight. *'Sii corragiosa, Chiara, ascolta il tuo cuore,'* she used to say: Courage! Listen to your heart.

Chiara inhales and slowly lets out her breath. Then she opens the DNA testing form on her computer.

'All right,' she says, 'I'm deleting your husband's contact

details. Only on this form, mind. And please be sure to tell him soon, won't you?'

In reply, the woman embraces her in a quick, tight hug.

'Thank God,' she says, 'and thank you - you're a lovely nurse. Thank you for understanding.'

A lovely nurse? The words echo in Chiara's mind for the rest of her shift. It would take more than an altered form for her to become the nurse she used to dream of being. A whole lot more.

13

STORE CUPBOARD

All that night, Chiara drifts in and out of vivid dreams. She sees Nonna rocking baby Gemma to sleep. She smells rosemary soap mingled with blood and fresh urine. She hears Katie's howl when they tell her baby Bella is dead.

The next day, she tracks down Salvador on the Delivery ward.

'Salvador,' she calls. 'Can I talk to you?' He freezes, and for a moment she thinks he's going to hurry away as if he hasn't heard. But then, all in one motion, he opens the door to one of the large store cupboards and sweeps her inside, pulling the door shut behind them.

It's totally dark. Chiara fumbles for the light switch, her heart hammering. Has she stumbled into a scene in one of those cheesy TV hospital dramas where the doctor kisses the nurse in the storeroom? She lunges for the door, but he's in her way. She feels for the light again, and his face is suddenly so close his beard brushes against her cheek.

'*Fermati!* Stop!' she manages, but at that moment the light snaps on, and she staggers sideways, almost falling over a box of speculums. Salvador holds a finger to his lips, his other hand extended in warning. His floppy hair is untidier than ever.

'Shhh!' His gaze is intense. He smells of newly-washed cotton with a hint of fresh sweat.

'What's going on? I only wanted to speak to you.'

'Sorry, I didn't mean to scare you.' He takes a step back. 'But it's not safe in the hospital; people are listening, and there are cameras everywhere.' He scans the windowless room as if someone might be hiding behind the boxes of IV fluids, or perched high on the top shelf. 'We're okay in here though,' he adds. 'At least, I'm fairly certain.'

Fairly certain? And if he's wrong?

'So what did you want to say to me?' he asks.

Chiara inhales. It's now or never. Nonna wouldn't hesitate.

'I've been thinking,' she says, 'about what you asked me. I tried to forget it, but I can't. All this -.' She casts a hand around the cannula sets and drug pumps, the syringes and security bracelets. 'I want to be more than this.' She pauses, and he nods slowly, waiting.

'So, I'll try' she says. 'If there's something I can do, to help the midwives? I'm terrified, but I have to try.'

She half expects him to say she's got it all wrong, that he doesn't know what she's talking about, before calling Security to arrest her. But he gives her a smile that lights up his improbably blue eyes.

'Amazing. Yes, I'm sure you can help. Perfect timing, as it happens; a request came through yesterday.'

'Yesterday?' She'd been thinking about next month, or the one after, when she's feeling ready.

'Listen,' Salvador goes on, ignoring her gasp of surprise. 'We can't talk here - it's too risky. Meet me at Cucina Piccola after your shift, and I'll give you the details, okay?'

She nods, speechless, wondering what she's got herself into.

'You leave the storeroom first,' he says, 'and I'll wait in here a few more minutes. We should avoid speaking to one another on the wards as much as possible from now on.'

She nods again, dry-mouthed.

'And Chiara - thank you! I knew you were kind and brave. See you later.'

As she goes to leave, he kisses her lightly on the cheek. Just politeness, of course; he's Spanish, after all. But later she catches herself replaying the moment and wondering. As if she didn't have enough to worry about!

———

'THERE'S A MIDWIFE OUT EAST. She lives on a boat.'

They're at the same table again, at the back of Cucina Piccola. Chiara takes a gulp of her coffee.

'Okay,' she says slowly. 'On the sea? What sort of boat?' She pictures the painted fishing boats of her childhood with their bright blues, reds, and yellows.

'No, not the sea. A canal boat. She's asked for a nurse to escort a patient. It's quite simple. You pick up the woman from her home and take her to the midwife's place to have her baby.'

'Where does the woman live? And why can't her family take her?' It doesn't sound simple. For a start, Chiara doesn't know her way around London; she's scarcely ventured more than a mile from the Genesis Centre.

'Wait a minute.' Salvador gets up, goes to the bar, and speaks to the proprietor. A moment later, loud music warbles through the trattoria. 'That's better. No danger of anyone eavesdropping. Now listen.'

Chiara leans in close and Salvador speaks into her ear, his breath warm:

'This couple who've contacted us - sterilisation is against their religion. And there are extra restrictions on their community. They're a Jewish family - Orthodox. There used to be

Jewish midwives in Stamford Hill but they were both arrested last month and haven't been heard of since.' He runs a hand through his hair. Chiara picks up her biscotti and puts it down again.

'Liz - that's the midwife's name - she usually asks for a nurse escort because your ID's good for travel, and you can help if there are problems on the way. But the nurse who went last time said she thought someone was following her, so she's reluctant to go again, for a while at least.'

Not a great endorsement then.

'Is it dangerous?'

'Well, you need to be careful. But if you take all the precautions it should be straightforward enough.'

Chiara tilts her head and gives him a long look.

'Really?'

'Okay, it could all go wrong.' He fidgets with his napkin. 'Look, you don't have to do this - we can probably find someone else.'

She chews her lower lip.

'But these people need help?'

'They're desperate. But I understand; it's too risky. I shouldn't have asked you.'

'No - I said I'd help.' She raises her voice as Dean Martin croons 'That's Amore' through the cafe's sound system. 'I'll do it, but only this once, okay? I can't afford to get too involved.'

He reaches across and brushes her fingers with his. Her skin tingles.

'Thank you, Chiara. They'll be very grateful. Now, I need to give you this.' He hands her a supermarket bag with something inside. 'Don't look at it now, just listen - there's a few things you need to remember.'

14

PERFECT FAMILY

'So how was the clinic?'

Martin kicks off his shoes and settles himself on the sofa. He looks tired. While he pets Louis, she pours him a whiskey - a large one on ice the way he likes it.

'Tell me about your day first,' she says. 'The clinic was fine - all good.'

He leans back and sighs.

'Same old, same old. Down, Louis, good boy! Usual grief from the boss, grief from effing Toby, more pressure to get the sterilisation numbers up.' He yawns. 'But I'm making progress on the midwife project. Don't worry, I won't go into detail. Some of it's not very pretty, but women need protecting from those charlatans. Besides, I need that promotion. Louis, down! I know you love your daddy, but I want to talk to mummy.' Having thoroughly licked Martin's face, the little dog trots away to his basket.

'Come and sit here, Rava, sweetheart.' Martin pats the cushion beside him. 'I want to hear all about your appointment at the Genesis Centre. I wish I could've been there, but there was no escaping that committee meeting.'

'There wasn't much to it really.' Rava does her best to sound casual. 'They weighed me, measured me, and took blood for all the tests. It's a beautiful building - luxurious.'

Nothing like the scruffy Infirmary in Aberdeen, where Mama spent her final weeks.

'Did you spot any celebrities?'

'I'm not sure.' She was too busy worrying about the baby and all the tests to notice her fellow patients.

'Next time perhaps.' He squeezes her shoulder. 'The Genesis Centre is fabulous; you'll be well looked after. Nothing but the best for our baby. So -.' He swirls the ice in his glass. 'Six million dollar question: Did you have another scan today? Have they told you the gender yet? I thought they might have said something last time.'

Rava replies a little too quickly.

'They said we can't be sure until we get the DNA results, which will take least a week, maybe longer. Warm in here, isn't it?' she adds, feeling her cheeks redden.

Martin raises an eyebrow.

'That's a bit poor. I'll have to insist on another scan; I'll give them a call tomorrow - pull some strings. It's not fair to keep you waiting. And I'll come with you next time.'

The heat reaches Rava's hairline. That can't happen.

'No, there's no need,' she blurts out. 'I had a scan this morning.'

'Oh fantastic. Why didn't you say?'

'I was going to tell you, but -.'

'But what? You did ask about the gender, didn't you?'

'Yes, of course.' What else can she say? She's played this all wrong.

'And?' He leans in and takes her face between his hands. 'What is it, boy or girl? You said it was all good, so I'm guessing -?'

'Yes,' she says. 'A boy. They said they think it's a boy.'

A boy. The words hang between them. Rava's never lied to Martin before - not about anything important. They've always trusted each other, shared everything. But before she can take it back, or even remind him about the DNA test, Martin plants his mouth on hers. He kisses her, hard and full, and she tastes the whiskey on his tongue.

'That's wonderful news,' he says when he releases her. 'Fantastic. You know, my darling, I wasn't sure about incubating. I was worried we weren't ready, but now - a boy - we can start looking forward.' He knocks back the rest of his drink and pours himself another, grinning from ear to ear.

'We could look at some bigger apartments if you like?' he suggests. 'At the weekend? Shall we see what's available?' He picks up his phone and starts tapping away at the screen.

'There's no rush,' she says. 'Let's not get ahead of ourselves; it's still early days.'

'You're right, I'm getting over-excited. But I've got a good feeling. I'm so proud of you, Rava, incubating our son!' He pats her on the stomach. 'Hey, come here, Louis-wooey. You're going to have a baby brother. You, me, Mummy, and baby Edward - we'll be the perfect family, won't we?'

'Perfect family,' Rava echoes, as Louis jumps up to join them on the sofa. It's what she's always wanted. But something sour burns at the back of her throat - the whiskey, maybe? She swallows hard, but she can't get rid of it.

PART II

15

THE JOURNEY

Chiara is ironing her uniform when the black phone buzzes. It gives her such a fright she almost drops the iron. She's been on edge, twitchy, sleeping fitfully ever since Salvador gave her the bag with the phone inside.

'Hello?'

'Hello. We were given this number, and the password "*Shifrah.*" Am I speaking to the right person?' The speaker sounds like an older woman with an accent Chiara can't place. German, perhaps?

'Yes, I'm the nurse.' Chiara presses the phone closer to her ear.

'Ah good, good. Devorah is labouring well - regular contractions. It is time for the midwife.'

The phone feels slippery in Chiara's hand.

'Are you sure?'

'Yes, of course. They said you could escort my daughter? How soon can you come? We were told you might be working.'

Chiara takes in her safe little room with her books lined up on the shelf and her bed neatly made. This woman doesn't know her shift pattern. She could say she's too busy, throw the burner phone in the river, and forget the whole thing. It would be somebody else's problem.

'Are you still there, please?' Behind the voice, a low moan rises, reaching a crescendo with a long, anguished 'oohhh.'

'Stay calm, Devorah. Breathe through it,' the woman says.

The cry fades, and a younger woman speaks:

'It hurts, Mama. It's getting stronger. Is the nurse coming?'

Chiara hears a high note of fear in Devorah's voice. The stray kittens used to mew in little, high-pitched squeaks, calling for comfort, and Nonna would tuck them inside her clothes to keep them warm. She was never afraid of being scratched or bitten. *'Pray, hope and don't worry,'* she always used to say.

Chiara crosses herself, crouches to unplug the iron, and speaks rapidly, before she can change her mind.

'Yes,' she says. 'I'm coming. I can come right now. Where do you live?'

Chiara removes her Femband and hides it at the back of a drawer. In its place, she straps on the fake band that came in the bag with the phone. Now they can't track her movements; at least, she hopes not.

THE HOUSE in Stamford Hill has a blue front door with peeling paint. Almost before Chiara has finished knocking, she is hurried inside, into a high-ceilinged hallway. The older woman from the phone call introduces herself as Naomi. She is plainly dressed in a dark skirt, black cardigan, sturdy slippers, and thick, flesh-coloured stockings. On her wrist is a yellow Femband - yellow, not gold - stamped with a Star of David.

'Come through,' she says, leading Chiara into a big, clean kitchen at the back of the house. Several children are playing in the garden outside, and the smell of baking hangs warm in the air. The scent pierces Chiara with a pang of longing. Nonna's bread was always soft inside, the sweet steam rising when you broke it open.

'I would offer you something to eat,' Naomi says, as if reading Chiara's mind, 'but I fear we have no time. They said the driver would be outside at six precisely, and he cannot wait. Stay here, while I go to fetch Devorah.'

Chiara sits in the kitchen with its well-used wooden cupboards, and two spotless sinks. From upstairs, the moaning she heard on the phone comes again. Is this what birth sounds like without doctors and surgery and anaesthetics? Nonna had all her babies at home, in the cottage, but by the time Chiara was born most Italian women went to hospital for delivery. It's safer, everyone says. She's never seen a baby born the old way.

Her stomach clenches, and she gets to her feet, looking at the front door at the end of the long hallway, her fingers fluttering in panic. She's here on false pretences. Maybe she should leave now, before -.

But as she steps into the hall, a door opens at the top of the stairs, and Devorah emerges. She's young - younger than me, Chiara thinks - and slender apart from the round football of her pregnant belly. She descends carefully, stopping halfway down to grip the banister rail with both hands. Here she stands still, swaying and making that low moaning sound, eyes closed, for thirty seconds or more, before continuing down.

'Chiara? Mum says you're here to look after me.' Devorah extends a hand, which Chiara shakes. Devorah has fair skin with freckles dotted over her nose and cheeks. She wears glasses with blue frames. 'First baby,' she says, pointing at her prominent bump, 'so Mum wants me to have a midwife for the birth. I'm not letting them sterilise me at the hospital - not that they give us Jews incubation licences anyway. We have to fend for ourselves.'

Chiara nods, not knowing what to say.

Naomi passes Chiara a small suitcase.

'We have already sent payment for the midwife,' she says. 'I wish I could come with you, but they say it's not safe. We must not draw attention. Everyone is so worried these days; my husband keeps saying we should move out of London, but our home is here, our community. We are used to being different, but things have become much harder since the new laws.' She casts a glance in the direction of the children in the garden. 'Have you worked with the midwife for a long time?' she asks Chiara.

'Um-hum,' murmurs Chiara, bending down as if to check her shoelaces. This doesn't seem like a good time to undermine the family's trust. Salvador's explanations were sketchy when it came to the midwife. He's never actually met this Liz, whoever she is. He said she's reliable, but how does he know, really?

Perhaps Naomi senses Chiara's uncertainty, because she places a hand on her shoulder.

'Thank you for what you do,' she says gravely. 'For us, this is very important. In our faith, children are a gift from God. We believe in family, not the rules of this Government.'

A rap at the door makes them all jump. Naomi opens it to reveal a man standing beside a battered jeep.

'Shifrah?' he says - the code word again. 'You ladies ready?'

Naomi embraces Devorah, squeezing her almost tightly enough to pop the baby out.

'Come back home soon, my darling, with your precious little one. I will be praying for you. May Adonai answer you in times of distress, may the name of the God of Ya'akov protect you.'

She kisses her daughter on both cheeks before releasing her, smiling with what Chiara suspects is a manufactured confidence.

'Go safely!' Naomi calls, as the two young women climb into the vehicle. Chiara can't be sure, but she thinks she sees tears on the older woman's cheeks as she stands watching the jeep disappear into the failing light.

———————

DEVORAH'S GROANS subside during the journey, which is a relief. Chiara's expected to take charge in an emergency, but she doesn't know what to do with no doctors or operating Theatres to call on. Every few minutes, Devorah becomes still and deepens her breathing, and Chiara clenches her own fists and jaw, but nothing more happens, thank God. Go faster, Chiara wills the driver.

When they reach the city limit, at the checkpoint, Chiara holds out her ID first, like the driver told her. She tries to look as if she travels in and out of London all the time. If anyone asks, she's to say she's on her way to work at the Romford Sealing hub. The soldier nods when he sees the Ministry of Population and Health logo and the words '*Registered Medical Staff*' on her card. He casts a cursory glance at the driver's ID, and waves them through, not seeming to notice the huddled shape under a blanket on the back seat. As they cross the bridge over the perimeter canal, Chiara realises she has been holding her breath.

Ten minutes later, the driver pulls up on a side street. Beige brick housing blocks line the road. Many of the windows are boarded up, and leaking drainpipes hang loose, trails of green-black slime staining the walls. Split bags of rubbish lie in smelly heaps beside overflowing bins.

'This is it,' the driver says. He hands Chiara a scrap of paper with a hand-drawn map and some scribbled instructions. 'Down that way, hang a left, and you'll see the river. You're looking for the Rosie Lee – long narrowboat with flowers down the sides. Shouldn't be far. Rip this note up and chuck it in the river, or burn it.'

Chiara helps Devorah out onto the pavement. The air is damp and the daylight is almost gone. The jeep drives away.

'It's not far,' Chiara encourages Devorah, hoping this might be true. Devorah plods slowly along the broken pavement, walking with her legs wide apart as if straddling a horse. Several times she has to stop and lean, panting, against a wall. 'Come on, we need to keep moving,' Chiara urges, doing her best to keep her voice steady.

An old man clutching a bottle shouts something Chiara doesn't understand. Two children, who look too young to be out on their own, pick their way through the jumble of dog mess and broken glass littering the road. A rat darts out of a rotting roll of old carpet. Chiara and Devorah turn a corner onto a side street ending in concrete steps. The steps lead up onto a bridge illuminated by a single streetlight.

The river beneath is a filthy brown, lined on both sides with boats of every kind. Painted barges, ancient fibreglass hulls, and cabin cruisers are moored along the banks for as far as Chiara can see. Smoke curls from their chimneys and hangs in the air.

On the far side of the bridge lies a mass of shabby improvised dwellings. In the gloom, Chiara surveys the outlines of caravans, tents, old buses, and wrecked boats propped up with stakes of wood. People mill around shacks made of wood, or corrugated iron, or cardboard. Skinny children sit on the roofs of broken-down cars and in the backs of trucks. This must be one of the camps Salvador told her about, where the black band people live.

Chiara rubs her eyes; she thought England was a rich country, but this scene reminds her of the refugee camps near the beaches in Sicily, where the boat people from North Africa end up, except that everything here is cold and drowned in mud. Groups of teenagers huddle near the water's edge, smoking cigarettes. A woman wearing flip-flops with a toddler at her side lowers a bucket into the oily river. The smoke from a hundred camp fires stings the back of Chiara's throat.

She squints at the map, trying to make sense of it, but the last instruction says only *'Rosie Lee, narrowboat'*. Chiara isn't sure what a narrowboat looks like. She'll never be able to find it in this chaos of boats and humanity, in the near-darkness, with Devorah huffing and moaning and stopping all the time. There's no alternative - she's going to have to ask someone. She shivers and pulls her coat around her, trying to feel brave.

'Wait here for a moment,' she tells Devorah. But Devorah grips Chiara's arm like a tourniquet and lets out a massive groan, her loudest yet. 'Shhh,' Chiara begs. 'Please, Devorah, it's not safe here. We have to find the midwife.' They are standing right underneath the yellow streetlamp, high on the brow of the bridge where everyone can see them. 'Please, let me -.'

But Devorah collapses onto her knees and yells aloud, clutching at her stomach.

'I can't do it,' she wails. 'I can't go any further. My baby is coming. Help me, Chiara!'

16

DNA

Martin's going to be late tonight. He was held up in a meeting, he said, so he's going straight from the office to his karate club. It's somewhere in Stratford, outside the city limits, and he often goes for a drink afterwards. With his Government car, he doesn't have to worry about the curfew. Daniel, Martin's driver, is on call 24/7.

Usually Rava misses her husband's company, but right now she's grateful for a quiet evening. She hasn't been able to focus at work all week, and her head feels as if someone's driving nails into it. How did everything get so complicated? All she wants is a happy family, but she seems to have stumbled into a mesh of lies.

Soon she's going to have to change her red 'unimpregnated' Femband for a blue 'incubating' one, and then everyone will know, including her boss and colleagues. And they'll all be asking if it's a boy or a girl. She's already been getting suspicious sideways looks. Her slender waist is noticeably thicker, and she still keeps rushing to the toilets to throw up.

'Is there something you're not telling me?' her friend Jess

asked yesterday, arching her eyebrows. Rava murmured something noncommittal, but Jess clearly wasn't convinced.

Alone in the quiet apartment, Rava opens the fridge, surveys its contents, and closes it again.Will this sickness ever go away? She makes a peppermint tea, flops onto the sofa, and buries her head in her hands. How can a creature the size of a kiwi fruit drain your energy like this?

Louis nuzzles at her knees. She ought to walk him - it'll be light outside for another hour - but she can't summon the strength. Besides, she needs to make the most of this evening alone.

'Not now, Louis. I'll take you out tomorrow.' She feels sorry for the little dog, shut up in the apartment all day. 'I'll fetch you a treat, okay?'

A few peanut-and-banana flavoured dog cookies settle him down. Not good for Louis's waistline, but Rava's got more pressing problems. Any day now, Martin will be asking about the DNA report; it's a miracle he hasn't already. If she says it hasn't arrived he might call the hospital to chase it up. And then what?

He might not realise she lied; the scan could have been a mistake. Would he believe that? It wasn't, of course; the DNA report arrived in her email box two days ago: *'Female foetus,'* it said, *'no chromosomal abnormalities detected.'* This was followed by a long list of syndromes she's never heard of and numbers she doesn't understand. She's read it over and over.

The peppermint tea is soothing. She sips it slowly, trying to decide. The simplest thing, surely, is to show Martin the report. The baby's thirteen weeks now; she's got bones, and kidneys, and vocal cords. And she's Martin's child too. He wanted a boy in the abstract, but he'll love his own baby, male or female, won't he?

Rava's almost convinced. But she keeps remembering how Martin reacted on their anniversary, when she first told him she was incubating. For a moment, before he had time to compose himself, his eyes looked like grey stones. It made her shiver, as if he was frozen inside.

He came round later, of course, and he's excited about the idea of a son - a boy to carry on his name. But she can't forget that icy stillness. He said he doesn't want a daughter.

Rava presses both hands over her belly. Are you all right in there, little one? I want to keep you safe. The problem is, it's easy for Martin to say no. He's signed the first lot of paperwork, for the incubation licence, but that's just the beginning. He still needs to pay all the hospital fees, and then, later, sign the parenting documents. *'Parenting is a privilege, not a right,'* says the slogan plastered on buses and in posters on the walls of the Genesis Centre. A child can't be registered without a father willing to provide for it.

Rava fidgets with her wedding ring, which has got a bit tighter recently. She goes to the kitchen and makes herself a piece of toast with jam. It tastes good, so she pops a second slice in the toaster. Maybe she needed the sugar, because her mind clears a little as she munches. She can't risk telling Martin, not yet. Once he knows, there'll be no going back. She needs to buy some more time.

She double-locks the front door before getting out her phone. Martin doesn't know her password, but she changes it, just in case. She must remember to clear her search history too. Then, with trembling fingers, she types: *'Fake DNA Health and Gender Report.'* A list of search results appears instantly; other people must do this too.

Rava clicks on a hopeful-looking provider. The service is surprisingly affordable, and there are reassurances about the report coming from a 'real' testing laboratory and so on, although this could be a pack of lies.

Rava reviews several more websites before coming back to the first one. She reads and re-reads the details, studying the sample report and comparing it with her real one. It looks convincing enough to her.

She's already thought about how to pay. Martin checks all their bank statements each month, so she asked Jess at work - who's pretty streetwise - how she can buy Martin a surprise present without him knowing the cost. Jess raised her eyebrows again, but suggested a prepaid debit card.

'But get yourself a bank account he doesn't know about too,' Jess added. 'It's basic common sense. I know you think the sun shines out of Martin's arse, but no man is perfect, trust me!'

Rava thinks this is going a bit far. Jess's had a lot of man trouble, so she's cynical. Martin's different; he's a good husband, always considering her needs. This business about the baby's sex is just an isolated problem.

She bought the debit card this afternoon with cash - *'to keep my options open,'* she told herself. If Martin asks why she needed cash she'll say she was sending money to Scotland for Aunt Nasreem's birthday.

Louis barks suddenly and Rava leaps to her feet. Is Martin home already? But it's only someone passing on the landing outside. Louis scrabbles at the door and comes to paw at Rava's knee, still restless for his walk.

'It's too late now, Louis,' she says. 'Tomorrow, okay?' Then, with her forehead screwed into a frown, Rava types her details rapidly onto the fake DNA request form.

She checks and double-checks it before pressing send.

'Allah have mercy on me,' she breathes. 'God help me, please, and keep my baby safe.'

17

ROSIE LEE

She appears outlined against the smoky sky: an old woman, wearing gypsyish skirts and a knitted hat, her features invisible in the gloom. With an oil lantern in one hand, and rubber boots on her feet, she looks at home on the marshes. Salvador said the Mafia are in charge out here; this crone might be a decoy, a trap.

Chiara moves closer to Devorah, trying to shield her from view, but the woman comes striding across the bridge towards them. Does she want money? Chiara fumbles in her bag for something to give her, to make her go away. The woman's eyes glint in the lamplight. Her face is creased like a rotten apple. Her nose is large and not quite straight. She smells of spices and the river. She looks like a witch from a fairy tale, or a nightmare.

Heart pounding, Chiara steps forward holding out her purse.

'Are you hungry?' she asks, trying to hide the quaver in her voice. 'Can I give you some money?' But the woman waves away her offering with a laugh, revealing uneven teeth. It is not an unkind laugh.

'So here you are at last. You must be Devorah,' she says, bypassing Chiara and resting a hand on Devorah's shoulder. 'I was expecting you an hour ago. It looks as if the walk from the drop-off point has worked wonders. Now let's get you somewhere warm.' Her voice sounds more like Sister Miller's than a beggar's; it's a voice accustomed to telling people what to do. 'I'm Liz,' she adds, 'the midwife. Calm down,' she adds to Chiara. 'I don't bite. Not often anyway.'

Liz is shorter than Chiara, and so plump she is almost spherical, bundled up in swathes of old shawls. She wears no Femband at all. With Chiara's help, she hauls Devorah to her feet. She takes Devorah's right arm and instructs Chiara to take her left, and together they cross to the far side of the bridge. By the time they get down the steps onto the far bank, Devorah is gripped by another surge of pain. She leans against Chiara, dragging at her shoulders.

'Stand steady,' Liz tells Chiara. 'You need to be strong for her.'

They make their way along the towpath beside the river, Devorah slipping and stumbling in the mud. Chiara is grateful for her sturdy work shoes, although she will have to clean and polish them back to a shine before returning to the wards.

The boats at the water's edge look dank and grey, nothing like the sunny fishing boats in long-ago Sicily. Their roofs are piled high with wheelbarrows and bicycles, plastic crates and what looks like heaps of rubbish. It's almost dark now, and Chiara can't read any of the names. She could never have found the right one on her own.

'Right-ho. Here she is.' Liz's lantern illuminates a row of big red flowers painted along the side of an old wooden vessel. A rosy glow peeks out from circular portholes. Liz hops aboard with surprising agility. She hangs her lantern on a hook and reaches out a hand to help Devorah. 'In you go,' Liz says, as Devorah squeezes through a tiny doorway and disappears.

Chiara waits on the chilly path. Liz hasn't asked her name or spoken to her except to give instructions.

'Shall I go now?' she asks. She's completed her task - to deliver Devorah to the midwife - but Liz is the sort of person from whom you ask permission.

'Is there somewhere else you have to be?' Liz heaves off her boots, grunting, and inverts them over a rack beside the door.

Chiara's not due back on shift for another two days.

'Not really,' she says.

'Well, why are you hanging about outside then? Can't you see I could do with a hand? I asked them to send a nurse. Are you a nurse? Whatever that means these days!'

Chiara steps onto the narrow deck. There is scarcely any space to stand. Every surface is crowded with shadowy objects: boxes, ropes and flower pots among them. The boards rock under her feet, and she senses the cold water beneath. Something soft and furry rubs itself against her legs.

'Come on then. We've got work to do. Leave your shoes out here, please.' Liz indicates the rack.

Chiara takes off her shoes and treads down three wooden steps into the belly of the Rosie Lee.

INSIDE IS WARM; a long, narrow space lit by candles and oil lamps. Chiara inhales herbs and beeswax, a heady mingling of rosemary with something earthy and female. The floor is soft under her bare feet. It's thick with rugs: multi-coloured ones, made from long strips of rags rolled up and stitched together, and others that might be animal skins. A low bed is covered with blankets and a hand-sewn patchwork quilt scattered with pink and orange cushions. Velvety curtains hang at the windows.

Lumpy bundles wrapped in white muslin are neatly

arrayed on the tiled kitchen surface, which has been scrubbed clean. An iron stove crouches in the corner with a wood fire burning. Liz fills a red enamel kettle with water and puts it on to boil next to a bubbling pot. Whatever is in the pot smells tasty. Chiara hasn't eaten since the sandwich she had for lunch before pressing her uniform. It seems a lifetime ago.

A mew reveals the furry presence to be an enormous ginger cat with long hair and a proprietorial stare. He paces up and down, taking in the presence of two newcomers to his home.

'All right, Gaskin,' Liz soothes him. 'Say hello to our friends, and then settle down.' He meets her gaze and then obliges, hopping up onto the bed and curling himself up in a corner. His purring fills the room with a throaty rhythm.

Devorah stands at one end of the narrow space, gripping onto a shelf and circling her hips. Her eyes are closed. Liz stands beside her, one hand on Devorah's back, the other resting on top of her huge baby bump. Her eyes are shut too, as if she is concentrating on something. She murmurs under her breath, but Chiara can't hear what she's saying. After a few moments, Liz removes her hand from Devorah's belly.

'Wow, that was a massive one,' she says. 'You are remarkable, my dear. All will be well. You are safe here. Now rest until the next surge comes.'

Liz turns to Chiara, suddenly brisk.

'Right then, let's get organised. Could you open that locker for me?' She points to a varnished wooden cupboard above the bed, and Chiara passes down folded sheets and towels, grateful for the simplicity of the task. Liz places a pile of towels to warm beside the stove and gets Chiara to spread what look like old plastic shower curtains over the rugs on the floor. They layer more towels on top. Together they help Devorah out of her coat and dress and into a long woven nightdress with a high neckline and buttons down the front.

'Modesty is important,' Liz tells Chiara. 'You need to think about each woman's background and beliefs, what makes her feel at home. She won't be able to let go otherwise.' She talks like a teacher. Chiara thinks of the Genesis Centre where all the patients have to wear surgical gowns, open at the back.

She's never seen so much packed into a tiny space. Narrow shelves above the sink are full to bursting with pots and jars labelled in curly handwriting. *Chamomile, Peppermint, English Lavender*, and *Clary Sage* all sit on the lowest shelf, with *Plantain Oil, St John's Wort Tincture, Shepherd's Purse* and *Motherwort* on the one above. There are rows of tall bottles and tiny ones containing liquids coloured leaf-green, amber, and purple so dark it's almost black. Everyone cooks with herbs back home in Sicily - or at least they used to - but this looks more like an apothecary's shop.

Liz tells Chiara to infuse two spoonfuls of herbs from a jar labelled 'First Stage Blend' in boiling water for four minutes. Then she must strain the mixture and add a spoonful of honey and a shaving of ginger root. A hint of lemon and a dusty suggestion of lavender rises from the brew. Chiara passes Devorah the steaming mug.

Liz encourages Devorah to kneel on the floor, with her chest and elbows resting on the bed. She instructs Chiara to kneel beside her and shows her how to massage Devorah's lower back, using her own body weight to flow with her movements. When she begins to tire, Gaskin pads across and settles his soft weight onto Devorah's buttocks.

'Ooh, that's lovely,' she says, 'it's like he knows exactly where it aches.'

'LET'S LISTEN TO THIS BABY'. Liz passes Chiara a wooden object from beside the muslin bundles. It looks like a tiny trumpet, surely too simple to be of much use. The Genesis Centre has ultrasound scanners and CTG machines to monitor foetal heartbeats. You have to do a CTG at every antenatal check after twenty-six weeks; Sister Miller says it's essential to have a good audit trail.

'May I have a feel of your tummy, my love, and then listen to your baby?' Liz holds Devorah's hand as she explains what she's going to do and why. Nobody explains much at the Genesis Centre. A doctor will sometimes turn up announced and pull on a pair of gloves when Chiara is getting a patient ready for Theatre. 'Just checking the presentation,' he'll mutter as he inserts a hand. The mothers - incubators - sometimes flinch or arch their backs, but they never dare complain.

Gaskin slinks obligingly out of the way as Liz and Chiara help Devorah onto the bed. He jumps onto Liz's rocking chair where he sits watching with his tawny tail curled around his paws. Liz covers Devorah's lower body with a folded sheet before lifting the nightdress to reveal her rounded belly. She uncorks a bottle and pours a little oil onto her hands. It smells of sage, and rose petals, and something warm - cinnamon, perhaps?

Liz massages the oil into Devorah's skin, taking her time, her age-spotted hands turning and sweeping like a dance. Sometimes she pauses or presses more deeply. As Chiara watches, the shape of a baby appears beneath Liz's hands as if she is moulding it from clay. There's the curve of the spine, the little bottom pointing upwards, the prod of a small foot.

'I'm having a good feel around to determine the position,' Liz tells Chiara. 'You must always do a thorough abdominal palpation before listening to the foetal heart. Otherwise you're just guessing. A good midwife knows exactly how the baby's lying before she picks up her pinard. Or even one of those ruddy CTG transducers.' She rolls her eyes. So Liz knows about modern machines, then? She must see the surprise on Chiara's face, because she laughs, showing those crooked teeth.

'Yep, I've worked in hospitals, back in the day. Been there, done that, got the effing t-shirt. Used to keep up with all the research every year for yonks. All the latest technology, and why it doesn't help. But they still do it anyway. I'll tell you all about it another time.'

Chiara nods, but she won't see Liz again after tonight. The last nurse thought someone was following her, Salvador said. Maybe that old man with the bottle wasn't really drunk at all; he could have been a Government spy. She swallows hard, willing herself to focus.

'Quiet little thing, aren't you?' Liz takes the wooden trumpet from Chiara. 'Come here. I want you to hear this.' Liz runs her hands over Devorah's bump again and selects a place on the left hand side. She rests the wide end of the trumpet on Devorah's skin and puts her own ear to the hole at the smaller end. Then she is silent, a smile slowly creasing her face. 'The sound of life,' she whispers. 'Listen.'

Chiara lowers her ear to the wooden cone. It takes a moment before she hears it. It's a small sound, but wonderfully alive. A horse galloping far into the mountains. A vibrating drumbeat. A joyful song from another country. This heartbeat sounds nothing like the wooshy thunder emitted by the hospital machines. This is an intimate whisper, a secret message, a call to prayer.

18

GROANING CAKE

The oil lamps burn through the darkest hours of the night while Chiara kneels beside Devorah, massaging her back and her feet the way Liz showed her. Devorah's belly tightens and hardens every three minutes with relentless regularity, but she no longer shrieks or screams. Instead, at the height of each surge, she closes her eyes and releases a long, tuneful mmmm as if she is singing to her baby.

Chiara struggles to keep her own eyes open. She's worked plenty of night shifts, but she's used to being on her feet rushing around. The dim, warm womb of a boat lulls her into a rare stillness.

'Slice of groaning cake?' Liz's voice startles Chiara.

'Sorry?'

'Groaning cake. Old recipe, handed down from generations back, when people knew how to treat labouring women. So called because -.' She grins. 'Because birth can be a noisy business.'

A cake crusted with brown sugar sits beside the stove. Liz cuts three thick slices and spreads them with Butterlyke. The cake is dark brown inside, sticky and delicious. Chiara can taste real eggs. It's the first home-baked thing she has eaten since leaving Sicily. She accepts a mug of terracotta-coloured tea, sweetened with honey, and Liz shows her the little hat she is knitting in soft, turquoise yarn.

'I try to knit a hat for every baby,' she says.

Galvanised by the tea, Chiara checks Devorah's pulse, temperature, and blood pressure with Liz's old-fashioned equipment. They had manual blood pressure cuffs at the old people's home in Palermo; Liz seems impressed that Chiara knows how to use it. Liz listens with the ear trumpet, which she calls a 'pinard,' every half hour.

Chiara tries to find the right place to listen for the baby's heart but it's difficult. She struggles to interpret the lumps and hollows of Devorah's abdomen so Liz places her hands over Chiara's and guides her.

'Here are the baby's buttocks,' she tells her. 'Here is his shoulder. His head is right down in the pelvis, too low to feel. He's on his way.'

When the clock above the bed shows three o'clock, Devorah grows restless. Her moans become broken cries. Gaskin wakes and begins to pace silently. Devorah can't find a bearable position, not even for a few minutes. Chiara soothes and rubs as best she can but Devorah pushes her away.

'No, I can't do it,' she wails. 'Make it stop!'

Chiara's pulse quickens. It's been hours, and still no baby.

'Liz? I think something's wrong,' she implores, but Liz only drags back her grey hair and secures it with a rubber band.

'You've been doing a good job,' she says. 'I think you might have the makings of a midwife, Chiara, and it's not every day I say that. Come on, let's do this together.' She heaves herself to her feet with a grimace, crouches beside Devorah, and takes her face in her hands.

'My love,' she tells her, 'your baby is nearly here. Don't be afraid. You are more powerful than you know, and women like you, your mothers and grandmothers, have been doing this for thousands of years. Can you get up off the bed?'

'No,' sobs Devorah. 'I can't move.' She lies rigid, fists clenched against the pain.

'Should I go for help? Do we need an ambulance?' Chiara's voice is unsteady but Liz shakes her head.

'They call this transition,' she says. 'It means it's almost time. Come on, Devorah, you've got this.'

Devorah places one foot onto the floor, then the other. As she stands, Chiara hears a soft splash, and a sweet, almond smell rises from the clear liquid flowing down Devorah's legs. Gaskin mews and leaps onto a shelf. Chiara's clothes are splattered with the waters.

'Sorry,' says Liz, passing Chiara a towel. 'I should've given you an apron; occupational hazard, getting wet.' She checks the baby's heartbeat again, then, satisfied, encourages Devorah to walk up and down the length of the boat. Devorah soon finds her rhythm, pacing intently, pausing to make low, grunting sounds with every surge. Between the contractions, she repeats something under her breath in a language Chiara doesn't know.

A brass rail runs the length of the kitchen surface. After half an hour of pacing, Devorah stops. She grabs the rail with both hands and drops into a deep squat, groaning more loudly than ever. What if someone hears? Chiara tries shushing her but Liz waves a dismissive hand.

'No stopping her now. She's got a universe to deliver, haven't you, my love? Go with it, Devorah.'

Devorah's shouts rise in a crescendo. She might be in agony or ecstasy; it would sound the same. She lowers a hand to the space between her legs. Her face is pure focus.

'He's coming,' she cries. Her whole body bears down. She bellows like a creature in a stable. She yells. And now there is a head: a wet, shining head rising up where before there was darkness. Liz shines a torch and at first Chiara can only see a purple dome. As she watches, the baby's face emerges. Devorah pulls herself upright and the whole baby tumbles from her. Liz catches him in her arms, gathering him into a warmed towel. He opens his mouth, throws back his head, and cries.

Liz dries the child and hands him to his mother, settling Devorah onto a heap of cushions. She helps Devorah loosen her nightgown and nestles the rosy baby between his mother's breasts. He quietens and begins to turn his head from side to side.

'Looking for his dinner already,' says Liz. 'Or is it breakfast? Congratulations, beautiful Mamma. You did it!'

Devorah strokes her son's body, kissing his head, holding him close. Her eyes shine. Chiara's mouth gapes wider than the baby's; she never imagined birth could be like this.

'Do you have a name for your baby?' she asks. She can't take her eyes off Devorah's glowing face and the way she cradles her naked child so close - so different from the empty, exhausted mothers at the Genesis Centre whose babies are wheeled away to be washed and dressed by the nursery nurses.

'At the *bris*, the circumcision,' Devorah tells her. 'We will name our son then. She lowers her head to the baby's and inhales his newborn scent.

Liz watches, seeming unhurried. Once or twice she touches the cord still attaching the child to his mother. Isn't she supposed to cut it? Devorah is still having pains, and after about twenty minutes, blood spurts from between her legs.

'Liz?' Chiara squeaks, but Liz calmly pulls on a pair of clean gloves and reaches for her muslin packages.

'Placenta's on its way,' she says. 'Devorah, my love, can you sit up a little bit and we'll get the bowl underneath you? Perfect. Now push.' Devorah screws up her face and grunts, and the big red placenta flops out, to be scooped up into an enamel dish and covered with a cloth. Liz unwraps her muslin packages to reveal sterilised surgical clamps and scissors. Clamping the umbilical cord, she cuts it and ties it off with a piece of red and blue braided cotton. 'All done,' she says. 'A beautiful birth from start to finish.'

'We need to keep an eye in case she bleeds,' Liz tells Chiara, 'but I haven't used any uterotonics and I don't reckon she'll need any.'

Chiara's brain is fuzzy with exhaustion. She makes a vague, questioning sound, and Liz looks at her sharply, cocking her head to one side.

'Look at you - all cross-eyed! Now, I might still have some suturing to do, but I reckon you've learned enough for one night. Gaskin can keep us company. You go and get your head down till morning. No arguments. I'll wake you once we're on the move; never like to stay too long in one spot. Next time you can catch the baby yourself.'

Next time? Chiara told Salvador she would do this only once. She ought to tell Liz she can't come back, but she's too tired right now. She devours another fat slice of the groaning cake before lying down in Liz's tiny spare cabin, the sights and sounds of the night blurring through her mind. Flickering candles, an enormous orange cat, the scents of sage and honey, the downy skin of a newborn. Weariness washes over her like a warm tide as her thoughts dissolve into a dreamless sleep.

19

VIP

Martin said there would be a TV crew, but Rava wasn't expecting quite so many long lenses and fluffy microphones. She pulls out her compact mirror to check her makeup. The Genesis Centre anniversary celebrations will be all over the news tonight.

The DBC are here - you'd expect the Government broadcaster - and Rava spots two or three commercial channels too. She throws Martin a worried look; he always says you can't trust the unofficial press. They're financed by fascists and extremists who want to undermine the Defender. But Martin nods and smiles. Maybe the non-DBC journalists have been promised some sort of deal in return for positive coverage. Everyone has a price, Martin likes to say.

The VIPs mingle, sipping champagne and making small talk. Dozens of chattering voices echo in the immense Atrium. It's a glorious space. Fifteen steps lead up from street level to the high triple entrance archway. Inside, the glass walls shine with reflected light from the forest of mirrored towers surrounding the building. The floor is white marble flecked with gold. Rava holds up a hand to shield her eyes; she should have brought her sunglasses.

Rava used to relish events like this, but her energy's low today. She'd rather not have come, but Martin insisted. 'This one's important,' he said. 'A chance to raise my profile and - let's face it, darling - you look much prettier on camera than me.' She giggled when he said that and tapped him playfully on the cheek.

A soothing backdrop of spa-type music wafts from invisible speakers. Rava is wearing a new dress from Jasper Conran in cerise silk with sparkly pink three-inch-heeled Jimmy Choos. 'We need to look the part,' Martin said when she questioned the extravagance of these purchases. The dress's soft folds conceal the new roundness of her lower belly, and the shoes look fabulous, but her ankles are aching already. Pregnancy makes everything more tiring.

Martin's in his Armani suit, which fits him beautifully. He's talking to all the important people. Just two or three times, when he thinks no one is looking, he pulls out a folded paper from his pocket and scans it before re-folding and replacing it. He's been working on his speech for days. Small beads of sweat glisten on his forehead.

Rava wishes he wasn't quite so wrapped up in his work. She'd rather have the baby at a cheaper hospital, or keep the two-bedroom apartment, than have him stressed out all the time. He's been coming home late every night and shutting himself in his study to take endless calls. Still, on the plus side, he scarcely glanced at the fake DNA report when she showed it to him. 'Well done, sweetheart. Our son's on his way,' he said before kissing her on the forehead and going back to his laptop.

So far, so good, but she'll have to tell him soon. The intermittent nausea of early pregnancy has given way to a constant, sick tension from the strain of keeping her secret. Hopefully if today's event goes well, he'll be more relaxed. If he's in a good mood, she might even tell him tonight. It's sixteen weeks now, and she'd have to go to the Fresh Start Suite for a termination under anaesthetic. Martin wouldn't put her through that just because the baby's a girl, would he? He loves her.

Rava hovers beside Martin, smiling hard. She spots several celebrities among the guests. A TV presenter munches on canapes as he chats with a famous actress. The actress had her baby here last year, and is going to make one of the speeches. She looks different in real life from her screen persona: older and heavily made-up, but still glamorous. Her golden Femband appears to be studded with diamonds. She stares vaguely across the room through long, violet eyelashes.

The small cafe is still serving espressos and cappuccinos to the building's regular customers. People drift curiously towards the roped-off VIP area, disposable coffee cups in hand. Some of the women point out the famous actress to their husbands.

'Enjoying yourself, my darling?' Martin enquires, mopping his forehead with a handkerchief. Rava nods and brightens her smile. A large, three-tiered cake stands on a table nearby, reminding Rava of their wedding day. One tier for each year since the Centre opened, Martin explains. Instead of a glamorous bride and groom, the cake is topped with a sugar stork carrying a basket in its beak.

Martin introduces Rava to the Centre Director, as well as two Senators, and the Chief Surgeon. The Surgeon holds onto Rava's hand for a little longer than necessary, offering effusive congratulations when Martin tells him his wife is a new client of the Genesis Centre.

'It's an honour to look after you, my dear. Charming.' His glance runs the length of her torso as if he's making a mental note of where to make his incision.

'How sweet!' The actress's voice rings out, and heads swivel towards the lifts where a line of nurses is emerging, each one carrying a baby. All the nurses wear crisp white uniforms, with snowy caps crowning their hair. The babies, bundled up in white blankets, all appear to be asleep. '*Oohs*' and '*aahs*' rise from the watching crowd, while the film crews press forward to capture the moment. Rava recognises the fourth nurse in line - she's the kind one who changed the email address on her hospital records - but if the nurse notices Rava she gives no sign of it.

Ten nurses form a horseshoe around the table with the cake. The babies are so quiet Rava wonders if they are dolls, until one of them wriggles and screws up its face, getting ready to cry. Before it can make a sound, an older, hard-faced nurse with immaculate blonde hair removes the waking baby, replacing it instantly with another sleeping infant.

The '*ting ting*' of a fork against a glass silences the chatter, and the Director begins the proceedings with a few words of welcome. Next, it's Martin's turn, as Under-Secretary of State for Women's Health, to cut the cake. He compliments the pretty nurses and makes a joke about tiers of cake and childbirth without tears, before launching into the main body of his speech:

'In the last three years, our flagship Genesis Centre has delivered over five thousand babies. Every delivery is a special event.' Martin indicates the well-behaved babies. 'Here, at last, we can guarantee a safe and pain-free delivery for every one of our incubators. Our world-class surgical teams run three award-winning operating theatres, staffed around the clock, headed by dynamic Chief Surgeon, Mr Vikram Gupta.' A nod towards the doctor is greeted with a patter of applause. 'I was astounded to learn,' Martin continues, consulting his sheet of paper, 'that, in just one year, our remarkable obstetricians use over one hundred and twenty thousand surgical instruments.'

A little gasp goes up from the crowd.

'All our incubators receive the very latest antibiotics and pharmaceuticals to guarantee a rapid recovery. Every newborn receives expert care from our dedicated paediatric team. We've replaced outdated, overcrowded hospitals with a modern centre of excellence. Let's take a moment to thank our dedicated and - if I may say so - very attractive nursing staff.'

Martin gestures towards the row of nurses. The applause is louder now, and a wolf whistle pierces the air. Martin beams into the nearest camera: 'Our next steps are clear. We have ambitious plans to expand what we have begun, creating a future where every child is healthy, every family wealthy. Safe births, secure futures. Here at the Genesis Centre we deliver sustainable -.'

'Justice for women!'

'Stop forced sterilisations!'

Martin falters mid-sentence as the shouts ring out. The camera lens wavers. Heads turn towards the cafe, where female voices begin to chant:

'Freedom for women! Freedom for birth!'

Hand-written placards appear above the crowd. One reads: *Freedom for Women: End Enforced Sterilisation.'* The other says: *'Midwives save lives.'*

The news reporters exchange glances. For a tense moment, nobody moves. Then, all at once, one of them breaks away from the pack and runs towards the disturbance, his cameraman close behind. Two more hesitate for a split-second before following like hounds picking up a scent.

'Freedom for women!' the cry repeats.

'- futures for a safe tomorrow. Thank you.' Martin completes his speech, but no one is listening. The colour has drained from his face. Even the DBC crew has started filming the unscheduled goings-on.

'Freedom for birth!'

The famous actress's personal minder appears from out of nowhere: a big man, dressed in black. He hustles the actress away from the commotion at breakneck speed. The Director speaks to someone on a crackling walkie-talkie. As the crowds part, Rava catches sight of the protestors: two women, one young, one older, both unremarkable-looking. Their faces are steady, their mouths open as they chant in unison:

'Freedom for women, freedom for birth!'

Brown-uniformed guards rush at the pair, brandishing weapons. The cafe customers abandon their drinks, and the crowd begins to surge towards the exits. Somebody screams. The older nurse shepherds her flock of pretty juniors back into the lifts. One of the babies is wailing. The Chief Surgeon is nowhere to be seen. A VIP drops his champagne flute, and yellow wine seeps across the floor. It looks like urine.

'Vermin! We had an arrangement.' Martin rips off his microphone and hurtles towards the TV crews, pushing his way past old people and children. Rava can't breathe, can't speak. Has he seen the guards with their guns? Martin tries to reach for the camera on the nearest man's shoulder. 'Stop!' he yells. 'Stop filming.' But no one takes any notice.

One of the guards grabs the taller of the two women. He yanks her hands up behind her back and her placard crashes to the floor but she keeps chanting. Her expression is oddly calm, as if she has expected this, prepared herself for it.

'Freedom for women,' she repeats with her companion. 'Midwives save lives.' For a split second, Rava could swear the woman meets her eyes.

But now more guards reach the protestors. Police in body armour and visors come running under the entrance arches, shouting. Someone snatches the second woman's placard, and there's a thump and a thud as both women are thrown face down onto the floor. One of the security guards aims a kick at the nearer woman's ribs. As she jerks and cries out, two or three more kicks go in - hard ones.

Rava winces and covers her eyes. When she looks again, the two women are being hauled away, their feet dragging along the floor. One has blood streaming from her nose. The other is limp, seemingly unconscious.

———————

MARTIN STANDS ALONE beside the cake. The VIPs and celebrities have vanished. His shirt is stained with sweat and his tie hangs askew. His right eyebrow twitches and quivers.

'Oh, Martin,' she begins, 'I'm so sorry.' He looks like a child robbed of presents at his own birthday party. 'Let's go home.'

She opens her arms to comfort him but he steps away. His lips are compressed into a tight line.

'You'll have to wait here,' he says flatly. 'I'll call Daniel to collect you. I've got stuff to sort out: major PR salvage job.'

'Is there anything I can do?'

'No, of course not. It's the Defender who needs to act - shut down the gutter press once and for all.'

Martin mutters something under his breath before swivelling to pick up the knife lying beside the cake. Rava's heart stops beating, but he only plunges it deep into the top tier, knocking the stork with its sugar baby sideways. Then he walks away without another word, passing through one of the security gates and disappearing into the lift.

Alone and a little dizzy, Rava finds a chair at the edge of the cafe. Customers start returning to reclaim their coffees and snacks. A cultured female voice speaks over the intercom, reassuring everyone that the incident is under control. There is no need for concern. Spa music resumes. People start queuing again for pastries, Earl Grey teas, and Americanos. In the middle of the Atrium, a cleaner mops blood from the marble floor.

20

BIRTHDAY CARD

Who were those women with the signs? Chiara couldn't see properly through the crowds and Sister Miller hurried the nurses away so fast. Were they former patients, or did they have connections with the midwife network? They were brave, that's for certain.

The atmosphere on the ward is edgy. Sister is in a foul mood, snapping at everyone from the domestic staff to the junior doctors. Even the consultants might not be safe. When it's finally time for her break, Chiara opens her locker to get her energy bar. Rummaging in her bag, her fingers close around something that wasn't here before. It's a square envelope, gummed shut. She draws it out cautiously and holds it at arms length as if it might explode. The envelope is pink, and the single letter 'C' is written by hand in the exact centre. Does someone have a key to her locker?

Chiara glances over her shoulder but she's alone in the windowless break room. Quickly, she rips the envelope open and pulls out a birthday card with a picture of balloons. But it isn't her birthday, not for months. Inside, someone has written in black ink with an old-fashioned fountain pen:

Greetings from Gaskin. Shall we meet again?

Underneath is a phone number. Chiara recognises the curly handwriting from the jars and bottles on the Rosie Lee. The back of her neck prickles, and she thrusts the card back into the envelope, shoving it deep into her bag, under her hat and scarf. But there's something else here: a small dense rectangle. A glance confirms her suspicions, and Chiara drops the cheap mobile phone as if it's on fire. She returns the bag to the locker, slams the door shut, and locks it.

Chiara sits down, heart racing, energy bar forgotten. She'd been starting to wonder if her night on the Rosie Lee was some sleep-deprived hallucination. The creaking boat, the outlandish old woman, the heavy scents of herbs, baking, and birth all seem like a dream, and the pristine corridors of the Genesis Centre the only reality. She's tried once or twice to catch Salvador's eye, but he always looks the other way. Did she imagine the whole thing?

But no; it was real; this phone and the card prove it. But to visit the Rosie Lee again? That would be insane. Chiara saw the armed guards in the Atrium; she's trying not to think about what might happen to those protestors. She's done her bit, and was lucky to get away with it. The birth on the boat was an amazing experience, but Mamma and Gemma are relying on her to keep her job. She needs to stay out of trouble.

CHIARA HEARS RAISED voices as soon as she leaves the break room. She rounds the corner to see Sister Miller holding onto a wheeled cot with both hands while a man shouts and gesticulates. The man's wife is gripping the other end of the cot; her face is blotched and swollen.

Chiara hesitates. She knows the wife: a sweet lady who's kept her baby girl in her room these past few days. Chiara's enjoyed helping her feed and dress her infant, Daisy, and watching the new mother's confidence start to blossom. What can have gone wrong?

Sister says something inaudible, and the new mother gasps and yanks the cot towards her. Sister snatches the cot back, glaring at the poor woman.

Chiara would be wise to sidle past and keep out of Sister's way, but this woman is one of her patients. She was going to be discharged home today with little Daisy. Is there a problem with the paperwork?

'It's temporary, I swear,' the man says, punching the air in frustration. 'This is some screw-up with the insurers. I'll be onto them first thing in the morning. Look at the state of my wife, for God's sake. Do you people have no compassion?'

Sister Miller's knuckles are white where she's holding the frame of the cot, and a couple of hairs have escaped from her perfect bun, but her voice is as calm as ever:

'Mr Marks, you signed our contract of care. You know the terms and conditions. As you say, I'm sure this problem will be temporary, and your neonate will be in the care of our expert staff. All you need to do, as I have explained more than once -.'

'Please, just let me stay with her.' The mother falls to her knees, still holding fast to the cot. Her cheeks are smeared with tears and snot. 'It's not Harry's fault he lost his job. He'll get another, won't you, love? Please, just let us have Daisy. We'll borrow the money - my brother will help - he's got his own company. Please!' As she wipes her sleeve across her face, the shiny new gold band glints on the mother's wrist. She's been sterilised; Daisy will be her only child.

The weeping mother spots Chiara hovering behind Sister Miller.

'Nurse Chiara,' she calls. 'They're trying to take my baby,

because we can't make the last payment. But you know I'd do anything for Daisy, don't you? You know I'm a good mother?'

Chiara opens her mouth, but Sister silences her with a glare. The mother tries to reach into the cot to pick up her baby, but Sister elbows her away. In desperation, the woman starts clawing at Sister's shoulders, crying out in a high wail. Sister unclips the walkie-talkie at her belt:

'Restraint team, please, for a hysterical patient. Serenity central lobby. With rapid tranquillisation. Security to attend'.

A response crackles back over the speaker.

'This is a travesty,' the husband says. He has to shout to be heard over his wife's howls. 'She's had her sterilisation, like you people want, and now you won't give us our baby. I'll be onto my lawyer first thing. You'll be hearing -.'

'Mr Marks, please keep your voice down! This is a hospital and our patients are trying to rest.'

As Mr Marks opens his mouth to retort, five nurses come running, bringing thick velcro straps and a wheeled stretcher. Sister nods towards the terrified woman, and the nurses grab hold of her. Before Chiara can fully take in what's happening, the mother is face down on the floor with two hefty nurses sitting on her back. As she writhes and yelps, one of them injects something into her buttock.

'Keep still, you silly bitch!'

The mother keeps trying to fight back, but the nurses fix straps methodically around her thighs, hips, chest, wrists, and ankles. They tighten and secure all the straps before rolling her onto the stretcher. A nurse holds the woman's head as she spits and swears, but as the medication takes effect her words start to slur and stutter. Soon she's muttering incoherently, head lolled to one side, eyes glassy.

As they wheel her away, Chiara turns to look for the husband, but he's gone, marched out by the guard, she assumes. Security do their work efficiently.

Sister brushes her hands down the front of her spotless uniform and straightens her cap.

'Thank goodness. I hate a disorderly ward; all this fuss interfering with our vital work.' She seems to notice Chiara for the first time.

'Ah, Nurse Chiara,' she smiles, her orange lips brighter than ever. 'Little job for you, my dear. Will you take the Marks baby straight to Neonatal Two please. The notes are in the cot.' She passes the cot to Chiara, nodding in the direction of the internal lift.

'Yes Sister,' Chiara replies. Too shocked to argue, she wheels the cot towards the lift, gripping it tight to steady the trembling of her hands.

21

DANIEL

'Mrs Robson?'

It takes Rava a moment to respond. There's a ringing noise in her ears, and the world sounds muffled and distant.

'Mrs Robson, are you all right? I saw what happened; it's all over social media. You weren't hurt, were you? Mr Robson called and said to collect you from here.'

'Daniel?'

A man in a chauffeur's uniform stands in front of her but his face is fading in and out of focus. Rava's not sure how long she's been sitting in the Atrium cafe. She begins to get to her feet, but bright specks float in her vision, or is it the gold in the marble floor? She stumbles - these stupid heels - and everything spins. Darkness clouds in, and she's going to fall, crack her head, like those women - when strong hands catch her by her shoulders and lower her firmly back onto the chair.

'Get your head down.' Daniel says. She recognises his voice - that odd melding of East London and Eastern Europe. 'Between your knees - that's it, now long breaths in and out.' She does as he says, and her vision begins to clear, the giddy nausea subsiding with each lungful of air. When she raises her head, Daniel is crouched at her feet. He's taken off his chauffeur's hat and there's a round black skull-cap on the crown of his ginger hair.

He gives her a relieved smile. 'Feeling better? You were white as a ghost just now. Good thing I was here. No, don't get up. Stay right there, and I'll fetch you a drink of water.'

He makes her drink it all, in slow sips, before she tries to stand again. This time, the world stays still.

'Okay, now hold my arm. I don't want you twisting your ankle. Car's right outside. Thank God for Government privilege, hey? I can leave that Merc anywhere and it never gets towed away. Don't rush down these steps, Mrs Robson. That's it, one step at a time.'

'Rava,' she manages. 'You can call me Rava.'

'Right you are, Mrs. But I'm not sure your husband would like it, mind. My wife, now, she has fainting turns when she's expecting, every time. Something to do with the circulation. Gotta get your head lower than your heart, see? You had a shock, didn't you? Poor Mr Robson - he wasn't happy when he called me up. And on his big day too.'

Daniel's torrent of conversation gets them down the steps, onto the Plaza, and right up to Martin's black Mercedes with its Government flag fluttering on the bonnet. The chauffeur opens the door and settles her into the capacious leather seat.

'Are you warm enough Mrs - Rava, ma'am? I've got blankets, if you'd like one? Easy to get chilled after a fainting fit.'

'I'm fine thanks, Daniel.' But he insists on tucking her in with a soft rug anyway.

WHEN THE CAR pulls up outside Rava's apartment building, she expects Daniel to help her out and then drive away. Instead, he turns off the engine and adjusts his rear-view mirror to look at her.

'May I come up to the apartment with you, ma'am?'

'Oh I'm fine,' she says. 'I'm much better now, thank you. I can go up on my own.' She tries to open the passenger door, but it's locked.

'Yes of course Mrs Robson, ma'am, I quite understand. But it's Mr Robson, you see. He asked me to fetch him something from his study - some papers. It's quite urgent, Mr Robson said.' Daniel clears his throat and blinks several times, still watching her in the mirror.

'Well -.' Rava hesitates. She knows Martin trusts Daniel; the driver's been working for him for years, since before Rava met Martin in fact. Daniel used to work for the Government car pool, but now Martin insists on having him all to himself. *I'm in a sensitive role, so I need someone discreet,'* is how Martin explains it. But Rava can't recall the chauffeur ever coming inside their apartment. He normally rings the doorbell and waits in the hallway. Why does he want to come in today, when she's on her own?

'I suppose so,' she says awkwardly. 'Do you know what it is Martin wants? Maybe I could fetch it for you?'

Daniel was kind to her in the Atrium, but now something seems odd, out of place, though she can't quite put her finger on it. Did Martin tell him to keep an eye on her, and what might that mean, now that she's got secrets?

'I'm afraid it's classified, ma'am. He told me where he'd left the folder. I have security clearance, you see.' Daniel blinks again.

Rava shivers, suddenly cold. Does Martin trust his driver more than his wife? She supposes she could call Martin to check; he's funny about people going in his study. But he was so angry earlier - the way he stuck that knife in the cake - and he said the papers were urgent.

'Okay,' she says. 'Come on up. It won't take long, will it?'

'Thank you, ma'am. Much appreciated. He's under a lot of pressure, you see. It'll only take a moment.'

They stand on opposite sides of the lift, embarrassed by the intimacy of the confined space. Rava gets out first on her floor and lets them into the flat. Daniel removes his shoes politely.

'Martin's study's in there.' Rava indicates the door.

'Thank you, ma'am. I'll be two ticks.' He disappears into the study, closing the door behind him.

Rava bends to take off the high heels, massaging her aching ankles. The pink Jimmy Choos are stunning but they're not designed for pregnant women. As she straightens up, Rava gets the strangest sensation. It's a tiny quiver deep inside her stomach, like a butterfly flexing its wings. She moves her hand down to touch it. Could it be?

She's not sure - it's only just sixteen weeks, but they say sometimes women feel it this early. The website says the baby can make facial expressions now, and flex its muscles, and hear sounds from outside.

'Is that you, little one?' she murmurs. 'Can you hear my voice?'

As if in reply, the gentle flutter comes again.

Goosebumps rise on Rava's neck and arms. She stands motionless, noticing everything: the late afternoon light slanting through the living room window, the waxy scent of the cleaner's polish, the tufts of the carpet between her toes. She will always remember this moment, even when she is an old lady.

'Hello, baby,' she says.

I must tell Martin, is her next thought, before she remembers that Martin isn't here, that he's dealing with a crisis, that he was furious when they last parted. She goes to find her diary to write it down, forgetting all about Daniel. When the study door opens she starts in shock. How long has he been in there?

'Thank you Mrs Rava, ma'am,' he says. 'That's all sorted. D'you mind if I use your toilet before I go?'

'Yes of course.' She can hardly say no, though he might make a bad smell in there, and she's desperate to be left alone. So much has happened in so short a time. While Daniel is in the bathroom, Rava retreats to the kitchen to make herself a fruit tea. Finally there's a sound of flushing and handwashing, and he's in the hall again, tipping his cap to her.

'Thank you, ma'am, and sorry to bother you. You take it easy, mind.'

He slips on his shoes, and he's gone. Rava hurries to spray air freshener and bleach the toilet. It's only later, lying on the sofa with some mindless TV show playing, that the thought strikes her: I didn't notice Daniel carrying any papers when he left. What was he really doing here?

She picks up her phone to call Martin, but thinks better of it. She shouldn't bother him. Daniel and Martin have known each other for a long time; they trust one another. She's the newcomer, relatively speaking.

Rava closes her eyes, exhausted. She's overthinking. A good night's sleep, and she'll feel much better. As she adjusts her position, the baby moves again - a definite wriggle this time.

'Don't worry, little one,' Rava says. 'I'll look after you, I promise.'

22

NEONATAL TWO

'Milk or meds?'

The nursery nurse doesn't look up from her phone. *'No Visitors,'* says the sign above the desk. Chiara hasn't been to Neonatal Two before, although she's heard it mentioned, often mouthed silently with a sideways look. In Neonatal One they treat babies for infections and jaundice, and some of the little ones delivered pre-term go there if they're healthy. That's where Salvador works when he's not in the children's wards, or Theatre, or doing checks on Serenity. But Neonatal Two - that's different. Chiara tried asking one of the other nurses what it's for, but the nurse looked uncomfortable and changed the subject.

The room is very warm. Six perspex cots are lined up against a pale green wall. Two of the cots are empty. The other four hold babies, all sleeping. One of them, the furthest from the desk, has a cannula for drugs or fluids protruding from a vein on his scalp. He looks yellow and very small - shrunken, in fact. A poster above the cots depicts a giant bottle of pink soap above a reminder to, *'Wash your hands for health and hygiene.'* Despite this, the room has a sour smell of nappies and stale milk.

The nursery nurse sits at the desk, scrolling through a social media feed. From the slump of her body, Chiara guesses she's been doing this for some time.

'Milk or meds?' the nursery nurse repeats with an edge of irritation.

Chiara doesn't understand the question. When she doesn't reply, the nursery nurse sighs, puts down her phone, and beckons with her fingers. She has long false fingernails painted candy pink.

'Notes,' she demands. 'Give us the notes. What's this one here for?'

Chiara passes her the folder and the woman leafs through the pages.

'Ah, Dad not paid the bill. Milk then. D'you know what she's on?'

'Defrosted breast milk. She had her last bottle at 3.00 pm, thirty millilitres. She's been taking it really well, haven't you Daisy?' Chiara strokes the little girl's peach-soft cheek.

'No fancy breast milk in here, sweetheart,' says the nursery nurse. 'Too pricey. She can have Creamygate like the others. Seven days, she'll get, unless they give her an extension. Sometimes they do.'

A whimper rises from one of the cots and the nursery nurse looks at her watch.

'Another hour to go yet, mate,' she says in the direction of the sound. 'Eight o'clock, next feeds. Easier to do 'em all at once,' she adds, addressing Chiara now. 'I prop up their bottles on pillows and they're away. Sorted.' She brushes her hands against each other in a gesture of satisfaction, the pink fingernails clicking.

'But that's dangerous, propping up a baby's bottle,' Chiara protests. 'And this one, Daisy, she's due a feed now. She can't wait that long. Shall I stay and feed her?' Chiara will get a telling off from Sister if she's delayed returning to the ward, but she doesn't like the way this woman is eyeing Daisy.

'Nah,' the nursery nurse replies. 'I need to get 'em into routine, otherwise it's mayhem in here. No peace for the wicked, y'know? I'll give her some meds if she cries, settle her down.' She returns her attention to her phone where a hamster is scrambling its way through a cardboard obstacle course. 'Aah, look at him, in't he cute, clever little bugger?'

Chiara didn't think nursery nurses were allowed to give medications. She lifts Daisy out of the cot and holds her against her chest, feeling the warm weight of her and the slight dampness of her nappy.

'What medications do you give in here?' she asks, trying to keep her tone neutral.

'Morphine mostly, once they're signed off as no feeds. Doctor comes and writes it up on their charts. It's the kindest way; they just sleep, peaceful like. But the ones on milk, I find a little dose once or twice a day keeps 'em happy. I'm on my own in here, see, so I've gotta keep it simple. Don't want them crying all the time.'

'No feeds? Are you saying you don't feed all the babies?' Chiara shakes her head rapidly; she must have mis-heard.

'It depends. Only sometimes - I just do as I'm told.' The nursery nurse won't meet Chiara's gaze. 'Sign here to say you've handed her over. And I need a scan of her security tag. Don't worry,' she adds as Chiara clutches the baby closer. 'These non-payment ones, they usually get it sorted and go home in a few days.'

'No - wait. What do you mean?' That baby in the end cot - its chest is barely moving. The smell is stifling: high and over-sweet.

'Watch out, you're smothering her.'

Chiara didn't realise how tightly she's holding Daisy. She loosens her grasp, and the infant begins to wail.

'Look sweetheart.' The nursery nurse is on her feet, arms folded across her large breasts. 'I just work here. I don't make the rules, but I do my best to keep these littl'uns comfortable, all right? If you got a problem with that, go speak to management. Like I said, most of this lot go home in a few days anyway, once the money's paid off, or mum persuades dad to sign his child support papers. It's mostly the ones brought in by the police, or if it should've been a lullaby and the doc missed it, and what kinda life was they gonna have anyway? Not down to me, is it?'

The nursery nurse's face is flushed, her phone abandoned on the desk. The baby in the nearest cot begins to cry along with Daisy.

'Now you've gone and set 'em all off.'

'I'm sorry,' Chiara begins. Then she stops, fighting the urge to turn and run. The stench of unwashed bottles and something worse is inside her nostrils and sticking to her skin. But she's a nurse - this isn't right. With an effort, Chiara makes herself walk to the end cot and look inside. The wizened infant lies silent, his jaundiced skin slack over tiny bones.

'Are you telling me he's being starved to death? I thought -. Don't they get adopted, or sent somewhere, if their parents can't support them?'

'Nah.' The nursery nurse shakes her head. 'That's what they want you to think, but mostly they end up here. Cheaper, see? This country's got too many people already, they say.'

Chiara swallows hard.

'And you're just sitting here? How can you do this job?'

'Sweetheart, I got bills to pay. Not all of us got a silver spoon in our mouths. I never had a chance to get no fancy nursing degree. I got a kid at home - four years old she is. Other half up an' left us two years ago, no child support nor nothing. They offered me double pay to come and work in here.' The nursery nurse glares at Chiara.

'But surely, there must be - ?' Chiara trails off.

'My daughter's not registered, is she? We couldn't afford one of them incubating licences. That means no school, no doctors, no nothing, unless I can save up enough to pay off the fines.' She blows out a contemptuous breath, as if this is close to impossible. 'I don't like it, course I don't. Sometimes I give a bottle to the ones down for meds, when I'm sure no one's coming, like. But it's only dragging things out, in'it? Just me being soft. Mostly I just try not to look at 'em. If it weren't me doing this job it'd be someone else. And it's way worse down the People's Hospital. The ones sent here's the lucky ones, that's what I tell myself.'

'Lucky!' Chiara can't take her eyes off the dying infant. His breaths are shallow and ragged. 'You call that lucky? And anyway, why don't - ?' The words stick in her throat. She hasn't yet witnessed another lullaby birth but she dreads it daily. If they inject defective newborns with poison in Theatre, why not do the same here?

The nursery nurse says nothing for a moment. She seems very interested in her long fingernails. When she speaks again, Chiara has to strain to hear her over Daisy's furious wails.

'It's not a nice job. Withholding treatment, they call it. Letting nature take its course. Sometimes they give them something to speed it up at the end, once they're past the point of no return. Policeman who brought him in, he told me about that one.' She jerks her head towards the baby in the end cot.

'His mum was in labour four days on her own at home. Teenager she was. Eventually the neighbours couldn't stand the screaming, took her down the People's, but it was too late. She didn't make it; lost too much blood, I think. No one come forward for him, and the Peoples' nursery was full, so he ends up here.' She shakes her head. 'At least I done my best to keep him comfortable, poor little mite.'

'But, surely it's not too late?' Chiara protests. 'If I could find someone, someone to adopt him, or -.'

Or what? Could she adopt him herself, take him home with her? But they'd want financial guarantees, and there's the two parent rule, and how could she get to work ?

'Sweetheart.' The nursery nurse lifts Daisy from Chiara's arms. 'Don't get yourself mixed up in stuff you can't change. That littl'un's on his way out, bless him. Let him go in peace. And now let me get on with my work,' she adds, her voice suddenly strident again. 'I don't need no hoity-toity foreign nurses telling me what to do, thank you very much. Coming in here, disturbing all my babies. Go on, get out of here, back where you belong.'

***

IT'S after 9.00 pm by the time Chiara gets home. She's too tired to cook, but she isn't hungry anyway. Her chest feels as if something enormous is pressing on her heart. She up-ends her bag onto the table and watches the contents tumble out. A couple of loose coins and a lip balm roll onto the floor. The burner phone lands on top of the heap.

This time it won't be just once; she knows that. This could land her in prison, or worse. But what else can she do?

23

CLOSING THE BONES

It's easier to find the Rosie Lee this time. Chiara arrives in daylight after a journey involving two trams and a long walk. Liz's boat looks cheerful in the morning sun with its painted roses and a little wind turbine spinning merrily in the breeze. Two chickens - one brown, the other grey - scratch and cluck in the grass beside the towpath. Smoke drifts from the chimney and Chiara thinks she can hear Liz's kettle singing.

Liz is on the roof tending vegetables and herbs growing in boxes. She looks up and waves when she sees Chiara.

'You found me! Beautiful morning.' She clambers down, a colourful apron tied round her ample middle. Her grey hair is piled up in an untidy bun. 'Right, plenty to do, as ever.' Liz dips a watering can into the river and douses her young cabbages and onions before leading the way inside.

As Chiara's eyes adjust to the semi-darkness, she makes out a young woman sitting in Liz's rocking chair with a baby in her arms. At her side sits a middle-aged Muslim lady, her head covered with a hijab. The young woman's feet are in a big bowl of warm water, the steam scented with peppermint and lemons. Chiara inhales; for a moment she can see the lemon trees in

Nonna's garden, and the feral cats prowling the baked earth. As if to complete the picture, Gaskin greets her with a loud meow.

'This is Madeleine and baby Tom, and Jamila, one of my fellow midwives.' Liz introduces them. 'And this is Chiara. Tom was born yesterday, and Jamila came over to help me, but she's been up all night, haven't you, my love?'

'We all have.' Jamila yawns; her eyes are tired behind her glasses. 'Nice to meet you, Chiara, but I'm afraid I need to be going now. I've been staying in a safe house in Newham, but there's been a security breach, so we're moving out this afternoon. See you again, I hope.' She gathers up her things, still yawning.

'Look after yourself.' Liz embraces her friend. 'And let me know if you need anything, all right? I can always pass on a message.' The two women step outside to exchange a last few words. Chiara gets the impression they have known one another for a long time.

Chiara admires the baby, who has fair hair like his mother. Liz returns alone a few minutes later.

'Right then,' she says. 'Madeleine's husband is coming for her and Tom tomorrow morning. They've a long journey planned: off to Wales to join a community up in the hills. Not an easy life, but Tom's her second, and they don't think London will be workable with an unregistered child, do you, my love?' Madeleine murmurs her assent. 'So now we need to close the bones,' Liz continues. 'Send you off whole and nurtured, Madeleine.'

Close the what? At the Genesis Centre new mothers get antibiotics, medications to stop their milk, sleeping pills, and six-hourly wound checks, but no one does anything to their bones. Did this poor woman break something giving birth?

'Don't look so terrified.' Liz passes the baby to Chiara. 'Can you change his nappy while I get the bed ready?' She busies herself arranging blankets and pillows. The baby is blissful and drowsy. After cleaning the sticky meconium from his bottom, Chiara kisses his forehead, breathing in his new baby smell. Liz tucks him into an old-fashioned rocking cradle. 'Sleep well, little one,' she says. 'Right, Madeleine, are we ready? Let's begin with your feet.'

Liz shows Chiara how to massage each foot with perfumed salt and oil, kneading them dry in a towel. Then Liz leads Madeleine to the bed, settling her onto her back. She kneels at Madeleine's side and rubs more oil into her soft tummy, still baggy from her pregnancy.

'Watch how I do it,' she tells Chiara, 'and then you can take over. Don't be afraid to go deep; her body will tell you if it's too much.'

Liz's hands are veiny and spotted with age, but they move with strength and skill. Her palms curve and wriggle over Madeleine's skin, her fingers spreading, kneading, pulling inwards towards the centre line.

'Birth is an opening,' she says, 'So now we close. I'm not religious, but I know this helps. It's an ancient tradition, used by birth attendants all over the world and handed down. We bring everything back together, honouring the mother. Your turn, Chiara.'

Chiara's movements are shallow and shy at first. When she pauses, worried she's doing it wrong, Liz places her own hands over Chiara's.

'Close your eyes,' she tells her. 'Don't think it, feel it. Handle the woman with love, with respect, and you'll know what to do.'

Gradually, Chiara begins to find her rhythm as Madeleine relaxes under her touch. When Chiara's wrists and shoulders are starting to ache, Liz produces a smooth, round pebble. She nestles the warmed stone into the dip of Madeleine's belly button.

'Beautiful,' she pronounces. 'Well done, Chiara. And now we wrap her.'

Together they bind Madeleine's hips with a long ruby-red shawl, pulling it tight and knotting it. Liz twists the knot to tighten the shawl until Madeleine's pelvis is held close. When Liz asks how it feels, Madeleine murmurs,

'Good; so good.'

They bind her ribs with another shawl, this one orange with long fringes. Liz unfolds one of her big patchwork quilts and lays this over everything, leaving Madeleine covered, swaddled, and secure.

While Madeleine and baby Tom rest, Liz leads Chiara out onto the deck at the front of the boat. *'The bow deck,'* she calls it. Chiara blinks in the April sun.

'We'll sit here and rest a while,' Liz says. The women sit in silence. Liz gazes across the water as if deep in thought, her knitting untouched in her lap. Chiara is full of questions, but this isn't the time; she'll ask Liz to explain later. This time and place is sacred, like the cathedral in Cefalu, full of candles and ancient mystery, or Nonna's chair where she used to sit and pray, the rosary beads always in her hands. Chiara watches the swan sitting on her nest near the opposite bank and loses herself in memories of home while the light dances on the river.

When Gaskin emerges onto the deck, this seems to be Liz's cue to move. She grabs onto the roof of the boat to haul herself to her feet.

'Let's go -,' she begins, and then falters. She wobbles for a moment, her face suddenly drained of colour.

'Are you all right?' Chiara asks, but Liz shakes her head and waves away Chiara's outstretched hand.

'I'm fine,' she says. 'Just a bit peckish, I reckon. Giving a massage takes it out of you. Come on, let's get the kettle on. A nice cuppa, and some bread and honey should do the trick.'

By the time they are back in the tiny kitchen, Liz has regained her bustling energy. 'We'll make a herbal blend for

Madeleine - stinging nettle and fenugreek to boost her milk production. And a pinch of fennel. Normal tea for you, Chiara? You're a natural with the massage, by the way, my love. Has anyone taught you before?'

Chiara blushes.

'Well, I used to look after the old people's feet, back in Sicily,' she says. 'And my Nonna's, when her legs swelled in the heat. I tried - I did my best.' Her voice fades to a whisper. 'My Nonna - my grandmother - she was a nurse once. I wish I could be more like her.'

Liz puts down her teapot and turns to look at Chiara. Her eyes are a very light grey-blue. She places a hand gently on Chiara's shoulder.

'You miss her, don't you?' she says. Chiara nods, not trusting herself to speak. 'Your Nonna was special; I can see that. And I'm glad you found me and the Rosie Lee. Would you like to learn to be a midwife, Chiara?'

Chiara nods again. Perhaps there was a reason she came to England after all.

24

ABERDEEN

The house in Aberdeen is even smaller and dingier than Rava remembers. It's as if she's gone back in time, treading on the same carpets, running a hand over the same embossed wallpaper, hearing the same boards creak as she climbs the stairs. The smell of garlic, spices, and onions rises from Aunt Nasreem's kitchen like it always did, pervading every room.

It's much quieter now the cousins have all moved out. Rava was an only child, and Aunt Nasreem's daughters are all married. She had no sons. Baba and Nasreem both look elderly and small, as if they've shrunk over the years along with the house.

Rava wasn't sure about coming, though she'd promised Baba. In the end it was Martin who persuaded her, rather to her surprise. He hasn't been keen on her visiting home in the past, and the flight permit is horribly expensive. When she was younger, you could make the journey by train, though it took a whole day to get here. But the railway tracks flooded too many times - they're all rusting away now - and the roads are completely gone in places. Scotland is another country: poor, fiercely independent, and increasingly cut off from the Defender's England.

'You should go,' Martin said, 'before you're too pregnant to fly. You're worried about your father and I'm snowed under at work. Three more midwife arrests last week but we haven't cracked the system yet. My contacts are playing games, and these old women are stubborn; tough to break even under refined interrogation techniques.'

So here she is, eating Aunt Nasreem's pungent cooking and wearing her most covered-up clothes. She stopped wearing the hijab soon after her move to London. Too many sideways looks in the streets, and besides, she wasn't that person any more. The demure little Muslim girl was gone forever. Perhaps she never really existed.

Baba sits at the table, pretending to eat his lentil stew. He's lost so much weight: his face is all angles, skin on a skull, and his clothes are almost comically oversized. He's animated though, asking lots of questions about Rava's work, her home, her husband.

Rava does her best to reply, trying to find answers that are more or less truthful but not too shocking. Yes, the bank lends money at interest, but it's all regulated by law and she works in HR. No, it's just her and Martin in the London apartment; his parents live elsewhere. Yes, Martin is always kind. He wanted to come to Aberdeen, but he's very busy with work at the moment. Baba nods enthusiastically.

'Thank God, thank God,' he repeats in response to everything she says. He has only three teeth remaining, but his smile is eager as a child's. 'A good husband is a great blessing. If God wills, Martin will come to visit with you in the autumn, after the child is born.'

Aunt Nasreem wants to know all about the baby. How many weeks is it now? Is Rava getting regular check-ups? Does she have clothes ready, and a crib? Fatima's old baby things are still up in the attic - would Rava like to sort though them?

'Maybe later. Thank you, Auntie.'

Rava's cleared her plate, mostly to encourage Baba who's still barely touched his meal, and her stomach is uncomfortably full. It's stiflingly hot, the radiators turned up to max, and the windows painted shut. As her baby shifts, a mouthful of acid reflux makes her gag. What would Martin say if she came home with a bag full of cast-off baby girl clothes?

After the plates are cleared away, it's time for Maghrib prayer.

'Will you join us, Rava?' Baba's expression is so wistful, she almost says yes. But then Aunt Nasreem chimes in:

'Motherhood is a great responsibility. You must set the example. How will your child learn Qur'an and Sunnah, except from you?'

Rava shakes her head.

'Sorry, but it's been a long day, with all the travelling, and I'm very tired. I will pray alone in my room.' She turns away so as not to see the disappointment on her father's face.

RAVA STAYS for three awkward days and nights. She sleeps in the bedroom she used to share with Fatima; it seems weirdly empty now she has it to herself. It's impossible to get comfortable on the lumpy mattress, and the yowls of the cats in the alleyway below wake her long before dawn.

She hears children's voices too, playing outside at all hours. Scotland doesn't have a Safe Futures Policy like England, and everywhere you see babies in pushchairs, toddlers tottering along on reins, and bigger children running and shouting. The public parks still have swings and slides, and there seems to be a school or a nursery on every street corner.

It's intriguing seeing so many children out in public. Half the time their parents scarcely seem to be watching them; what if someone were to snatch them away? Rava admires the cute infants and the energetic toddlers, but she can't help noticing the mothers' harassed faces too. And the noise - she hadn't realised children could be so loud! She spends ages one afternoon searching fruitlessly for an adult-only cafe. In London, whole zones are designated child-free, but things are different in Scotland.

SHE CALLS HOME, hungry to hear Martin's voice and homesick for her neat, modern apartment. But Martin rarely picks up, and when he does, he sounds distracted.

'I miss you,' she tells him. 'Is Louis all right without me? I'll be back soon.'

'I miss you too,' Martin replies, but he sounds as if he's reading from a script.

'The baby's kicking lots now. I'm feeling it all the time.' She has to remember not to say 'she' or 'her'. What if she makes a mistake?

'That's good,' he says, but when Martin hangs up, Rava feels hollow, conscious of the growing gap between them. She needs to sort this business out, and soon. What would Baba say if he knew she was lying to her husband on a daily basis?

BETWEEN PRAYERS and the meals he can't eat, Baba sleeps much of the day. He does his best to hide the fact he's in pain, but Rava notices him wince when he coughs or gets up from his chair. When she asks Nasreem about his treatment, her aunt knits her brows.

'We can't afford it,' she says. 'Not the chemo. Abdullah has painkillers, but there are better treatments for those who can pay. He could live longer, I think -.' Nasreem raises her eyes. 'Your husband, Rava? Is his work going well?'

Rava knows what she means, but she can't ask Martin for money, not now, while he's working so hard to provide for their child. And while she's not being honest with him. The blood rushes to her cheeks.

'I'll do what I can, Auntie. I'm due a bonus myself at work in a few months. Perhaps I can help then.' If Martin agrees. If it isn't too late. But what else can she do?

Nasreem nods.

'We will pray to God. If God wills -.' She stops speaking, stoops over the vegetable rack, and comes up with a handful of carrots. Her eyes are bright with un-shed tears. 'Right - there's work to be done. Can you help scrub these please, Rava?'

Together, the two women prepare the evening meal.

ON THE LAST DAY, Rava opens the scratched and battered wardrobe in the corner of her room. The clothes she left behind still hang from the rail as if they've been waiting for her: long tunics, loose trousers, abaya dresses, hijabs. She lifts them out, one by one, and heaps them onto the bed. Faint aromas of the past rise from them: turmeric and henna, with a hint of Baba's tobacco. The necklines are modest, the colours muted. She buries her face in the soft folds.

For years she's thought she was free in London, far from her religious family, this narrow house, too much routine, and never enough money. But now, with the baby coming, and everything so complicated, she aches to begin again. If only she could go right back, to when Mama was alive, when she was a little girl, still innocent. Impossible, of course.

Rava glances at the clock. Then she takes a shower and selects a sage-green abaya. The fabric flows gently over the curve of her growing baby and the long sleeves conceal her Femband. Covering her hair with a hijab, she makes her way downstairs to join Baba and Nasreem.

'May I pray with you?'

Baba's smile almost splits his face in two.

'My daughter!'

It's been so long, Rava was worried she might have forgotten how to pray. She's never stopped believing in God, but she fears he stopped believing in her a long time ago. Today though, reciting the familiar words, folding her hands over her heart, prostrating herself, she feels safe in a way she's missed so badly. God is great, I am small. God protects me.

Please let it be true.

AT THE AIRPORT, Nasreem thrusts something into Rava's hands. It's a paper bag with something inside.

'For the baby. It was your mother's.'

Rava opens the package while she's waiting at the boarding gate. Inside is a tiny white dress, hand-embroidered, smocked and frilled, adorned with pink satin ribbons. Rava gasps. She spreads the garment on her knees and examines the exquisite stitching, smoothing the delicate cotton lawn. It's beautiful.

'Ooh, that's pretty,' comments the lady in the neighbouring seat. 'Been shopping? D'you know someone who's incubating?'

'It's me,' Rava replies proudly, lifting her sleeve so the lady can see her blue wristband. 'And this is a family heirloom, for my daughter.'

My daughter. The words echo in Rava's head all the way back to London.

My precious daughter.

25

ZOE

Chiara's life begins to resemble a spy movie, with burner phones and cryptic notes appearing on a regular basis. Sometimes, when she goes to collect patient medications from the hospital pharmacy, an extra package turns up in the box for Liz or one of her fellow midwives. Chiara can't work out who leaves the notes or provides the stolen drugs.

'Don't ask, and don't try to find out,' Liz tells her. 'It's safer that way.'

It might be Salvador, but he never meets her gaze when they come across one another on the wards. She keeps hoping he might invite her to Cucina Piccola again; once or twice she finds herself walking past the little trattoria and looking in through the windows, but there's no sign of him of course. Silly of her; she doesn't have time for this nonsense. Anyway, there must be other hospital staff secretly supporting the network.

Chiara visits Liz at every opportunity, whenever she has time off work. She's stopped taking extra shifts at the hospital, and sometimes she stays two or three days on the boat. Her heart still beats faster every time she sets out to find the Rosie

Lee, but these days she smiles to herself, wondering who will be on the boat today.

The narrowboat travels the canals and rivers north and east of London, never staying long on the same mooring. Liz is always busy, and there's always something new to learn. Once you get past her gruff exterior, Liz is a patient teacher. When a baby emerges with his cord wrapped twice around his neck, Liz shows Chiara how to ease the pulsating loops over the baby's head as he slides into the world.

One night a gentle Somali woman births her baby bottom-first: *'by the breech,'* Liz calls it. Liz helps the woman onto her hands and knees, and Chiara watches, fascinated, as first the baby's bottom, then its legs, chest, both arms, and finally the head appear. It's as if the baby knows what to do. The next day Liz demonstrates with a doll and a model pelvis what to look for at a breech birth, and how to intervene if the head gets stuck.

'Otherwise, keep your hands off. The effing doctors always want to interfere.' Liz snorts. 'They're always in a hurry to cut women up and take over. Pay proper attention, watch the signs, and most healthy breech babies will birth themselves.'

When there are no mothers or babies on the boat, Chiara reads. The Rosie Lee is full of books. There are so many piled high in Liz's cabin and stashed under the beds, it's a miracle the boat doesn't sink. Nearly everyone reads on their electronic devices nowadays, though Nonna had her Bible and her prayer book with pages thumbed soft as rose petals. Liz's books look equally well-loved. Some have faded lettering, and crumbling spines held together with yellowed tape. The titles sound like poetry: *'Spiritual Midwifery', The Female Pelvis', 'Culpepper's Complete Herbal.'*

'Go ahead, read whatever you like,' Liz says. 'They don't teach you nurses much that's useful these days, in my opinion.' Chiara reaches for a slim volume: *'Supporting Women for*

Peaceful Birth.' She settles onto a cushion on the big bed and loses herself in a world of purple lines and placentas, instinct and intuition.

Liz teaches Chiara her recipes. Together, they pound calendula flowers with soothing comfrey to make a balm for bruises and swelling after a long birth. There's an energy elixir for labour: honey mixed with apple juice and warming spices. A peppermint infusion can help a woman pass water; lavender prevents panic. Liz shows Chiara how to harvest herbs by moonlight, tying their stems with twine and hanging them up to dry.

Valerian is good for sleep; eyebright for coughs, colds and inflammation. They brew nettle tips into nourishing soups, and camomile into teas. When the elder bushes come into flower, Chiara harvests the frothy, lace-like blossoms to make a tea for constipation. She kneads bread dough into loaves to feed hungry new mothers and learns how to bake the groaning cake, rich with fruit soaked in tea and brown sugar.

The eggs for the cake come from Liz's chickens, Vic and Soo. These feisty birds are entirely unfazed by Gaskin, though he likes to eye them thoughtfully and stretch out his claws towards them. But he soon turns tail and retreats if they come pecking too close, jutting their sharp beaks in his direction. The hens spend their days foraging around the long grass and bushes beside the river, returning to their nesting box on the Rosie Lee to lay their eggs in warm straw and to roost at night. Liz is meticulous about shutting them in at dusk.

'Foxes are everywhere,' she says.

SOMETIMES LIZ and Chiara travel to clinics organised by volunteers in decaying buildings outside the city limits. It's not a crime to provide general medical help, so Liz offers remedies, bandaging, and advice for anyone in need - mostly the elderly, the poor, and unregistered children. Pregnant women come along too for their antenatal check-ups.

Chiara practices palpating a mother's abdomen to feel how and where a baby is positioned. She learns when a head is well settled into the pelvis ready for birth, and when a foetus is wedged at an awkward sideways angle.

'Come and see me again in two weeks,' Liz tells the tired-looking woman with the sideways baby. 'If the baby's head down by then I'll look after you, but if it's still across your belly like this you'll have to go to the People's Hospital for a C-section.'

Chiara gasps. The free People's Hospital is notoriously dirty and understaffed. Surely Liz can't be serious about sending this woman there?

Afterwards, Liz explains:

'If that woman labours alone with a transverse foetus, her uterus will rupture and she'll die. Part of our job is knowing what we can't do.'

'But -?'

'The People's is a shithole, but it's all we've got. If she's married and her husband's in work they might let her keep the baby. They'll sterilise her, of course, but she'll be alive. What do you expect - a fairy tale ending every time?'

Chiara's stomach feels hollow.

'I thought we could help everyone,' she whispers.

'Sorry.' Liz shakes her head. 'If you think I've got a magic wand, think again. This isn't a fairy story; it's a war, and we're fighting in the trenches. We can't win every battle, but we don't quit either. There's an ancient story about midwives refusing to knuckle under when a king told them to kill all the male babies. And there were midwives in Nazi death camps, risking their lives daily. Nothing changes. Don't expect it to be easy.

'Midwives are warriors. We don't give up. We don't bow to

the powers that be. Women and their babies rely on us - you might say life itself depends on us. So we keep fighting - warriors till our last breath. Don't forget that, Chiara.'

CHIARA ARRIVES one afternoon to find a young woman rocking and moaning her way through a labour contraction. As the pain ebbs, she hammers her fists on the floor.

'I don't want no effing baby. Changed my mind. Can't you pull it out or something?'

The girl looks about Gemma's age - fifteen or sixteen - but her resemblance to Chiara's sister ends there. This mother-to-be has intricately braided hair, angry eyes, and dozens of little scars running the length of her left forearm. A black wristband marks her as a 'Molly' - one of London's female menial workers. She wears a tiny t-shirt which barely covers her breasts, and a printed cotton sarong tied round her hips. Her pregnant belly looks huge on her skinny body.

'Get it out of me!' she wails.

'Ah, Chiara, you found us all right then. This is Zoe. Make yourself a cup of tea and I'll fill you in.' Liz sits in her rocking chair, a notebook on her lap. She smiles at Chiara, but doesn't get up; her face looks paler than usual.

Chiara busies herself with the kettle while Liz tells her about Zoe:

'First baby, full term, so far as we can tell. She's staying with her grandmother at one of the big camps on the marshes. Works as a cleaner in the city. She arrived here alone and in labour this morning, and she's been having strong regular contractions for at least the past eight hours. Membranes intact.'

A piercing yell cuts across Liz's voice.

'All right, Zoe, you're doing well. Keep breathing through it, my love.' Liz nods towards the pinard on the kitchen surface. 'Will you listen to the baby, Chiara, and do a full set of observations? That's it, lean into it, Zoe.' She reaches across and places a reassuring hand on Zoe's shoulder but Chiara senses a hint of disquiet in the tilt of Liz's eyebrows.

The baby's heartbeat is a healthy one hundred and forty-eight beats per minute, and Zoe's pulse, temperature, and blood pressure are all normal. But the young girl's pupils are dilated and her fists clenched. Between her pains, she paces the kitchen like a caged animal.

'I need Jajja,' she sobs. 'I should've stayed home with Jajja. I wanna go home!'

'Who's Jajja?' Chiara asks as Zoe's fingernails bite into her wrist. 'Can we get her for you?' Zoe's not much more than a child.

'My granny. No. Too old - don't wanna worry her. But I - oooww!' Zoe grabs Chiara's other wrist and wrings them both. The Rosie Lee vibrates with her cries, and Chiara hopes none of the inhabitants of the nearby boats decide today is the day to call the police. They're moored in a quiet spot, and few if any of the river dwellers want to get involved with the authorities, but you can never be certain.

26

NOT QUITTING

All through the night, Zoe's belly hardens like granite every two or three minutes. Liz encourages her to eat oatmeal biscuits and gives her homemade cordials laced with pain-relieving herbs. Chiara massages Zoe's back, hands, and feet. Zoe paces and rests, rests and paces, but there's no sign of her baby.

Morning comes, and Gaskin emerges from his favourite sleeping spot in Liz's cabin. The chickens cluck to be let out, and the Rosie Lee grows warm in the sunshine, but still Zoe's baby isn't here. Zoe cries and asks for her Jajja, but with less energy now. She lies down and whimpers.

Liz examines Zoe and says that the baby's head hasn't descended deep enough into Zoe's pelvis. She gets Chiara to feel how the foetus is facing upwards, with its spine curving towards Zoe's back. It needs to turn to move down into the birth canal.

'Well done, Zoe,' Liz says. 'You're doing so well.' But the old midwife's face tells a different story.

'Come outside for a moment. Let's get a breath of air.' Liz leads Chiara out into the bright day. The boards of the deck are warm underfoot. Liz unlatches the coop, and the chickens flap and scuttle off the boat into the long grass beside the river.

'I'm not happy,' Liz says. 'She's too young. Won't tell me her age, but she can't be more than seventeen - maybe less. These girls aren't fully grown, pelvis is too narrow. She's probably never had a decent diet, not enough protein or calcium. No iron, so she's at risk of a bleed.' Liz stares at Vic and Soo who are scratching and pecking for worms.

'What are we going to do?' Chiara's throat is dry.

'I don't want to send her to the People's if we can help it.' Liz seems to be talking to herself. 'But - I'm going to call Funmi - old partner in crime. Get a second opinion. Could you grab me a fresh phone from the locker, my love, and then go sit with Zoe?'

Liz spends several minutes speaking on the phone. Snatches of her conversation drift in through the doorway. She uses the shorthand and incomprehensible jokes you use with a friend you've known forever:

'Shepherd's - more, d'you reckon? ... Would you ARM yet? ... Yeah, I need your fingers! You been busy?'

Chiara runs a cloth under cold water and sponges Zoe's forehead. She's offering her a drink when Liz returns with a new air of determination.

'Okay, Funmi thinks we should get her mobilising again. Reminded me of some of our old tricks. Got to be worth a try.'

They give a dose of shepherd's purse tincture to intensify the contractions. Zoe makes a face at its musty, old-broccoli smell, but swallows it with a spoonful of honey. Then they help her off the bed and onto all fours on the floor.

Liz and Chiara wrap a long shawl around Zoe's hips. Taking one end each, they wobble her bottom vigorously from side to side. Liz says it's called '*shaking the apple tree*'. Then they do the same with the shawl around Zoe's belly.Then back to the hips again. Afterwards, Liz feels the baby's position again. She thinks perhaps it has turned a little, has moved lower down, but still not low enough to be born.

They try lots of different positions. Zoe sits on the toilet with her feet on two wooden blocks leaning forwards onto Chiara's shoulders. They take turns to walk her up the steps to the deck and down again. When Zoe needs to rest, Chiara helps her lie down on her left side on the cushioned floor, her right leg raised and supported to open her pelvis.

Chiara checks the baby's heartbeat every fifteen minutes. It's always between one hundred and forty-five and one hundred and fifty-five beats per minute. Until it isn't.

As the day cools towards evening, the baby's heart starts racing at over one hundred and sixty-five. Liz's lips tighten. It's a bad sign; the infant is losing its ability to tolerate the relentless squeezing of Zoe's contractions. Half an hour later, the heartbeat is up to one hundred and sixty-nine. The sunlight is fading.

'Do you want to go home, Chiara?' Liz asks. 'Didn't you say you're working at the hospital tonight?'

Chiara looks at Liz. There's a lop-sided look about her, as if she's struggling to stand up straight. Her face is ashen, her eyes dark-shadowed.

'I don't want to leave you,' she says. 'You look so tired.'

'You mustn't get yourself into trouble, my love, not on my account. I'm a tough old bird; I'll be fine.'

But the slump of Liz's shoulders contradicts her words.

'No,' says Chiara. 'I'll tell work I was sick. I'm staying to help you.'

'If you're sure,' Liz says gruffly. But she doesn't argue; only bends and busies herself with something on the stove. When she straightens up, Chiara wonders if she can see a tear in the old woman's eye. Or is it a trick of the lamplight?

ANOTHER HOUR PASSES. The baby's heart gallops at one hundred and seventy beats per minute. Liz tells Chiara she is going to break the waters.

'Don't like doing it if I can avoid it,' she says, 'especially with a high head and a narrow pelvis. There's a danger of the cord coming down in front of the baby's head. That can cut off the foetal blood supply, and then we've got a real emergency on our hands. But we need to get the head down onto the cervix and I've tried everything else.'

They have no difficulty now getting Zoe to lie down on her back. She's limp with exhaustion.

'You're seven centimetres dilated,' Liz tells her. 'Well done, Zoe. Just a little bit further to go.'

Zoe groans.

'I thought you was going to tell me it's coming out now. Can't you send me down the hospital, get them to cut me open?'

'If you go to the hospital you'll have to wait hours before anyone can help you. I think we should break the bag of water around your baby now. Is that all right?'

'Yeah, whatever.' Zoe shrugs with a teenager's weary indifference. 'Just get it out of me.'

Liz closes her eyes and takes a long breath in and out. You might almost think she was praying.

'Chiara, can you put on gloves, and then unwrap that long package please?'

Chiara does as she is told. The object inside the sterilised muslin parcel looks like an elongated, flattened crochet hook. She passes it to Liz.

'Okay Chiara. Now, listen carefully. Place your hands onto the top of Zoe's uterus. That's right. Now, when I tell you, press down towards me.'

Chiara places her hands onto Zoe's belly. As it hardens with the next contraction, Liz speaks:

'Okay, now. And keep that pressure on till I tell you to stop.'

Chiara presses down as a flood of greenish liquid pours out, soaking into the towels piled beneath.

'Okay, now let go, and pass me the pinard.' Liz palpates Zoe's belly, which has changed its shape; the lump of the baby's bottom is lower now. She finds the place, presses the pinard stethoscope to Zoe's skin, and listens. Relief softens her features.

'Still one-seventy. We haven't trapped the cord, thank God. Otherwise the foetal heart might've dropped to fifty or worse.'

Chiara takes her turn to listen. The heartbeat sounds like a distant, hurtling train.

'Now what?' she asks.

Liz grips the rail on the edge of the kitchen surface to haul herself back to her feet. Beads of sweat stand out on her forehead.

'Now we get this baby out.'

THEY GIVE Zoe a mug of sweet raspberry leaf tea, holding it to her lips and encouraging her to drink. After a few sips she revives enough to complain about the wetness between her legs. Then she cries out in pain.

'Okay,' Liz says when the surge subsides, 'it's going to be intense now, strong pains - good pains to bring your baby. But he's getting tired now, like you. We need to get him out. Or her - we'll find out soon. Are you ready?'

Zoe gives them a sharp look.

'It's a she - little girl - that's what I want. Got a name 'n everything.' Zoe grasps the mug for herself and drains it in a few gulps, adding, 'I'm not a kid, you know. I'm gonna do this.' She lifts her chin and squares her thin shoulders. 'Let's do this.'

Zoe seems to find a second wind. She gets up and moves spontaneously, her mouth set in determination. She sways and gyrates her hips in the birth dance of a thousand generations. Somewhere, deep in her body, she recalls the knowledge of her fore-mothers. Her baby's heartbeat keeps going at between one hundred and sixty and one hundred and seventy beats per minute. Like his mother, he's tired, but he isn't quitting.

Zoe's moans shift into a deeper, earthier pitch. There's a new urgency about her. She rocks from side to side, eyes closed in concentration.

'Need the toilet,' she announces. 'Gotta do a massive crap.'

Liz smiles.

'It's your baby's head,' she says. 'Do you want to push?'

Zoe nods. Screwing up her face and letting out a mighty cry, she squats and bears down with all her strength.

Liz brings out her little birthing stool to support Zoe as she pushes. The baby's heartbeat drops to seventy, then fifty, and Chiara bites her lip. Zoe brays like a wild donkey. The liquid draining from her is thick and green, tinged with blood. The baby has opened its bowels; it is in distress.

'Keep going,' Chiara says, 'you're almost there.'

With an almighty cry, Zoe pushes again, and a head rises up between her legs. It is covered with tight curls of dark hair. Chiara reaches forward, and the baby shoots out into her hands. It is big, and wet, and slippery. Chiara rubs it with towels. It's a girl. She is not yet breathing.

'Keep rubbing her.' says Liz. 'Well done, Zoe.'

Chiara holds her own breath as she dries and stimulates the infant. Zoe has the little girl she wanted, so long as -.

'Let me hold her,' Zoe says.

'Just a moment; she needs a little encouragement.'

Liz produces something that looks like a rubber bulb with tubes protruding. She puts one end to the baby's nose and the other to her own mouth and sucks. Vile-looking green liquid fills the bulb. The baby splutters. She wriggles. Liz has a plastic mask ready to help her breathe, but before she can use it the baby opens her mouth and cries as the air fills her lungs.

Chiara watches her colour change from greyish blue to a warm, rosy brown. Her eyes blink open. She is vigorous, beautiful, and alive.

'What a lovely baby.' Chiara exclaims. 'Zoe, you did it!'

27

ON THE NEWS

Martin's key in the door makes Rava jump, and the oil in her cooking pan spatters onto her dress. As she rinses her hands, Louis runs yapping to the hallway. It's only 5.30; why's he so early? Thank God she's finished her prayers.

Martin bursts into the kitchen, holding out a bouquet. He's grinning, excited. He thrusts the flowers at Rava before taking her in his arms and kissing her. The baby shifts, and a flutter of hope rises inside her. Something good's happened - he's happy - perhaps she can tell him today.

'Congratulate me!' he cries. 'I'm going to be on the news, and it's a win this time. All my little ducks are lining up.' He kisses her again. 'You're going to be so proud of me, sweetheart. It'll be on at six; I rushed home so we can watch it together. You've been so patient with all these late nights. No need to cook - I'll take you out to dinner later. What d'you fancy? Indian? Chinese?'

Rava turns off the stove and starts tidying away the half-cooked meal.

'I don't mind - whatever you like. Is it your promotion?' If they're making him Junior Minister, then surely he'll be all right about the baby. Rava feels unusually light, as if her feet might float off the floor.

'Shall I find a vase for the flowers?' He selects a too-small one and half fills it with water before putting it down again. 'It's another arrest, but a juicy one this time. This old hag knows all the ringleaders, and we caught her in the act, so we've got hard evidence.'

'Evidence?'

'The midwife had a client in her flat, just given birth. Umbilical cord attached. It's a clear-cut contravention - no way she'll wriggle out of it - so we got the press involved. Time to make a splash.'

'Oh!' Rava's hand flies to her mouth. She pictures a newborn, wet from birth, still joined to its mother.

'This is the breakthrough I've been waiting for, Martin goes on. 'I know I've been distant these last few weeks, but it's a delicate operation. I'm having to pull a lot of strings, keep a lot of people happy. That's politics. Information is power, and sometimes you have to deal with unsavoury characters to get what you need. But today it's paid off. Come here, Louis.'

Martin scoops the little dog into his arms. 'Your daddy's been very clever, Louis. We're going to be moving up in the world. That promotion's pretty much in the bag. We need to get on with looking at larger apartments. There's a new tower going up in Holborn, very prestigious: excellent security, swimming pool and gym, rooftop garden, dog creche. You'd like that, wouldn't you Louis? And we'll need a third bedroom of course, for the son and heir.'

Rava squeezes Martin's hand. She'll tell him soon ,when the moment's right. She busies herself finding a larger vase. The flowers smell cold, as if they've come out of a fridge.

MARTIN INSISTS they switch on the TV before the news begins. They watch the last few minutes of a game-show where the contestants have to remove an item of clothing whenever they get a question wrong. The studio audience finds it hilarious. As the closing credits roll, Martin puts an arm around Rava's shoulders and sits Louis on his lap. He's poured himself a whiskey. He drums his fingers on the table as the theme tune plays for the news, then fidgets through the first item about the removal of elderly people from Sussex villages.

'This is old news,' he grumbles. 'Should've accepted alternative housing when they had the chance, shouldn't they? We're only rounding them up for their own safety. Settle down now, Louis. Ah, this is it. Shh!' He holds up a hand as if Rava might interrupt.

A reporter appears on the screen, standing in front of a dismal, graffiti-covered tower block.

'A midwife was arrested today and charged with attending an illegal birth outside an authorised healthcare setting. Funmi Ikande, aged sixty-three, was discovered in the building behind me assisting a woman to give birth to her third child, in direct contravention of the Safe Futures Policy, and Ministry of Population and Health directives. Home births carry a high risk of mortality for both mother and child. This arrest is an important step forward in the Government's continuing commitment to deliver safer births and healthier families.'

The TV screen shows a woman in handcuffs being marched up to the back of a police van. She looks older than sixty-three, limping, and doubled-over as if in pain. Her hair is dishevelled, and there's a purple swelling around her right eye. She's trying to argue with the officers, jerking her head towards something or someone. Blue lights flash from an approaching ambulance. The clip ends abruptly.

Rava shivers but Martin doesn't seem to notice. He points excitedly at the TV.

'Look, it's me!'

Martin stands next to the reporter. He's wearing a dark suit with a sombre tie.

'Martin Robson is Under-Secretary of State for Womens' and Reproductive Health at the Ministry of Population and Health,' the reporter continues. 'Martin, can you explain the significance of this arrest?'

'That was the question I primed him to ask.' Martin leans forward, intent on the screen.

The on-camera Martin inclines his head before looking into the lens with a grave expression.

'Yes.' He pauses for effect. 'Illegal midwives are responsible for a growing number of deaths among England's most vulnerable families. Some of these -.' He gestures as if struggling for the right word. 'I hesitate to call them butchers, but I'm afraid that isn't too harsh a name for them. Some of these elderly women claim to have medical qualifications, but in reality criminals like Funmi Ikande are more accurately described as witches.

'Midwives deceive the public with dangerous, often poisonous, home-grown drugs, and medieval practices. Their victims suffer agonising pain attempting so-called natural birth. Tragically, not all of them survive. I'd like to show you -.' Someone passes Martin a handful of objects which he holds up to the camera: a kitchen knife, a pair of scissors, and a long steel knitting needle, all smeared with blood. 'These implements were found in Mrs Ikande's home.'

Rava gasps. The camera pans to the reporter, who raises his eyebrows.

'Appalling. So are you suggesting that Funmi Ikande wasn't working alone? Are there others like her still at large?'

The at-home Martin nods and takes a swig of his whiskey.

'Yes, I'm afraid so.' The on-screen Martin touches the corner of his eye, perhaps to wipe away a tear. His face fills the frame.

'Women are brought into our hospitals every day with appalling injuries sustained at the hands of midwives. Our heroic doctors do everything possible to save them, but, tragically, some of these victims of the underground home birth industry are beyond help. Women are dying. Babies are dying. But we at the Ministry of Population and Health have pledged to put an end to this scourge.'

Martin pauses and the reporter speaks:

'Thank you Martin. Is there anything our viewers can do to help?'

'Yes. Women need our protection. I'd like to express my gratitude to our police and enforcement agencies for their tireless efforts to put charlatans like Mrs Ikande behind bars. Women and babies need our protection. We anticipate Mrs Ikande will provide information leading to further arrests. But I appeal to the public. Please, if you have any information relating to illegal pregnancies or births, we'd like to hear from you. You can call the number coming up on your screen now, or visit the Ministry of Population and Health website for more information.'

A number flashes across the screen, and the news cuts to the next item: the Defender opening the refurbished Opera House in Covent Garden. Martin switches off the TV.

'What did you think? Came across all right, I reckon - got the message out there, loud and clear. Pity it wasn't on first, but you can't have everything.' He finishes his drink and pours another.

Rava keeps seeing the old woman being forced into the van. She goes to turn down the air conditioning; she feels cold all over. There's something wrong with the news item; something missing.

'That knife,' she asks. 'Did she cut the poor woman open?'

Martin shrugs.

'I dunno. Might be a bit of poetic licence to drive the point home. The place was a mess by the time I got there. There was plenty of blood, and I needed something for the cameras. Found those bits and pieces in the kitchen, so yeah, they were in her home.'

'But -.' Rava's baby kicks, and her mouth floods with saliva.

'Okay, a bit over the top perhaps.' Martin spreads his hands. 'But this is important, Rava. Imagine if that was you and our baby, Edward, in that awful slum. It's breathtakingly unhygienic. I'm doing this to protect you, my darling, and all the other incubators.'

Rava bows her head.

'I know,' she murmurs. She thinks she might be going to throw up. Martin's fingers brush her cheek.

'You're freezing. Are you feeling all right? Sorry, have I been insensitive? I was so excited, making progress at last, but maybe I shouldn't have let you watch. It's upset you, hasn't it?'

Rava swallows.

'I'm all right - tired, that's all. I'm glad your work's going well - you looked very smart. Could you get me a glass of water, please darling?'

'Of course. Your wish is my command!'

When Martin's standing at the sink with his back to her, Rava realises what's been bothering her.

'What happened to the baby, Martin? Did it survive? And the mother - the one the midwife was looking after - will she go to prison too?'

The poor woman must have been terrified.

Martin finishes filling the glass and brings it over. He kisses Rava's forehead and both her cheeks before replying:

'Oh my darling, you're so thoughtful, so sweet. I've been assured the incubator was fine; very grateful to be rescued. I expect they took her to the People's Hospital.'

'And the baby?'

Martin sighs.

'They didn't tell me. Confidential health information. But nothing for you to worry about, my love. They're all in good hands.'

He sits down beside Rava.

'Now, speaking of babies, it's high time I got more involved with our Edward. When's your next scan, my love? I'm going to clear the diary to make sure I'll be there. I want to see him for myself.'

28

BLOOD TESTS

Chiara longs to tell Gemma about the Rosie Lee but Liz says her personal phone might be monitored. Besides, Gemma can talk of nothing but their plans to leave Sicily. Mamma's brother, Uncle Francesco, has found work in Milan, and he's persuaded Mamma and Gemma to join him there. Mamma's accepted a pitiable price for the cottage, so it's really happening.

Chiara still sends money home when she can, but it's harder now she's dropped the extra shifts.

'Don't worry, things are looking up for us now, *grazie, Santa Maria!* You're still young, Chiara. Enjoy your freedom,' Mamma says.

Freedom. What would Mamma say if she knew the truth? Every day at the Genesis Centre is a long march down a white corridor, never looking to left or right, never allowing your imagination free rein. Chiara does her best to focus on nothing but this IV pump, that drug calculation, the anti-embolism stockings for the lady in bed four. The red Femband tracks her every movement.

She reminds herself, over and over, that she's in debt, that she'd be homeless without this job, that Sister threatened her with criminal prosecution. But she isn't sure she can keep it up much longer.

Liz has been unusually subdued since her friend, Fumni, got arrested. Chiara contacted Liz the day after she saw it on TV, but Liz told her not to come to the boat.

'Stay away for at least a week, maybe two,' she said, her voice flat. 'And think long and hard about whether you want to come back at all.'

Chiara did go back though, as soon as Liz would let her. She missed the excitement too much, and the joy of helping women birth their babies, and the escape from the Genesis Centre, even for a few hours.

'NURSE, you haven't completed these notes correctly. Your patient observations are missing from page eighteen. And I had a complaint about you yesterday.'

Sister Miller stands in the middle of the corridor, brandishing a set of patient notes. Her orange lips are set in a thin line.

'Sorry Sister? What was the complaint Sister?'

'One of our wealthiest patients was very unhappy at having to wait over two hours for you to come and remove her wound dressing. She said you promised to come back in five minutes, and then disappeared. She also said you yawned in front of her.' Sister's features form a caricature of appalled incredulity.

'Sorry, Sister Miller, I was late for the antibiotics round.'

It's probably true about the yawn; Chiara was up all the night before helping a mother give birth to twins on the Rosie Lee. She hangs her head, hoping Sister hasn't noticed the shadows under her eyes.

'Look at me when I'm speaking to you, Nurse. Do you want

your patients to get sepsis and die? The rules are there to protect you. One single mistake, and the whole thing can unravel in no time.'

'Yes, Sister. Sorry, Sister.'

'Since that unfortunate incident at the anniversary celebrations we are all under additional pressure to demonstrate excellence. Some of our clients are very important people with a lot of influence. Pay more attention to the indications on their files, please. A purple *V* for a VIP client. It really shouldn't be difficult.' The mole on Sister's right cheek quivers.

'Yes, Sister.'

Chiara wonders if she dares walk past Sister to continue her chores. She takes a hesitant step forward, but Sister halts her again, hand raised like a police officer.

'I haven't finished, Nurse.'

'Sorry, Sister.'

'Your days off are supposed to be for rest and recuperation. If you're out all night with your boyfriends, how can you perform at work? Nursing is a vocation, not a hobby.'

'Yes, Sister Miller.'

'Correct these before leaving tonight.' Sister thrusts the offending set of notes into Chiara's hand. 'You were doing so well, but things seem to have gone downhill these past weeks. Have you thought about that sterilisation yet? We often find it settles young women down, helps them focus on career and so forth.'

'I'm still thinking, Sister.'

'Well, don't leave it too long. You're a bright girl - I thought you had promise. All right - run along now.'

With a sigh, Sister turns back towards her office, her kitten-heels click-clacking on the polished floor.

A COUPLE OF WEEKS LATER, Chiara walks into the neonatal examination room to see Salvador bending over a baby. He's got his back to her but she knows it's him from the faded cartoon scrubs and the soft Spanish voice:

'Sorry, baby. Nearly finished, I promise.'

Chiara's stomach does a little somersault. She feels awkward, though she's not sure why. Didn't she want a chance to talk to Salvador? She finds herself thinking about him sometimes, late at night, as if he's a puzzle she can't solve.

'Well done, *chico*. You did great.' Salvador applies a plaster to the baby's heel. He straightens up, sees Chiara, and his face changes.

'Sister sent me.' She doesn't know why she sounds so defensive. 'She told me to come and assist with the heel prick tests.'

'Okay.' A slow smile spreads across his features, and he goes to pull down the blind over the square of glass in the door. 'We're good - there's no camera in here. How are things with you, Chiara?'

'Busy.' They exchange glances.

She's clumsy to begin with. She drops the first test card on the floor, and they have to start again, pricking the poor baby on the other foot. After she's wheeled the cot back to the nursery, she hurries to the toilets to splash her face with cold water. Why does she always have to turn red at the slightest embarrassment?

But when she returns, he cracks a silly joke, and she starts to relax. Between doing the tests, and updating the notes, the pair of them chat about safe, normal things. Salvador tells her funny stories from when he was a student in Madrid, and about the football team he plays for when he's not on shift. He prides himself on his goalkeeping skills.

They compare their favourite movies. Salvador likes action and thrillers; Chiara does too, though she can't share his love of disaster movies. It turns out they're both fans of the old *Godfather* films.

'There's an awful lot of violence,' Salvador admits, but I just love that whole Italian family thing. The countryside, and the big family meals and celebrations.'

'Exactly,' she agrees. 'It's crazy, but those films make me feel homesick. They were all filmed in Sicily - the churches, the streets, the villas. Tourists used to come and take pictures . You know that villa in the first film, with the well in the courtyard? It's still there, after all this time, not far from where I grew up.' She looks up at him, her gaze soft with the memory.

'Really! Perhaps you will show me some day?'

'Perhaps.' She hesitates before adding shyly, 'Your eyes? Where does that colour come from?'

He grins.

'Blue eyes run in my family. A Celtic ancestor, perhaps? You like them?'

She blushes, but speaks her thoughts aloud:

'The abandoned shipyards in Sicily are full of borage flowers in spring - exactly that shade of blue.'

'Nice to know I look like a post-industrial wasteland!'

'No, I didn't mean -.' She clasps a hand to her mouth, but he's laughing, and she joins him, giggling helplessly over the next set of notes. It makes a change to be laughing at work.

CHIARA HOLDS each baby in her arms while Salvador pierces its heel. She hums the lullaby Nonna used to sing when Gemma was little, and the infants scarcely cry at all.

'You have a gift with babies,' Salvador says. 'I should work with you more often.' Chiara turns pink with pleasure.

'Would you like a coffee?' he asks after she's returned the last baby to the nursery. 'I think we've earned one.'

'Good idea. I'll go to the machine. How d'you have it?'

He rolls his eyes.

'Not that shitty machine. It spews out dirty dishwater. I'll get you a decent coffee from the doctors' mess. Black or white? Sugar? Shot of vodka in it?'

'Vodka?' She giggles again, but he only raises his thick eyebrows.

'You'd be surprised how many of the doctors need vodka to get through a shift. Plenty of them rely on other drugs too.' He runs his fingers through his hair. 'This job's not easy.'

The coffee is delicious, hot and strong. Salvador asks Chiara about her family, and she tells him about Mamma and Gemma's plans to move north, and how much she misses the village by the sea.

'And your family?' she asks. 'Who do you have at home?'

Salvador reaches into the pocket of his scrubs. He brings out his wallet and extracts a thin sheet of folded paper, smoothing it out to reveal a childlike drawing in coloured pencils. Two people stand hand in hand under a yellow sun. One has a beard and dark, shaggy hair; the other is shorter, wearing a skirt and round, red-rimmed glasses. Underneath, in wobbly letters, the artist has written: *'Estoy con mi hermano.'*

'I am with my brother,' Salvador translates. 'My sister drew it - Mariana. She has Trisomy 21 - Down Syndrome.'

'Ah, that's beautiful. Do you miss her?'

Salvador stares at the paper.

'*Sí, claro.* Of course, all the time. I wish she could come here, even for a little break in the summer. Mariana doesn't do well in the Spanish heatwaves; she's got damaged heart valves. When I first came to England, I thought one day I might bring her over, but I hadn't understood how things work here. In England she'd be an Incurable. She'd be signed up for Peaceful Rest within weeks. Days maybe.'

Chiara blinks hard.

'But I thought people had to consent for Peaceful Rest? Surely, if she has a learning disability - ?'

Salvador shakes his head.

'A kindly Rest Advocate would tell her it's for the best, she'd agree, and that would be that. Mariana trusts everyone. Family members aren't allowed to object - that would be coercion.'

'Coercion? Chiara's ribs tighten. 'But surely -?'

Salvador makes a growling sound deep in his throat.

'Don't be so naive, Chiara. Haven't you seen what goes on here, in this fancy hospital?' He raises his coffee mug and thumps it down on the table so hard little drops of brown liquid fly out and spatter the pile of unused test cards. 'We used to treat babies who failed one of these tests, but you know what happens to them now, don't you?'

Chiara flinches. She glances nervously at the door, gesturing to Salvador to lower his voice.

'Is there nothing we can do?'

Salvador clutches handfuls of his hair.

'If I wasn't such a pathetic coward. Mariana thinks I'm some kind of superhero. She's got no idea. They'd know it was me, and - I'm not ready yet. I do a few things for the network, but Mariana relies on me sending money home.' He stares at the picture for several seconds before folding it, giving it a kiss, and replacing it into his wallet. Then he drains his coffee and starts tidying the test cards. 'They've got all the power,' he says. 'We do all we can.'

Do we, though? Chiara wonders.

A sharp rap at the door shatters the quiet.

'Are you finished in there, Nurse Santori? We've got three new admissions on the ward so hurry up please. And open that blind! How can I keep my patients safe if I can't see what's going on?'

Chiara jumps to her feet.

'Yes, Sister Miller. Coming, Sister Miller.'

29

HOME TRUTHS

'Martin? Oh, I'm so glad I caught you. It's Louis - I'm worried.'

'Louis? Oh my God, what's wrong? He was fine when I left this morning. Did you take him out in the heat?' Martin's voice rises so sharply Rava has to hold the phone away from her ear.

'Yes, I -.' He'll be angry, but she has to make this convincing. 'I'm so sorry, Martin. He was whining for a walk, so I took him out, only along the street, but he started this noisy breathing, so I brought him back, but now he's -.'

'You idiot, Rava. What were you thinking? It's thirty degrees out there! Frenchies are sensitive to heat - I've told you plenty of times. Let me hear his breathing. Have you called the vet?'

Rava glances at Louis, who is curled up asleep in his basket, cool and content, having been inside the air-conditioned apartment all day.

'I think it's settling down a bit now.'

'Let me hear. Have you given him a drink? Not too much, mind - little sips. I can't hear him panting.'

'He was a minute ago, before I called you. He was making a funny noise, rasping.' Those are the symptoms she looked up online.

'Has he been sick? Does he seem disoriented?'

'I'm not sure, maybe. I'm sorry, Martin, it was silly of me. I thought he might like some fresh air before I left for the scan. But now - I don't want to leave him like this.'

'Of course you can't leave him. He could start fitting. Dogs die of heatstroke. Did you call the vet?'

'Not yet; I thought I should call you first.'

Martin groans.

'I'll do it. I'll coming straight home. In the meantime, keep offering him water and sponge him down with a cool cloth. Cool, mind, not icy. Call me if he gets any worse.' He calls out to his secretary: 'I need my car now, Sonia. Emergency at home. Cancel my one o'clock.' To Rava he adds, 'I'll be there in half an hour. Have you turned up the air-con?'

'Yes Martin, but - what about my scan this afternoon at the Genesis Centre? You were going to come with me?' Rava holds her breath.

'Well, I can't be in two places at once. You'll have to go on your own; they'll charge us an arm and a leg to reschedule.'

She exhales.

'I'm sorry, Martin. I didn't mean to hurt him.' She doesn't have to fake the shakiness in her voice; she hates lying to Martin, hates making him angry, but she didn't know what else to do. If he comes to the scan he'll see the baby's a girl; even thinking about it makes her sick with worry. He'll have to find out eventually, but not yet. She can't risk it yet.

Martin sighs.

'Okay. Look, I need to call the vet. Daniel is on his way to pick me up. Don't leave till I get home.' He hangs up.

Thank God!

Rava's shoulders drop in relief. She unclenches her fists and strokes Louis's smooth flank. The little dog opens his blue eyes and looks at her, ears pricked back.

'Thank you, Louis,' she says.

Inside her, the baby girl nudges and flutters, like a fledgling testing its wings.

MARTIN IS in a somewhat better mood by the time Rava returns home from the Genesis Centre. The vet pronounced Louis to be in excellent health, complimenting Rava on taking all the right steps to reverse the effects of overheating. Martin sits cradling the dog in his lap while Rava carefully answers his questions about her scan.

'D'you think he's got my profile? Limbs all in proportion? No health concerns? Not that I'd expect any after that excellent DNA report. You and I are obviously ideal propagators, my love!' Martin squeezes Rava's leg. 'Sorry I was a bit stressed earlier, but Louis is delicate, and I've got so much lot on at work. That knob Toby -.'

He launches into a long description his colleague's plot to steal the Junior Minister promotion. Martin's making progress with his midwife project, but it's too slow, he says. The women arrested are refusing to give information. He needs another breakthrough, and soon.

'Are you worried about the protests?' Rava asks. The demonstration at the Genesis Centre has been followed by a smattering of small protests outside hospitals and health centres across London.

'Yes and no.' Martin picks at his fingernails. 'They're just a handful of extremists - religious loonies, mainly. We've got good regulations to prevent harassment around healthcare settings. But there's always the risk of copycats, and we need to keep getting our message across. If it was down to me, I'd put tighter controls on the press; people need to see the big picture. We're working for a better world. Some people are just selfish.'

After dinner, Martin disappears into his study saying he has important work to catch up with. He's been irritable recently, and Rava worries that there's something he's not telling her. His interest in karate has re-kindled and he's spending a lot of time at the club, but it doesn't seem to relieve his tension. He's started smoking again - although never in the apartment - and he comes home late night after night, often going out again after dinner. When he finally comes to bed, he keeps Rava awake with his endless tossing and turning - as if the baby pressing on her bladder wasn't disturbance enough.

LATE ONE AFTERNOON, there's a knock at the door. Rava is resting on the sofa after a tiring day at work, but she hurries to answer. Daniel stands in the lobby holding an enormous box.

'Oh, hello Daniel.' Rava smooths her dress over her bump, conscious of her bare feet and dishevelled hair.

'Special delivery, Mrs Robson, ma'am. May I come in?'

'Er - yes, of course.' She stands back to let him enter, and the chauffeur carries the package into the lounge.

'Mr Robson ordered it for you, madam. He wanted you to have it straight away. He sends his apologies, but he's going to be home late again tonight. He also asked me to check something in his study. Do you mind?'

What can she say? The back of her neck tingles, as if someone's watching her from behind.

'Only be a minute, ma'am.'

Daniel disappears into Martin's study, closing the door behind him. The large box sits in the centre of the room. She doesn't want to open it while Daniel is here; it might be something private. She sits back on the sofa and fiddles with her phone, waiting.

'All sorted. Would you like me to help you unpack it?' Daniel straightens his jacket as he emerges. He glances up at the crystal light fitting - an extravagant purchase from two or three years ago - and then across at the window blinds.

'No thank you. I'm fine.' Why's he hanging about? Has Martin sent him to check up on her?

'If you're sure, ma'am? And is everything all right with you and the baby?'

'Fine, thank you, Daniel.' Just go, she urges inwardly.

'Right you are. Could I just grab a glass of water? It's like an oven out there.'

Rava gets to her feet, but Daniel reaches the sink ahead of her. He seems to know his way around the kitchen cabinets. Has he been here before, when she was out? Rava shivers as if the glass of cold water has been tipped down her spine.

Daniel uses the bathroom, like last time, and finally he's gone. Rava opens the box, still wondering about Daniel and his uninvited interest in her pregnancy. She removes layer after layer of environmentally friendly packaging to uncover - oh, it's a baby's cradle!

The crib is beautifully made from silky white oak, hand finished, traditional and modern at the same time. Exactly what she would have chosen, in fact. She saw one just like it in 'Future Mother' magazine. Maybe she even pointed it out to Martin.

With a little squeak of excitement, Rava rips off the rest of the wrappings. It's tricky bending forward over with her growing bump, but at last she lifts the cradle out of the box. She runs her fingers over the artistically distressed surface, inhales the new wood scent. Then she sees it: carved into the oak at the head end and picked out in blue paint are the words:

'Edward - Our Son.'

Rava takes a step backwards, one hand clasped to her mouth. She collapses back onto the sofa, holding her belly.

Oh, little girl, this is too much! We're living a lie, you and me. And he's going to find out - he'll have to. Oh please God, let Martin forgive me. Let him understand!

30

JAJJA

The containers stretch away into the distance with dirt tracks running between them. They're laid out in an enormous grid; some are stacked two or three high. The heatwave has baked the earth hard, but these paths must be a quagmire when it rains. Some of the containers have doors or windows cut into the sides; others are completely open at one end, revealing huddles of people sitting inside. A tangle of electric wires trails overhead.

The camp is bordered by a high fence topped with barbed wire and a stinking ditch running alongside. Heaps of rubbish are piled everywhere. Chiara sees children sifting through the debris, searching for anything they can sell. A thin woman drags a huge net full of rags, her shoulders bent under the strain. Flies and mosquitoes buzz in the hazy air.

Chiara and Liz are here to visit Zoe and her baby. Their guide through the maze of containers is a small boy who was assigned to them at the gates by a pot-bellied man with a gun. The boy is six or seven years old, barefoot, wearing a tattered t-shirt and grubby shorts. He runs eagerly ahead, halting now and then to let Liz and Chiara catch up. Chiara carries the bag with the blood pressure cuff, Liz's notes, and the rest of the equipment. Liz walks with a list to one side, her breath audible. Once or twice, she pauses to wipe sweat from her face with a handkerchief.

They cross another ditch on a single-plank bridge. The water beneath them is black and scummy with floating refuse. A fat rat crouches fearlessly at the water's edge. Around the next corner, the boy points at a rusting green container sitting on top of a red one. A ladder leads up to a doorway covered by a curtain.

'Here you are,' he announces. He turns a cartwheel, bows, and grins up at Liz and Chiara. His teeth are thin with decay and he has sore patches on his ankles, but his smile is childish and hopeful. Liz gives him more money than Chiara expects, and the boy darts away whooping with delight.

Liz huffs and puffs as she climbs the ladder, with Chiara following behind. Inside, the space is oppressively hot. One end is curtained off to make a sleeping area. There are two chairs in the living space: an upright wooden one, and a swivel office seat with stuffing bulging through rips in the cover. A rug made from strips of rag covers part of the metal floor.

In one corner, a life-sized statue of the Madonna stands with arms outstretched. Both her hands are gone, leaving jagged holes at the wrists. Her blue-and-white robes are gouged with deep scratches. A string of rosary beads hangs around her neck, and a bunch of daisies in an old jam jar has been placed at her feet.

Chiara makes out an old woman crouching over a camping stove in the shadows. She looks ancient, her hair snowy white, her clothes loose on skeletal limbs. When she straightens up and adjusts her enormous glasses, she looks like an elderly insect.

'Liz!' the old lady exclaims, 'Welcome, welcome!'

Liz knows the camps well; apparently she's come across

Zoe's grandmother before, because the two women embrace like old friends.

'This is Chiara, my student.'

Chiara holds out her hand, English-style, but the old lady hugs her too. For someone who looks so spindly, her embrace is surprisingly soft.

'Welcome, Chiara. I am Jajja - everyone calls me Jajja. Come, sit.'

Chiara sits, and Jajja returns to the stove. A stack of wooden pallets functions as shelves for a few mismatched plates and mugs. Several buckets sit in a corner. A single electric bulb is strung up by its wire looped over a hook above an old-fashioned sewing machine, the sort that works by a foot treadle. Chiara's Mamma had a sewing machine like this; she used to make scarves and bags to sell to the tourists before the flights were banned.

Jajja brings two steaming mugs of tea. There is too much sugar, and no milk, but Liz, normally fussy about her tea, drinks without complaining. Next, Jajja offers them each a small bowl of food. Chiara hesitates; this might be all Jajja's family has to eat today. She snatches a look at Liz, who nods firmly, takes her bowl and digs in. Chiara follows her lead. It's rice with a few shreds of vegetables, flavoured with pepper and chilies.

'Thank you - it's delicious.'

While they eat, the old lady sits on the rug watching them. Chiara tries to give up her chair, but Jajja is insistent.

'You helped my Zoe,' she says. 'You are honoured guests. I only wish I could pay you.'

'Nonsense,' Liz tells her. 'We don't expect anything. People bring us what they can. If someone needs clothing, do you turn them away, Jajja?'

Jajja's grasshopper-like face opens into a wide smile. She has no teeth at all, and her eyes are hugely magnified by her glasses. She begins to laugh, her bony shoulders rising and falling.

'Ah never,' she proclaims. 'Everyone comes, to me - half this camp.' She waves her arm as if to take in the whole world. *'Jajja, I need a shirt. Jajja, I have holes in my coat. Jajja, I have a child, and nothing to put on his back.* It is a gift to help friends in need. As long as God gives me my hands, my eyes, my sewing machine, and clean rags, I turn no one away. Some pay with money, some bring a potato, or a little rice. Everything is good.'

'Exactly - it's all good. And we're the same. That was very tasty.' Liz returns her empty bowl to Jajja. 'So how are Zoe and the baby?'

As if on cue, a wail comes from behind the curtain.

'Hey Chiara, Liz - come and see her.'

The curtain twitches at one corner to invite them in. The bedroom is lit by a candle stub in a saucer. Zoe sits on a low bed made of pallets, her baby at her breast.

'She don't never stop feeding,' she says, stroking the infant's head with absorbed tenderness. She looks as tranquil as the Madonna. It's hard to realise this is the same teenager who flooded the Rosie Lee with ear-piercing yells.

'What have you called her?' Chiara asks.

'Dembe,' Zoe tells them. 'It's Jajja's mum's name, from back in Uganda. We're dead proud of her, aren't we, Jajja?'

Jajja brings Zoe a heaped bowl of the rice and vegetables.

'I feed her in the old way,' Jajja says. 'One month warming food, rub with oil, rest. Eat now, Zoe.'

Zoe takes the bowl with a very teenaged eye-roll.

'She won't let me go out,' Zoe complains. 'I gotta get back to work soon up the city - bring in money, but she keeps saying rest all the time.'

'You will do the month,' Jajja says with gentle insistence. 'Then if you want to work, I can care for the child. No hurry though.'

'Sounds like a plan. How old are you Zoe, really?' Liz gives her a sideways look, but Zoe only shrugs.

'Don't matter,' she says. 'I can work. I'm strong - I can look after Dembe, and Jajja too.'

Liz nods.

'Okay, let's check you over. How's the feeding going? Plenty of wet and dirty nappies?'

Zoe laughs.

'They don't stop coming. Little shitting machine, aren't you?' She kisses Dembe's curly head and her snub nose. 'Milk in, poo out, all day, all night. That's our life now.' She giggles. 'Hamid, my boyfriend, he's come to see her. Said he was proud of me, and he's going to give us some money when he can, like. But he's just a kid really.' Zoe shakes her head with the world-weariness of an old woman. 'We can manage, can't we, Jajja?' A murmur of assent comes from the grandmother.

Satisfied that Zoe and her baby are doing well, Liz and Chiara take their leave. As they are about to set off down the ladder, Jajja comes scuttling towards them, holding something.

'Thank you, thank you,' she says. Her eyes glisten behind her glasses. 'For my Zoe, our little Dembe, so grateful. I made these for you. I hope they fit all right.'

Liz takes the folded fabric from Jajja's hand, unfurls it, and holds it up to the light. It's a skirt, stitched from pieces of many garments into a multicoloured swirl of patterns and shades. There's a flare to it, and a braided drawstring at the ample waist. Jajja has created it perfectly to fit Liz's short, plump figure. Who would have thought such a lovely thing could be made from rags? Liz pulls Jajja into another hug.

'I think this one might fit you,' Jajja says, offering another item to Chiara, 'but if not, come back and I'll alter it, make it just right for you.' She hands Chiara another skirt, this one longer, with a slim waistline. Like Liz's, it's made from a myriad of scraps and fragments. The colours are greens and blues, golds and turquoises, chosen to flow together. If Chiara half-closes her eyes she can see the beach and the sea back home on a summer's day.

'Oh,' she gasps. 'It's so beautiful. But are you sure? I didn't really do much.'

'Yes, you did, Chiara,' Liz breaks in. 'You worked very hard to help Zoe. In fact, I'm not sure I could have done it without you.' She grasps both of Jajja's hands. 'These clothes are wonderful, Jajja. Thank you so much. We'll think of you and Zoe whenever we wear them.'

Jajja makes a little half-bow, her hands clasped together. 'You are welcome any time, both of you. Our home is simple, but we do our best to make it a place of shelter.'

As Chiara and Liz pick their way back across the litter-strewn pathways of the camp, they are soon surrounded by a chattering gaggle of children. Liz gives them home-baked oat cookies and laughs at their terrible jokes. Chiara's thoughts turn to Nonna. Jajja's rosary beads, her kindness, and her insistence that everything is good, all remind her so strongly of her own dear Nonna that her chest aches.

Nonna's fingers were ice cold when Chiara found her. If only she'd been stronger, if she'd had more to eat. If only Chiara had been there when she had the stroke. It was after Nonna died, that Chiara applied to work in England; she wasn't much use to anyone at home. And now she is leading this double life, helping Liz one day and working at the Genesis Centre the next, trying to pretend she doesn't know about the Lullaby births, the forced sterilisations, and what happens in Neonatal Two. What would Nonna make of it all? Would she be proud of Chiara, or ashamed?

'Look out,' calls Liz, tugging at Chiara's arm. Lost in her memories, she has almost stumbled into the rotting carcass of a fox.

LATE THAT NIGHT, Chiara watches the news on her laptop. Three more midwives have been arrested: two in north London, and one somewhere in Essex. That's way too close for comfort. At least one of them must know Liz; maybe all of them. It would only take one to betray her. Funmi's solid, Liz said, but a network is only as strong as its weakest link.

On a sudden impulse, Chiara opens her bedside drawer and takes out Nonna's rosary beads. Sitting on her bed, she makes the sign of the cross:

'Nel nome del Padre, e del Figlio, e dello Spirito Santo. Amen.'

Quietly, under her breath, she prays all five joyful mysteries, just like Nonna taught her. Afterwards, she gets into bed, pulls up the covers, and closes her eyes. Whatever happens next, she's going to need all the help she can get.

31

NOT MOVING

'Move, baby, move!'

Rava lies on her left side on the sofa. She's drunk the cold sugary drink the website suggested, and eaten some sweets too. She's even tried ice cubes on her bump. Now she's waiting, concentrating, but still nothing.

She doesn't know when her baby last moved. She's been busy at work and worrying about Baba - Aunt Nasreem says he can't always get out of bed now, and Martin's still stressed about his promotion.

The baby was active the night before last; the kicking kept Rava awake. But since then - oh, she must be a terrible mother, not to have noticed! Yesterday she was rushing around, and then Martin took her out for dinner, and afterwards she was so tired she fell straight to sleep. It was only this morning, in the shower, when she didn't feel the usual wriggles, she started to worry.

Could it have been something she ate? She's tried so hard to be careful, but there are so many rules, so many things that aren't safe. Maybe that meat in the restaurant wasn't properly cooked - not that it was real meat anyway? Or did she sleep on her back by mistake? She must have done something wrong.

'Come on, baby!' Rava places both hands on her bump, straining to feel something, even the slightest nudge. But no - nothing. She's been lying here almost an hour. It's no good - she'll have to go to the Genesis Centre. *'Don't delay,'* the website says. *'Seek urgent medical help if you can't feel your foetus moving.'* What if she's waited too long already?

She orders a taxi. Should she call Martin? She twists a strand of hair around her fingers, scared to face this alone, but still more afraid he might find out the truth. Besides, he's got important meetings, and she might be making a fuss about nothing. The website says the hospital will monitor the baby's heartbeat and then likely send her home again. But it also hints at worse outcomes - much worse. Rava wraps her arms around her body as if she could keep her daughter safe with a hug.

What should she take? She grabs a bag and starts throwing things in almost at random. Her e-reader ? As if she could focus on a novel! A bottle of water, her keys. She checks her phone - still no taxi. Maybe she should take a nightdress? They won't keep her in, will they?

In the bedroom, she freezes, staring blankly at the tasteful decor and designer silk bedding as if she's a stranger here. Then, on an impulse, she fetches a chair and climbs up to reach the high shelf in the wardrobe.

She lifts down a stack of handbags and winter sweaters. Behind these, right at the back, lies the copy of the Holy Qur'an she brought back from Aberdeen along with the baby dress Aunt Nasreem gave her. Hidden treasures.

She unwraps the Qur'an, kisses it, and sets it down reverently on the dressing table, next to her silver-framed photograph of Mama. She kisses Mama too. Please let my baby be all right! She tries to pray, but her mind keeps jumping to her baby.

Are you all right, little one? Please move. Please move for Mama.

Rava goes to the toilet. When she wipes herself, there's something on the tissue. It's reddish brown, only a smear, but blood. Her legs start shaking. She's heard the phrase, 'knees knocking,' but she never knew it was a real thing until now.

This can't be happening; she's only twenty-five weeks.

She grabs her phone, but the taxi's stuck in traffic. The ban on private cars has done little to help London's congestion with so many people living here and the buildings higher and higher. She tries another operator, and another.

'Sorry, Miss, gridlocked out there. Going to be forty-five minutes minimum.'

Should she catch a tram? She goes back to the toilet: more blood. Her whole body trembles. It's no good, stop wasting time. She'll have to call Martin. His Government car can use the priority lanes and cut through the traffic.

She dials his number, and it rings twice, three times, four. When he answers, her words tumble out:

'Oh Martin, I'm so scared!'

A NURSE LEADS them into a room with a sunrise picture covering one entire wall. She tells Rava to lie on the couch and wait for a doctor. Then she's gone. Music tinkles from somewhere unseen.

'Has he moved yet?' Martin squeezes Rava's hand. He's loosened his tie and slung his suit jacket over the chair.

Rava shakes her head.

'You should've called me sooner. I know I've been preoccupied, but it's all for you and little Edward, my love. I want us to be a family, happy and healthy together - you know that, don't you?' He rubs the back of his neck as if it's sore.

'Yes, Martin.' She's been so stupid. Why didn't she trust him? Martin's face is creased with concern. He loves her and the baby; of course he does.

'Mr and Mrs Robson?'

A man in scrubs enters the room and extends a hand to Martin.

'A pleasure to meet you, Sir. I'm Doctor Thakur. So, what's been happening?'

Martin tells the doctor about the baby not moving, and the bleeding, and then Rava has to lie on her back, legs open. The doctor inserts something metallic and peers inside her with a bright light.

'Hmm. I can see a bit of old blood, but the cervix is tightly closed, so hopefully you're not going into labour. Let's have a listen.'

He squirts cold gel onto Rava's stomach and slides the probe across her skin. The listening device crackles and rumbles while she holds her breath, shoulders rigid, fists clenched, eyes squeezed tight shut.

More rumbling, gurgles, and sounds like scrunching paper emanate as the probe digs in hard. Please God, please don't let -. And then, just as she's almost given up, there it is: the racing, thrumming gallop of her baby's heart. Thank God!

'She's alive!'

The words slip out before Rava realises she's spoken. Martin loosens his grip on her hand and, for a few, breathless seconds, no one speaks.

'DOES THE HEARTBEAT SOUND NORMAL?' Martin asks when the doctor turns off the device.

'Well, we'll need to do some more tests - monitoring and so forth. Did the pre-natal screening show up any problems? When did you say you last noticed movements, Mrs Robson?'

'I'm not sure; I can't remember.' Rava buries her face in her hands, overcome. What if the baby's not all right? What if she's sick, or dying? And did Martin hear what she said, calling the baby 'she'? Hot tears flood her fingers.

'Try to relax - this may not be anything serious. I'll fetch the portable ultrasound to do a full check of the foetus.'

Doctor Thakur leaves the room.

'Don't cry, my love.' Martin strokes Rava's hair; maybe he didn't hear? 'We're in good hands. I'm worried about Edward too, but the DNA report was excellent, and you've had the best care from the start, so let's try to be hopeful.'

Rava's throat tightens; that perfect DNA report was a fake. Was there something in the real one - some terrible problem she didn't understand? But the doctors saw the real report, didn't they? They would have told her. Maybe it's the stress of keeping her secret - her lies have damaged the baby. It's her own fault; all her fault. Her shoulders shake with her sobs.

'My darling!' Martin embraces her, solid and close, with his comforting smell of cologne and cigarettes. He rushed here to be with her. She presses her forehead to his chest and lets her tears soak into his shirt.

How silly she's been not trusting him. Martin's always looked after her, hasn't he? Before she met him, she was scratching a living in London, barely making the rent each month on a miserable studio apartment. Now she has designer dresses, a luxury home, and she's having a baby - God willing - at the glamorous Genesis Centre, all thanks to Martin! She'd be nothing without him.

He lets her cry until her sobs subside. Then he passes her tissues while she sniffs and wipes her eyes, his arm still around her shoulders. She's almost composed herself by the time the doctor returns with a nurse, and a big machine on wheels.

'Right then,' the doctor says. 'Let's have a proper look. Lie down again please, Mrs Robson.'

IT's good news - excellent in fact. Dr Thakur spends a long time looking at the baby's heart and other organs. He measures its limbs, watching it lunge and dance in its watery world.

'It looks very lively now; might you have been distracted yesterday, and failed to notice the movements?' he suggests.

Yes,' she agrees, feeling foolish. 'I had a lot on my mind. But the bleeding?'

'Oh, that's just a bit of old blood from the cervix; have you and your husband perhaps had intercourse recently?'

Blushing, Rava admits that yes, they did, last night. Martin looks absurdly pleased.

When the doctor pronounces everything healthy, Rava cries again with relief. They want her to stay for another hour to monitor the foetal heartbeat, and to return next week to repeat the checks, but there's every chance her incubation can proceed as planned. Light-headed with relief, Rava reaches down to caress the bulge of her baby's bottom. You're going to be all right, little one.

Martin's been quiet throughout the examination, but now, just as the doctor's about to switch off the machine, he speaks:

'I know it's not medically necessary, Doctor, but this is the first scan I've been to. Ridiculous work commitments, I'm afraid. Would you mind showing me - I mean, I know he's a boy from the DNA test, obviously, but can I just take a look?'

'Yes, of course, Sir.'

Doctor Thakur picks up his probe again and rolls it around. Silence. He squirts on more gel and presses harder. Rava's bladder is fit to burst; she has to clench to avoid wetting herself. She closes her eyes, wishing she could be anywhere but here.

'I'm sorry,' says Doctor Thakur after a long pause. 'The foetus has its legs open, it's in a good position and, well, I've had a good look, but - this isn't a boy.'

Silence. Martin gets to his feet.

'What do you mean, not a boy? That can't be right; I've seen the DNA report: *'male foetus,'* it said. I didn't think you people made mistakes like that. All these months we've been paying your fees. Can you check again, please?'

The doctor straightens his clothing and fiddles with the controls of his machine. Then he turns the screen to face Martin and Rava.

'We could order more blood tests, but take a look for yourselves.'

Rava and Martin look, and it really is very clear: the baby is unquestionably a little girl. Martin sits down, his eyes flicking to left and right, his face puce.

'I don't understand. How could this have happened? You know who I am, don't you?'

'Yes, Mr Robson, sir,' says the doctor, glancing nervously at the nurse.

'I need to speak to management - someone more senior, right away. This is a travesty. How could this be allowed to happen? I'll be suing for damages; you people have no idea!' Martin's brows furrow and he rubs at the reddened patch on his neck.

Doctor Thakur hurries off, doubtless glad to have an excuse to escape. The nurse stands in the corner looking terrified. Martin's eyebrow twitches. Rava lies on the couch, her skin still coated with sticky gel, the baby girl shifting and turning inside her.

'I don't understand,' Martin repeats.

Rava stretches out to touch him, but he sits motionless as stone.

'I'm sorry, Martin,' she whispers. 'It will be all right, won't it? She's still our baby.'

Martin doesn't reply.

32

RED BUTTON

'Can you help me, Nurse? Something's not right.'

The woman's breath comes in long gasps. She clutches at her stomach, her eyes bulging in panic. Chiara hurries to her bedside.

'What is it?'

'Oh, oh! Pain. In my stomach. So much pain. Oh! It's going now. Oh Nurse, that was so bad. What's wrong? What's happening to me?'

'Can I feel your tummy?' Chiara places a hand onto the woman's abdomen and locates the round swell of the baby's bottom under its mother's ribs. The uterine muscle is softer now, but even as she soothes the terrified woman it begins to tense and harden into the next contraction. 'It's okay. Look at me, and keep breathing - nice long, slow breaths - and again. Good, that's right.'

It's obvious what's happening. This woman is thirty-seven weeks pregnant, and she's in labour. Here at the Genesis Centre, everyone has their C-section by thirty-eight weeks at the latest. All the obstetricians say it's dangerous to let a pregnancy continue beyond that point. The foetus might suffer from postmaturity syndrome. It might die inside its mother - sorry, incubator! - when it could safely have been delivered. Or, worse still, the incubator might go into labour at home, where she could go into shock from the pain, or bleed to death.

The Genesis Centre prides itself on sparing its incubators the horrors of labour. Birth at the Centre is meant to be pain-less: a smooth, sweetly-scented experience delivered by obse-quious staff to the sounds of spa music. That's how the advertising presents it, anyway.

But sometimes labour starts unexpectedly. Chiara has seen this before. Panic-stricken patients are wheeled into the Ante-natal ward complaining of gripping pains in their stomachs. They shake and scream, rocking back and forth, pleading for help. After a quick examination, they are whisked into theatre to have their babies extracted and their sterilisations completed in the nick of time. Afterwards, they are tearful with gratitude, showering the staff with chocolates and heartfelt thanks. They have been snatched from a cliff edge, pulled from under the impending wheels of a train.

Stories abound at the Genesis Centre of the trauma of natural birth. Everyone has a mother or grandmother who was made to give birth in the old way, back before safe, modern healthcare. Nurses share tales of week-long agonies and shredded vaginas, shaking their heads over the enormity of it all:

'It's shocking,' someone will say. 'For decades they knew how to do perfectly safe C-sections. But instead they let women suffer all that torture and damage. Disgusting, when you think about it.'

Everyone agrees.

'Medieval,' they say.

'Vile.'

'Wicked.'

'Barbaric.'

Chiara keeps quiet and says nothing. No one would believe her anyway.

THE WOMAN CRIES OUT AGAIN. Her uterus contracts hard, and her shrieks transmute to a low, guttural 'uurrrh.' Her face is flushed and screwed-up as if she's already pushing.

Chiara knows what she is supposed to do. There are rules for this situation, as for every eventuality at the Genesis Centre. She should pull the red emergency button on the wall. Loud sirens will sound, and a team of medics will come running. They will rush the woman into Theatre, administer a general anaesthetic, whip out her baby, and cut and tie her fallopian tubes. It will all be over within a matter of minutes. Chiara moves towards the red button.

But something stops her. Maybe she's groggy from last night's birth on the boat, or dazed from the long journey back to the city centre. Almost certainly she isn't thinking straight. It was a beautiful birth last night. A young mother breathed her second baby into the world by candlelight. There was no rush, no hurry. The air smelled of new life, sage, and lavender. Chiara wrapped the woman and her child in Liz's home-knitted blankets and watched the newborn suckle, with Gaskin purring beside them. The peace was palpable.

Chiara's hand, stretched out towards the red button, returns to her side. She walks to the door and closes it.

'Do you mind if I have a look,' she asks the woman, 'to see what's going on?'

'Just help me, Nurse,' she whimpers. 'Whatever you need to do. Am I going to die? Ooohh!'

The woman's belly is tight and hard as a football. Her baby is deep in her pelvis.

'I need the toilet. I'm going to - uurrhh!' The woman bears

down, her whole body pushing. An unmistakable smell of faeces fills the air, sure sign of an imminent birth. 'Oh God. I think I must have -.'

Chiara untucks the snowy sheet from the foot of the bed.

'Can I check down here?' she asks.

The bed is soaked with amniotic fluid. Chiara lifts the woman's nightdress and is greeted by the sight of a baby's head about to crown. It will be here with the next contraction.

'You're doing fine,' Chiara says. 'Everything's going to be fine. Your baby's coming now, it's nearly here. You've done it all by yourself.'

The woman's mouth drops open, and her hands scrabble at the air.

'No,' she gasps. 'It can't be. Get me a C-section. Quick!'

'There isn't time. Your baby's right here. Now, look at me and listen to my voice. I'm going to look after you. You can do this yourself, I promise. When the pain comes again, I want to you pant gently, like this, okay?'

The surge grows under Chiara's palm. The woman fixes her eyes on Chiara's. They pant together. And now the head is coming, stretching the space, filling, rising. Chiara supports the woman's perineum with her fingers, using the end of the bedsheet to wipe away the mess. There's no time even to put on gloves, or to fetch any sort of equipment. Somewhere on the ward there's an emergency delivery pack, but only doctors are allowed to use it.

As the baby's head is born into Chiara's hands, the woman throws back her head and screams. It sounds as if she is being murdered. Chiara registers the sound of feet charging down the corridor, but all her attention is on the infant still emerging. The shoulders are born, and now the baby is here, wriggling, turning pink, and crying. It's a little boy, perfect and full of life. She rubs him dry with the bedclothes as best she can, and tries to pass him to his mother, but the woman's hands flail help-lessly in the air.

When Sister Miller, two doctors, and three nurses burst into the room, Chiara is holding the naked newborn. The bed is a mess of body fluids; the mother shouts something incoherent. Chiara has blood all over her hands and on her white uniform.

'Nurse, what in heaven's name is going on? Why did you not pull the emergency button immediately? Mrs Durscombe, I can only apologise. This should never have been allowed to happen.'

Someone grabs the baby from Chiara. A cluster of medics surrounds the bed, calling for instruments, drugs, and back-up. *Hurry! Hurry! Cannula. Catheter. No time to lose!* The cord is cut, and the baby bundled away to be weighed and measured, assessed and medicated.

'Can I see my baby?' the mother calls, recovering herself now, but no one replies. An anaesthetist comes running to treat her for the shock, injecting a sedative that makes her flop back slack-mouthed onto the pillows. Sister Miller calls for a haema-tologist to assess the blood loss. *Quickly please!*

The consultant obstetrician arrives in his smart suit, flanked by a gaggle of students. He inspects the woman's vagina and shakes his head. She will have to go straight to theatre for removal of the placenta and sterilisation. He can only hope there will be no long term damage. Physical damage at least. He would not be able to speak for the psychological trauma.

AFTER THE WOMAN is wheeled away, Chiara is sent to change her clothes and report to Sister's office. She sits on the hard chair listening to the clock tick on the wall while Sister types something lengthy on her computer. The air is heavy with Sister's perfume. Chiara studies her hands in her lap. After what seems like forever, Sister makes a phone call, requesting someone from Human Resources to come and take notes and to act as a witness. It takes the HR person - a man with thinning grey hair and a laptop - more than ten minutes to arrive. Only then does Sister address Chiara.

'Nurse Santori, I have been trying to take a charitable view of your attitude. But I have had serious doubts about your professionalism for some time now. I have been keeping your file updated with all the relevant information, and it is not a happy story.'

Sister Miller pauses to glare at Chiara, her orange lips pressed together. Chiara inspects her own fingernails. She feels as if she's jumped out of a plane without checking first to see if she has a parachute. She ought to be scared, but instead there's this crazy sense of lightness; she wonders if she might be able to fly.

'You seemed to begin well at the Genesis Centre,' Sister continues. 'I had high hopes for you. You were willing and hard working, and, most importantly, you did as you were told. You seemed committed to our patients' safety. But recently all that has changed. Today's disgraceful incident is the culmination of a catalogue of insubordination.'

Chiara opens her mouth to say she's sorry. But then she realises she isn't. She's not sorry at all for trying to spare that poor, frightened woman a totally unnecessary surgery. She's not sorry for helping that little baby find his own way out into the world. So she closes her mouth again.

'I have had to reprimand you numerous times regarding lateness, incorrect uniform, and lack of attention to detail. You are insufficiently deferential to senior staff and important patients. Your sick leave record is concerning, to say the least. Several times I've caught you yawning at work, looking as if you are struggling to stay awake. The Genesis Centre does not accept sloppiness or laziness in its nurses. We're saving lives here. Do you have anything to say for yourself?'

Chiara looks out of the window. A swallow darts past with forked tail and blue-black plumage.

Sister speaks a little louder as if Chiara hasn't understood:

'I know the transition isn't easy for you foreign girls. Health-care in southern Europe sadly comes nowhere the standards we expect in London. It's a steep learning curve for you, I realise that.' She sighs. 'Do you know how many people would give their eye-teeth to work in a world-class facility like this? I have tried to be patient, offered opportunities for further learn-ing, paired you with experienced nurses, but still you seem to insist on going your own way.

'Recently, I have sensed an arrogance about you, Nurse Santori. You don't listen. You seem to think you know best.' Sister waggles a slim forefinger as she reaches the climax of her tirade. 'But this morning's incident takes my breath away. Chiara, what on earth did you think you were doing? There is an emergency button on the wall. You know how to use it, don't you? Really there is no excuse, none at all, for failing to call for help in a major obstetric emergency.'

She pauses to draw breath, and Chiara speaks. All these months, she's been holding her real thoughts in, keeping quiet. It's enough; she can't do it anymore.

'It didn't seem like an emergency to me. It seemed like a normal birth.' She speaks so softly that Sister has to ask her to repeat herself. 'It was a normal birth. The mother was fit and well, and the baby was coming. It happened very fast and I needed to give them all my attention. I was going to call for help as soon as the baby was born, or if there was a problem.'

'Normal birth? There's nothing normal about women dying in agony. Some of the things I used to see, back in the old days!' Sister picks up a pen and starts turning it over and over. 'Listen, Nurse, I have no idea what goes on in the back streets of Sicily, but in England we know vaginal birth is highly dangerous, traumatic, and illegal except in exceptional circumstances. If you had simply pulled that emergency bell, we could've got that mother into Theatre and prevented a major incident. I fully expect a legal suit with the hospital likely having to pay significant damages. The paperwork alone will take me weeks.'

Another heavy sigh and a vigorous shaking of the head. Chiara is gratified to notice that a couple of strands of Sister's lacquered blonde hair have come loose from her bun and are dangling in front of her cheek.

'I cannot employ nurses who ignore the most basic safety protocols. Even now, you have offered no apology, no excuse for your behaviour. Are you sorry?'

If Chiara loses her job she'll still owe all that debt to the hospital. And there's the threat of criminal investigation over the lullaby birth. She'll have nowhere to live, no income, nothing to send home for Gemma and Mamma. She ought to be terrified; she ought to grovel to Sister, begging and pleading for another chance. But she can't say sorry; she just can't. It would be a lie, and she's so very tired of living a lie.

'No, Sister Miller,' she says. 'I'm not sorry I helped that woman birth her baby. She didn't need a C-section. The baby was already coming.'

Sister Miller gives Chiara one last withering look.

'Very well, Miss Santori.' Sister turns to the HR official: 'Please arrange for the termination of Miss Santori's nursing contract with immediate effect. I will email you my report shortly. I think a laundry role will suffice for the outstanding liabilities, don't you?'

'Laundry?' Chiara echoes.

'Even in these cases we do our best to be generous. You will be offered menial work to pay off your debts to the Centre. I hope you will embrace that opportunity with a better attitude. The alternative would be most unfortunate. Now, go and clear your locker, and don't ever let me see you on my wards again.'

PART III

33

A LETTER

Martin assumes it's the hospital's fault at first. Doctor Thakur returns with the Chief Surgeon and Martin asks them question after furious question:

'Whose fault was this? Who mixed up the DNA results? Do you realise the impact of this incompetence? Look at my poor wife!'

Rava twists her hands together and says nothing.

But then Martin demands to see the nurse who drew the blood for the test. It was that young girl - the kind one with an Italian accent - who altered the form when Rava begged her. She'll be hauled in here and punished, and it will all be Rava's fault.

'I'll send for her right away,' says the Chief Surgeon, picking up the phone.

'Wait!' The stink of un-flushed toilets rises from nowhere, and Rava covers her face. Hasn't she ruined enough lives already?

'What is it?' Martin asks.

'Martin.' She speaks in a whisper. 'It wasn't the nurse. It was me.'

Hugging herself with her arms and rocking from side to side, she tells him the truth.

'Don't be angry, Martin. I only wanted a bit more time for the baby to grow. I knew you'd love her when she was bigger. It's nobody else's fault - only me. I'm sorry, Martin.'

His look then - she'll never forget it. The shock in his eyes - astonishment that she could've betrayed him, but something else too - something cold and unyielding, like steel.

'After all I've done for you,' he says.

Then he gathers up his things and walks away.

MARTIN ISN'T in the apartment when Rava gets back. The baby kicks all night and Rava spends the long hours staring into the dark, praying that Martin will forgive her. All she wants is for the three of them to be a family.

But there's no sign of Martin next morning. Rava stays home all day, and all the next day, waiting. Louis whines endlessly for his 'Daddy', scratching at the door to be taken out, but Rava daren't leave the apartment in case Martin comes and she misses him. She calls his phone countless times, but he won't pick up.

On the second evening, an envelope drops through the door. Rava picks it up and sees her name on it in Martin's handwriting. She rushes out to the lobby calling his name, but he isn't there. The lift has already gone. Through the window, she sees his black Mercedes driving away. She strains her eyes, but she can't tell if he's inside or if Daniel came alone to deliver the missive.

Dry-mouthed, she rips open the envelope and takes out a letter typed on crisp Government stationery:

Dear Rava,

I hope this letter finds you well.

I have reflected on what you told me at the Genesis Centre. It was a great shock to learn that you have been dishonest with me. I had always believed our relationship to be one of complete mutual trust. I was wrong.

I have been very clear with you about my wish for a male child, if indeed we are to procreate at all. The choice to incubate is an immense responsibility on our overcrowded planet with its dwindling resources. With so many choosing the selfless path of non-parenting, I ask myself what right we have to do otherwise.

Females are weaker, more economically and emotionally dependent, and more expensive to raise than males. They pose an inherent risk to the planet by their hormonally-driven desire to bear offspring, which progressive societies are only now beginning to bring under control. For all these reasons, I believe it would be wrong for us to bring a female infant into the world.

I suggest you opt for an immediate Fresh Start termination, which I will arrange for you to have at the Genesis Centre in comfort and with the best medical care. I will not insist on you being sterilised at this point, as I can see how important it is for you to have a child. We all make mistakes, and I want to be generous.

If you continue with the current pregnancy, you must understand that I will not sign registration papers for a female child. You would be sterilised for a neonate which you would be unable to support, and would not be allowed to take home from the hospital. The child would most likely go to an institution, assuming it passed the necessary quality checks. I am sure you will see this is not a kind or desirable outcome.

I very much hope you will see sense and choose our future together. A flood of female hormones has doubtless made it difficult for you to think clearly in recent months.

Emotional discussions will only make this harder, so I will stay

in a hotel to give you space. Let me know when you have reached a
decision.

> *Yours,*
> *Martin*

RAVA READS the letter three times. Then she folds it again and
again, pressing down on every crease as if she could make it
disappear. She sits for a long time, frozen in place, until Louis's
relentless snuffling and the baby bouncing against her bladder
force her to get up.

'You don't understand!' she cries to the empty room. 'You
haven't felt her moving inside you. You don't know what it is to
be a mother. I love you, Martin, but I love our baby too, and I
can't kill her, I just can't.'

34

STILLBIRTH

Chiara's first emotion after Sister Miller fires her is a heady wash of relief. No more drugging new mothers so they barely recognise their own babies; no more wheeling cots to Neonatal Two; no more terror that the next delivery might be another lullaby birth. She empties her locker with vague thoughts of going back to home to Sicily, maybe it's not too late to stop the sale of the cottage? She could work in Palermo again, perhaps. But next morning, a long email from HR sets out the bitter reality.

Chiara's passport will be held by the Ministry of Population and Health until her debts to the Genesis Centre are fully repaid. She should report to the hospital laundry tomorrow to work a fourteen-hour shift, forty percent of the wages for which will be deducted towards her debt. She no longer qualifies for registered medical staff housing, but the hospital can offer her accommodation at a rent exceeding the remainder of her paltry wage. Credit can be extended in cases of hardship.

She'll be enslaved for the rest of her life.

After a sleepless night, Chiara packs her belongings into her rucksack, leaving her Genesis Centre uniforms hanging on the rail, and her scarlet Femband and nurse's ID card on the bedside table. Then she catches a tram to the city limit where the soldier on the checkpoint nods her through, thank God. They're much less bothered about people leaving the city than entering.

She makes her way to the Rosie Lee. It's a long walk on a sweltering day, but when at last she sees Liz on the deck watering her carrots, Chiara breaks into a run. Moments later, she's pouring out her story to Liz, who smiles and nods as if she'd been expecting this for some time. After a good cry, a mug of tea, and a hunk of bread and honey, Chiara moves her rucksack into the tiny spare cabin.

'I don't want to be a burden,' she protests weakly. 'And what if the hospital people come looking for me?'

'You're no burden, my love, and I reckon the effing Ministry of Murder's got more to worry about than a missing laundry operative. There's not many people I'd want to share my space with, but you've got a good heart for this work, and I can use an extra pair of hands. If you're sure you want to stay, that is?'

Chiara gives Liz a hug.

'Yes, please.'

As weeks lengthen into months, Chiara starts to feel at home on the Rosie Lee. She wakes each morning under a patchwork quilt, listening to the clamour of geese flying overhead, rocked by the gentle motion of the boat on the river. The Genesis Centre seems a thousand miles away.

More people than ever come to the old narrowboat for help, and Chiara grows adept at the skills of a midwife. She recognises the curve of a baby's spine, the location of its head, shoulders, knees, and feet, all from the evidence of her own eyes and hands. She knows exactly where to place the pinard, and how to tell whether an unborn infant is thriving. The height of the fundus of the uterus tells her the gestation of a pregnancy. She learns the power of touch and reassurance.

She becomes expert with the wood-burning stove, stoking it to exactly the right temperature to bake the loaves to a golden crust and soft, sweet-scented middle. She makes firm friends with Gaskin, and Liz pretends to be offended when he starts laying his offerings of dead mice and birds outside Chiara's door instead of her own.

Liz teaches her to manage the boat: how to steer between tightly-packed neighbours and fellow travellers, always alert for obstacles in the river. In Sicily, Chiara left the boats to the men and boys, but now she learns all the tricks for negotiating locks single-handed. She can angle the craft deftly under bridges and moor up in a tight space. She knows how to check the engine oil, re-fill the water tank, and clean weeds from the rudder and propellors. Chiara is shocked to learn that Liz can't swim, but Liz only laughs and says the water's too dirty for bathing anyway.

If Chiara wants to call home, she has to use one of the burner phones and throw it away afterwards. She tells Mamma and Gemma everything's fine; she's sorry she can't phone more often but she's so busy with work right now. She hates lying to them, but the truth would be too dangerous, Liz says.

Most weeks they hear of another midwife being arrested or disappearing. Every colleague lost is a bitter blow, but Liz only stiffens her spine and works harder, squeezing in another clinic, staying up all night for another birth. Her friend Jamila, whom Chiara has met several times, stops answering messages and seems to have vanished without trace.

'Perhaps she's lying low for a while,' says Liz, but her face betrays her unspoken fears.

Liz can be chatty one evening and completely silent the next. Sometimes she disappears for hours without telling

Chiara where she's going or when she'll be back. She's used to living alone, Chiara reminds herself, when Liz is distant or moody.

'Did you ever have children yourself?' Chiara asks one day. Liz never talks about her personal life.

'A long time ago; we're not in contact any more.' Liz rubs at her left side as if it's sore.

'Oh, you must miss them!"

'I've always kept myself busy. Now, let's get those instruments sterilised. Have you refilled the water tank yet?' She gets up and starts scrubbing the kitchen surface. 'That woman will be here within the hour, and it's her third baby, so it's going to be quick.'

MOST BIRTHS END JOYFULLY, with a wriggling baby opening slate-coloured eyes to find its mother's face. Most, but not all. A woman arrives one morning with cramping pains and bleeding. She is accompanied by her sister.

'I didn't know where to take her,' says the sister. 'We were scared of going down the People's.They cut you up there, don't they? Please don't let anything happen to her; she's all I've got.'

Chiara knows something is very wrong the moment she places her hands on the pregnant woman's stiff belly. The infant is small - twenty-eight weeks, perhaps? - and as still as a tomb. She finds the place and listens with the pinard: silence. She moves the pinard to another spot, tries again, still nothing.

'When did you last feel your baby move?' she asks as gently as she can. The mother's skin has a greenish tinge; her face is gaunt.

'I've not felt him for three or four days. He's dead, isn't he?' She makes little hiccupping cries, clinging to her sister, who holds her close.

'I'm so sorry, hun. It's not fair, is it?' The sister's eyes are red-rimmed. 'I lost my little girl last year,' she tells Chiara. 'She was nearly two, but she got this fever - meningitis, they said, but the hospital wouldn't admit her. Not registered, see. I had her at home, on my own. After that, I wanted to end it all, but Trish and her partner took me in, didn't you, hun? We was all going to move to Scotland next month - start again - but there's no point now, is there?' Her face crumples, and the two women rock together, their tears mingling.

A stillbirth is a slow, quiet business, with no heartbeat to listen for. Liz brews her strongest pain-relieving elixir, lacing it with liquid morphine. The woman labours through the night in her sister's arms, her face empty. Chiara turns the lamps down low, and the river laps against the sides of the boat. The baby comes at daybreak, emerging in its caul of membranes. Chiara breaks the soft globe of waters, cuts the cord, and hands the tiny lifeless boy to his mother.

'He's beautiful,' she tells her. 'I'm so sorry.'

Together, the two women wash and dress the child, speaking to him the whole time, telling him how precious he is, how loved. They wrap him in one of Liz's knitted baby blankets, cuddle him, and tell him stories of the life they dreamed of spending with him, while the reflections of the ripples on the river dance up and down on the wall of the boat.

Next day, Chiara and Liz close both mothers' bones while the infant lies between them in Liz's old pine crib. Chiara sings him Nonna's lullaby:

> 'Dormi riposa sutt'a 'na rosa
> alla susuta ti dugnu na cosa
> ti vogghiu beni, ti vogghiu beni
> chiudi l'ucciḍḍi ca 'u sunnuzzu veni.
>
> T'a cuitari, t'a cuitari

comu si cueta l'unna dû mari

comu agghi' a ddiri, comu agghia a ddiri

l'occhiu ti joca e a 'ucca t'arridi.'

'What does it mean?' The mother's eyes are swollen and red from crying.

'It's an old Sicilian song about a baby sleeping under a rose. It means he's precious and loved.'

The mother reaches out for her child, and Chiara picks him up, carefully because he is fragile, and places him onto her chest.

'Thank you,' the mother says. 'I don't know what we'd have done without you. You made us feel precious too.'

THAT EVENING, Chiara takes a long walk alone. She finds her way to Abney Park, an ancient, long-abandoned cemetery, where giant yew trees shade the paths, and brambles tangle among crumbling tombstones. She pushes her way past trails of wild clematis and through hanging curtains of ivy, not knowing what she is looking for or why she is here. Cracked memorials and faceless stone angels shelter under green leaves. Old stones lean against fallen trees.

She's almost lost herself in the winding pathways when she ducks beneath a low branch and emerges into an open, sunlit space at the very heart of the graveyard. Surrounded by long grass, a ruined chapel stands open to the sky. It's high summer, still light, and the song of a blackbird rises and falls from somewhere unseen. Chiara sits on the grass and listens. She sits for a long time before making her way back home to the Rosie Lee.

35

IT MEANS HOPE

R ava Robson
    To: MartinJRobson@MPH.gov.uk
    Moving out
Dear Martin

I'm sorry, but I can't bring myself to terminate the pregnancy and kill our baby. I love you, but I love our baby too.

My friend Jess at work says I can stay with her for a while, so I am moving out of the apartment. Please come home to look after Louis. He misses you.

I love you, Martin, and I still want us to have a life together with our baby. I am very sorry for not being honest with you. Please, please let me know if you are ready to talk.

I love you,
Rava

JESS LIVES on the edge of the city in Hoxton. She's junior to Rava at the bank, but she has her own modern one-bedroom apartment because she's got a gold band and gets paid the enhanced rate for Sealed women.

'I respect your choices and all that,' Jess says, 'but I reckon kids aren't worth all the grief. Your Martin'll come round though once he sees you mean business. You gotta show men what's what! Till then, you're welcome to sleep on the couch.'

Rava thanks her profusely and offers rent, which Jess refuses, 'for now.' Jess has boyfriends over on a regular basis; they're all friendly and polite, but there's only one bathroom, which often smells bad, and no privacy. The couch is hard, and Rava wakes with backache every morning. She misses Martin and thinks every day about going back to him. She still calls and messages every few days, begging for a chance to talk things over, but he doesn't reply.

THE BABY KEEPS GROWING. She kicks and wriggles all the time, thank God, and Rava starts to get breathless when she climbs the stairs. The heartburn gets worse too, but Rava doesn't mind. She loves to lie down and watch her belly change shape: a small foot jutting here, an elbow there. Her little girl is getting stronger day by day.

Rava has a name for her now - a secret name that she hasn't told anyone else:

'You're Amani,' she murmurs, cradling her bump. 'My sweet baby Amani.' Amani was Mama's name; it means 'hope.'

When Amani gets hiccups, Rava strokes and soothes her. She sings her songs that Mama used to sing. Sometimes she talks to her about Mama and Baba, and Martin too. She tells her daughter how much they all love her. One day, if God wills, this will be true.

'HEY ISN'T THAT YOUR BLOKE?'

Jess points at the TV screen, and yes, it's Martin on the news again. He's freshly shaved and wearing an open-necked shirt; Rava can almost smell his cologne. The interviewer says something about an increase in demonstrations against the Population Policy and Martin nods sagely.

'People need to be patient,' Martin says. 'This Government defends the right of every qualifying couple to have a child, but we need everyone to play their part and plan sustainably. We have to limit the number of incubation licences issues each year to prevent overcrowding and homelessness. But there are so many achievements to celebrate: births are safer than ever, and our polling shows a steady increase in satisfaction with women's healthcare. I want every child to be welcomed into a thriving and loving home. Every family matters. Every -.'

Rava snaps off the TV.

'Sorry,' Jess says. 'I didn't mean to upset you. He's still not listening?'

Rava grinds her fingernails into her palm

'He says he cares about families, and all the time -.'

Jess gives her a sideways glance.

'D'you have, like, other plans? I mean, that bump's getting kinda big.'

Rava shakes her head.

'I keep hoping he'll change his mind. I don't know what else to do.'

'Have you thought about a midwife?'

'You what?' Rava doesn't think she can have heard right. 'A midwife! Are you insane? They cut women up with knives, Martin says -.'

'Yeah, yeah, calm down. Your Martin says a lot of things. Friend of a friend of mine, she went to a midwife last year after her man left her in the lurch - said it was the best thing she ever did. The midwife's mates helped her get away to Wales afterwards with the kid and everything.'

Rava's chest tightens.

'How could I trust anyone? It's all illegal - run by the Mafia, Martin says, and anyway, Martin's had most of them arrested by now. Even if I wanted to, I wouldn't be able to find one.'

She rubs a hand over her belly to soothe the baby. Jess laughs.

'You're such an innocent, Rava! There are plenty of people who know people. Let me ask around - don't worry, I'll be discreet. Don't you think you should have a Plan B, just in case?'

'I don't know. It sounds so risky, and what if Martin found out? He already thinks I've betrayed him. Plus, what midwife would trust me, if they knew who I'm married to?'

Rava grinds her fingers so hard beads of blood appear on her palm. The baby head-butts her bladder once, twice, then lies still.

'Promise me you'll think about it,' Jess insists.

36

A VISITOR

The sun peeps through the curtains, filling the cabin with rosy light. Chiara stretches and wriggles her toes against the sheets, contemplating whether to get up and make coffee or lie here a little longer.

An insistent mew and the scratch of claws at the door tell her Gaskin is hungry for his breakfast. She lets him in, and he jumps onto her bed: a big, furry shape, purring throatily. She snuggles down for a few more minutes, promising Gaskin she'll feed him in a moment, greedy boy, when the rhythm of the cat's breathing is broken by a loud '*tap, tap, tap.*'

Someone is knocking on the roof of the boat. This early? They usually get a call when a labouring woman is on her way, and Liz would have woken her if they were expecting anyone. An emergency perhaps?

Chiara's skin prickles. Gaskin thuds down off the bed and streaks away.

What if it isn't a labouring woman?

'*Trust no one,*' Liz tells Chiara almost daily. '*Always ask for a password. The police could come with a warrant at any time, or they might send a spy; they need evidence to convict us.*'

The knocking comes again, louder this time.

Chiara pulls on a sweater over her nightdress, and tiptoes into the kitchen. There's no sign of Liz; she must still be asleep. Gaskin is on the steps scratching at the bow doors.

'Hello?' calls a man's voice. 'Anyone in there?'

Chiara gives Gaskin a frantic look, willing him to be quiet. Maybe, if she keeps very still, the man will go away. Shallow breaths, don't move, don't rock the boat.

But Gaskin lets out a loud meow, and a nose appears flattened against the glass, peering in through a gap in the curtains. He's less than an arm's length away. Chiara glances about as if there might be some magic hiding place on the boat. But, short of jumping overboard, there's no escape.

The voice calls again:

'Is that you, Chiara? Let me in.'

She knows this voice: the Spanish accent, the hint of humour, the way he says her name.

'Salvador! What are you doing here?'

She rushes for the door. It's been months; she thought she'd never see him again.

'Chiara *amiga*! Are you going to let me in? It's a beautiful morning and I'd kill for a coffee.'

'How did you find me?' She fumbles for the key on its hook, pulls back the bolts, and flings open the double doors. Cool morning air fills the boat with the scent of water, and Salvador steps onto the bow. He's tall, bearded, and smiling, and Chiara is suddenly conscious of her bare legs under the jumper, her naked feet, her bed-tousled hair.

'Can I come in?'

She nods, and he has to bend almost double to step down inside.

'Hello, boy, what's your name?'

Gaskin is rubbing his nose insistently against Salvador's legs.

'His name's Gaskin. You'd better take your shoes off; Liz is strict.'

Salvador seems huge in here. There's warmth coming off his skin, and a fresh smell of sandalwood soap and summer morning. He gives her a conspiratorial grin.

'Never mess with a midwife!'

Salvador removes his shoes. He's wearing jeans and a cotton shirt with the sleeves rolled up, open at the neck. His pupils widen as he gazes around Liz's kitchen, taking everything in, just like Chiara did that first time.

'Wow, this place is like something in a storybook. So many bottles, and books, and you! For ages I thought you'd gone back to Sicily, but here you are - a midwife and a free spirit.'

Chiara blushes. Gaskin is mewing again and pawing at the cupboard, so she squats down to look for his food. It's a chance to hide her face too.

'Oh, I'm not a proper midwife yet, but I'm learning.'

'Fantastic! How long have you been here? When I got the message, last week, I couldn't wait -.'

'Morning. Are you my latest drug mule?'

Liz emerges from her cabin, squinting at Salvador through her half-moon glasses. He removes a canvas bag from his shoulder and unpacks the contents.

'Four boxes of syntocinon,' he says, 'and just one pack of syntometrine. There's some ferrous sulphate, and co-codamol, but I couldn't get any antibiotics - sorry, but it's getting harder every time. The pharmacy's started doing more random checks, and hardly anyone's willing to do the drop-offs. That's why you've got me.'

'Much appreciated,' says Liz. 'That'll keep us going for a few more weeks.' She casts a sharp glance at Chiara. 'And do I gather you and this gentleman aren't entirely strangers?'

'Er, yes. We worked together at the Genesis Centre.' Chiara's ears feel impossibly hot.

Liz puts the drugs into the fridge and closes the door with a snap.

'Effing Genocide Centre, more like.' She rolls her eyes. 'Cup of tea - what's your name?'

'Salvador,' he says, with the slightest hint of a bow. 'And I'd love a coffee, if it isn't too much trouble?'

'Chiara makes the best coffee,' Liz says, nodding in her direction.

Chiara fills the red kettle and spoons coffee into the pot.

'Shall I make toast as well?' she offers. 'Tea for you, Liz?'

Liz grunts her acknowledgement and asks Salvador if he has any news of contacts at the hospital. He does, but it isn't good. The Filipina nurse who's escorted several women to the Rosie Lee was taken in for questioning last week. They let her go eventually, but she's too frightened to help again. A porter who was carrying messages has been fired and accused of sexual indiscretions with patients.

'No one's talked, yet,' Salvador says. 'No one's given anyone else away, but I worry it's only a matter of time. Too many people know too much.'

Liz agrees, wincing and rubbing at her left side. After giving Salvador a burner phone and a wish list for more drugs and equipment, she retreats to her cabin. She's been spending a lot of time in there recently; she says her back's giving her trouble.

Chiara makes the toast. As she passes Salvador the black-berry jam, their fingers brush together and she feels an exquisite lurch in her stomach.

'Shall we go outside to eat this?' he suggests. 'It's a lovely day.'

They sit side by side next to Liz's pots of marigolds, heart-sease, and fennel. The toast is crisp, the coffee smooth and good. Swallows dart and dive overhead. The chickens rummage and cluck in the bushes. Gaskin purrs in the sun.

The deck is small, and Salvador sits so close Chiara can feel him breathing. The hairs on his forearms catch the light. His hands cradle his mug.

'Is it true a midwife can deliver a baby when the mother is standing up?' Salvador's forehead wrinkles in disbelief.

'Of course. And it's not the midwife that delivers the baby; the women give birth themselves. I got a big lecture from Liz about that. Babies aren't parcels and we aren't postmen, she said. Or storks!' Chiara smiles.

'I guess you're not allowed to call them incubators either?'

She giggles.

'Don't let Liz hear you saying that!' She glances up at his face and he's looking right at her. Her stomach makes that happy little leap again.

'Tell me,' he says. 'What's it like, being a midwife? You must have some amazing stories.'

And she does; lots of stories. Chiara stretches her bare toes on the warm deck, rolls up the sleeves of her sweater, and talks. It's so good to have someone to talk to; someone who listens, and stares at her so intently, asking all the right questions in the right places. Her words bubble up and spill over as she tells him all about the births, and the clinics, and the visits to the camps.

There was Zoe, and another teenager too. There were the twins born last month to a couple determined to keep both their babies a chance in defiance of the one-child-per-couple rule. Then there was the woman who swore for ten straight hours, using words Chiara had never heard before. They both laugh about that one. And Salvador is rapt as Chiara describes the Jewish mother of six whose daughter slid silently into the world, and that tiny Indian lady who spoke no English, and the Muslim father who whispered holy words into his newborn baby's ear.

Salvador asks question after question. He wants to know about Liz's methods and her herbal remedies. He would love to look at her books. He is interested in what Chiara has learned about supporting new mothers to breastfeed.

'We rely so much on artificial methods at the Centre,' he says. 'The old skills are gone.'

'Maybe you should come and help us on the boat!' The idea is so thrilling, Chiara takes Salvador's hand and squeezes it. 'You would be marvellous with the babies.'

'Liz might have something to say about that. She might not want some questionable Spaniard elbowing in on her operation. Besides -.' He hesitates. 'I'm not sure I have your courage.'

'Courage? No, not really. I just help Liz, that's all. It's much nicer working here than at the hospital. Sometimes there are sad things, like when that baby died, but mostly it's fine. You would like it.' Please, she thinks.

He is silent for several seconds. Then he rests a hand on her knee, his touch as light as a leaf.

'Chiara, you know this is dangerous? They're hunting midwives, and if they catch you - it won't be fine.' He's almost whispering. She lets his hand rest there, feeling the warmth of his skin on hers, scarcely daring to breathe.

'Liz is very careful. We'll be okay.' She needs this to be true.

'Please be careful, Chiara. I'd hate anything bad to happen to you. You're - I think about you a lot, you know? I've missed you.'

She looks up at him, straight into his blue eyes.

'I think about you too.'

37

MIRACLE DRUG

Rava stares at the piece of paper. It's covered with lists, charts, and crossings-out: all her attempts to find a way forward. She can't have the baby here at Jess's, and the midwife idea is terrifying. It's no good: if Martin won't change his mind, she'll have to go back to Scotland. She'll be right back where she started, in the cramped old house full of memories.

Aberdeen is cold and grey, in darkness for half the year. No one has any money since the the oil industry closed down. It's a place she thought she'd escaped forever, but Martin's right - she can't raise her baby here. Amani would have no birth certificate, no right to education or healthcare, no future. They'd end up in one of those terrible camps, eating rats and begging.

With a heavy heart, Rava picks up her phone.

It takes several rings before Baba answers. He's sitting in a green armchair which looks cartoonishly huge, but it's Baba who's shrunk.

'Rava! It's so good to see you. And how is my granddaughter?' Baba's face looks like a skull, but his eyes still burn brightly.

'Well, Baba, and growing. She kicks all the time. Look!'
Rava lowers the phone to show her father her bump, big and
rounded now.

Baba beams.

'Allah be praised! And is your husband well?'

'Yes, Baba. He is well. And you, Baba? How are you?'

Baba shrugs and spreads his hands.

'Don't you worry about me. You take care of yourself and
your little one, and your good husband. When the child is
born, *inshallah,* perhaps I will see her.'

'Yes, Baba. Baba, I've been thinking - I might need to come
and stay with you and Aunt Nasreem for a while, if that's all
right?'

Baba's smile spreads to all four corners of his face.

'Allah be praised! When will you come, my daughter?'

'Well, I'm not sure yet, Baba, but I've been thinking about
maybe having my baby in Aberdeen.'

Baba blinks. Then he tugs at his ear.

'I'm sorry, my old hearing! I thought you said -?'

'It might be the best way, to have her in Scotland.'

The old man rubs both eyes.

'And your husband -?' he asks, confused. Then he calls out:
'Nasreem, come quickly! Rava is coming home.'

'What is it, Abdullah?' Aunt Nasreem bustles into view, still
wearing her apron and rubber gloves. 'Ah, Rava - how is the
baby?

'She's coming home, to have the baby here.'

'No, you're getting mixed up, Abdullah; that's not right.'

'No, Auntie, that is what I said. I'm not certain yet, though.'

Aunt Nasreem's eyes widen as Rava tries to explain. The
hospitals in London are very good, yes, but they have lots of
rules and restrictions. No, Martin can't come; he's very busy
with his work. Yes, she knows it's late in the pregnancy to be
flying, but she's sure Allah will protect her and the child.

Nasreem turns pink with excitement. She knows a nurse at Aberdeen Maternity Hospital; she will make enquiries. She still has the old cot up in the attic, and all Fatima's old baby clothes. She thinks she can borrow a pram from the neighbours. Has Rava got her flight permit yet? That can take a while, can't it?

Rava's throat tightens. Un-Sealed women aren't eligible to fly without a husband's or employer's certificate, and a permit would cost most of her savings, if she could get one at all. The alternative is a precarious journey by jeep.

'Not yet, Auntie. Like I said, I haven't decided yet; it's just a possibility, that's all.' Perhaps she shouldn't have called, but she needed to know they'd say yes.

'Marvellous news. Marvellous,' Baba keeps repeating, but he's turned very pale and sounds breathless.

'Abdullah, you must rest now,' Nasreem says. 'All this excitement is exhausting you. Wait, Rava,' she adds, 'there is something I need to ask you.'

With many goodbyes and blessings, Baba shuffles away to lie down. Aunt Nasreem closes the door and her face creases into a frown.

'What is it, Auntie? Is it Baba?' Rava swallows hard.

Her aunt nods.

'It's bad,' she says, her lower lip trembling. 'He gets tired so quickly, and the pain is very bad. But the doctors have talked about a new medication - miracle drug. They think it could give him another six months at least, maybe a year, or more.'

'Oh that's wonderful.' Baba could see Amani smile and sit up. He might even see her walking. But Nasreem dabs at her eyes with a crumpled tissue.

'It's the cost,' she says. 'We have already borrowed everything we can. I don't want to ask Fatima and her husband; things are hard for them right now. And if I speak to Abdullah, he will tell me not to bother, he is old, and all that rubbish!' She rolls her eyes. 'So, I was going to ask you, Rava. Do you think, perhaps, your husband can help?' Her hopeful face fills the phone's small screen.

Rava closes her eyes; her breath feels trapped inside her. Martin won't even speak to her, and she has so little money of her own. If she goes to Aberdeen, it will be to watch Baba die.

'Rava?'

'I'm sorry, Auntie - I don't know. I will try, but -.'

'Thank you, Rava; I know you have it in you to be a good daughter. The doctors need -.'

She names the amount and Rava suppresses a gasp. It's almost exactly the sum she'll get paid at the end of August, with her annual bonus on top of her salary, but by then the baby will be almost due.

She runs her fingers through her hair, trying to think straight. She has all her jewellery, but if she goes to Aberdeen she'll need a black-market permit as well as a plane ticket. And Jess is starting to hint about rent. If only she'd set up her own bank account months ago, she could've saved more. Jess was right all along.

'Let me know as soon as you can,' Aunt Nasreem presses. 'The doctors say the sooner the better, to start the drugs, for the best chance of remission. And Abdullah is so very sick.'

'I will try,' Rava repeats.

AFTER THE CALL, Rava sits for a long time making calculations in her head. If Martin doesn't change his mind, she'll have to support herself and Amani as well as paying for Baba's chemo-therapy. She can't bear the thought of being a burden on Baba and Aunt Nasreem; they can barely make ends meet as it is. If she carries on working at the bank for another two or three months and earns her bonus, she might just be able to save enough before the baby arrives.

Her employer offers loans at preferential rates to its staff, so Rava applies, but incubating women are not a good risk.

'If your husband completes an application, I'm sure it will be fine,' says the lady behind the desk. Rava thanks her and leaves.

Baba needs his medication straight away, so she takes her gold jewellery to a pawnbroker's shop on one of the seedier streets behind Jess's place. A man with a face the colour and shape of a potato runs a nicotine-stained finger through her necklaces, the keepsakes she inherited from Mama, and most of the jewellery Martin gave her. She keeps hold of her wedding ring and the big anniversary diamond in case Martin comes back.

The man offers less than she'd hoped.

'I'll come and redeem it all,' she insists. 'I get my bonus in August.'

The man nods and writes down the redemption price, which is eye-wateringly high. When she tries to protest, he points to her blue Femband and shrugs.

Everything will be fine, she reassures herself. And when Aunt Nasreem calls, sobbing with gratitude, Rava knows she's done the right thing. Whatever else happens, Baba will have his treatment.

For herself and Amani though, she will have to look at all the options. Waiting until August means she is cutting things very fine indeed.

38

THE MIDWIFE'S CLINIC

I s this the right place? The doors of the church are bolted, and the graveyard is deserted. Rava consults the instructions Jess gave her: *'Go round to the left.'* She glances about, but she can't spot any Mafia types hiding behind the tombs. A path leads her under an enormous tree and through a gate to a dilapidated hall.

She turns the iron ring handle and the door swings open to reveal a long room smelling of damp and disinfectant, with people sitting on rows of chairs. Several small children run noisily up and down on the bare floorboards. A white-haired lady stands behind a table.

'Are you here for the clinic, dear?'

She peers at Rava, whose pregnancy is difficult to conceal now, even under a chador.

'Yes,' Rava whispers. She doesn't dare say she's come to see the midwife.

'Have you been before?' The lady consults a list. 'What's your name, dear? You don't need to worry; we're all friends here. I'm Peggy Newton. I've been at Our Lady and Saint Joseph for forty-five years, through thick and thin. Rather thin these days, I'm afraid, but we carry on.' She holds out a veiny hand for Rava to shake.

'Rachel Fazel.' No one must guess who she really is.

'There's a bit of a wait,' Peggy says when she's written Rava's fake name and real date of birth on an index card. 'Hand this to the nurse when it's your turn, and strap this on.' She holds out a black Femband - the sort the cleaners wear.

'Do I have to?' She left her blue Femband at home, so no one can track her, but her long sleeves conceal her bare wrists. Black bands are for the outsiders: people who live in the container camps and on the marshes.

'I would if I were you, dear. It'll get you back into the city; they do more thorough checks on the way in. And just in case we get any problems here. That's it. Now, Maureen over there will keep you plied with tea and biscuits. Oh, and the loos are down the far end, through that door. Did you bring a wee sample?'

Rava shakes her head. What sort of problems, she wonders?

'Take this then.' Peggy hands her a small plastic bottle.

The toilets are clean, thank God; Peggy must be good with the bleach. Her sample done, Rava sits on one of the chairs towards the back. One corner of the hall is partitioned off with screens on wheeled frames. Every now and then, someone emerges from behind the screens, the next person goes in, and everyone shuffles up another seat.

Rava expected the clinic to be full of pregnant women, but more than half the people waiting are elderly. A scrawny old man sits hunched over his stick in the chair beside her, wheezing in hoarse gasps between spasms of a bubbling cough. Rava pulls her veil close over her mouth and nose, praying she doesn't catch anything.

Three patients have swollen legs wrapped in bandages. There are children with sticky eyes and crusty rashes. A girl who looks barely eighteen cradles a thin baby in her arms.

Rava keeps a tight grip on her Gucci handbag, which she should have left safely back at Jess's place. Everyone here is poor. Only one other woman is obviously pregnant.

'Am I in the right place?' Rava asks when the lady called Maureen brings her tea in a thick-rimmed mug. 'I've come for -.' She points to her stomach.

'For the midwife, yes lovely,' Maureen assures her. 'She's a nurse too, you see, so everyone comes with their problems. Liz won't turn anyone away; point of principle with her. So of course it gets busy, but what can you do? People've got nowhere else to turn, since they closed the health centres outside the city limits. Unsupported territory, see? Supposed to be evacuated.' She spreads her hands in exasperation. 'If you're over sixty, you've got zero chance of being re-housed; supposed to sign up for peaceful flaming rest, aren't you? Burden on society and all that. Hah! We'll see about that. Ginger nut, lovely?' Maureen extends the plate of biscuits. 'Go on, take two. You'll be here for a while yet.'

The queue moves slowly. Several times, Rava almost gets up to leave; it's only the thought of having to explain herself to Jess that stops her. She didn't want to come, but Jess more or less insisted. She's made several remarks about the small size of her apartment and not wanting to get mixed up in anything illegal. She's terrified Rava might go into labour in her living room.

'And then what would we do?' she said. Rava didn't have an answer. Martin still hasn't been in touch, and it's proving harder than she'd expected to get a flight permit for Scotland. Her employer sent off the application - you're allowed to visit a dying relative if your husband or employer countersigns the forms - but nothing's come back yet. And the baby will be due soon.

The chair grows hard under her buttocks. Rava twists her wedding ring round and round on her finger. She keeps checking the clock on the wall; it took ages to find this place and she'll need to return before curfew.

The baby presses against her bladder and she has to get up twice more to use the dank toilet. Her lower back aches. When at last the old man with the cough comes out from behind the screens muttering, 'Thank'ee kindly, nurse,' Rava gets to her feet.

BEHIND THE SCREEN, Rava does a double-take and stops dead. Standing in front of her is the young nurse from her first appointment at the Genesis Centre. What on earth is she doing here? Is this a trap? Does Martin know about this?

Rava's first instinct is to turn and run, but bright spots are dancing in front of her eyes and her legs feel woolly.

'I'm sorry,' she falters. 'I know I've missed my check-ups at the hospital, but my husband you see -.'

The room starts to sway.

'Hey, it's okay - you're safe here.' The nurse takes her arm and leads her to a chair. 'Sit down.'

As Rava's head begins to clear, another voice breaks in:

'Thirty-two weeks or thereabouts, I should say. Welcome, my love.'

THE MIDWIFE IS OLD. She's shorter than Rava and moves with a stiff, one-sided shuffle.

'Have you got a sample?' she asks, holding out her hand. There's something weirdly familiar about her pale eyes, though Rava's certain she's never met the woman. She's not the sort of person you would forget, with her crooked nose, colourful shawl, and commanding tone of voice. 'What's your name, my love?'

'Rava Robson. No, no, I mean Rachel!'

Idiot! Fool! How could she make such a stupid mistake?

'Rachel,' the midwife repeats deliberately, squinting at Rava's index card. 'Don't worry, my love, you wouldn't be the first person to turn up here with a complicated story. There's not much I haven't seen, believe me.'

'Have I seen you before?' asks the young nurse. Rava squirms and adjusts the veil of her chador.

'I'm Chiara,' the nurse says, 'and this is Liz. I used to work at the Genesis Centre, but I've left now. Long story!'

The nurse has kind eyes; she was kind before.

'Did you say Robson? Rachel Robson?' the old midwife asks. She waddles closer, adjusting her shawl as if her shoulder is painful. Then she grasps a pair of half-moon spectacles hanging on a cord around her neck, perches them on her nose, and peers at Rava.

'Yes - no. The thing is, my friend told me to come here. I'm having a baby, and my husband - he doesn't - I can't make him understand.' Rava's voice wobbles.

'Husbands!' The midwife rolls her eyes. 'Let me guess, either he's threatening you with something, or he's walked out, or he's got cold feet about the baby, or some combination of the above - am I right? This effing system gives the husbands way too much power. Now listen, I've been helping women have babies since before you were born. I'm unshockable. And Chiara here's solid. She left that sodding Genesis Centre for some of the same reasons you're here. Abuse of women, is what it boils down to. So, tell me all about it.'

Hesitantly, Rava tells Liz and Chiara the bare bones of her story. She's careful not to say Martin's name, or to mention what he does. What if they think she's a spy? It would only take one more mistake. Martin says the midwives are backed by the

Mafia; they might have security waiting behind the scenes, ready to deal with anyone they don't trust.

'And so Jess said I should come and see you, so I've got options,' Rava concludes. 'But I don't know - I'm still hoping my husband -.' She trails off.

Liz sniffs loudly but refrains from further comment about Rava's husband.

'Okay. Coming to see me doesn't commit you to anything; it just gives me the chance to explain what I can and can't do for you. Your friend's right - it's good to have options, especially these days. I can do an antenatal check-up today, if you like? And if you think you might want me at your birth, I need to assess whether you're suitable - clinically suitable, I mean. If there are complications, we might need to look for alternatives. How does that sound, my love?'

Rava hadn't even considered that she might not be suitable for the midwife. But the old woman's business-like tone is reassuring.

'How much do you charge? I've had to borrow money, you see, and my friend's started asking for rent, but I'll get my bonus at the end of August.'

'It's okay,' says Chiara. 'Don't worry.' Her glance strays to the Gucci bag but her smile seems genuine.

'Sure,' says Liz. 'We're here for everyone. I don't give a monkey's about your background, who you're married to, or any of that nonsense. You're a human being, you need help - that's it. That's my only religion, by the way, but I'll respect yours, no problem. As for money, people pay what they can. Chiara and I have to eat, and we have some expenses, but if you need us, we're here. End of.' Liz's weatherbeaten face is fierce. 'So, shall we get down to business?'

Liz has a long list of questions about Rava's pregnancy and her medical history. Rava does her best to answer everything, but there's one question she dreads, and here it is:

'Have you had any previous pregnancies, miscarriages, or terminations?'

Rava pulls her veil closer.

'One termination, when I was seventeen.' The words come out in a monotone as her nostrils flare with the stink of the school toilets and the hot tang of blood. She squeezes her eyes tight as if this might shut out the memories. 'I didn't have a choice,' she says.

'Women rarely do,' Liz comments drily.

'It's okay,' says Chiara, reaching out and taking Rava's hand. 'We're here to support you; it's been a difficult journey, right?'

In reply, Rava only bites her lip; she mustn't cry in front of these strangers. She swallows the water Chiara brings and tells them she's okay to carry on.

When all the questions are done and her urine and blood pressure checked, Rava climbs up onto the couch. There's no scanning machine like they have at the Genesis Centre. Instead, Chiara uses her hands to feel Rava's baby. Firm but tender fingers caress the lumps and bumps of her belly.

'Here's your baby's bottom, on the right side under your ribs. This is her back, and I think that's a foot over there. Her head's well down already, in a lovely position for birth. Is it okay if I listen to her heart?'

'Oh, yes please.' Rava's fascinated that Chiara can tell all that without machines, and amazed when the young nurse produces a wooden trumpet and presses it against her skin.

'Can you hear her? Is she all right? It's so long since I've been to the hospital.'

Chiara passes Rava a stethoscope and helps her position it. A quiet, insistent gallop thrums in her ears, and now the tears start to come. All these weeks, she's been so worried, so alone, but her little Amani is well and alive. She cries happy tears, wishing she could stay here forever, tuned into her baby, the pair of them wrapped in Chiara's gentle attention.

But soon she is up and rearranging her clothing.

'Everything seems normal,' Liz says. 'I'm sure I can help you, if you want me to. Now, pay attention please, because this is important.'

Liz hands her a brown envelope with something heavy inside and launches into a detailed explanation. Rava listens to all the instructions and warnings, and asks several questions. The midwives weren't what she'd expected; maybe, if she's really stuck, she might consider coming back.

She's just about to leave when Liz asks:

'Your husband? Is Robson his surname too?'

Rava's stomach tries to turn itself inside out. She'd almost convinced herself Liz wasn't bothered about her mistake, but of course that name will have set alarm bells ringing. Martin's often in the news, talking about the scourge of illegal midwives. And Liz is obviously hot on security; the lecture she's just delivered about phones and passwords made that perfectly clear. If she guesses, or even suspects -.

'I'm sorry, I have to be going now. The curfew.' Rava makes for the gap between the screens, then has to turn back because she's forgotten her stupid rich-bitch handbag.

'This must be yours. Very nice.' Liz hands it to her. 'Sorry, I didn't mean to scare you; there are lots of Robsons, I'm sure. Go carefully, and call whenever you need us.'

Rava grabs her bag and flees. In the churchyard, she trips on a tree root and only just saves herself from landing bump-first on a gravestone. Not daring to look back, she gathers up her chador and breaks into a breathless half-run. Her Gucci bag, heavier by the weight of the midwife's burner phone, thumps rhythmically at her side.

39

SUNSHINE AND MOONLIGHT

'I've got something to tell you, Chiara. Can we go for a walk?'

This is the fourth time Salvador has turned up at the Rosie Lee in the last few weeks, but today he looks different. It takes Chiara a moment to realise he's trimmed his beard. He's wearing a plain white t-shirt, slim jeans, and a serious expression.

Chiara folds the dough she's been kneading into a tin and covers it with a cloth. Then she knocks on Liz's cabin door.

'Do you need me this afternoon?'

Liz is half-lying, half-sitting on her bed, propped on a heap of pillows. Her knitting lies untouched beside her. She winces as she shifts position to blink at Chiara.

'Is it that boy again?' Liz raises her eyebrows, then shrugs. 'I'm not your boss, my love. Go and enjoy yourself, but be careful, mind. No names, no places, no details.'

'Yes, I know. But Salvador's one of us, isn't he? He brought a big box of syringes today from the Genesis Centre, and he says he can get more medications next week.'

'He's been very helpful all of a sudden.' Liz lets the words hang between them.

'What d'you mean?'

'Come on, Chiara. I wasn't born yesterday. Why do you think that lad's turning up here every other day? You're pretty, he's charming. If I was young again -.' Liz winks, and Chiara blushes.

'Is your back hurting?' Chiara asks. 'Shall I get you some paracetamol before I go?'

But Liz shakes her head.

'No, I'll be getting up soon. Got laundry to sort, and tomorrow's clinic to prep for. Go on - he's come all this way to see you. Just don't do anything I wouldn't!' She manages a wry smile before sinking back onto her pillows and closing her eyes.

CHIARA AND SALVADOR walk side by side along the river bank. Last time he took her to Cucina Piccola, risking a fake black Femband to get her into the city. They chatted about their homes, families, and dreams for a better future. Salvador grew up near the sea, like Chiara. The cottage is sold now, and she told him how badly she'll miss the village with the harbour, the stray cats, and the smell of the sea. Mariana, Salvador's sister, is doing okay; her health seems better this year, and she's been on a trip to the mountains. Salvador would love children of his own one day, but it seems impossible, with the world the way it is.

But today the chatter falters and they walk in silence. Salvador seems to be lost in his thoughts; he's got news, he said. Chiara turns over the possibilities: another member of the network has been compromised? Salvador thinks he's been followed? He's going back to Spain? Her fears grow heavier with every step.

They pass under a bridge and emerge into a meadow. Six cows graze behind an electrified fence, but the land beside the river is green and peaceful, dotted with yellow flowers. There are no tents or shacks here - the owner of the cows must keep the land cleared - and only two boats are moored at the next bend of the river. The long grass tickles Chiara's bare toes in her flip-flops.

When they reach the centre of the field, Salvador stops.

'Chiara,' he says, then hesitates.

'You said you had something to tell me?' she prompts. Might as well get this over with.

'Okay.' He takes a deep breath. 'I've done it Chiara - finally. I've quit my job at the Genesis Centre. I handed my notice in yesterday. It was you - you inspired me.' He grins triumphantly.

'Oh that's wonderful.' But her voice comes out flat. She ought to be pleased - he's doing the right thing - but she knows what this means. He'll be leaving the country, going home to Mariana. He's come to say goodbye.

'When are you leaving?' The words seem to stick in her throat.

'I have to give two months notice.' Salvador stares at the cows. 'I feel terrible that I've left this so long. I'm a coward, Chiara. I hate myself for what I've been doing, with the babies who fail the checks, you know? But I still kept putting it off. I told myself all their lies: that it's for the best - that we're relieving suffering, saving the planet, and doing it all for a better future. But I knew that was a load of crap. Tomorow, I told myself, or next week, or after I get my next pay check.' He turns to face her. 'But seeing you on the boat, working with Liz, risking your safety - you showed me the way, Chiara. I woke up yesterday and knew it was over. I'm going to be free of that evil place at last.'

'That's good. I'm glad. Your sister will be very happy to get you back.' Chiara forces her lips into a smile.

'My sister?' His brows crease as if she's not making sense. 'No, I'm not going home. At least, I thought - oh, this is awkward, but, I wanted to stay and help you and Liz. But maybe I got the wrong idea?'

'Stay and help us?' Chiara echoes. 'But how will you support Mariana? We can't afford to pay you.'

Salvador gestures as if his words are lost in the air.

'I don't really have a plan, Chiara. I had to quit; I couldn't do it any longer. I felt dirty, vile; you must despise me. Of course I worry about Mariana, but I have some savings, and I could get some other job here. I don't mind what I do. If I go back to Spain the money's terrible, and besides -.'

He takes a step closer, examining her face as if he's seeing her for the first time. His hair is shorter as well as his beard: no floppy curls any more. He looks older, but in a good way. He clasps both of Chiara's hands in his.

'Besides, I would miss you, Chiara. But of course, if you want me to leave, I understand.'

He loosens his grip on her hands.

'Please don't leave.' She reaches up to touch his cheek on the smooth place above where his beard grows. His eyes shine, and she realises they're wet with tears. He's so kind and gentle with the babies. Yes, he's done bad things, but he didn't want to; that's not who he is. He was trapped by the system and he's sorry now; it was the same for her.

'Salvador,' she says. He doesn't move, so she presses her face against his chest. His heart beats steady and strong. His arms come around her, and she nestles into the warmth, the solidity, the big, safe size of him. He starts kissing her hair. She breathes him in, and he smells like the new-washed linen Nonna used to hang out in the sun.

She turns her mouth up towards his, but he hesitates, almost pulls back.

'Chiara - you're so sweet, so good. Are you sure?'

'Yes,' she tells him. 'Yes.' And because he is staring at her as if she's a gift he doesn't deserve, she kisses him, hard and certain. When he kisses her back, she knows he has wanted this for a long time, just as she has.

It's late by the time Chiara returns along the towpath towards the Rosie Lee. The sky fades from blue to deep midnight, scattered with a handful of stars. A bright half moon sails in and out of the clouds, and a breeze drifts across the river. Chiara's legs and feet are cool, but her shoulders and arms luxuriate in the warmth of the jacket Salvador insisted on draping around her. He wanted to walk her home, but he has an early shift in the morning, and she told him she'll be fine.

He took her to a cafe after they left the meadow, but she wasn't hungry. She was full up with happiness. They sat with fingers intertwined, gazing at one another as if they'd never seen another human before. He'll come back as soon as he can. His notice period will be tough, he said, but he's planning to steal as many drugs as he can for the network before he leaves. She made him promise to be careful.

The lamps on the boats reflect on the river as Chiara strolls dreamily along, still seeing Salvador's face, still feeling his arms holding her. Under her breath she hums an old song about being in love. She feels so light, so perfect; her body is fizzing as if she's come alive for the first time. If she wanted, she could walk on the water.

She rounds the last bend to find the Rosie Lee moored under a willow tree. Liz will have gone to bed hours ago, but she hasn't lit the lantern, which is odd. Didn't she think Chiara would be back tonight? Perhaps she was called out to a birth? Chiara feels in her bag for her key, but she's startled by a low clucking from the shadows beside the path. A moment later, Soo, the dappled grey chicken, struts out from under the bushes. Why isn't she safely shut up in her nesting box? Liz never leaves her beloved hens out at night. Something's wrong.

Chiara bends to pick up Soo, who squawks and fusses in her arms. She calls out Vic's name; please don't let a fox have caught her. The moon dips behind a cloud, and Chiara shivers despite Salvador's jacket. She's flooded with a cold sensation, an urge to look over her shoulder, as if someone is watching her. Her skin prickles, but this time it's not with the thrill of being in love. She drops the struggling chicken and rubs her eyes. Something's different - something about the boat.

A sudden whirr of wheels makes her stumble sideways. Soo protests noisily, but it's only a cyclist riding home along the towpath. His lamp flashes past the flank of the Rosie Lee, lighting it up, and, all at once, Chiara sees.

In crude, black letters half a metre high, someone has painted along the side of the old narrowboat, obscuring the red roses:

'BURN THE WITCHES. SEND THEM TO HELL.'

Chiara gasps. She can't breathe, and her flip-flops seem to be stuck to the ground. With trembling fingers, she finds her phone and turns on its torch. She reads the words again slowly, tracing each letter in turn. Her knees start shaking. Who did this? What else have they done?

The lantern on the prow has vanished, and something else is hanging from the iron hook. The thing looks like a tattered flag swinging slowly from side to side. An old towel, perhaps, or a rag hung up to dry? Chiara steps onto the deck, peers more closely, reaches out to touch whatever it is. Something soft and wet. Something furry.

The cloud slides away from the moon and she staggers backwards in horror. The hanging thing is the carcass of a cat.

Gaskin has been strung up by his front paws. His head is thrown back, his mouth gaping, teeth protruding in a frozen, silent yowl. Someone has slit his belly open and his entrails are dangling, trailing blood onto the wooden boards of the boat.

40

LIQUID MORPHINE

Chiara rushes into the boat for a knife to cut Gaskin down. She bangs on Liz's cabin door and shouts her name, but it takes far too long before Liz appears, clutching at her left side, her eyes glassy. She doesn't seem to understand what Chiara is saying. In the end, Chiara has to lead her outside, into the moonlight, to see for herself.

Gaskin is stiff and cold. They wrap him in towels and Liz cradles him in her arms. She strokes his thick fur and talks to him, whispering about kittens and tigers. Later, she starts rambling about her friend Fumni, who still hasn't been heard from months after being arrested. Next afternoon, Liz is still sitting there, blank-faced and motionless. Chiara has to coax her into letting go of the corpse and lead her back to bed like a child.

Chiara buries Gaskin at one of his favourite riverside hunting grounds. She searches high and low for Vic, Liz's beautiful Rhode Island Red, but the chicken has vanished, either stolen or fallen prey to foxes. And poor Soo hasn't laid a single egg since that awful night. She cries with high-pitched, insistent peeps, missing her sister.

Despite hours of scrubbing with bleach and hot water, the writing on the side of the boat proves impossible to remove. Chiara has to buy thick black paint from a man on Hackney marshes. It takes three coats, and the painted roses disappear along with the letters, but at least the job is done.

'Who did it?' Chiara asks. 'If they know we're midwives, why don't they arrest us and have done with it?'

'It was a warning. Thugs paid to come and scare us.' Liz scowls. 'Evil bastards; I'd rather they'd taken me, but oh no, that would have been too easy. They'd rather torture an innocent creature instead.' She aims a furious gobbet of spit at the river. 'Right, I'm going to lie down for a bit - my back's killing me. No, I don't need a massage; just leave me in peace, okay?'

Liz hobbles off to her cabin. She's becoming more irritable, criticising Chiara for burning the bread, failing to water the herbs at the right times, and not tying the ropes properly. And that was just yesterday!

Some days Liz sits in her chair for hours without speaking. Sometimes she knits, or writes in her notebook, but more often she stares unseeing. Her hands lie empty in her lap with no cat to stroke. It is as if she is waiting for something, without hope.

Late one night, when Chiara can't sleep, she goes to the kitchen to make a drink and sees Liz sitting in near-darkness, her face taut with pain. The bottle of liquid morphine stands uncorked beside the sink. Chiara starts to say something, but Liz waves an impatient hand at her to go away and leave her alone.

CHIARA SPENDS every spare moment with Salvador. Sometimes she goes to his apartment and they spend the evening snuggling on the sofa and watching old movies. He gives her a spare key 'just in case.' He's managed to get his hands on a supply of 'burner' black Fembands which Chiara uses with grateful caution, but she's still nervous going into the city, especially so close to the Genesis Centre. Last week there was another demonstration - three women with placards - and Salvador says it's happening all over London now. Pressure is building, he says.

When they can, they take long walks together hand in hand, sometimes returning to the meadow where they first embraced. He fills her thoughts night and day; it's agony saying goodbye. They kiss and cling to one another till the very last moment.

'Let's find somewhere to live together,' he says, 'when I finish my job. It's only a few more weeks.'

'But what about Liz?'

'We'll work something out; I've got a friend who might be able to help. But let's not waste time worrying now.' He covers her mouth with his and her troubles vanish.

41

MARTIN'S OFFICE

'I'm afraid he's in a meeting, Mrs Robson.' Martin's PA smiles coldly, her lips framing perfect teeth.

'I'll wait.' Rava sits on one of the slippery chairs. 'I've got plenty of time.' She'll sit outside Martin's office all day and all night if need be. First she had to work up the courage to come, and then she almost couldn't persuade the woman on the desk downstairs to let her into the lift. It was the pregnancy bump that swung it; the woman seemed terrified Rava might give birth right there on the lobby floor.

'Well, the thing is -.' The PA steeples her fingers, her golden Femband glinting. 'He did say, if you showed up here, not to let you in. It's not appropriate, you see; this is a professional environment and Government property.'

Is my husband Government property? Is my baby?

'But I've tried everything else. He won't answer my calls or my messages.'

'Mrs Robson, this is really none of my business.' The PA starts typing very fast, her nails flying over the keyboard. She answers the phone several times in her irritating posh-girl voice. Would Martin still love me, Rava wonders, if I sounded like that? Would he love me if I'd been to a fancy university? If I had a gold band?

Half an hour passes, forty minutes. Rava's back hurts; this chair is agony and she needs the toilet, but she won't budge. Her carefully-chosen dress - one of Martin's favourites - is much too tight and itchy. It's been nearly an hour when the phone rings again.

'Yes, of course, right away, Mr Robson.' The PA glares at Rava before getting up from behind her desk and entering the door marked *'Under-Secretary of State: Mr M. A. Robson.'*

Rava seizes her chance. She leaps to her feet and follows the PA into Martin's inner sanctum.

'Sonia! What's going on?' Martin's pale eyes widen. 'Did you let my wife in here?'

The PA looks over her shoulder and gasps.

'Oh, I'm terribly sorry, Sir. I told her you didn't want to see her, but she -.'

'Martin, please!' Rava breaks in. 'I just want to speak to you; what choice did you leave me except to come here? You never answer my messages; how can I explain if you won't listen? I want us to be together - you, me, and our baby. We need to talk.'

Martin's eyebrow flickers. He looks tired; the ashtray on his desk is overflowing.

'Shall I call Security, Sir?' The PA - Sonia - hovers beside Rava, literally breathing on her neck.

'Please, Martin!'

Martin sighs. His head droops, and for a moment Rava sees his softer, more vulnerable side. Sometimes he used to have nightmares and cling to her, trembling, in the hours before dawn. He never told her what his dreams were about; he said he couldn't remember.

'You're still pregnant.' It's a statement, not a question.

'Martin, I couldn't; this baby's almost ready to be born.'

'I told you not to contact me unless you want a Fresh Start termination. Have you changed your mind.'

'But why, Martin?' She squeezes her palms together. 'Why can't you love both of us?'

'I've already explained; I'm not going to repeat myself. But, since you're here, I've been been thinking, Rava: perhaps I've been too harsh.'

'Yes?' Rava bites her lip. Is this it? All along she's believed, if she could only see him face to face -.

'I've been wondering, Rava, if you're not well?'

'What d'you mean? My ankles are a bit swollen, and I'm worried about everything, but I'm okay.

'Have you had any check-ups lately?' He leans in towards her.

'Well, no, except - no. You stopped paying the fees at the Genesis Centre, so I couldn't go, could I?'

'All right. Listen, Rava, have you heard of something called antenatal psychosis?' He narrows his gaze.

'No, I don't think so, but -.' Her heart starts to race.

'It's a rare condition, but serious. It can threaten the incubator's life, as well as the foetus. Often goes hand in hand with hypertension and pre-eclampsia, I'm told. Have you been checked for those conditions?'

'Well, no, but -.'

'I'm worried about you, Rava. What sane woman runs away from a safe home and a husband who working his guts out for her? Pregnancy's much more dangerous to your mental health than people realise; it's an abnormal state. The foetus gradually takes over like a parasite, sapping your resources. Some women never recover. I think you need help.'

Rava looks at Sonia, who nods her head gravely.

'Are you saying I'm crazy for wanting to keep my baby?' Rava's voice rises to a madwoman's pitch.

'No, not necessarily. I'm not a doctor, but I think we should get you checked over for your own safety. Let the experts decide. The People's Hospital has a special unit.'

'The People's Hospital? But I heard they don't do antenatal care.' She's heard terrible things. Martin wouldn't send her there, would he?

'Yes they do, for registered incubators. Of course, its not as comfortable as the Genesis Centre, but for this sort of thing they're the experts.'

'What sort of thing? There's nothing wrong with me.' Rava clutches her head; her fingers are clenched into claws.

'We don't know that, do we, my love?' Martin's voice is cautious and low as if he's dealing with a dangerous wild animal. 'I think you need to be in a safe place, with professionals to watch over you. Why don't I call Daniel, and we could head over there? I can cancel my meetings.' He glances at Sonia, who nods.

For a moment, Rava almost agrees. She's missed Martin so much, and he sounds kind, concerned. Maybe she is going a bit crazy with all the stress. Maybe this has all been a massive misunderstanding.

'Well,' she begins, but then Amani kicks. Not just a little wriggle, but a hard, frantic pummelling on the inside of Rava's ribcage. Rava lowers a hand to soothe her. 'Hey, what's the matter in there?' The baby elbows her again.

'What is it?' Martin asks.

'The baby; she's moving. Martin, if I come with you to the People's Hospital, will you sign the paperwork for the baby, so we can keep her?'

Martin rubs at his lips.

'It's your health I'm worried about, my darling. Let's get you somewhere secure. We can discuss everything else once you're feeling more yourself.'

'But I am myself!'

'No, you're not. The woman I married was sweet, gentle, and trusting. You've changed, Rava. You don't even take care of your appearance properly. I'm going to be a Minister soon, and I need -.'

' - a wife you can be proud of.' Rava completes his sentence. 'Well, maybe that's not me. I don't know who's changed - me or you. But all I ever wanted was for us to be a family. Why don't you marry Sonia here instead - she might be more what you're looking for?.'

Sonia tuts and straightens her skirt.

'Calm down, Rava.' Martin makes a grab for Rava's wrist, but she twists away.

'Leave me alone!'

Mustering the last shreds of her dignity, Rava makes for the door. Sonia steps towards her, but Martin shakes his head.

'Let her go for now,' he says. 'This is a distraction from our real work.'

RAVA FIGHTS her way through the crowds, breathless and sweaty. There are even more police about than usual. She doesn't dare look back towards the Ministry. Only when she's several streets away does she retreat to a cafe to use the wash-room. She orders a herbal tea and sits in a corner, trying to compose herself. What happened? she asks herself, over and over. How can that cold, distant official be the man she married? Has Martin's job eaten him up and spat out a monster?

She ought to go back to work, but she can't trust herself not to start crying. She feels dizzy and sick with a pounding, throbbing head. Perhaps there really is something wrong with her? No, she needs to go back to Jess's place. Besides, she's got things to do: flight permit or not, she's going to have to find a way to get to Aberdeen, and quickly.

On the other side of the cafe, a man with ginger hair nurses a coffee. Rava's too wrapped up in her worries to notice him until she starts gathering her things to leave. It's only then, with a jolt of shock, that she recognises him: it's Daniel. Martin must have sent him to follow her.

42

CODE WORD

'You need to leave, Chiara.'

Liz emerges from her cabin, clutching at a shelf to steady herself. Her face is a muddy shade of ash.

'Leave?' Chiara drops the sheet she was halfway through folding.

'Yes, you're young. Whole life ahead of you, and all that. You should get out while you still can. Either move in with lover boy, or go home to Italy, but keep yourself safe, my love. They're closing in; it's all over except the shouting.' Liz shrugs lopsidedly as if this was only to be expected.

'But Salvador's still looking for somewhere to live, and the Genesis Centre still has my passport, and besides, what about you, Liz? How will you manage on your own?' Liz is too weak these days to chop firewood, or fetch water in plastic cans, or manage the heavy lock gates on the river. She scarcely has the strength to steer a course with the tiller. Narrowboat life is tough.

But Liz waves a hand dismissively.

'I managed for years before you showed up. And it won't be for much longer. Trina out Romford way got hauled in for questioning last week. They let her go, but now she won't open her door to anyone, poor thing. There's scarcely any of us left. I think we're pretty much the last, you and me.'

Chiara feels seasick, as if the Rosie Lee has hit stormy waters.

'And listen,' Liz goes on, 'That doula they picked up in Dartford - fierce as you like, but she's got a child of her own. What happens when they start threatening her kid? We've been lucky, but the network's starting to break down. Two more arrests last week - someone's bound to crack.'

Chiara shivers.

'It's that Martin Robson, isn't it? I keep seeing him on the news saying how much he cares about women's health.' Chiara pictures the handsome, sharply-dressed man with the pale face. 'Why does he hate midwives so much?'

'He's an angry man.' Liz's voice sounds distant, as if it's echoing from underneath the boat. 'No, you should go, Chiara, as soon as you can. Don't worry about me. There's some old stuff I need to clear up.'

'But you're not well, Liz. I love Salvador, but I don't want to leave you. You remind me of my Nonna.' The jars and bottles on the shelves blur together. 'And I love being a midwife,' she adds in a strangled voice.

Liz removes her glasses and stares at Chiara as if she's seeing her for the first time. The hollows under her eyes are the colour of old bruises. She is shrinking like drying fruit.

'This can't last,' she warns, but her voice is softer.

'Just a few more weeks,' Chiara pleads, 'until Salvador's worked something out.'

Liz purses her lips, but she doesn't say no. She pats Chiara on the shoulder.

'Talk to him,' she urges. 'We may not have that long. There's something I need to do - one last shot - and I don't want you getting mixed up in it. But -.' She spreads her hands wide. 'I'm not going to throw you out, but you need to understand we're on borrowed time, okay?'

'Okay?' What does she mean - borrowed time?

'They're waiting to catch us red-handed, with a birthing woman on board, so we have to be extra careful. No re-using phones, no calls when we're with a woman, triple-check everyone's identity?'

'Yes, I know. I'm always careful.'

Liz says this stuff all the time.

'Good. Now, one more thing, and this is important.' Liz fixes Chiara with a glare. 'If the shit hits the fan, you run, okay? Don't come back for me. Don't even look over your shoulder. Just run.'

'Oh but I couldn't -,' Chiara begins, but Liz isn't listening.

'Meconium,' she pronounces. 'Baby shit. That'll be the code word, got it?'

'Meconium?'

'If it all goes down, and you hear me say meconium, leg it, Chiara. Run. I know you're a fast runner, girl. No questions asked, okay? And do not -.' Liz stabs the air with her finger to emphasise each word: 'Do not come back for me.'

43

A GREY STONE COTTAGE

'Look, it's perfect!'

Salvador points to the picture on his phone. A grey stone cottage leans drunkenly against the side of a grassy hill. Its slate roof is draped with an old tarpaulin and the windows are boarded over, but Chiara's seen worse in Sicily.

'Where is it?' she asks.

'Wales. It's a country to the west of England - semi-independent, but in practice it's much freer. The authorities here leave it alone: too much trouble. We'd have to work hard - grow our own food and so on - but my friend says there's a village nearby and a growing local community. The house is available, and there's no doctor or midwife in the area, so we'd be welcome - needed, in fact. What d'you reckon?'

'How would we get there? Is it far?' The news is full of stories of impassable roads and murderous bandits who prey on travellers foolish enough to stray outside the cities.

'Easy. I'll buy a four-wheel drive - old LandRover or something. It's not half so bad out there as they want you to think. We can leave next week as soon as I've finished my last shift at the Genesis Centre.' Salvador bounces from foot to foot in excitement. 'This is our chance, Chiara!'

Chiara enlarges the photo with her fingers. It could be a pretty cottage with some love and care. They could paint the window frames and the door, plant some flowers, make a little garden.

'It won't take long to turn it into a home,' Salvador says, reading her mind. 'We can do the repairs together. It'll be a place of our own.'

A place of our own. A lump rises in Chiara's throat. Might that really be possible?

'But what about Liz? And your sister in Spain? And we - we haven't known each other very long.'

'Chiara, listen to me.' He places his hands on her shoulders. 'Liz told you to move out, yes?'

'Yes, but -.'

'And Mariana might be able to come and live with us once we've got the house sorted. They say it's easier in Wales for disabled people. Perhaps your sister could come too?'

'Well, maybe, but I don't know if -.'

'And we'll be away from London - no more armed police, no more demos, and surveillance. The nights will be quiet, and the cottage is near the sea.'

'Oh!' Chiara imagines the sound of waves on a beach; a clean beach under wide open skies, like in Sicily. She dreams of living beside the sea again.

'And,' Salvador goes on, 'you and me - I know it hasn't been long, but these are special times, don't you think, when everything happens fast? Ever since I first saw you, Chiara, I've hoped, I've believed -.' He cups her face in his hands. 'Chiara, I'm serious about us; you're the best thing that's ever happened to me. I want us to have a future together.'

He pauses, and she nods several times, struggling to form words.

'Me too, *amore mio*,' she says at last. 'That's what I want too.'

He brushes aside the strands of hair that have fallen across her face.

'So - what I mean is - when you're ready, one day - might you consider marrying me?'

In reply, she flings herself into his arms. His shirt grows damp as she sobs her 'yes' into his chest.

44

ONLINE CHECK-IN

'I 'll be there at the airport with Baba.' Aunt Nasreem is almost gabbling with excitement. 'I've got everything ready: your bed's made up, and Julie at the maternity hospital says you can make an appointment as soon as you're here.'

'Great. How are you doing, Baba?'

'Fantastic!' Rava's father holds up a skinny arm in a strong man gesture and grins. Most of his teeth are missing, but he's gained a little weight and there's more colour in his cheeks.

'He's so much better,' Nasreem says. 'The pain is completely gone, isn't it, Abdullah? And he's got so much more energy. The doctors say it's been a wonderful result from the chemo.'

'God is good,' Baba adds. '*Inshallah*, I shall see my grand-daughter. I pray every day that I will hold you both in my arms, Rava: you and your baby. Is your husband well?'

'Yes Baba. I'll be there tomorrow, Baba. It'll take me a while to get through immigration, so don't rush, okay? Don't exhaust yourself; we'll have plenty of time to be together.'

'*Inshallah*. I will be praying for you. Travel safely.'

'I love you, Baba.'

Rava hangs up and allows herself the luxury of a yawn and a stretch.

'We're going to Scotland, Amani!'

The baby shifts; she can't have much room in there anymore. Rava's skin is stretched tight over the bump, and her belly button has popped outwards. She can't quite believe it, but everything seems to be falling into place. Her bonus came through three days ago, and it was slightly more than she expected. She's been back to the potato-faced man at the pawn shop and redeemed all her jewellery. The price was extortionate, but she couldn't bring herself to let it go, especially the things from Mama; it's all she has left of her.

Best of all - and this seems like a miracle - Rava's got her flight permit. It came through last week, and she bought her ticket straight away. Technically, she's too pregnant to fly - she had to lie about her due date on the permit application - but she'll wear a large chador which should hide everything. On Jess's advice, she bought a fake doctor's letter online which says she's fit to fly.

She knows she's left it late, but the baby isn't due for another three weeks. All she needs to do is get on that plane. It's a short flight to Aberdeen: not much more than an hour. Then she and Amani will both be safe.

RAVA GOES ONLINE to check in for tomorrow's flight. She's not carrying fireworks, gas cylinders, or party poppers. She has her flight permit and ID for female travellers. Documents to show at airport security: passport, birth certificate, marriage certificate, flight permit, certificate of fertility status. Yes, yes, yes - wait! Marriage certificate? She didn't realise she needed that. Have they changed the rules again? She re-reads the list, her heart beating faster.

Maybe they won't check? But here it is in black-and-white:

'We take security seriously for the safety of all passengers and staff. Female travellers will not be permitted to pass through security without all the following identity documents ...'

Rava takes a great gulp of air. She leafs through her folder of paperwork as if the missing certificate might magically materialise inside. But she knows; of course she does. She brought all her personal papers with her when she moved out of the apartment, like Jess said, even though it seemed excessive and she was sure she'd be going back. But it didn't seem right to bring the marriage certificate; that belongs to Martin too. Now, though, she'll have to go back to the apartment and search through Martin's things. Her skin prickles, and Amani lies ominously still.

PART IV

PART IV

45

PEACEFUL REST?

I t's a still day on the river, hot and heavy. A miasma of oil and rotting vegetable matter rises from the water's surface. Chiara sits on the deck, half-heartedly fanning herself with a book about nutrition in pregnancy. It's been unusually quiet on the boat these past few days; maybe people are too frightened to come here any more, preferring to take their chances alone at home. Chiara couldn't blame them. The Rosie Lee feels temporary, fragile, like over-ripe fruit about to split open.

In five more days, she's leaving for Wales with Salvador. She's tried to persuade Liz to come with them - her health might improve with clean air and fresh food - but so far the stubborn old midwife has refused to consider it. Chiara will keep trying though; she owes it to Liz to care for her in her retirement. She pictures them there together, a little family. It will be almost like being home again, except better because Salvador will be there.

She glances at her phone: no messages from Salvador. Which is okay, she tells herself. He's busy working extra shifts to maximise his savings for their new life together. And he's still looking for an opportunity to snatch one last haul of medications from the Genesis Centre pharmacy. Forcing herself to put the phone aside, she opens the book and tries to read, but the words aren't going in. It's pointless anyway, advising women to eat iron-rich foods when they're barely surviving on potatoes and stale bread. She's about to fetch herself a drink of water when she hears sounds of stirring from Liz's cabin.

Liz has scarcely got up these past few days, except to use the toilet or brew herself mugs of strong tea laced with morphine. Chiara expects her to make her usual slow, fumbling way to the bathroom before returning to bed, but she's wrong. Liz emerges onto the deck, fully dressed, with her hair combed and tied back. Her face looks a little less sallow than usual, and she doesn't mutter her usual expletive as she bends down to put on her shoes.

'Are you going out?' Chiara can't hide the surprise in her voice.

'Uh huh.' Liz buckles her sandals with self-absorbed focus.

'Are you sure you don't want to rest? If we're running out of water, I can fetch some. Or shall I go and see if the shop has any flour?'

'No. No need.' Liz steps off the boat without a backward glance and walks away at a half-decent pace. listing only slightly to one side. She doesn't acknowledge the two old men who live in a tent under the bridge, but makes her way wordlessly up the slope towards the road.

Chiara hesitates. Liz might want some fresh air, but she's so obviously unwell - what if she were to collapse out there on her own? If she needed to see a pregnant woman, or sort out a clinic, surely she would have said? Chiara's been doing most of the work anyway, and she knows all their recent clients. Something's not right.

Chiara takes a furtive look inside Liz's cabin. There's a sour smell, and the bed is unmade, piled high with pillows and blankets. A packet of pills sits on top of the locker: *Dexamphetamine Sulphate, 5 mg.* Two tablets are missing from the packet. Chiara has her suspicions, but she looks it up in Liz's formulary to make sure: amphetamines. Liz has always been good at getting her hands on drugs. Now she's taken a large dose of stimulants and disappeared. But why?

Is it to do with her health? Has she gone to look for a doctor, or more medication, or - a horrible thought hits Chiara. Liz has always been disparaging about the Peaceful Rest programme - killing off the old and useless, she says - but what if her illness is really bad? The adverts are there all the time, on social media and the video billboards: '*Find comfort, rest and loving support at a Peaceful Rest Centre near you.*' Would Liz do that, without even saying goodbye?

What was it she said the other day? Something about having to deal with her own business, and everything being over soon. Was this what she meant? Did she want Chiara to move out so she could end her own life? A chill creeps over Chiara's skin. No, not on her own. Not like this. They don't let relatives or friends into the Peaceful Rest Centres in case they try to 'coerce' you to change your mind.

Nonna died on her own and I wasn't there to hold her hand. I came home from work and her fingers were curled and cold.

Chiara grabs a black Femband. She might be wrong, but she has to find out. Liz is her friend - the best friend she has in London, apart from Salvador. Yes, she can be grumpy, and infuriatingly distant at times, but so what? I'll care for her right to the end if she needs me, like I should have done for Nonna.

When she reaches the road, Chiara looks left and right, but there's no sign of Liz. A woman sits at the street corner with a plastic carton beside her.

'Have you seen an old lady go past? Just a couple of minutes ago. Short, wearing an red shawl?'

The woman points across the bridge towards the city.

'Seemed to be in a hurry,' she says, revealing a toothless mouth. 'Any spare change, sweetie?'

'Thanks so much.' Chiara drops a couple of coins into the beggar woman's carton and hurries on. In the distance, she spots a red figure plodding steadily towards London's dense forest of skyscrapers. Yes, that's her! Chiara picks up her pace.

LIZ KEEPS MOVING, pausing only a few times to catch her breath. Chiara follows at a distance, doing her best to shelter in door-ways or behind heaps of rubbish when Liz stops. She daren't confront Liz until she is certain where she's going.

When they reach the checkpoint, Liz shows something to the soldier on the barrier, who nods and lets her through. A Peaceful Rest authorisation letter, perhaps? There are Centres outside the city limits too, but they let you choose your place of death as a final treat.

Chiara's burner Femband gets her past the barrier - she'll have to discard it as soon as she leaves the city - and she follows Liz to a tram station. It's easier here to hide behind other trav-ellers. Liz boards the next tram, and Chiara hops on at the back behind a group of women in Orthodox Jewish dress. She should have brought a hat or scarf to cover her hair.

Liz gets out at The Strand. Tower-blocks line the streets; their mirrored surfaces hurt Chiara's eyes after the softer shades of the river. Shoppers and city workers throng the busy walkways. Chiara glances about nervously for any hospital staff who might recognise her. Don't get distracted, she scolds herself, as she follows Liz past acres of plate-glass windows full of designer dresses, handbags, and steel kitchen appliances.

Liz seems refreshed from her tram ride and has picked up her pace despite the oppressive heat. Those amphetamines must be powerful, but how long can they last? Liz seems to be heading for Whitehall, but why come all this way to be euthanised? She must have passed three or four Centres already. Chiara gnaws at her finger-ends, trying to make sense of it. A few moments later, Liz walks right past the entrance to the Charing Cross Peaceful Rest Hub without a sideways glance. Chiara shakes her head: she was wrong. Liz is here for something else.

46

ELECTRONIC DOCUMENTATION

L ouis leaps up at Rava, yelping and barking before she's half-opened the door. He looks podgy and floppy around the jowls. There's a chewed patch on the sofa and another on the rug. He must be here alone every day until late, poor little dog. Rava lets him lick her hands and face.

'Martin?' she calls, just to be sure, but he's at work. The apartment smells stale. She tiptoes from room to room like a burglar, gathering up one or two last items: a photograph from the day they got engaged; a bottle of perfume; a picture of Louis when he was a puppy.

She was worried Martin's study door might be locked, but it opens straight away. He must have got used to having the place to himself. Feeling as if she's being watched, Rava goes straight to the filing cabinet. For a horrible moment, she thinks Martin must have changed the combination, but when she tries again, the lock clicks open. Thank God!

The folder marked *'Personal and Family'* is still there in the bottom drawer. She sinks to her knees and rifles through it. Right at the back, she finds it: the all-important piece of green paper certifying the marriage of Martin Anthony

Robson, bachelor, to Rava Fazel, spinster. Easy. She slips the certificate into her bag, closes the cabinet, and locks it.

Rava straightens up and rubs her aching back. As the baby bunches and squirms, a new sensation grips her. It's a tightening across the top of her belly, as if someone has wrapped a scarf around her stomach and pulled on it. It doesn't hurt, not really, and a few seconds later the feeling has passed. Right, time to be going.

She glances around the room, checking she hasn't disturbed anything. Will she ever come back here again? A trace of Martin's amber cologne pierces the stale-cigarette smell, and she pictures him looking at her the way he used to. Even after all the things he's said and done, she still can't quite believe it's over.

I can't leave without saying goodbye. On an impulse, she picks up a pen from the desk and searches for something to write on. She'll leave him a note; it's the least she can do.

There are no papers on the desk; *'clear desk, clear mind,'* Martin likes to say. So she pulls open the top drawer. Inside is a plain cardboard folder. Without thinking, Rava opens it and pulls out a sheaf of papers.

A printout lies on top with long lists of names and numbers. Some names have been altered, or crossed out, and figures amended in Martin's neat handwriting. He's used green ink to make the changes. Something to do with the hospitals, Rava supposes. She's about to replace the papers, when a note falls out. It's written in blotchy biro in an entirely different hand:

> *Dear Martin,*
> *For electronic documentation supplied as agreed:*
> *Licences: 673*
> *Certificates: 981*

Registration Portfolios 359

BESIDE EACH ITEM is a considerable sum of money. The letter concludes with the words:

Usual arrangements,

and an illegible scrawl. Underneath this, Martin has drawn two lines with his green pen, scoring deep into the paper, and added the words:

Done, but no more.

Beside this is a little drawing, also in green. Rava can't make out what it is at first, but when she looks again she sees it's a tiny man suspended from a hangman's noose.

47

THE PINNACLE

A shiny glass tower called *The Pinnacle* dominates Whitehall. Several Government departments have their offices here, including Housing and Resettlement, Transportation, and the Ministry of Population and Health. The Defender doesn't work here though; she lives at the Palace surrounded by private parks. Chiara took pictures of its famous marble facade on a sightseeing tour when she first arrived in London.

Today, the granite-paved square outside the Pinnacle bustles with men in suits and women in high heels. Police with guns patrol the street corners. Sunlight sparkles off the fountains. Chiara feels out of place, but plump little Liz in her scarlet shawl stands out like an interloper from another planet. Surely she didn't mean to come here? Has her illness made her confused? Enough is enough; she has to stop Liz now - she should have confronted her sooner.

Chiara dashes forward, but before she can reach her, Liz has marched past the weird, blobby works of art, past the security guard, and right up to the revolving glass doors. A moment later, she is swept inside, vanishing into the steel-plated heart of Government.

Chiara gasps. She halts so abruptly she almost bumps into an irritated-looking man with a bald head. It's not safe here. Has Liz gone mad? Chiara covers her face with her hands, fighting to control her breathing. Don't run; don't panic. You need to know what she's doing.

Step by nervous step, Chiara edges up to the Pinnacle entrance and peers inside. The guard has moved from his post by the door and is standing beside the reception desk, eyeing Liz with suspicion. An enormous flower arrangement stands at the centre of the lobby. Important-looking people hurry in and out of the lifts.

Before she can change her mind, Chiara lets the turning door draw her in. The blast of air conditioning does nothing to slow her racing pulse. She ducks behind the bird-of-paradise blooms and twisted bamboo stems, praying the guard doesn't look this way.

Liz is arguing loudly with the receptionist.

'I need to see him today,' she demands. She's got her elbows on the polished surface, leaning in.

'Do you have an appointment, Madam?'

'No. But I have to see him today.' Liz uses what she jokingly calls her *'midwife voice'* - the one you don't argue with.

'Well -.' The receptionist looks at her screen. 'Martin Robson is a very busy man. He has a full schedule of meetings. But I suppose I can make enquiries. Whom shall I say is here?'

Liz places both hands on her wide hips.

'Just tell him it's Liz,' she says. 'He'll know who I am.'

Chiara clasps a hand to her mouth as the floor shifts like quicksand under her feet.

48

UNFINISHED BUSINESS

The dewy young receptionist is rattled. She does her best to hide it under that glued-on smile they obviously teach them in receptionist school, but Liz can see the girl's shapely bosom rising and falling a little too fast. Liz isn't surprised; she knows she looks out of place in her old shawl and grungy sandals. Everyone at the Pinnacle wears designer suits and smells of money.

'Do you have identification, Madam?'

Liz can't resist a smirk; it's a long time since anyone has called her 'Madam.'

'Nope. But you can tell him I'm missing my cat if you like.'

The receptionist's eyes widen, and her candy-pink nails fly to her lips. She peers up at Liz from beneath unfeasibly long eyelashes.

'Sorry, did you say - cat?'

'Yes. Martin Robson had my cat murdered.'

The girl flinches. Poor thing; she's not going to want to relay that to the boss, is she? Martin's doubtless a total shit to work for.

'I'm sorry, but you're going to have to leave. Mr Robson would be very angry if -.'

'I bet he would.'

Liz has had enough. She doesn't have time to be messing about. Out of the corner of her eye, she spots the next lift arriving on the ground floor and spewing out an assortment of well groomed ladies and gents. With perfect timing, she turns tail and ducks inside, ignoring the receptionist's startled squeaks.

She presses the button marked Executive Level and whizzes up to the heights. Here the carpets are inches deep, and the modern art on the walls will have cost an arm and a leg. Another excessively made-up woman guards a waiting area with uncomfortable-looking chairs, but Liz walks quickly past. Halfway down the corridor, she finds a door conveniently labelled: *'Mr M. A. Robson.'* She raps at it with her knuckles.

'I'm busy right now, Sonia,' calls a voice from within.

Liz opens the door. The room is spacious and bright, with a view of all the posh parts of the city. Martin's sitting behind a desk. In the moment before he looks up she sees that his hair is turning grey. She closes the door behind her and strides up to the desk.

'Afternoon, Martin,' she says. 'It's been too long. We need to talk.'

MARTIN RECOVERS QUICKLY; Liz gives him full credit for that. He sweeps all the papers on his desk into a folder and locks them inside a drawer. Then, without making eye contact, he says,

'Who let you in here?'

'I let myself in. The woman downstairs did her level best to protect you, so please don't blame her. This is all my doing.'

Liz lowers her bulk into one of the oh-so-swanky leather chairs.

'Why are you here? I thought I told you -.'

'Yes, you told me. Sixteen years ago you told me you never wanted to see me again. And I've stayed away all this time. But we've got unfinished business, you and me. Plus, I was under the impression you've been looking for me. Thought perhaps I could save you the trouble.'

Liz catches him stealing a glance at her. His right eyebrow twitches; that old problem hasn't gone away then.

'I've got nothing to say to you. Can't you see I'm busy? There's nothing between us. I have a new life now. A new life.' He mutters the words like a mantra.

'Nonsense. There's a great deal between us. Look, Martin, I'll admit I was angry about my cat.' He opens his mouth to speak, but she interjects. 'Oh, don't tell me you weren't behind that. You're right at the head of the witch hunt; I've seen your media appearances. Not that you got your own hands dirty, of course, but it's not worthy of you, Martin. I loved that cat. Why couldn't you just come straight for me?'

'I didn't -.' he begins, then, 'This wasn't the way I wanted it.'

His face twists into an expression Liz can't read, and she wonders for a moment if she misunderstood. Was the graffiti and Gaskin's killing some random mob violence? But no matter; she's not here for revenge. She needs to compose herself, get this right. She won't get another chance.

Liz takes a deep breath. A fierce gripping in her side tells her those drugs are wearing off.

'Martin, I came to say sorry.'

Martin rolls his eyes.

'Yeah, right,' he mutters, sounding like an angry teenager. 'Do you think you can blackmail me, is that it? I've got friends more powerful than you can dream of.' He reaches for a button on his desk.

'Please, Martin. Let me say what I came to say, and then throw me out if you must.'

'You think saying sorry is going to change anything?'

'Probably not, but I need to say it anyway. I haven't been well, Martin. I've been thinking about the past, and the way things turned out. We got on all right at first, didn't we? And let's face it, you wouldn't be here, in this exalted position, without me. But things got complicated, and the whole midwifery thing took over, and I'm sorry.'

Her words hang in the air. His lip flickers, and she notices how tired he looks.

'It's a bit late for that now. I'll never trust you again.' Martin's voice is almost level, but Liz knows him too well to miss the wobble of self-pity. He clenches his fists. 'Why have you come here whining, trying to justify yourself, after the way you abandoned me? I don't care if you're sorry. It won't change anything. And so what if your disgusting cat died? Did you cry all night over its corpse? Was it your precious baby?' Martin spits out this last word as if it might poison him.

'Yes, I cried,' Liz says. Grief comes easily nowadays, with her choices worn so thin. She stares up at Martin, taking in his diamond cufflinks, his sharp suit, and his clean hands with their bitten fingernails.

'Are you happy, Martin?' she asks him.

He seems surprised by the question. He says nothing. Then he swallows, and she can see his Adam's apple move up and down in his throat.

'What's happiness got to do with anything? Does happiness save lives? Anyway, what would you care? I'll be glad when I've put a stop to you and your cronies messing about with what doesn't concern you. Why can't you just retire? Wouldn't that be more fitting at your age?'

'I would love a leisurely retirement, but my skills are still needed, more's the pity. If the Government cared about the nation's health, it would provide adequate maternity care and genuine choice for all. Until they do, desperate women will keep knocking at my door. What can I do? Turn them away?'

'Send them to the hospitals for a legal caesarean section. Haven't you heard about the Safe Deliveries policy? No one buys your lies about natural births any more.'

Liz laughs.

'Safe Deliveries? When did you last visit the People's Slaughterhouse? Or watch healthy young women being sliced open for no good reason at your Genocide Centre, come to that? Female fertility's a messy business, isn't it? You want it sanitised out of existence.'

Martin's hand moves towards the button again. Liz squeezes the arms of her chair.

'Martin, listen. I'm getting away from the point. I'm sick, okay. I won't be able to carry on much longer. Everything's a mess, and I know why you hate midwives so much, and I wondered if we might be able to work something out, you and I? Some sort of reprieve? I came here -.'

Liz falters. A coil of pain is weaving in and out of her ribs like a flesh-eating worm. She rehearsed a whole speech on the way here. How she never meant things to turn out this way. How they used to make things work between them. How she'd love a chance to try again.

But Martin flicks an invisible speck of dust from his lapel. His mouth twists into a sneer.

'I told you already,' he says. 'It's too late. You don't under-stand what's at stake here. There won't be any reprieve, as you call it.' He pauses, and maybe Liz imagines it, but she thinks she sees his lip tremble. 'It's all much too late,' he repeats, looking stricken, and she wants to comfort him but of course he won't let her. 'Is that all you came to say?' he finishes.

Liz lowers her head, catching her breath against a fresh bite of pain.

'Right. That's all then. I have important work to do, safeguarding the nation's health. No one needs you anymore. Sonia will see you to the lifts.'

He walks to the door, opens it, and stands there waiting for Liz to leave.

Liz doesn't move. Her whole left side seems to be on fire, and if she stands up she might scream. He snaps his fingers at her.

'Come on, I don't have all day. Don't you have some filthy breeders to be getting back to?'

'Why don't you just arrest me now?' she asks.

'Oh, I think you know, or you wouldn't have marched in here bold as a crow. I need hard evidence so I can close you down for good. Don't worry - it won't take long; soon there'll be no more midwives, no more pandering to women's fantasies, no more births outside Government control. People will thank me then - all the sacrifices I've made! I never needed your help, Liz. Never.'

His eyebrow jumps.

'This is over. Finished. You'll never see me again. Now get out of my office before I call Security to drag you out.'

49

BRAXTON HICKS

I t's oppressively hot outside, with thick clouds gathering and a sense of the sky pressing down. A late summer storm is coming, but please God, not yet, not until she's safe in Aberdeen. The tram is crowded and Rava has to stand all the way back to Jess's flat. Just once, when she's nearly there, her belly tightens again like it did earlier. Nothing to worry about, she tells herself. It's not time for the baby to come yet; these are just those 'Braxton Hicks' practice contractions they tell you about.

She packs and re-packs her bags, triple-checking every-thing. The taxi is booked for eight in the morning. She and Jess hug and say their goodbyes, and Rava promises to send pictures of the baby. She gives Jess one of her gold necklaces to say thank you, and Jess says 'you didn't need to,' but puts it on and looks pleased.

All evening, Rava wonders if the tightening feeling will come again, but it doesn't. By the time she settles down to try to sleep for the last time on Jess's uncomfortable sofa, she's almost convinced she imagined it.

50

INTERFERENCE ON THE LINE

Chiara kneads her forehead with her knuckles. She's sitting on a bench on the New Embankment, gazing out over the wide, muddy Thames. She's lost track of how long she's been here, but the light is beginning to fade. It won't be long until curfew, when the police round up any Mollies with black bands lingering on the city streets. She needs a plan.

Did Liz simply mean Martin Robson is onto them - that he knows she's a midwife? Did she go to hand herself in? But something in her tone implied more. *'Just tell him it's Liz,'* she said to the receptionist, as if she and Martin were on first name terms - as if they actually knew each other. Liz never talks about her past, but she used to work for the Government hospitals. Could she and Mr Robson have been colleagues once, when she was a senior nurse and he a raw, young manager? Does she know something about his past?

Maybe Liz hoped to make a deal. Might she have information that could embarrass that horrible man? Or - no, surely not, it's unthinkable - but Chiara owes thousands of pounds to the Genesis Centre where she's supposed to be working in the laundry. If Liz returned a runaway to the authorities, might they agree to leave the Rosie Lee alone?

No, Liz would never do that, would she? Perhaps she offered herself to protect Chiara, or someone else? But that wouldn't work; if Liz has handed herself in, Chiara won't be safe. They'll come for her next. Is that why Liz kept urging her to leave the boat?

But why didn't she tell Chiara what she was planning? Liz has said some strange things these past few weeks:

'*You need to leave, Chiara.*'

'*There's some old stuff I need to clear up.*'

'*Martin Robson will know who I am.*'

What did she mean? Liz can be distant and downright difficult sometimes, but Chiara's always thought she could trust her. Now, though, she can't be sure.

She dials Salvador's number again. He'd know what to do, but she's been calling him for hours with no reply. The phone rings three times and goes to voicemail, like all the other times. Gritting her teeth, she dials again, with the same result. Did he say he was working a late shift today? She could go to his apartment, but she's left his key on the Rosie Lee and he might be working all night. Hanging about outside the Genesis Centre doctors' accommodation would be asking for trouble.

With a sigh, she gets up and makes for the nearest tram station, calling Salvador's number several more times on the way. If she returns to the Rosie Lee, will the police be waiting there to arrest her? But where else can she go? Nowhere feels safe.

Finally, as she joins the hordes of black and yellow-band workers crowding into the station to go home, he picks up. Thank God!

'Salvador. I've been calling and calling.'

There's a pause and a crackle, and she presses the phone to

her ear, straining to hear over the noise of an approaching tram.

'Chiara? Is it you?' He speaks very slowly, and there's something different about his voice - thick, as if he's got a cold.

She cuts in on him.

'I'm so worried, Salvador. It's Liz - she went to the Pinnacle. The MPH building. Wait - it's too busy here.' Chiara spots a toilet sign at the far end of the platform. She dashes inside and bolts the door, inhaling a sharp reek of urine. 'Are you still there?' In the hot little cubicle, she spills out her story.

'So, I don't know what's going on, or where to go now,' she finishes. 'Should I come to your apartment, d'you think? The boat might not be safe.'

He's silent for so long she thinks they've been cut off.

'Salvador? Can you hear me?' The phone indicates that the call is still live, but there seems to be interference on the line. 'Salvador?'

She's about to hang up and re-dial when he speaks.

'Don't come here. Chiara. Not tonight. Go back to the boat.' Again that thick voice, as if he's drunk, or been taking drugs.

'Is something wrong, Salvador?'

Another gap, another crackle, then he says,

'I'm not feeling well. Sorry, Chiara, but you should stay away. You don't want to catch this.'

'Oh no! Shall I come and look after you? D'you need me to bring some paracetamol?'

'No, Chiara!' He speaks so fiercely she flinches. 'Don't come. It's a sickness bug, okay. Look, you've most likely misunderstood, with Liz. She's a good person. You should -.' He stops speaking, and she thinks for a moment she can hear voices in the background, but it's only the crowds out on the platform. The rattle and whine of a tram drowns everything out for several seconds.

'Sorry, what did you say?' she tries again. 'I'm worried, Salvador - you sound really sick.'

'Go back to the boat, Chiara.' He pronounces each syllable carefully, as if he's having trouble getting his mouth round the words. 'And don't call me again tonight.' He hangs up.

Chiara stares at the phone. Her eyes sting and water from something more than the ammonia rising from the filthy floor. Uncomprehending, she unlocks the door and steps outside into the bustling, lonely city.

51

TO THE AIRPORT

Rava wakes early and goes to the bathroom to pray. It's difficult to prostrate herself now she's so big, but she does her best. She will need God's help today. The familar dawn prayers take her back to her childhood with Mama at her side. God willing, she'll be in Scotland tonight. All she has to do is get to the airport and board the plane.

As she stands up, a sudden pain makes her catch her breath. It's like those tightening sensations yesterday, but stronger, as if invisible hands are pressing on her belly. She holds the edge of the washbasin and takes deep breaths, trying not to make any noise. Jess had a boyfriend over last night and she mustn't disturb them. The pain soon passes, and she goes to the kitchen; she ought to eat something before the journey.

She pours cereal into a bowl, but she isn't hungry. Just nerves. But as she lifts the spoon to her lips, she knows she's going to throw up. She barely makes it to the bathroom. Vomiting makes her feel a bit better, but another tightening sensation grips her while she's cleaning up the mess. It's nothing, she tells herself. It'll be gone in a moment. Only Braxton Hicks.

Rava drinks a glass of water; she must have eaten something that disagreed with her, that's all. She checks her luggage for the last time. These are all her possessions now; she's had to leave so much behind. On top of her few clothes and toiletries lie her copy of the Holy Qur'an in its linen wrappings, her most precious photographs, and Mama's white baby dress. From the side of the bag, she pulls out a brown padded envelope. Is it worth taking this? The case is heavy and her backache is worse than ever this morning.

She upends the envelope and tips out the little black phone the midwife gave her, along with a slip of paper with a few words in curly handwriting:

Heartsease. 065775 35290. 064398 87012.

The password is the name of an English flower, the midwife said, and the phone numbers are for contacts in her network. Rava's kept it all this time, just in case, but she won't need it now. Still, best not leave it behind, in case Martin should find it.

A buzz on her phone tells her the taxi has arrived, so she shoves the envelope back in her bag, puts on her shoes, and hauls her baggage down to street level. But as she steps outside, a fresh pain seizes her, so sharp and sudden she can't suppress a gasp. She clutches her middle, only looking up several seconds later to see the taxi driver staring at her with concern.

'You all right, Miss?' he asks. 'Not going to give birth in my cab, I hope!' He laughs nervously, and Rava does her best to smile. Does she really look so pregnant? She thought the chador hid everything.

'Where're you off to then, love?' he asks, picking up her case. 'They said Heathrow Airport, but I'm wondering if they should've said the hospital.' He raises his eyebrows.

'Ha, ha! No, Heathrow, please.' Rava settles herself on the back seat, clutching her smaller bag with the documents and all her gold jewellery inside. The traffic is bad, and it's stuffy inside the car.

'Would you mind turning up the air conditioning please?' she asks. Don't throw up, she tells herself over and over. She sits very still and forces herself to look out of the window; Mama always said that helps with motion sickness. Music blares from the radio as Rava mops sweat from her forehead.

They make it as far as Chiswick before she has to ask the driver to stop.

'I'm so sorry, but I need the toilet. Would you mind?'

The petrol station washroom is beyond disgusting. That awful smell hits her the moment she gets inside. Un-flushed faeces float in the bowl, reminding her - Oh, God, no! She falls to her knees and vomits, closing her eyes to fight the flashback. This cramping pain; it was like this, all those years ago, in the college toilets when she was seventeen. There was so much blood. She heaves again, and again.

At last, Rava drags herself to her feet, but at once another pain begins to rise and spread, her abdomen clenching down on itself, rock hard. She drops back to her hands and knees, allowing herself a little moan as she sways back and forth. This can't be happening.

A 'toot toot' from the taxi outside penetrates her conscious-ness; she needs to get moving. As soon as the pain subsides, she washes her hands and splashes her face with cold water. The Genesis Centre doctors said vaginal birth is extremely dangerous. Come into the Centre immediately, they all said, if you have any regular tightenings, any discharge of blood or mucus, any abdominal pain. You could bleed to death, they told her.

But if she goes to a hospital now, she'll miss her flight, and they won't let her keep the baby. She won't get another chance, and neither will Amani. These pains might turn out to be nothing; they stopped overnight, didn't they?

Back in the taxi, the traffic slows to a crawl.

'What time did you say your flight was, Miss?'

Rava clenches her teeth as another pain takes hold. If she can keep quiet, if they can get to the airport soon, she can still get on the plane. It takes ages to have a baby the old way, doesn't it? Once she's in Aberdeen, Aunt Nasreem will know what to do. This is probably a false alarm; it has to be.

The music fades out on the radio as the announcer cuts to the newsroom:

'Several arrests have taken place outside medical centres across London this morning. Extremist religious and far-right groups have taken to the streets demanding a downgrading of the Government's Safe Futures policy. The Minister for Population and Health issued a statement this morning, reminding us all that limiting family size is essential to ensure the wellbeing of biodiversity and our beautiful planet Earth. Meanwhile, wildfires continue to blaze in Cambridgeshire -.'

'Ruddy tree-huggers!' The taxi driver snaps off the sound. 'I reckon you're doing the right thing, love. Can't be easy though, with all these sodding rules and restrictions. You sure you're all right back there?'

'Yes. Are we nearly there?'

The rain begins as they approach the motorway exit. First a few heavy drops hit the windscreen, then a noisy spattering, then a torrential roar. Even with the wipers at top speed, the view of the road ahead is all but obliterated.

'Coming down cats and dogs,' says the driver. 'Hope it doesn't - .' The rest of his words are lost in a crack of thunder.

The traffic stops and starts, and it's another fifteen minutes before they pull up outside Terminal 5. The wind tugs at Rava's skirt as she climbs awkwardly out of the car.

'Got your passport and all that?'

'Yes, thank you. How much do I owe you?'

It's more than she expected. She'll have to sell some gold once she gets to Aberdeen.

'Thank you,' Rava says again, and picks up her heavy case, but as she does something shifts inside her. There's a sharp pain, the strongest yet, and she feels warm, wet fluid running down her legs.

'Oh my God,' she cries, 'it's really happening!'

52

STORM SURGES

Rain pummels the roof of the Rosie Lee. It's almost midday but the sky outside is black. The ducks have disappeared, and a million raindrops pit the river's furious surface. As Chiara watches, an island of rubbish spins past the boat, rushing downstream on the current. Sodden rags tangle with shards of wood and discarded bottles, all topped with a mildewed flip-flop.

Chiara tugs back the curtain and presses call on her phone. Straight to voicemail. Again.

She imagines Salvador lying on the floor, passed out in a pool of vomit. It might be serious; there's been typhoid in some of the camps. She should go to him, but she dithered earlier, her brain glitching after a sleepless night, and now the storm has broken. She chews at her fingers, pacing the tiny kitchen; the narrowboat has never felt so small.

Liz's door is closed. She returned late last evening looking terrible. '*Tomorrow,*' was all she could say in response to Chiara's barrage of questions before tottering into her cabin. Chiara crept in a little later to offer a bowl of soup, but Liz was fast asleep and snoring.

A crack of lightning turns everything blinding silver. Chiara switches on Liz's old-fashioned radio. The reception crackles and sputters.

'*Storm surges ... anticyclonic conditions ... severe storm warning. Heavy rain, strong winds, and flooding in low-lying areas are expected over the next twenty-four to thirty-six hours, posing a significant risk to safety and property. Citizens are advised to stay indoors and avoid all non-essential travel. As a safety precaution, London's city perimeter checkpoints will be closed except to emergency services.*'

Chiara knows exactly what Liz would say to that: '*Safety precaution, my arse!*' She pictures the thousands of people evacuating the camps all along the marshes: mothers piling bedding into wheelbarrows and strapping babies onto their backs; children dismantling tents and shelters; old men pushing their possessions in shopping trolleys. Many will make for the the city with its tall buildings, flood barriers, and perimeter canals, only to be turned away.

Chiara sighs, picks up her phone, and tries Salvador again, with the same result. At least while the storm lasts, she and Liz should be safe from the authorities. The security services will have more than enough to occupy them for the next few hours. After that?

I'll get my things together, she decides, ready to leave later. She'll go to find Salvador as soon as the storm dies down. She goes to her cabin and is pulling out her rucksack from under the bed when a tumultuous banging erupts right over her head.

SHE THINKS it's thunder at first. The rain hammers relentlessly as lightning shatters the sky. But the banging comes again, and this time there's a rhythm to it - something human - that makes Chiara's heart race in response. It's Salvador, here at last, knocking for her to let him in out of the rain. She's at the door at once, turning the locks and pulling back the bolts.

'One moment,' she shouts. 'Thank God you made it. Did you -?'

She swings open the door and stops, taking in the shape huddled on the bank. It isn't him. At first the disappointment is all she can register, but then she sees it's a woman - a heavily pregnant woman wearing something tent-like and sodden. Her head and neck are covered, but a few strands of hair cling to her terrified face. Rain runs down her neck and streams off the bottom of her dress.

'Is this the midwife's boat?' she asks. 'I called the number, and a man came in a jeep and brought me here. He made me throw away my Femband. But it was so far, and there are so many boats.' She clutches at her middle, pain contorting her expression. 'Oh God, help me please!'

'It's okay - you've found us. Come inside, quick, out of the rain. Is anyone with you?'

'No. I am alone.'

Chiara helps the woman onto the Rosie Lee, holding her cold hand down the steps. She heaves inside the woman's large case and her smaller holdall, wondering how she managed all this luggage on her own and in this state. Water puddles on the floor as the woman starts to shudder and sob.

'I thought I was going to die. I thought the baby would come in the car, or out there in the storm. Oh!' She lets out a long, anguished moan which rises to a scream.

A slug of guilt hits Chiara low in her gut. She's been so busy trying to contact Salvador she forgot to check the work phone for messages. She should have gone out to meet this desperate, half-drowned woman from where the driver dropped her off.

'Will I die?' the woman asks, wide-eyed, after the contraction passes. 'They say women bleed to death; if God wills, I accept it. But please, if you can, save my baby!' She glances left and right like a hunted animal. 'I was trying to get to Scotland, but - .' She grits her teeth and screws up her face. 'Ya Allah, another!'

Her cry rises shrill above the drumming of the rain. Chiara thinks fast. She needs to get the room warmed, the bed and floor covered, blankets and towels ready. And this petrified woman needs to feel safe enough to give birth.

'I'm Chiara. What's your name?' she asks, when the surge is over.

'Rava.'

Chiara takes hold of Rava's hands and looks into her eyes.

'It's okay,' she says. 'You don't need to worry any more. I'm here, and I won't give up on you. Yes, that's right, take some long, steady breaths. I'm going to look after you, Rava.'

BETWEEN RAVA'S CONTRACTIONS, which are coming every three minutes, Chiara lights the lamps, stokes up the stove, and helps Rava change into a long, clean nightdress.

'How many weeks are you? When did these pains begin?' She recognises Rava now: the pretty, petite woman who asked about finding out her baby's sex at the Genesis Centre all those months ago. The one who didn't want her husband to come to her scans. And she came to the church clinic - two months ago, was it? - and vanished again.

Rava's fear clings around her like static. Chiara can hear it in her shallow breathing, see it in her widened eyes, smell it behind the traces of expensive perfume.

'Is my baby okay?' Rava asks as the next surge rises, her fingernails digging hard into Chiara's wrist.

'We'll check in a minute. Are you having a boy or a girl, do you know?'

Rava responds with an anguished wail.

'A girl,' she gasps, after the pain peaks, 'But something is wrong. It hurts so bad.'

'It's all right; these pains are normal. See, that one's going away now. Can you come and lie down here, Rava, and let me feel what's going on?'

Chiara begins her examination, doing everything she now knows so well, talking to Rava as she goes to reassure her. Everything seems healthy. The contractions are strong, and the baby girl's head is low in her mother's pelvis. Chiara listens to her heartbeat with the pinard before settling Rava into the rocking chair with a hot water bottle behind her back. Then she goes to knock on Liz's door; sick or not, loyal or not, they're alone together for now. And Chiara might need her help.

When there's no reply, she goes in and shakes the old woman to rouse her. Liz looks a hundred years old, white-faced and limp, all yesterday's vigour long gone.

'What is it, my love?' Liz asks blearily. But as soon as she comprehends the situation she scolds Chiara for not calling her sooner. 'I'm fine,' she protests when Chiara offers to fetch some painkillers. 'Stop fussing over me and get yourself back to the woman.'

When Liz is up and dressed, Chiara tells her what she has done so far to care for Rava. Liz nods approvingly. It's amazing how a birth always seems to reinvigorate the old midwife. Once she's reviewed Rava's vital signs and listened to the heartbeat herself, Liz sits down to knit a soft, mauve hat for the coming baby. She watches, saying little, but creating a calm atmosphere by her mere presence, while Chiara tends to Rava.

As the minutes lengthen into hours, Rava finds her rhythm, greeting each surge with a long, low moan instead of a scream. Chiara prepares Liz's labour elixir, sweetening it with the last of their honey, and offers it to Rava in small, frequent sips. She mixes a few precious drops of frankincense essence into safflower oil and rubs the blend into Rava's feet. She sterilises all the instruments for a birth in the large pan on the stove. The baby is well-positioned, her heartbeat reassuringly lively. The rain on the roof steadies to a constant, soothing patter.

ONCE OR TWICE, Rava begins to say something about her husband.

'I tried everything. I begged and pleaded, but he said I was going crazy. He sent someone to follow me, and - oh!' She bows her head as the next contraction rises.

'All right,' Liz says, her hand on Rava's shoulder. 'Let it go for now, Rava my love. Once your baby's here, we'll have plenty of time to sort things out, don't you worry.'

As soon as the surge is over, Liz clicks her tongue, and goes to poke up the stove, muttering something uncomplimentary about men under her breath.

BY LATE AFTERNOON, the storm is still blowing, rocking the Rosie Lee on the rising current. The weak daylight is almost gone.

'Can I get you a cup of tea, Liz?' Chiara asks. Liz's face creases into a smile.

'Thank you - that would be perfect. You make an excellent cuppa, and you'd be amazed how few people I've said that to in a long life.' Chiara fills the red kettle as Liz adds, 'Nice and strong, mind.'

'Yes, I know.' Chiara spoons tea leaves into the pot.

'And another thing,' Liz goes on. 'I've been meaning to say this for a while, my love, but anyway, here it is. You're one of the best nurses I've ever worked with - kind, caring and brave - all the things that matter. And you're a ruddy good midwife too. Your Nonna would be proud of you.'

'Really? Are you sure?' Chiara's heart does a little leap in her chest.

Liz rolls her eyes.

'Have you ever known me flatter anyone? Whatever happens, Chiara, remember that Nonna of yours and you won't go far wrong.'

'I will. Thank you, Liz - I can't tell you how much that means. And I was meaning to ask -.'

But at that moment, Rava lets out a long, unmistakable bellow. Her labour has reached the pushing stage.

53

EVERYDAY MIRACLE

Rava kneels on all fours in the rosy, sage-scented belly of the Rosie Lee, her head lowered, her bottom rocking from side to side. Amniotic fluid drips from her, sweet like almonds. Powerfully and gently, she eases her child into the world with Chiara and Liz beside her. Liz has her hands poised to welcome the baby.

'Yes. Yes,' Liz says. 'She's almost here, Rava. I can see her beautiful head. She's coming. Breathe softly now.'

Together, the three women form a circle, sharing the everyday miracle. Liz and Chiara watch and wait. Rava pants, her body opening. Liz's face is pink in the lamplight. She holds a warmed pad of clean linen in her hand, and now she applies it to Rava's perineum to give support as the head crowns.

Rava's voice rises into a great cry, and, like the sun edging its way over the horizon, the baby's head slides into view. Clear fluid drains from the infant's nose and mouth. The little face turns towards Rava's thigh, and, for a moment, mother and child pause, amazed at where their long journey has brought them. Then Rava pushes again, and Liz's hands are ready, and the child is here. Amani throws out her arms and shouts to greet the air.

She is perfect.

54

A LOCKET

'Can I hold her?' Rava reaches out, still gasping from the burning fullness and the hot, sudden release. 'Here you are!' The baby is slippery, warm, wriggling, alive. 'Is it you? Are you mine?'

'That's right, put her on your chest, nice and close.' Liz helps Rava nestle the baby between her breasts, snuggling her in with a warm towel. Rava strokes her damp hair in wonder, kissing her over and over. Amani has pink cheeks and a velvety head that smells like sweet saffron cakes. Her grey eyes are wide open, solemn and trusting.

'A gorgeous little girl,' says Liz. 'Congratulations; yes, she's all yours.'

'Oh, thank God. Thank God!' The baby's tiny face is peaceful, her skin impossibly soft. She has limbs, toes, fingers - everything.

'You're mine. I'm your Mama.' Amani turns her head towards Rava's voice.

'Is she hungry? I don't have any bottles or anything.'

'You can feed her yourself,' Liz says. 'Let her take her time and she'll find her own way, you'll see.'

Rava's not sure; people say breastfeeding hardly ever works. But the baby flips her face from side to side, squirming and digging her toes into Rava's belly. Soon she opens her lips wide and takes in a big mouthful of breast. A tiny tongue laps at Rava's skin, and soon the baby is sucking long, deep gulps as if she's been doing this forever.

Rava bends her head and whispers the holy name of God into her daughter's ear, just as her own dear Baba did when she was born. Amani's father isn't here, so Rava must take his place. She prays the Arabic prayers for God's blessing and protection, and when Amani pauses her sucking to listen, Rava feels a stab of love, pure and intense. She would die for this child.

Delivering the placenta hurts more than she expected, but Rava would gladly go through the whole birth again to have Amani here in her arms. With the baby still at her breast, she borrows one of the midwives' burner phones to call Baba and Aunt Nasreem. It's a poor connection and she struggles to hear what they're saying, but there's plenty of relief, joy, and praises to Allah.

'Thank you so much,' she tells Chiara and Liz after hanging up. 'You saved both our lives; I can never thank you enough.'

'Nonsense, you did it yourself,' Liz says.

'You breathed her out so calmly,' Chiara adds, 'You knew just what to do.'

'It was amazing. I had no idea what birth was like; everyone told me you need an operation. I was so scared, but in the end it was beautiful. Thank you, thank you.' Rava makes a prayer gesture with her hands.'

'You're more than welcome. Do you have a name for your little one? She's got lovely eyes.' Liz takes off her glasses, polishes them on her skirt, and puts them on again, staring at the baby's face.

'Amani. It was my mother's name.'

'Amani,' echoes Liz. 'That's beautiful. Is your mother still alive, my love?'

'No, she passed away when I was twelve.'

'Oh, I'm sorry.'

'Yes, I still miss her, especially now.'

'I know.'

For a few moments, nobody speaks. The wind howls outside, and Amani suckles, her mouth soft but remarkably strong. Liz breathes with an audible wheeze.

'Now, you must be hungry too, Rava. Let me see what we've got.'

But as Liz gets to her feet, she sways and her face turns a doughy white.

'You sit down, Liz,' Chiara interjects. 'I'll sort it out.'

Liz sinks heavily into the rocking chair. She must be tired, of course, but Rava can't help noticing the bluish tinge around the old lady's lips and the careful way she supports her left side with her right hand. When Mama was sick, towards the end, she had that same glassy, faraway look.

Chiara gives Liz something to drink and suggests she goes to lie down, but Liz only shakes her head. She seems to want to stay close to Rava and her baby. And she was right about Rava being hungry. When Chiara brings homemade bread, thickly spread with jam, Rava devours it as if she hasn't eaten for weeks. Only when she's savoured the last crumbs, and Amani is milkily asleep in her arms, do her thoughts turn to what happens next.

'I missed my flight,' she tells Chiara. 'I was going home to Scotland, but now -.' Rava looks at Amani, so small and help-less, and her chest tightens. 'My husband said he won't sign the papers for her, because she's a girl, so I won't be able to get her registered, and I don't have anywhere else to go. She'll need a passport.' Rava's voice wobbles; it's impossible. She's missed her chance to get Amani away to safety.

'Try not to worry,' says Chiara, resting a hand on Rava's shoulder. 'We have helped people before. There are safe houses, and drivers.' Her glance flies to Liz, who is still staring wordlessly at Amani.

'I've spent nearly all my money. I had to pay for my father's treatment.' She can't even afford another taxi back to Jess's place, not that Jess would let her stay there with a baby. 'I have some gold, though. Perhaps it will be enough? It's in my bag over there.'

Chiara hesitates, but, when Rava insists, she picks up the holdall and rummages inside. Her eyes widen as she pulls out the heavy gold necklaces, Mamma's filigree brooches, and the box with the diamond ring.

'There's more,' Rava tells her. 'Find it all, please.'

Chiara protests that it's too much; that they'll help her whether she can pay or not, but Rava is adamant. She'd sell every last thing to keep Amani safe.

'Will it be enough, do you think?'

'More than enough,' Chiara says slowly. She finds a wooden bowl and heaps the gold into it. It spills over the sides. 'Liz? Do you think we can find a contact to help?'

Rava and Chiara both look at Liz, who opens and closes her bloodshot eyes several times. She raises a hand to tell them to wait a moment, pulls out a tube of tablets from somewhere in her clothing, and swallows a handful of them. Only then does she perch her half-moon glasses onto her nose and peer into the bowl, poking at the necklaces with a shaky finger. She fishes out an old ring with a small red stone in a heart-shaped setting and holds it up to the light. Rava doesn't think that one's worth much; she's not even sure where it came from.

'Liz?' Chiara asks again. 'Rava needs us to make arrangements, to get them to Scotland?'

But Liz still doesn't answer. She puts down the ring and roots around in the bowl again as if she's looking for something. Breathing heavily, she selects a locket on a fine gold chain. It's tangled around a chunkier necklace, and she untwists it carefully, taking her time.

It's a pretty little piece, but very old-fashioned. Rava's never worn it. Liz holds the locket between her thumb and forefinger, turning it over. There are letters engraved on the back.

'Where did you get this?' Liz asks, almost accusingly.

'Martin said that was his mother's, I think.'

Silence hangs in the air between the flickering lamps and the sleeping baby. Rava clasps a hand over her mouth. This is worse than last time! She promised herself she wouldn't mention his name. If they guess, they won't trust her - how can they? The midwives have been good to her, kind, not asking questions, but now Liz's whole body is shaking. With fear? Fury? She thinks Rava's a spy. She's going to throw them out - her and Amani - into the storm.

Liz removes her glasses and rubs at her eyes. She buries her head in her hands.

'What's the matter, Liz?' Chiara asks, looking scared herself.

Liz looks down at Amani, then back at the locket. Her cheeks have a new flush of colour.

'Martin?' she says. 'Your husband's name is Martin? Martin what?' With a fingernail, Liz prises open the locket, taking care not to let whatever is inside fall out. Rava didn't even know it opened.

'It's not what you think,' she mutters desperately. 'I didn't have anywhere else to go.'

'Is it Martin Robson? The Under-Secretary of State for Womens' Health? You're Martin's wife, aren't you?' Liz leans in much too close, inspecting Rava with a new intensity. Her breath smells sour.

'It's not my fault.' Rava clasps Amani close. 'He doesn't know I'm here, I swear. I've told you the truth. Please, let me stay here with my baby, at least till the rain stops.' She shrinks away from the angry midwife, but there's nowhere to hide.

'Martin Robson?' Chiara jumps to her feet. 'You're married to that man?' She looks almost as panicked as Rava feels.

'Martin Robson,' Liz repeats. She puts down the locket and takes a long breath, in and out. 'It's all right, both of you. No one needs to run away, at least not yet. I didn't mean to scare you, Rava, but it was such a shock, although, I had suspected, once or twice. But I told myself I was going crazy; it couldn't be. And perhaps I should've come clean with you, Chiara, but I didn't think it could matter, at least not now. Anyway, Martin Robson -.'

Liz mops at her forehead with her handkerchief.

'It's a long story,' she says, 'but Martin was my little boy.'

55

ALFIE

'I didn't dare believe it.' Liz picks up the locket again. Inside are two curls of fine, blonde hair. 'My twin babies.' Her crumpled cheeks are wet with tears.

'But I don't understand.' Chiara backs towards the door. 'Are you saying that terrible man is your son? Is that why you went to the Pinnacle? I thought you were going to hand yourself in - or me perhaps?'

Liz shakes her head. A gust of wind rocks the boat on its mooring. Rava holds Amani close; she's not sure who anyone else is anymore.

'It's more complicated than that. Sit down, Chiara, and I'll do my best to explain.'

Chiara frowns, but she perches on the step, keeping close to the exit. Amani stirs and starts rooting for Rava's other breast.

'You're a hungry one, aren't you?' Liz's voice is tender as she helps Rava reposition the baby. 'I never imagined this; I don't deserve it, that's for sure. I supposed Martin might have a child one day, though it didn't seem likely, given his views.' She snorts. 'But I never thought I'd get to see my grandchild, let alone help her into the world.'

Her grandchild. Rava wonders if she might be dreaming. Liz is Amani's grandmother?

'I've never been religious,' Liz says. 'But this -.' She gazes at Amani, who is feeding contentedly, oblivious to the emotions she has stirred. 'This is a gift I never expected.'

In a low voice, pausing now and then to sip at her tea or wipe her eyes, Liz begins her story.

'THIRTY-NINE YEARS AGO, the twins were born. You never forget a night like that. Martin slipped out no trouble, but the second twin, Emily -'. Liz's mouth contorts. 'Let's just say things went wrong. She was starved of oxygen: damaged. Floppy and feeble, with her lolling head and her sideways arms and legs as thin as twigs.

'At first, the doctors thought she might do all right. It would be a lifetime of care - my life as good as over - but what could I do? I loved her. Endless hours of physiotherapy, all the hospital appointments, surgeries, tube feeds - I did it all. I massaged her hands and feet to stimulate the circulation. I stayed up all night, every night, keeping watch on her oxygen levels. Marriage fell apart, of course; he didn't have the patience. It was a relief, to be honest, when their dad packed his bags and left; I didn't have the energy for the rows.'

'How did that affect Martin?' Rava asks. 'Is this why he doesn't want a girl, d'you think?'

'Part of it, I expect, but the whole population-reduction bollocks is inherently anti-female. I fed Martin, kept him clean, and all that, but I don't remember much of it; all my worries were focused on Emily. Martin smiled, rolled over, and crawled at all the right ages. A textbook healthy infant. He was bright - used to stack up bricks in neat little towers and line up his toy cars. A bit late talking maybe, and slightly on the small side, the health visitor said, but he seemed massive compared to Emily. And never any trouble.' Liz sighs.

'When Emily turned two, the doctors' faces changed. She'd had so many infections, they said. Her lung function was damaged. There was too much strain on her heart and kidneys. She'd stopped gaining weight, despite the high-energy feeds. Her oxygen and her meds were all maxed out. I begged and cried; I even prayed. But the doctors shook their heads. Take her home, they told me. And people said, *'Perhaps it's for the best.'*

Liz fingers the gold locket, silent for a long moment.

'Well-meaning friends said I should be grateful I still had a healthy child. And other crap like that. Of course, Martin was never ill.' Liz shakes her head. 'It wasn't his fault, poor kid. But whenever I looked at him - those grey eyes and long lashes - I saw Emily's face on the wrong body. It felt like he was mocking me. So when he whined for my attention, I told him to go and play. And after a while, he stopped whining. I knew, deep down, he was too well-behaved, too quiet.

'That first year after Emily died, I only wanted to join her. But gradually - it was like waking up with a hangover - the fog started to clear. I remembered this lovely nurse from when Emily was tiny. She used to sit and hold my hand; never talked a load of patronising rubbish like the rest of them. She made a difference. So once Martin started school, I applied for nurse training. It would fill the long days, if nothing else.

'Martin grew into a skinny kid, clever, picky about his food, wore glasses. I think he got bullied at school; some of those boys were total shits. I offered to speak to the teachers, but he begged me not to. You'll only make things worse, Mum, he said.' Liz shifts her position, and winces.

'I qualified as a nurse, and then a midwife, worked all the hours. I loved it, though the pay was never great. We lived in a cottage on Mersea Island, right out on the Essex coast. It used to be joined to the mainland by a causeway.'

Liz's shoulders drop and her eyes seem to lose their focus. Thunder rumbles somewhere in the distance.

'When Martin was nine or ten years old, he found this dog. Alfie, he called him. Alfie was a scruffy mongrel with a grey, whiskery face, and sad eyes, and he followed Martin everywhere. No one else claimed him, and Martin seemed happier, so I paid out the extra for dog food each week. Maybe Martin told Alfie his worries; he never talked much to me.

'I was working in Colchester back then, before all the floods and fires. It was getting tougher to be a midwife - constant legal cases and Government investigations. You had to watch your back all the time. C-sections were rapidly becoming the norm, but it wasn't the law, like now. A few women still had home births; those were always my favourite. Of course nowadays we're all supposed to worship the great god Technology!'

Liz makes a spitting sound and rolls her eyes so violently Rava worries she might strain a muscle.

'Anyway, I thought Martin would be safe when I was at work because he had Alfie to keep him company. Alfie was an excellent guard dog, very loyal.' Liz takes a swig of her tea.

'Martin was almost fourteen when the first big flood happened. The weather forecast was bad, but we were used to storms on the island. We had no idea what was coming. A woman went into labour somewhere on the mainland, so off I went, leaving Martin alone in the cottage. And that was the night the sea breached hundreds of miles of defences. It was apocalyptic.

'I was desperate to get back to Martin, but the phones weren't working and most of the island was underwater. Parts of the causeway were washed away; no one had imagined the tides could reach that high. At least our cottage was on top of a hill; Martin would have the sense to stay indoors, I hoped. I tried and tried to call him. I tried to borrow a boat, but every-thing was chaos.' Liz shudders.

'By the time I made it home, the cottage was in darkness. I found Martin hiding in the big cupboard in the upstairs back bedroom, sitting with his back to the wall all curled up and hugging his knees. He was soaking wet and shivering, and he wouldn't speak - not a word.

'I had to drag him out of there; he was taller than me, and heavy. I dried him, and wrapped him in blankets, begging him to tell me what had happened. In the end, he found a scrap of paper and wrote down one word:

'ALFIE.'

'Alfie always slept on Martin's bed, but he wasn't in the cottage. I searched the garden and the shed, and next morning, after most of the water had gone down, I walked halfway round the island, calling his name. The destruction was horrific; huge trees swept away, houses destroyed, cars upturned, and boats in the street. I knocked on a few doors, but no one had seen a wispy grey-and-white dog. Everyone had bigger things to worry about. Thirty-eight people had drowned on Mersea Island alone.

'Alfie's body washed up two days later. Martin found him - he'd been searching through the debris on the beach - and brought him home. My poor boy sat rigid, red-eyed and awake for a day and a night with the corpse in his lap, clutching at handfuls of Alfie's hair. When at last Martin fell asleep, I dragged the stinking carcass into a wheelbarrow and took it down the lane to bury on a piece of waste ground. I worried for weeks in case Martin found the place and dug it up.

'Martin's speech came back, but he wasn't the same. None of us were. You couldn't feel safe - couldn't trust the dry land under your feet. No one trusted the old Government any more;

everyone was scared. Then along came the Defender promising a new heaven and a new earth. Of course we all voted for it; even I did, back then. We thought there'd be a rebuilding programme all down the east coast, with improvements to the sea walls and maybe our causeway replaced with a bridge. There was going to be fabulous healthcare, free university education, and hardly any crime.

'The protected cities policy went down well at first; it was all voluntary, and people got nice new homes at affordable prices. But then they started talking about a points system, and there were rumours about coastal defences being abandoned. Mersea Island's population collapsed overnight as everyone scrambled to get a foothold in a safe city. Before we knew it, the local school was closing.

'I suggested moving to Colchester, more for Martin's sake than mine; I'd grown fond of the island over the years. But Martin wanted to go to boarding school. They were offering scholarships for bright children from coastal areas to be educated in London, and Martin was always ambitious. Plus, he was furious with me.

'"You've never given a shit about me, have you Mum?" he said. "You only ever wanted a girl, and after she died you replaced her with everyone else's babies."

'What could I say? He was at least half right. So off he went, to a fancy school and a life I could never have given him. I'd lost my son, and most of it was my own fault.'

56

FULL OF SURPRISES

'Did he come for the holidays?' Rava asks. Martin's never wanted to talk about his family; that was something the two of them had in common. London's the perfect place to re-invent yourself.

'Less and less,' Liz replies. 'He found friends to stay with, and before I knew it he was off to university. I missed him - cried a lot the first year - but you can get used to anything. In many ways, it was easier. I was working long shifts in the hospital, and the few times I saw Martin, we were both treading on eggshells.' Liz stares into the middle-distance.

'Did you lose touch altogether? Did you know he was married?' Chiara has questions too.

'He got First Class honours from City of London University.' Liz's lips form a sad smile. 'I went to his graduation, but he barely acknowledged me. Not long after, he sent me a message telling me not to contact him again. Broke my heart, but what could I do? So I followed his career online - watched him climb the ranks of the Defender's Party. He's been in the news quite a bit, especially this last year. But I never saw him again in the flesh, until yesterday.'

Chiara tries to interject, her face pink with frustration, but Liz holds up a hand.

'I'm coming to that,' she says, 'but first, yes, I knew he was married, though I didn't know his wife's name. Five or six years ago, wasn't it?'

'So when did you suspect Rava?' Chiara demands. Rava flinches.

Liz takes a long swallow of her tea.

'It's okay, Rava, don't worry. Chiara, I'm sorry, but let me explain my own way. When you came to the clinic, Rava, and gave your surname as Robson, I did wonder. And you had that posh bag - just the sort of thing Martin's wife might carry. But the way you were dressed confused me; I never thought Martin's wife might be Muslim. You didn't come back, and I've not been too well, these past weeks. Had a lot on my mind. But then you turned up here.

'When you said about your husband not wanting a girl, I thought, yes, that could be Martin. But I still assumed I was going crazy. But the locket; it was a gift to me from my mother - those are her initials on the back. And this little one -.' Liz's voice catches as she gestures towards Amani. 'There's something about her mouth, and her eyes; she reminds me so much of Emily.'

Liz is crying properly now. Rava gazes at Amani's face.

'Liz,' Rava says, 'I'm so sorry about everything that happened. I don't think it was all your fault, not at all, but even if it was, you've more than made up for it. All the babies you've saved! And now you have a family again.' She wraps Amani in a blanket. 'Would you like to hold her?'

Liz nods several times and wipes her eyes. She takes her granddaughter and lays her lovingly in her lap, cradling her head in both hands.

'Do you want a pillow to rest her on?' Chiara asks, but Liz doesn't seem to hear. She caresses the tiny child as if she's never seen a newborn before, stroking her forehead with the tips of her fingers, taking in the long lashes, the cloud-soft skin, the delicate ears. As Rava watches, Liz's face - *my mother-in-law,* she marvels - seems to grow smoother, her bearing stronger, as if a spell has cast her back to her youth.

Amani's eyes flutter open, and she looks up at Liz, grave and knowing.

'Hello, my love,' Liz greets her. 'Well, isn't life full of surprises! I'm your Granny.'

57

RESTLESS

Chiara's still got unanswered questions, but this is a holy time, as Nonna used to say. She sits quietly, watching and wondering, while Liz holds her granddaughter. At last, Amani begins to whimper.

'Here, she needs her Mum,' Liz says, passing her back to Rava. 'I just need a little rest, and then we'll - oouf!' Liz tries to get up, but collapses back into her chair, clutching at her left side. Chiara's throat tightens.

'What is it, Liz?'

Liz's breathing is ragged. She gestures with her right hand towards the tap and starts fumbling for her painkillers.

'Didn't you take some tablets not long ago?' Chiara asks. 'And Liz, I'm sorry, but, yesterday, when you went into the city? I'm still confused. Are we safe?'

'Give me some water first.' Pain strangles her voice.

Liz swallows another handful of pills. She closes her eyes and blows out each breath, her hands bunching up her skirt. When she looks at Chiara, her face is shiny with sweat. She speaks in a taut staccato.

'Okay, I'll keep this short. I'm sick. Have been for a while.

Cancer. Too far gone to do anything. Don't want their peaceful effing rest. Was planning my own ending - scuttle the old Rosie Lee and go down with her. Just needed you safely out of the way, Chiara. Not your mess.'

'But, Liz -.'

'Hear me out. I wanted to see my boy one more time. Say sorry. But he didn't want to know. Too busy trying to save the world.' Liz mops her forehead with a trembling hand. 'So that was that. All over, I thought. Until now. Suddenly, I've got a grandchild and a daughter-in-law to look after. We'll sort this all out somehow. Have to. But first, a little rest.'

Liz reaches shakily for the edge of the kitchen surface with her right hand. Refusing Chiara's offer of help, she drags herself to her feet. Her eyes roll upwards, and Chiara is scared she might fall. But after a few shuddering breaths, Liz gathers the shreds of her strength.

'I need to lie down. Wake me in an hour,' she mutters, and staggers to her cabin.

IT'S EASIER to work than think, so Chiara busies herself changing sheets, tidying equipment, and cleaning the kitchen. She checks Rava's bleeding, which is minimal, and gives her some chamomile tea. Rava sings Amani a lullaby - something low and sweet in a language Chiara doesn't know. The baby is soon asleep. Rava's reluctant to put her down, but they all need to rest, so Chiara tucks Amani into the cradle at her mother's side.

'Try to get some sleep. She's had a good long feed, and it's been an exhausting day.'

Rava's eyes are dark-shadowed, but she can't settle.

'Poor Liz - she looks so sick. Do you think Martin might come here? He had someone following me not long ago; he said I was psychotic. But he didn't use to be like that - he's changed; I think he's in some sort of trouble. I'm worried, Chiara. I need to get to Scotland with Amani. How soon can we leave?'

Chiara's head and limbs ache; she scarcely slept last night for worrying about Salvador.

'Let's sort things out in the morning. Try not to worry now.'

'But the gold - will it be enough? We need to go soon before Martin finds us. Did you say there is a safe house? How much will it cost?'

'I'll contact someone first thing in the morning. Now, why don't you lie down?' Chiara stifles a yawn.

'Please look after the gold for me. If there's any left over, you can give it back once you've made the arrangements. I know I can trust you, Chiara.'

'I'm sure there's no need -.'

Chiara tries to object, but in the end she scoops the gold jewellery into a drawstring bag and puts it in her own pocket alongside Nonna's rosary beads. It's the only way to pacify Rava. She'll give it back tomorrow.

WHEN EVERYTHING IS clean and Rava is sleeping at last, Chiara pulls on her raincoat and wellies. She needs to clear her head.

It's still raining outside. The river laps only a few centimetres below the level of the bank and the mooring lines have grown dangerously tight, so Chiara jumps ashore to slacken them. Soft mud squelches under her feet. Her task completed, she gives the Rosie Lee an affectionate pat on her old wooden flank.

There's no sound from inside the boat. Chiara's fingers close around the phone in her pocket. *'Never make a personal call when there's a woman on board,'* Liz always says. *'They want to catch us in the act.'* But the roads will be flooded from the storm, and Salvador's sick. She won't be able to rest until she knows he's all right. Perhaps he's been trying to call her. It can't hurt to try just once.

There are no missed calls. Her stomach feels as if someone is tying it into knots. Her hands are cold from wrestling with the ropes, and she has to stab at the phone's rain-spattered screen several times before it responds. She holds her breath - it'll probably go to voicemail - but then he speaks:.

'Chiara? S'you?' His words slur drunkenly together. He must be really ill.

'Salvador, how are you feeling? I've got so much to tell you, about Liz, and Martin Robson, and this woman - you'll never believe! I tried calling you earlier, but you didn't pick up, and I wanted to come over, to see how you are, but the the storm was so bad, and then this woman came, and -.'

Salvador makes a sound somewhere between a grunt and a moan, as if he's been punched in the stomach.

'Oh, *amore mio,* you sound so poorly. I can't come right now; we've got a newborn on the boat and Liz is sick. Will you be all right until tomorrow?'

There's a moment's silence; a bad signal, slow to connect in this weather. Then comes a crackle, and she can hear him breathing. He must have got the TV on because she can hear voices in the background.

'Salvador? Can you hear me? Shall I come over in the morning, after we've found a safe house for this mother?' She pulls the hood of her coat closer around her face. There's more crackling, and then he says,

'Don't come here. I'll come to you. Where are you?' It seems to cost him an effort to pronounce each word.

'No, Salvador, you're not well enough to travel, and there'll be floods. I'll come to your apartment as soon as I can. You stay in bed.'

'Where are you?' he asks again. *Never give out our location when there's a woman on board. Not to anyone.* Chiara hesitates. He sounds so sick; he might be delirious.

'Don't worry about us,' she says. 'We're fine; you look after yourself.'

'Where are you? I miss you, Chiara.'

She pictures him, ill and alone. How high is his fever? Could it be typhoid?

'I miss you too, *amore mio.* So much! Now listen, we're about a mile north of Tottenham Lock, moored up near the old bus depot. But please, don't try to come tonight; go to bed and rest. Call an ambulance if it's really bad. I'll call you again in the morning, I promise. Now listen, I have to go; I have to keep an eye on the new mamma and her baby. Salvador?'

She waits, but the line has gone dead. She tries again, but this time there's no reply. It's 1.00 am, and the towpath is deserted; nobody will be out in this weather. Time to get warm and dry inside. But as Chiara pulls off her boots and hangs up the dripping raincoat, the knot in her gut tightens.

58

SPLINTERING

'Welcome to Aberdeen and thank you for choosing to fly with Net Zero Airlines. Please check you have all your hand baggage before disembarking.'

Rava joins the queue of people pressing to get off the plane. At the door, she realises she's left something behind. She wants to go back, but the crowd pushes her out into the rain, and she has to carry on, down the steps and onto the tarmac. At the bottom, Baba is waiting to meet her.

'Where's the baby?' Baba asks. 'You told me you had a baby.'

Rava looks down at her empty hands. There's a huge hole inside her; how could she have forgotten? She turns and tries to go back up the steps and onto the plane, but the people are still coming down. Hundreds of faceless people. And her legs won't move.

'Oh no!' she begins, and looks back at Baba, but he has turned into Martin. Martin's expression is blank, but as she watches his eyebrows, lips, and cheeks all start to twitch and convulse.

'You have to come with me,' Martin says. 'You're not well. The baby was a parasite.'

He tugs at Rava's clothing, and the ground wobbles under her feet as if it's melting. She tries to pull away, but she trips and falls onto the sticky, melting tarmac. It clings and creeps like glue, sucking her under.

RAVA OPENS HER EYES. Her heart is racing. She rubs at her face, but there's no melted tar. She's lying in an unfamiliar bed under a low, wooden ceiling. She feels sore, and there's a pad between her legs. A dream; it was just a dream. No need to be scared: Amani's here, sleeping at her side. Rava reaches out to touch her. The room shifts, but that's just the river; they're still on the midwife's boat.

The interior is dimly lit by a single oil lamp. She can just make out Chiara, asleep in the chair, her head lolled onto her chest. Rain thrums on the roof. Rava checks her watch and shifts her position, trying to get comfortable. Only a dream. But then the boat wobbles again - a sharp, sideways roll - and she hears something. A man's voice.

She sits up, hyper-alert, and listens. She can hear several voices now, right outside. She can't catch what they're saying, but they're very close. A powerful instinct tells Rava to pick up her baby. She pulls the little hat Liz knitted onto Amani's head, as if this will keep her safe. Amani stirs and begins to cry, but Rava shushes her to be quiet. She puts her to the breast and listens again, holding her breath. Have the men gone? Did she imagine them? The inside of her mouth is dry.

Suddenly, the white beam of a torch tracks across the window, its light piercing the curtain.

'I think there's someone -,' Rava begins to say, her voice shaky, but before she can finish, the boat lurches, as if someone heavy has jumped aboard. A heart-splitting shout shatters the quiet:

'Police! Stand clear of the door!'

Amani shrieks. The whole boat shudders, and Chiara leaps to her feet. A crashing thud and a horrible sound of splintering bursts open the door. Before Rava can move or speak, men crowd into the narrow space, trampling, smashing and yelling:

'Get on the floor! Now! Armed police!'

Blinding lights. A rush of cold air. Men in body armour, stinking of sweat. A woman's voice screaming. Red and blue flashing lights. Guns.

Rava wraps her arms around Amani, trying to shield her. A hand tears at her shoulder.

'Baby's here, guv! Give me the baby!'

'No, she's mine! Leave us alone!'

'Stop it! Liz, stay where you are!' Chiara's on her knees, a man standing over her.

'Shut up, bitch!' The man aims a kick and Chiara falls silent.

Amani is frantic, arms and legs flailing. Rava tries to hide her under the blankets, but the man yanks them away. The scream comes again, hurting her ears and her throat. It's me, Rava realises. I'm the one screaming. Someone shines a torch into her face; she's blinded.

'Get off! Let go of me!'

The man's fingers are bruising her shoulder. He's pulling her out of bed; if she falls she'll crush the baby, but she mustn't let her go. She tries to make herself rigid.

'Chiara, help me!'

But one of the men has Chiara by the wrists and he's dragging her to the door. Dogs howl and yabber nearby. The man makes a grab for Amani.

'Give it here, you stupid cow.' Rava shakes her head, tears burning. 'This is a crime scene, so do as you're effing told.'

She tries to twist away, but the man has both her shoulders.

'Look at me, bitch.' She bares her teeth, yelling wordlessly at him, and he lands a stinging slap on her cheek. In the shock, she loosens her grip on Amani, only for a split second, but it's enough. The man snatches her away.

'No!' Rava's on her feet, vaguely conscious of a hot gush of blood between her legs. 'Give her back!' She tries to claw at the man's arm, to bite him; she screams and pleads, but he carries Amani away through the door into the cold mist outside.

'Give her back!'

Rava tries to go after him, but another man grabs her from behind.

'Shut up and keep still!'

She tries to struggle but the man's too strong. He clamps a hand over her mouth. Amani's gone. Flashes of light shine on her empty cradle.

'This one's the breeder, coming out now.'

The man shoves Rava forwards, through the narrow belly of the Rosie Lee, past Liz's stove, past the shelves of jars and bottles, and the rocking chair. He forces her up the steps, out into the wind and rain. Cars, lights, and men are everywhere. Sirens blare. Where's Amani? Which way did they take her?

Another man grabs Rava and lifts her down off the boat. Her bare feet slip in the mud.

'Where is she? What have you done with her?' There are so many vans, so many people. She stumbles on the hem of her nightdress, sobbing and begging:

'I'll do whatever you want. Please, give me back my baby.'

'Oi, listen to me!' Another man, his face too close, his breath foul. 'Quieten down. No need for hysterics. We're taking you to the hospital. Come with me.'

'Have you got my baby? Is she in that ambulance? I won't go without her.'

'All right, listen,' the man says. 'I'm going to hand you over

to the paramedics. You've convinced me you're the mum, what
with all that yelling. It's not you being arrested, all right? Just
the old witches. Come on. They'll take your baby down the
hospital too, sort you both out from there. And guess what?
People's Hospital's all full up tonight, so they're taking you
down the Genesis Centre. Luxury pad, where all the celebs go.
Lucky, or what? You've hit the jackpot, girl.'

59

MECONIUM

'*O Dio mio!* Where are they taking her?'

The doors of the ambulance slam shut behind Rava. Chiara can still hear her screams, calling for her baby.

'None of your business, bitch.' The policeman twists Chiara's wrists. He smells of dog overlaid with cheap after-shave. Her calves throb where he kicked her to bring her down, but she makes herself focus on the bodily pain. It hurts less than everything else.

She can't believe it, can't take it in. They hauled her out here into the rain. So many lights, so many people - but his was the first face she saw. He was standing right there, beside one of the cars, lit up in the blue flashes. He looked different, with a swollen eye and bruises on his cheek, and she tried to tell herself it wasn't him. It couldn't be. Not Salvador. She was hallucinating; she'd made a mistake. He would never -.

But then he looked at her, and she knew: Salvador betrayed her. He betrayed them all.

She called out his name, but he turned away. The policeman dragged her over here to the riverside and she stopped trying to struggle. She looked back one more time, but Salvador was gone.

Rava's ambulance drives away, sirens wailing. The water at Chiara's feet churns and rushes, thick with half trees and pieces of people's homes. She told Salvador their location. Tangles of weeds and plastic and strangled masses of what might be human hair whirl past like a giddying fairground ride. Salvador brought the police. The water might top the lock gates, gushing out of control. She trusted him. Liz is dying. They dragged Rava out, screaming for her baby. There was blood on her nightdress. We were going to get married, have children together one day. He betrayed me.

The policeman presses himself against her, and Chiara realises sickly that he's enjoying this. He speaks into her ear: 'Didn't know some of you witches was young girls.' His breath is wet. Chiara squirms, trying to loosen his grip, but he jabs a knee into her thigh, so that she pitches towards the foul, surging water. As she gasps, he jerks her back. 'Gotcha.'

A shout comes from the boat and the barking of the dogs rises to a crescendo. Catching her breath, Chiara looks up to see Liz emerging onto the prow deck. She's struggling to get through the narrow doorway. No, that's wrong; she's holding onto the frame with her good arm, resisting, while someone shoves her from behind. She's going to fall; she'll break her ribs. Her mouth is moving, but Chiara can't hear what she's saying over the wind and the baying of the hounds.

A second later, Liz comes hurtling out like a cork ejected from a bottle. She grabs at the hook where they hang the lantern and stands there, swaying. The headlamps from the cars are trained onto the deck, and in this cruel light Chiara sees how Liz has changed since their first meeting all those months ago. Her face looks like a deflated balloon, skull-thin and greenish-yellow. She's thin and gaunt, her teeth almost all gone. Her hair has escaped its bun, frizzing out into a wild, white halo.

The dogs quieten, the wind drops for a moment, and Liz's voice carries across the water:

'I'm the midwife. I'm the one want. Arrest me, and let the others go.' She sounds calm and steady, as if she's talking Chiara through a tricky birth complication.

'I don't think so, Grandma. Come on.' A police officer pulls at Liz's left arm, her bad one, and she doubles over in agony. Chiara can't bear to watch. She closes her eyes, but Liz is speaking again. She's calling out one word, repeating it, syllable by syllable:

'Mec-on-i-um.' Meconium. It's their code word. Liz wants Chiara to run away, but how can she? Can't Liz see she's being held here? The policeman is a hard, sweaty wall behind her; he's pulling her arms up her back. Her head's spinning, dizzy, red and blue lights inside her brain, circling. If only she hadn't called Salvador. If only -.

Another shout rings out:

'Hey! Come back!'

Then another voice, sounding alarmed:

'Help over here! The old cow's making a break for it.'

The policeman holding onto Chiara gasps. He takes a step backwards, momentarily letting go of her wrists. She looks up at the boat, and her mouth drops open. A bright-haired figure stands on the roof of the Rosie Lee, silhouetted against the sky. How? Chiara screws up her eyes, and looks again. How did Liz get up there? She must have surprised them, broken free. Did she pretend to be weaker than she felt, to put them off their guard? Liz was always good at clambering around the boat, until recently, but even so. A burst of adrenaline, maybe?

The men rush up after her, but they're not used to the river and the boat is pitching crazily. One of them wobbles as if he's about to fall. They hesitate, and Liz edges away from them along the roof, balanced precariously above the water. She can't escape that way. What's she doing?

As the wind roars, Liz calls out again, and her voice is strong, ringing over the storm:

'I'm the midwife. I'm the one you want. Come and get me!'

Then, as the men lunge towards her, Liz jumps.

60

RUNNING

She hits the water with a splash. The boat lists violently and the men stagger, arms flailing almost comically. Liz's white head appears, hurtling past Chiara's feet, then disappears, before bobbing up again. She's being swept downstream, rolling over and over like a log. She can't swim, and she's sick, with a bad arm and shoulder.

'Liz!' Chiara squeaks, knowing her friend can't hear her.

There are two - three more splashes as police officers plunge into the river. One swims a clumsy front crawl in Liz's direction, but a large sheet of floating plywood sweeps him off course. Straining her eyes, Chiara thinks she can see Liz spinning on the current. All those shawls and skirts must be weighing her down. She rolls over one last time before vanishing into the blackness.

Chiara takes a step, then another, before she realises no one is beside her. The man who had hold of her wrists has rushed to join the others chasing after Liz. Chiara's alone. No one's paying her any attention; all the police are running along the towpath, calling for ropes and lifebuoys. They're shining torches onto the river, sweeping their beams to and fro.

'If it all goes down, and you hear me say "meconium," leg it, Chiara. Run. Don't come back for me.' Liz's words come back, a clear command in her head. Red and blue lights dance on the river, almost festive, like a carnival. Nothing else makes sense, so Chiara runs. She turns her back on the water, and the lights, and Salvador, wherever he is, and runs into the moonless night.

———

SHE HARES UP THE TRACK, trying to stay in the shadows. She's barefoot; there was no time to find her shoes when they dragged her off the boat. Barks and yelps echo on the air; if the dogs have her scent they'll be on her any second, bringing her down with their teeth. Unless it's a bullet in her back. Will she hear the shot before she feels it? Something sharp rips the sole of her foot, but she doesn't pause, mustn't stop. Keep running.

Gasping for breath, she follows the road uphill under a line of pylons. She's exposed up here, but the marshes are flooded, cutting off the way back to the river. Her lungs sob and wheeze. The braying of the dogs fades, but she daren't slow down; the men will surely be after her. They'll want to bring in a midwife, and she's the only one left. Her feet sting as if they're being sliced open and something's thumping against her thigh. She thrusts a hand into her pocket and finds Rava's gold, bashing and bruising with every step.

Lights blaze up ahead from one of the power stations burning rubbish to fuel the city. Instinct tells her to stay in the dark places, so she runs between empty warehouses, some with fires burning inside. Refuse workers and scavengers live in these broken buildings. Would they offer her shelter or greet her with the jagged stump of a bottle? She can't risk it; there might be a price on her head already.

In a shadowy corner, she pauses to catch her breath,

bending half-double and gasping. But a sudden cracking sound makes her heart stop. They're behind you. Keep running.

She staggers on, past stinking mountains of waste and empty, flooded marshes. Rain plasters her hair to her face, her clothes to her body. Her feet are red balls of agony. She flinches at every sound. At every turning, she heads what she hopes is away from the river, away from the city, but nothing looks familiar anymore.

Her foot catches on a stone, and she flies forwards, grazing her hands and knees, but she picks herself up and keeps going. Soon she falls a second time, landing heavily on one hip. Throbbing stripes of pain dance in front of her eyes: mauve, orange, and lime. It's almost a disappointment when the colours fade and she has to get up again and carry on.

The road ends at an empty yard, ringed by high wire fences. The gates stand open and Chiara limps inside, following the fence towards a distant building. She doesn't think she can go much further. She can't feel her feet anymore, which is a relief, but she keeps stumbling and tripping. More than once, her vision darkens and she has to grab at the wire to steady herself.

At last, she reaches the skeleton of a burnt-out car, and the building beyond. The windows are boarded and graffiti covers the walls. No lights are visible, and she can't hear any sounds from inside. The main door is bolted and barred behind a heavy steel grille, but there's a porch with an overhanging roof around to the side. She half-walks, half-crawls towards it.

The porch is in deep shadow. Low walls border a wide concrete step creating a sheltered space almost long enough to lie down in. Chiara reaches gingerly into the corners, feeling with her fingertips: dead leaves, damp cardboard, rags, and - *Mamma mia!* - something soft. Animal? Human? She shrinks back, pulse racing, but it's just an old blanket. She tugs at the edge of it, and something small and terrified scuttles out from underneath. A mouse. Only a mouse.

Chiara creeps into the darkest corner of the porch. She slumps with her back against the door, out of the rain at last. Are they still coming for her?

She listens and watches for a long time, starting at every sound. At last, when she can watch no longer, she lies down and curls herself up like a foetus under the mouse-eaten blanket, knees to her chest, hands over her head.

Behind closed eyes, she sees his face, blotched and damaged in the blue lights. Salvador. What did they do to him? What has he done to her?

PART V

61

A SCENT OF LILIES

Music seeps from invisible speakers. The same tune tinkles over and over, irritating Rava's brain like rats scratching behind the walls. Her body feels bloated and fuzzy, and the room keeps coming in and out of focus. She was never a drinker, not even in her rebellious teens, but this must be what a hangover feels like: dry mouth, pounding head, sore everything.

She sits up carefully and blinks, taking in a hospital room with a locker, a washbasin, and medical equipment on the walls. Someone must have dressed her in this gown and fastened the plastic identity tag onto her wrist. She rubs her eyes. The tag bears a long number, but no name. The ceiling and walls are white, and there's a faint scent of lilies, over-sweet and artificial. Rava knows that scent; it pervades the Genesis Centre.

How did she get here? She touches her right cheek and flinches; it's tender and bruised. What happened last night? It's all jumbled together: her feet covered in mud; blood on her legs; a man slapping her, and - her baby! That man took her

baby! All at once, she remembers; how could she have forgotten, even for a moment? What kind of mother is she?

They said Amani was in the ambulance, so she went inside,
and someone gave her an injection, and then, after that,
nothing.

She screws up her eyes against the whiteness. What have
they done with Amani? There's no cot here, no baby. What
about that door in the corner - could she be through there?
Rava stands up too fast and the room pulsates. The corner door
opens onto a small bathroom - no baby. Saliva floods her
mouth. She stumbles to the toilet and throws up.

When she's done, Rava sits back onto her heels, shuddering. The ends of her fingers are numb. Her gown is open at the
back and there's a blood-soaked pad in her knickers, but there's
no time to sort that out. Her breasts are tight; Amani is hungry,
crying for her somewhere. She has to find her.

The main door to her room has a square window. It opens
onto a wide, white-floored corridor where the tinkling music is
louder.

'Help me!' Rava calls, but her voice comes out in a barely-
audible croak. Her tongue feels too big for her mouth. 'Can
someone help me?' she tries again. 'I need to find my baby.'

No one comes, so she sets off towards a distant sound of
voices, one hand on the wall in case the dizziness gets worse.
She manages only a few steps before a nurse appears. Thank
God!

'Can you help me find my baby? I don't know where they've
taken her.'

The nurse has a striped uniform, a large mole on her right
cheek, and bright orange lipstick. She raises her eyebrows, then
unclips a walkie-talkie from her belt and speaks into it:

'Assistance outside room twenty-two. Our mystery patient is
up and wandering. Twenty milligrammes of Diazepam please.

Thank you.' She takes hold of Rava's hand. 'You're up earlier than expected, my dear. Come on, back to bed. You need your sleep.' She steers Rava back through the door into the little white room.

'But I have to find my baby,' Rava protests. Specks of light flicker in her vision, making it hard to focus. 'She needs feeding. Where have you taken her?'

'Sit down. You look very pale. We can't have you collapsing, can we?' The nurse ushers her onto the bed.

'Is she here in the hospital?'

'Please try to relax, dear. You've been through quite an ordeal. We were concerned about your blood loss last night. I'm surprised your medication has worn off so quickly, but don't worry, we'll look after you.'

Another nurse enters bringing a plastic cup with some tablets.

'These will help, but first, what's your name, my dear? Nobody seemed to know when they brought you in.'

'My baby,' Rava repeats. Why doesn't this nurse understand? 'I had a baby last night - a little girl. A policeman took her. What have you done with her?'

'There, there,' says the nurse, patting Rava on the back. 'Settle down, dear. First things first. The police will be in later to take your statement, so you should get some rest before they arrive.'

'But -.'

'Listen. The neonate is being looked after while we care for your medical needs and sort out the legal position. Let's face it, you were breaking the law, and women who use illegal midwives don't generally have incubation licences, now do they?' The nurse's lips form a chilly smile.

'Oh, but I do!' Rava leans forward, willing the nurse to understand her. 'We do have an incubation licence for the baby. I was going to have her here at the Genesis Centre, but my husband - we had a disagreement and I didn't know what to do.'

'Really?' The nurse arches her eyebrows so high they disappear into her blonde hair. 'So what happened to your blue Femband? If you have a licence I should be able to find you on the records, shouldn't I? What's your husband's name, dear?'

Rava hesitates. Martin will be angry, especially if he knows she went to Liz, and he's always said he won't sign the forms to keep a girl. But maybe, just maybe, when he sees his daughter - sees how much she looks like him? Maybe he might change his mind?

'Martin Robson,' she whispers.

The nurse does a double-take. The mole on her right cheek wobbles.

'Sorry, dear, I must have misheard you. I thought you said -.'

'Martin Robson,' Rava repeats, louder this time. 'He works for the Government, at the Ministry of Population and Health. He -.'

The nurse cocks her head to one side.

'Are you sure you're telling me the truth? Because you're in quite enough trouble already, delivering with unauthorised assistance. The police don't often bring charges against the incubators in these cases - too lenient, in my opinion, encouraging people to take shocking risks - but there are exceptions.'

'Yes, it's true. I'm Rava Robson, Martin's wife. And I don't care what you do to me, but I have to see my baby. Please!' Rava tries to stand again, but the nurse pushes her back onto the bed.

'All right then, Rava. Mr Robson is an exceptionally busy man, especially right now, but if you insist, I will contact his staff and we'll take it from there. I do hope you're not wasting his time.' She sighs and shakes her head. 'Come on now, hop back into bed.' She pulls back the covers.

'What about my baby?' Rava doesn't budge.

The nurse sighs again.

'The neonate went upstairs to the paediatric ward last night.'

'Is she sick?' Rava's heart races. 'She's here, upstairs? Can I see her?'

'That would not be appropriate, all things considered.' The nurse's voice is bone dry.

'But she'll be missing me; I'm breastfeeding.'

The nurse laughs.

'A neonate can't miss anyone; their brains aren't developed yet. Now, lie down.' She proffers the tablets. 'Swallow these like a good girl and have a nice little nap. Meanwhile, I'll make enquiries about your *"husband"*.' She makes air-quotes with her fingers.

Rava shakes her head.

'I'm not taking any more drugs. I need to see my baby.'

'As you wish then. I'll leave them here in case you change your mind.'

The nurse goes to leave. Rava tries to follow her, but she's too slow and the door slams shut in her face. A key turns in the lock with a clunk.

'Get some rest,' the nurse mouths through the window.

Rava calls, shouts, and hammers on the glass with her fists until they're sore, but nobody comes.

62

A PLACE OF SHELTER

An insistent *miaow* wakes Chiara. Gaskin? No, it can't be. Her next thought is: my feet! Her legs end in a pair of throbbing, purple monstrosities. As if that wasn't bad enough, her back aches from lying in a huddle on the concrete slab, and she's been bitten or stung all over. Mosquitoes or mice - who knows? Her tongue sticks to her dried-out mouth.

A feral cat pads into view, mewing hungrily in the morning sun.

'Sorry *micio*, I've got nothing to give you.'

It's hot already. Steam smelling of old urine rises from her blanket. Last night - no, don't think about last night. Don't think about Rava in her bloodstained nightdress. Don't think about Salvador turning his back on me. Don't think about the baby. Or Liz. Don't think about Liz.

Chiara stretches each protesting limb in turn. Her thigh is bruised from the heavy bag of jewellery in her pocket. It's still here though; at least no one robbed her in the night. Nonna's rosary beads are here too. Chiara pulls them out and looks at the tiny figure on the crucifix with nails in his hands and feet. *'Don't expect it to be easy,'* Liz said.

'Help me,' Chiara whispers, kissing the man on the cross. 'And Nonna, wherever you are, pray for me, and for all the others.'

———

THE YARD IS DESERTED, but she can't stay here; she needs water, and food, and a safer place to shelter until she can think what to do next. Shelter? The cat miaows again, sounding eerily human, and a remembered phrase drops whole into Chiara's head:

'Our home is simple, but we do our best to make it a place of shelter.'

That was what Jajja said. Zoe's grandmother promised shelter to Liz and Chiara if they ever needed it. Chiara shrinks at the thought of asking for help from someone so nearly destitute herself. Besides, what if the authorities follow her there, bringing trouble for Jajja and Zoe? She tugs at her tangled hair, but she can't think of anything else; she's out of options. She's not even sure she can find her way to Jajja's container camp.

Chiara inspects her feet. What she sees makes her want to cry, but she clenches her teeth and suppresses a yelp as she extracts a shard of glass and a pile of gravel and grit from her bloodied soles. She inspects and rejects the stinking heap of rags in the corner, choosing instead to rip strips off the bottom of her shirt to make bandages. She binds up her feet, creating makeshift sandals, before attempting to stand. At first, the pain makes her light-headed, but it settles. Breathe through it, she tells herself. You can do this. You're stronger than you think. That's what she always tells the birthing mothers; time to find out if it's true.

Despite the heat and the gruesome stains, Chiara drapes

the old blanket around her head and shoulders. It'll make her harder to identify, and if she can't find Jajja the blanket will cover her for another night. Hunched and hobbling, Chiara makes for the gate at the far side of the yard, glancing frequently over her shoulder.

She follows the sun, heading south. So much of the land is still flooded that the landscape looks unfamiliar, and she has take long detours to find passable roads on higher ground. Displaced people are everywhere, pushing their possessions in wheelbarrows and shopping trolleys. If only Chiara had a trolley, she could lean on it as she totters along; the best she can find is a branch to use as a walking stick. As the heat builds, she's tormented by a thirst so ferocious she fantasises about drinking from the foul floodwater. An old woman offers her a swig from a bottle of nameless alcohol, but Chiara shakes her head.

She wants to discard the blanket; it's so heavy, so horribly hot, but what if they're still looking for her? Two or three times, someone taps her on the shoulder and she flinches in terror, but it's only beggars asking if she can spare a coin or two. She almost laughs. She's got a pocket weighed down with gold, but if anyone sees it they'll knife her for it. People are murdered daily for less.

At last, she enters familiar territory. A crumbling church tower looms into view, and she passes a long-condemned housing block, notorious as a haunt of violent criminals. But it's still a long walk to the camp. Chiara's feet protest at every step. The thirst burns. She plods onward, walking on glass, walking on jagged rocks, walking on scalpel blades.

'Look out, love!' A one-legged man shouts up from where he's sitting on the pavement. Chiara has almost stumbled into a barrier closing off yet another flooded street. 'You lost, sweetheart?' He gives her directions and she shuffles on, envying him his crutches.

The shadows are long by the time she approaches the high, rusted gates outside the shoddy settlement where Jajja and Zoe live. Or lived; it was months ago when Chiara last came here, and people move on all the time. Puddles cover much of the ground, and the tracks are thick mud, but at least the camp isn't underwater.

The guard on the gate touches his rifle like a mother patting the head of a child. He squints at Chiara, looking appraisingly up and down her body. She shrinks under her blanket; surely she looks too ravaged to take his fancy?

'I'm a friend of Jajja,' she says, realising only now she doesn't know Jajja's proper name. 'I think she lives here - Jajja and Zoe?'. Hundreds of people live here; thousands most likely. But to her amazement, the guard nods and releases the gate. He cocks his head towards the interior of the camp.

'Give Jajja my regards. You know where you're going?' he asks. Chiara shakes her head.

'Gabe,' calls the guard, 'take this lady to Jajja's place.' The same skinny boy Chiara remembers from last time comes running up, skirting the puddles.

'Follow me,' he announces. *I've made it,* Chiara thinks, and starts forward after him, but her legs won't obey her. Her bones have turned to water. She staggers, her hands flailing at the air, but there's nothing to hold onto. *Almost made it,* she tells herself, as the earth rises to slam into her face.

63

I WANT TO FORGIVE YOU

'Have you seen the baby? Is she all right?' The nurse has barely shown Martin into her room before Rava shoots out her questions.

Martin stares at her.

'I came straight here from the office. When they told me you were the woman brought in last night, I didn't know what to think. Didn't believe it at first. Are you trying to ruin my career?' He sits down in the chair and scratches his neck.

'No, of course not; I don't even remember how I got here. They've taken the baby, Martin. Please, will you ask if I can see her? They'll listen to you.' She presses her hands together. 'I'll do whatever you want.'

Martin looks at his shoes; they're so shiny he can probably see his face in them.

'Really? You're the one who moved out. I was heartbroken, and all over an unborn foetus that I never wanted in the first place. What do you expect me to do?'

'I know you're angry with me, and I'm sorry, but the baby, Martin? Is she still on the neonatal ward? I need to feed her.' Rava's voice is hoarse, her throat raw from all the screaming.

'You're living in fantasy land, Rava. I dropped everything to come here today, despite you having walked out on me, stubbornly refused to see reason, and then, to top it all, massively embarrassed me by running off to my mother, of all people, for an illegal delivery.' His eyebrow twitches.

'Won't you at least go and see our baby? She's beautiful, and she looks so much like you.'

'How did you find my mother? Was it your plan all along, to humiliate me?' Martin claws at the back of his neck as if trying to draw blood.

'No. I didn't know. Where's my baby, Martin? I told them we had an incubation licence.' She sounds like a broken record, but she doesn't care.

'How could you not have known? I mean, what are the chances?'

'Honestly, I had no idea Liz was your mother. You never told me anything about her. I was trying to get to Scotland but I went into labour. All I wanted was a normal family, a normal life, but you made it impossible.'

Martin screws up his forehead; there are bright spots on his cheeks.

'Daniel drove me to her boat yesterday. The police were clearing it out, looking for evidence. What a mouldy old wreck, crawling with germs! I knew my mother liked squalor, but this was something else. Daniel was so shocked he threw up on the towpath, and I can't say I blame him. She's dead, by the way. You killed my mother.'

Silence falls between them. Rava swallows; it's true then. One of the nurses said the old midwife had drowned, but she hadn't wanted to believe it. No one's mentioned Chiara, but she must have been arrested; there were so many police.

'Was it all worth it, d'you think?' Martin asks.

Rava hangs her head. Has she been selfish, insisting on keeping this baby, despite everything? Their marriage, their future together, Liz, Chiara - so many sacrifices - and now they've taken Amani too.

'The police?' she whispers. 'The nurse said I have to give them a statement?' She's done so much damage already; must she make things even worse for Chiara?

But Martin only grunts irritably.

'Not much point at the moment. The police ballsed the whole thing up from start to finish, and I don't want news getting out that my wife was involved. I'll tell them you're not up to it yet, okay?'

'Thank you, Martin.' Tears well up behind her eyelids. Martin takes her hand and she doesn't have the strength to pull it away.

'What happened to your rings?'

'I - never mind.'

Thank God, he doesn't press the matter. He looks at her, and she looks at him properly for the first time in ages. His face is grey and strained, and he's lost weight. She used to think he was the love of her life.

'I'm sorry, Martin,' she whispers. The clock ticks on the wall and the endless music plays.

'I feel sorry for you, Rava,' he says at last. 'As I said before, I don't think you're well. You need psychiatric help. I know this has been difficult for you. Unplanned incubation is never a good idea; I should have insisted on a Fresh Start right away.' He pauses. 'But it's not too late. I want to forgive you, Rava.'

He comes to sit beside her on the bed, caressing her hair before planting the gentlest of kisses on her forehead. Her shoulders soften. She still loves him, doesn't she? She's missed the old days, and their lovely home, and she never really wanted to go back to Aberdeen. She moves in a little closer.

'What about the baby, Martin?' she murmurs. She's not giving up; she can't.

He sighs.

'How about I try to get you a picture? Would that make you feel better?'

'Oh, yes please! I need to know she's safe.' Rava clasps her hands together. If he sees Amani, surely he'll change his mind. She's so sweet and innocent.

'But we should shelve any decisions until you've had a proper rest and a full assessment of your mental health. Incubation takes a lot of out women. I know how you feel about the People's Hospital; clinically they're excellent, but it's not exactly the Ritz. What if I look for a nice private facility? I believe there's a Perinatal Care Home in Ealing that might be suitable - quality food, private rooms, all that sort of thing. Then we could think again about our options once your hormones have been rebalanced. How does that sound?' He pats her thigh.

'But who will look after Amani? Can she come to the home with me?'

'Who's Amani?'

'Oh - that's what I called her - the baby. But we could change it, if you like?' Rava's voice falters.

'Let's see.' Martin stands up. 'I'm sorry, Rava, but I have to get back to the office. There's a lot at stake right now; the promotion announcements are due next month.'

'Is everything all right at work, Martin?'

'Yes of course.' He brushes the air dismissively. 'Everything's under control. It's the silly season, that's all; the hot weather, and then the floods. And Daniel has been a bit off; said he wasn't well and needed to go home early last night. That's all I need right now - unreliable staff! ' He rolls his eyes. 'Right then - I'll ask the nurses to get you a photo, okay, and we'll take it from there.'

AFTER HE'S GONE, Rava paces the room. They've locked her in again, *'for your own safety,'* but she can't sit still; the idea of rest is ludicrous. She replays the conversation with Martin, trying to make sense of it. She wants so badly to trust him. Could it work? If she agrees to go to the care home for a few days, might he change his mind about Amani?

A rap at the door breaks into her circling thoughts. The nurse with the orange lipstick turns the key and enters.

'I believe this is what you wanted.' She holds out a piece of paper. Rava snatches it hungrily.

'How is she? Is she crying for me? Have they fed her?'

'See for yourself. She's fine.'

The nurse departs, and Rava scans the paper. It's a photograph of a newborn in a hospital crib. The baby is sleeping; she has long eyelashes, and tufty hair sticking up in all directions. She looks healthy, well-fed and content. There's only one problem.

It's not Amani.

64

TWO TYPES OF POWER

'One more spoonful.'

Jajja's soup is spicy, with beans and chunks of carrot.

'And some bread.' Chiara takes a bite, chews, and swallows. It's good. She tears off another mouthful, ravenous after three days of fever. 'You look better this morning. Some colour in your cheeks.' Jajja smiles her toothless smile as she sets the bowl aside. 'Time to change your bandages.'

'I can do it myself,' Chiara protests, but Jajja is already unwinding the wrapping from Chiara's left foot.

'Ah that's better; swelling's almost gone.'

'Thank you. You've been very good to me.' Chiara flexes her ankle and wriggles her toes; her feet feel as if they belong to her again. 'I need to get up soon. I'll find somewhere else to go, don't worry.' Although she does not know where.

Jajja washes Chiara's feet in a basin of warm water, taking her time. The silence is broken only by the soft trickle of pouring water. At last, as she binds up the healing wounds with clean strips of rag, Jajja says,

'No hurry, my darling. No hurry at all. You and dear Liz, we never forget what you did. Our home is your home. Stay as long as you like.' She pads away to empty the basin.

'Thank you, Jajja.' Chiara sinks back onto the bed. She doesn't know how she made it through the camp and up the ladder on the day she arrived. She found herself lying here in Jajja's container, with Zoe squatting beside her. Jajja was sponging her forehead with a cold cloth, and Zoe was asking questions she couldn't answer. A baby was crying; Chiara thought it was Rava's baby, until she remembered Zoe has a baby too - little Dembe. Chiara tried to get up straight away, but the pain was so bad she fainted. She's been resting here ever since, cared for by Jajja and Zoe, drifting between brief, bitter periods of clarity and feverish nightmares.

'I have your gold safe.' Jajja reappears, drying her hands on a towel. Her intonation suggests the faintest hint of enquiry.

'It's not mine,' Chiara replies. Then she realises Jajja might think the gold is stolen, and, in a way, it is. 'It came from - it belongs to a mother. She had a baby, on the boat with Liz, but then -.' Chiara's voice quavers. 'I don't know how to give it back,' she concludes.

'No need to tell the whole story.' Jajja kneels beside Chiara. 'We know you have a good heart. I only wondered, if you wanted to go home to Italy, to your mother? There is enough, and some to spare, I think.' Her eyes stray to the Madonna statue. 'I know of a man in the camp who helps with such things.'

'The Genesis Centre still has my passport.'

'Passports can be arranged, with gold.' Jajja nods gravely. Does she want Chiara to leave? The police might come searching the camp for her. Chiara tries to picture Mamma and Gemma, but they seem impossibly far away, somewhere in Milan now, she thinks. Besides, the gold isn't hers; it belongs to Rava and her baby.

'No need to decide now,' Jajja adds. 'You stay here as long as you like. I'm only saying, in case you're homesick. You take it easy now. Zoe and Dembe will be back later. And there's plenty more soup in the pot - help yourself.'

Jajja heads out to the communal camp kitchen where she helps prepare soup for the hungry and destitute. Chiara lies down, but when she closes her eyes, images swirl like the rubbish in the river. Will she ever stop seeing Rava's anguished face, bereft of her baby; Liz pitching head over heels into the torrent; Bella, the lullaby baby killed by lethal injection? And Salvador, whom she'd thought was her the blue-eyed hero? Even if she returns to Italy, she'll never be able to leave this country behind.

'ALL RIGHT, little monster, we're home. Quit yelling and get sucking.'

Chiara wakes from a shallow doze to the sounds of Zoe's voice and her baby's wails. The cries end abruptly as Dembe finds her mother's milk. Chiara pulls back the curtain that separates the bed from the living area.

'You feeling better?' Zoe asks.

'Yes, thanks.' And it's true, physically at least. 'Do you have a phone, so I can check the news?' Chiara needs to find out what happened to Rava and her baby. And Liz too. She's certain Liz drowned; she saw her sucked under, knows she never intended to survive that final plunge. But they might have found her body.

Zoe adjusts the baby in her lap and produces a cracked smartphone from her pocket.

'You know all that news crap is a pack of lies, yeah?'

Chiara nods, but she's already fumbling with the unfamiliar mobile. Even with all the Government filters and censorship, there must be some clues to what happened.

It doesn't take long to find a news report from three days ago. 'Last Midwives Scuttled,' is the headline. A reporter stands in front of the Rosie Lee interviewing a police officer while figures in masks and white overalls swarm around the old boat.

'The search for the body may take several days,' says the officer. 'The river was in full spate after the weekend's heavy rain.' The camera zooms in on a frogman with an oxygen tank strapped to his back. 'A second midwife has gone to ground,' the reporter says, 'but a search is ongoing. Police believe there are now very few, if any, clandestine midwives remaining in London and the South East.'

Chiara shivers.

The report switches to a shot of the Atrium at the Genesis Centre, all white marble and modernity. Apparently the 'victim' was taken there to recover from her ordeal; she has given a full statement to the police and is receiving the best medical care. There are no pictures of Rava, and no mention of her name. And the baby? Chiara wonders. As if in reply, another image flashes up: a row of hospital cots, each containing a sleeping newborn.

'The infant is being cared for by specialist staff at the Genesis Centre pending ongoing enquiries.'

Something jolts Chiara's attention and she stops the video. That poster on the green wall above the cots: a big bottle of soap and a hygiene slogan - Chiara's seen it before. She watches the clip again, and a third time, scanning for every detail. That looks like Rava's baby all right. She's got an IV drip in the back of her hand. Fluids perhaps, for dehydration, or an antibiotic infusion? Chiara doesn't think so. The drug being pumped into Amani's veins - she'd swear to it - is morphine. And the green-walled nursery - she's certain now - is Neonatal Two. Where babies are left to die.

The phone drops from Chiara's hand and lands with a clatter on the metal floor.

'What's the matter? You feeling queasy again?' Zoe looks alarmed. 'Shall I get the bucket?'

Chiara shakes her head.

'I need to think,' she says.

IT'S three days since Amani was born. Three days in Neonatal Two. Are they feeding her, or is it a morphine-only diet? How long can a baby survive without milk?

'I know I can trust you,' Rava said, when she insisted Chiara take her gold. Instead, Chiara called Salvador, who led the police straight to the Rosie Lee.

Chiara leans out of the hatch window. The air is acrid with smoke and the stench of excrement. In the crowded camp, weary women haul water in plastic buckets. Dogs sniff around for rats. A tiny, grimy girl, maybe three or four years old, crouches over a heap of rubbish beside the ditch. She is searching through the filth with a stick, looking for anything she might be able to sell, or eat. Will this be Dembe's fate in a few years time? Was it really a kindness to help her into this world?

Perhaps the Government is right after all, and the midwives do more harm than good. Perhaps they should be stopped. There is less land to live on now, with all the flooding and the climate problems. Perhaps it is right to manage the population and stop people having babies. The Defender wants a safe and healthy future, she says, and everyone has to make sacrifices for that. People protest for choices and freedom, but is it worth it, if they end up in squalor like this?

Chiara stares up at the sky. At the Genesis Centre, everything was clean and calm. She wore a uniform and followed protocols. Someone was in charge. Everything was under control. It was safe.

Turning back into the dim room, dazed from the sunlight, she stumbles into the plaster Madonna. She grabs at the figure to stop her from toppling. The jagged ends of her arms, where the hands have been lost, crumble into dust at the edges.

'Did you see Jajja out there?' Zoe's voice has an edge of concern. 'I keep telling her she's too old to be cooking up soup for everyone that can't find no work, but you know what she's like. I was gonna go, but she told me to come back here and feed littl'un. She'd give away the clothes on her back, Jajja would.'

'No, I didn't see her.' Chiara sits down on the rug, her vision adjusting to the container's dim interior. Nonna was like that before her arthritis confined her first to the cottage, and then to her chair. Nonna used to bake an extra loaf every day for the refugees who came by boat from Tunisia. She fed all the stray cats too; nothing Mamma said could deter her. If Nonna lived here, in this camp, she'd be out in all weathers, just like Jajja, helping people even poorer than herself.

Chiara sighs. That's all very well; she's tried her best, but she's got nothing left. The police are after her. Liz is dead, Amani is dead or dying, and Salvador wasn't who she thought he was. The gold? No, she can't use it for herself; it doesn't belong to her. She's homeless and penniless, with nothing and no one to call her own.

Nothing. What was it Nonna used to say? Nonna loved old proverbs and sayings. When she told her magical stories about shipwrecks and angels, giants and princesses, she always ended with what she called *'qualcosa da ricordare'*: something to remember. Chiara pictures her grandmother leaning towards her, eyes shining:

'There are two types of power in this world, my chica. There is the power of the people who have everything. And then there is the power of the ones who have nothing. Most of us have the second kind

of power. Especially here in Sicily. And that is the best kind, because God himself helps the helpless. Remember that.'

Chiara sees her Nonna's face, not pale and cold in death, but alive, with a shrewd smile and dark, eager eyes. She feels Nonna's warm hand squeezing her own fingers. She hears the rocking chair creak.

'Du' su' i putenti,' she hears Nonna whisper. *'Two types of powerful. Be the second kind.'*

'Where did Jajja put the gold?' Chiara asks slowly.

'In there.' Zoe points to the life-sized Madonna statue. 'You wanna buy a ticket out of here?'

Chiara smiles.

'No,' she says. 'I've got a better idea.'

65

CLEANERS

E arly next morning, two young women join the stream of Mollies heading for the city. Maids, toilet attendants, and shop assistants throng in their hundreds out of the camps and slums. They have put on neat uniforms, ready to keep London cleansed and fragrant for another day. Chiara and Zoe are both wearing hospital scrubs. Chiara's are several sizes too big, and her borrowed shoes rub at the sore patches on her feet. Her hand keeps going to the back of her neck, prickly and exposed without her long hair. She asked Jajja to cut it off last night.

'Are you sure about this, Zoe? You've got a baby of your own to think about.'

'No sweat. You're gonna need a mate in there. Lucky I'm still working up the city.' Zoe's been working casual cleaning shifts in the city hospitals: mopping floors, wiping down walls, and bagging up soiled linen for the laundry. It's heavy work, but the job comes with a Ministry of Health ID pass and a free uniform. 'Perks of dealing with other people's shit!' she jokes. 'And I'm going to study for something better, as soon as I get the chance.'

'Yes, but, if we get caught - .' They talked about this yesterday, but it feels more real now.

'Chill. We won't get caught. We're just a couple of cleaners, taking out the laundry. Invisible. They treat us cleaners like ants - just one faceless mass. When did you ever look at an ant's face?'

Chiara hopes Zoe's right. There are so many worries: the city checkpoints, the hospital security systems, the babies' electronic wristbands. Something's bound to go wrong; it's crazy even to try.

They cross a road and approach the perimeter canal. Chiara hands the hunk of bread Jajja insisted on giving her 'for your lunch' to an old woman sitting outside a shop. A long queue of people waits to cross the barrier. All the women have their black Fembands visible, ready to be scanned. As she and Zoe join the line, Chiara fingers the little belt-bag strapped around her waist.

The water level in the canal has dropped with the receding floods. Old tyres, scraps of wood, and assorted plastic detritus litter the margins. A sour smell cabbage rises from the mud. Shapeless things float in the water, and, with a wave of nausea, Chiara pictures Liz gyrating, rolling, sucked under.

They've almost reached the barrier when the whole line has to stop for a shiny, stretched-limo with blacked-out windows. Its heavily-tattooed driver leans out and hands something to the soldier, who nods and waves the car though.

'Mafia,' Zoe mutters.

The line shuffles forward again. Chiara lowers her gaze, praying that her dodgy black Femband will work, and that the soldier won't look too closely at her ID card. It belongs to a cousin of Zoe's ex-boyfriend who works in the Genesis Centre mortuary. She's called Humairah, and it's her day off today, but she thinks the pass will work. Chiara hopes so; if she gets caught, Humairah could be in trouble too. The photo on the pass is blurry, but it shows a round-faced woman who looks nothing like Chiara.

Chiara tries to look as if she's just on her way to another day's work, but her insides are churning. She's used fake black bands before, but what if today's the day it goes wrong? She's so nervous, she might do something stupid and give herself away. When they get to the front, the soldier pinches Zoe's cheek and makes a dirty joke. Chiara braces herself for something similar, but the man just glances at the MPH logo on her pass and waves her through.

'See, no sweat!' Zoe tells her. 'Yeah, I'm used to that crap,' she adds, jerking her head towards the soldier. She rolls her eyes. 'Come on. We've got a job to do.'

They board a tram, squeezed between care assistants and low-ranking office workers. Chiara keeps her gaze on the grubby floor. What if someone recognises her? She's wanted by the police. Her cropped hair should help, and she's thinner now, but it would only take one former colleague to look properly at her face.

'Hey, we're here.' Zoe tugs at her arm, and they hurry off the tram, pressed along by dozens of sweating bodies. It's the Plaza station, outside the Genesis Centre. Chiara glances ahead, but something's not right. There are more vehicles than usual, more people in uniform. Men with guns, and dogs.

'*Mamma mia!* How did they know?'

The Plaza is full of police. Chiara grabs Zoe's wrist so hard that Zoe squeaks. Blue lights are flashing everywhere. Chiara can't move; she tries to exhale, but her windpipe is closing up. Dogs. Red and blue lights, flashing. They've come for her.

'Chiara, what's the matter?' Zoe's voice comes from far away. 'It's okay; it's often like this these days. Hey, Chiara - listen to me!'

Chiara tries. She listens, but all she can hear is the rush of the river, the splash of Liz hitting the water, and the sound of screaming.

66

DO YOU REALLY REMEMBER?

Rava's breasts are about to burst, so tight and swollen she can't bear to touch them. The nurses keep bringing medication to stop her milk, but she won't take it, like she won't take their sleeping pills and tranquillisers. Amani's still here somewhere, and she has to find her.

'What have they done with her?' she asks, for the thousandth time. Martin doesn't reply. His phone rings, and he glances at the screen, swears, and switches it to silent.

'Effing work can't leave me in peace for five minutes. Come on, hurry up and get dressed.' He nods towards the clothes he brought in for her. 'Daniel is waiting outside.'

'I'm not leaving. Not without my baby.' She sits on the side of the bed, rigid.

'Rava, you've been discharged; you can't stay here. I've moved heaven and earth to get you into the True Self Sanctuary; that's the right place for you now. They'll get you properly rested and medicated, and it's very safe and secure.'

She clenches her jaw. Her eyes are gritty from all the crying. She's barely slept for what seems like endless nights and days.

'That picture wasn't my baby. I've told you; I've told all the nurses, but no one will listen. You all say I'm crazy, but I know what my own baby looks like.'

Martin sighs. His phone vibrates, but he ignores it.

'We've been over this. All the neonates are tagged and labelled. The nursing staff are professionals; I think we can trust them to keep track. You only saw it for a few hours in the dark when you were in a disturbed state after a brutal trauma.'

'It wasn't brutal; it was beautiful. And she's not an 'it,' Martin; she's our baby.'

Martin picks at his fingernails.

'Rava, do you remember what happened?'

'What do you mean? Of course I do - look!' She points to her nightdress, wet with the milk leaking from her breasts and running down her body. 'I had a baby, and someone took her away.'

But he shakes his head sadly.

'My darling, you're not well. The staff say you've been refusing your medication, and I think you've been blanking things out. I've done my best to protect you - we all have - but you need to understand -.'

'Understand what?' She's too hot and too cold all at once. 'What do you mean, Martin?'

'Rava, listen to me.' He comes and sits beside her on the bed. His voice is gentle and kind.

'No!' She covers her face, pressing her fingers into her forehead.

'Rava, I'm sorry, but you've been hallucinating. The mind can do strange things - even simulate physical symptoms, like this discharge.' He touches her sodden chest. 'You've lost track of the timeline; it's a common trauma response. Listen Rava - your neonate died shortly after delivery.'

'No. No - you're lying!' Her heart jumps and races, but it's not true. He's trying to confuse her, manipulate her. 'She was fine; I know she was.'

'Try to listen, Rava. The foetus was born in very poor condition, and these self-styled "midwives" are hopelessly ill-equipped to diagnose problems, let alone treat them. My poor old mother was way past it. The ambulance staff said it should have been obvious the neonate was struggling; they did what they could, and they tried to tell you, but -.'

'No, that's not right.' She flails at him, trying to claw at his face, to erase what he's saying, but he takes hold of her arms and forces her to look at him.

'How much do you really remember, my love? You haven't been sleeping, have you? And the paramedics had to give you something, they said, because you were so distressed. Some of these drugs have an amnesiac effect.'

'No - but - the picture - .' Even as she says it, she knows she's not making sense.

'My darling, you said yourself the picture wasn't your baby. The staff said it might not be a good idea, but you were so frantic, I wanted to comfort you. Now, though, I have to tell you the truth. Physically, you've recovered remarkably well, but you need expert psychiatric care. You're delusional, Rava.'

'Stop lying to me! Go away!'

She shuts her eyes, but in the hot blackness she doesn't know any more. She doesn't remember how she got here; doesn't know what they did with Amani after they took her off the boat. And maybe - oh God, no! - could that be why they haven't let her see Amani all this time? They said she was upstairs, but did they ever say she was alive?

A hammer cracks her skull. Could it be true? Is Amani dead? Why is he only telling her now? A high-pitched keening leaks from her ragged throat.

67

JUST A DEMO

'Breathe in and out. Slower - yeah, that's right. It's just a demo, I swear; they're not here for you. Come and sit down a minute.' Zoe leads Chiara to a bench under the station canopy. 'People were looking at something on their phones on the tram,' Zoe goes on, 'but you were too stressed to notice. Some hoo-ha about one of them lying Government pricks. Like we didn't already know they was all con artists!' She snorts. 'Looks like they might be expecting a bit of trouble.'

Chiara nods, head down, still fighting to get air into her lungs. They're not here for us. Not for us. Slowly, her fists unclench and the ringing in her ears abates. She opens her eyes and scans the Plaza.

There must be thirty or forty police here already, and more arriving all the time in black vans. Some of them are wearing body armour and helmets with visors. They already outnumber the little group of people with placards standing outside the Genesis Centre.

'Intimidation,' Zoe says. 'They do this all the time; you've not been in the city much recently, have you? Sometimes they

make arrests; sometimes the protestors give up and go home.'
She shrugs.

Chiara starts to get to her feet, still a little light-headed.

'Are you up for this?' Zoe asks, her brows drawing together.
'Coz we can quit now if you want? Maybe you're not ready. We
could come back tomorrow; it might be quieter then?'

Chiara almost agrees. They'd be insane to go ahead with
this many police right outside the hospital doors. They could
come back tomorrow, or the next day; it might be safer - no one
could blame her. She can't risk another panic attack inside the
Genesis Centre; it wouldn't be fair on Zoe.

'Well?' Zoe waits for her answer. 'Tomorrow then?'

Chiara reaches into the pocket of her scrubs, where Nonna's
rosary beads nestle alongside Humairah's security pass.
Humairah might need her pass back tomorrow. And the
soldiers on the checkpoint might look at Chiara's face tomorrow. And by tomorrow, Amani might be dead. This is the fourth
day already. She gives the beads a little rub between her fingers
and whispers,

'*Madre di Dio, prega per noi.*' Then she straightens up. 'Today,'
she says.

Zoe grins and gives her a thumbs-up, so Chiara unzips her
bag, pulls out two medical face masks, passes one to Zoe and
puts the other on herself.

They skirt the police vans to join the stream of hospital staff
crossing the wide Plaza.

'Keep walking,' Zoe hisses in Chiara's ear. 'Don't look
round. This is just another day at work, remember? Demos
come and go.'

Chiara keeps moving, but plenty of her fellow-workers are
staring at the busy scene, and she can't help snatching a glance
or two.

There are ten protestors now - maybe fifteen. More than
she's seen before, and they're not dispersing, despite all the

police. In fact, more are arriving: men and women, young and old, variously dressed, some of them carrying home-made signs. They join the group in twos and threes, staring scornfully at the police vans. Many of them look angry. An elderly woman shakes her fist.

'*Safe Futures = State Murder!*' reads one of the placards.

'*End MPH Corruption Now!*' says another under a picture of a rat with a man's face.

'*Who gains from the One-Child rules?*'

and, most shockingly of all,

'*BURN YOUR FEMBAND!*'

THE POLICE ARE SETTING up metal fences and talking on radios, as if they're waiting for instructions. A murmur rises from the growing crowd of demonstrators. Young Muslim women wearing hijabs stand alongside white-haired old ladies. A family with a toddler joins the group; who brings children to a demo? What could have happened to trigger this sort of defiance?

As they draw near to the steps leading up to the Genesis Centre, Chiara keeps her face lowered. But a voice from the huddle of protestors catches her ear: a woman with an unusual accent? Where has she heard that before?

'I had to be here today,' the voice says, 'after everything that's happened.'

Chiara stops. It is; it must be. Ignoring Zoe's frantic admonitions, she turns and looks straight into the eyes of a slender woman with a pale, freckled face and blue-framed glasses. Devorah!

It doesn't make sense, but it's true. The very first mother Chiara led to the Rosie Lee all those months ago is standing here, outside the Genesis Centre, holding a sign that declares simply: *'Choose Life!'* Devorah's head is covered with a bobbed wig and a little hat, and her eyes sparkle with rebellion.

For a split second, the two women stare at one another. Devorah smiles. Chiara gasps.

'Why -?' she begins. But Zoe tugs at her arm.

'Come on!' she urges.

Chiara returns Devorah's smile before hurrying on, up the stone stairway, under the central arch, and into the Genesis Centre.

68

IS THERE A PROBLEM?

Rava sits in the chair, hands in her lap, not moving. If she can sit like this forever, if she tries very hard, she won't have to feel anything. Not ever again.

After what might be ten seconds or a thousand years - what difference would it make? - Martin returns.

'Did I leave my phone in here? You were making such a noise, I left to let you calm down. How are you feeling now?'

Stupid question. Nothing.

He rests a hand on her shoulder. She doesn't respond. She's leaking milk, blood, tears, but it doesn't matter. Nothing matters anymore.

'You're obviously very upset, so the nurses say you can stay till this evening, or tomorrow if need be, until you've got over the shock. They say we shouldn't rush you. That's kind, isn't it?'

Her face is a mask. Don't move; don't think. Don't feel.

He pats her leg.

'I hate to see you like this, my love. Try to get some rest. The nurses will give you something to help you sleep. Ah, there it is.'

His phone lies face down on the locker. It's been buzzing

and vibrating quite a lot. Martin picks it up, looks at the screen, and freezes. His eyebrow starts twitching. Sweat appears in large beads on his forehead, and his mouth opens and closes like a landed fish.

Is he having a heart attack?

'No - there's pictures - who could have? Oh my God!' His speech dissolves into a torrent of swear words as he buries his head in his hands. When he looks up again, his face is a sickly green. He clutches at his stomach. A tic in his cheek joins his frantically working eyebrow.

'Is there a problem, Martin?' Rava's voice is level and low.

He flaps a hand at her distractedly and starts scrabbling away at the device, eyes bulging.

'I've got to get out - they'll be looking for me - can't mess with these people. Not after last time.' He's muttering, speaking to himself. 'What's the quickest way? Think, for God's sake!'

He dials a number and lifts the phone to his ear.

'Daniel, are you still there? Daniel? Thank God! Listen, urgent change of plan. I'll be outside in five minutes, okay? Come to the door to meet me, and don't be late.'

Martin swabs his face with his handkerchief and switches off the phone. Then he walks to the window, opens it, and throws out the device. They're dozens of storeys high; heaven help any poor pedestrian down below if it lands on their head! But Martin doesn't look down. As he makes for the door, he starts, as if he's only just noticed Rava's still in the room.

'Sorry,' he says. 'Something's come up. Trouble. Some total bastard's dropped me right in it.'

Still gripping his stomach, he opens the door and glances left and right several times, up and down the corridor. 'Stairs might be safer,' are the last words Rava hears as her husband disappears.

SHE SITS for several more minutes after he's gone. Some part of her brain registers that he's left the door unlocked. Faint noises rise from the Plaza outside; was that someone shouting? Amani is - no, don't think it. Don't say it, not even inside your head. Think about something else, if you have to think at all. Martin? What's going on with Martin?

Very slowly, as if she's stiff after gruelling exercise, Rava gets up and switches on the TV. She flicks through shopping channels, movies, dating and cooking shows until she reaches the Government's DBC news channel.

'Breaking News: Mafia-led conspiracy infiltrates Ministry of Population and Health,' is splashed across the screen in red.

A reporter stands outside the Pinnacle building where Martin works. A sizeable group of angry-looking people has gathered. Some of them have climbed up onto the modernist sculptures.

'The Defender expressed her disappointment at this morning's leaks,' the reporter says. 'She has pledged a full investigation in response to questions about pictures and video footage circulating on social media which to show the Under-Secretary of State for Women's Health entering into corrupt arrangements with known mob bosses.'

The mob? Mafia? Rava's hand flies to her mouth.

A banner crawls across the bottom of the screen. *'Health Ministry under attack by fascist groups,'* it says. *'Allegations of underworld payoffs.'*

For a fleeting moment, a black-and-white photo appears. Rava catches her breath because there's no mistake: it's Martin. His features stand out in sharp profile against a moonlit sky. He's outdoors somewhere, at night, shaking hands with a bulky, bald-headed man.

'The unsubstantiated allegations relate to illegal trades in incubation licences and child registration documents,' the reporter goes on. 'Groups opposed to the Government are attempting to smear the Ministry of Population and Health by suggesting that high-ranking Ministry officials have been involved in corrupt practices. The Defender has pledged to root out any rogue employees to uphold public trust in the Ministry's essential and world-leading work.'

Even as Rava watches, more people are joining the crowd. Their shouts cut across the reporter's words:

'Liars! We've all seen the pictures.'

'Hypocrites! Telling us what to do, while they're breaking the rules themselves.'

'Shut up and tell the truth.'

The reporter's eyes shift sideways.

'We are hearing reports of people gathering outside Health Ministry buildings,' he continues. Rava's eyes widen. 'The Defender appreciates the public's desire to support our ground-breaking health services, but there is a risk that dangerous extremists might take this opportunity to disrupt public order. For your own safety, therefore, please stay off the streets at this time. Remain at your home or place of work, and keep calm.'

'Safe Future, State Murder!' One of the men sitting atop the sculpture begins to chant, and others in the crowd join in. The reporter loosens his tie and consults his notepad.

'Our Defender's commitment to the nation's health and security knows no compromise. Stay tuned - I'll be keeping you updated as the situation develops. This is Marcus Hungerford for the DBC, bringing you the news for your safe and happy future.'

Rava turns off the TV. Even through all the DBC's obfuscations, the truth is obvious: Martin is involved in something corrupt. He's been lying. She sits, taking this in, her pulse fluttering. Martin lied. He lied to his bosses, to the public, maybe - who knows? - even to the Defender.

With a shiver, she recalls the papers she found in his desk

drawer. There were lists of documents supplied in return of money: licences, certificates, and registration portfolios. '*No more*,' he wrote at the bottom, next to that little hangman figure. He wanted to stop. He must have got mixed up in something, and it spun out of control. Maybe he never meant things to go so far.

But one thing is certain: he lied. He told her how important it was to keep the rules, to save the planet, to set an example, but all the time he was meeting the Mafia and helping supply the black market. And if he can lie to all those people - to the whole country, in fact - he could lie to her too.

Rava springs to her feet as if she's been struck by lightning. If Martin was lying to her about Amani - if he even might have been lying - she's wasted far too much time already. She has to do something, now, before it's too late.

With shaking hands, she discards her soggy nightdress and pulls on the turquoise dress he brought her. It'll be easier to get out of here wearing proper clothes. She slips her feet into her shoes. Okay, that'll do; she's ready.

Martin has his own problems, but she doesn't have time for him now. She's made up her mind. Whatever they tell her, however many tricks and traps they weave, Rava knows one thing for certain. She can feel it in her gut, in her breasts, in her belly: Amani is still alive. And Rava isn't leaving this place without her.

69

THE STAIRWELL

The Atrium is wider, higher, brighter than Chiara remembers. Are there more guards here than usual? Workers file one by one through the security gates outside the lifts. Isn't that the doctor from Serenity Ward? And there's the healthcare assistant who always complained about equipment not being put away; someone's bound to recognise her.

She holds her breath as they approach the gate. If the red light flashes, she'll have to pretend she left her pass at home; no way can she let a guard scrutinise her borrowed ID. But when she waves Humairah's pass at the sensor, there's a flash of green and a beep as the glass gates slide open. Zoe follows, and they're in. So far, so good.

Doctors, nurses, and assorted hospital staff squeeze into the mirrored lift. None of them look at Chiara or Zoe. Perhaps the scrubs and surgical masks really make them invisible? But as the lift flies upward, Chiara's stomach lurches so violently she wonders if the cable might have snapped.

They step out onto the forty-fifth floor where signs direct patients to *'Expectancy Antenatal Clinic,' 'Ultrasound,'* and *'Fresh*

Starts.' Security is usually a bit lighter here, with no babies on this level, and pregnant 'incubators' coming and going all day long. From here, Chiara and Zoe plan to take the internal stairs up to the more heavily-guarded paediatric floor. There are no cameras in the stairwell, so far as they know.

But today, a guard stands outside the lifts. He speaks into his walkie-talkie, one hand on the holster of his taser gun. Something to do with the demonstration on the Plaza? Will Devorah and her friends be safe out there?

Heads down, Chiara and Zoe hurry past the guard and into Expectancy. Here sit the usual couples hand-in-hand outside the consultants' rooms, the fathers' palms resting proudly on their wives' swelling bellies. The mothers' designer outfits attest to their wealth and suitability to breed. They need only to pass all the tests, complete the paperwork, and produce flaw-less infants.

'Nurse!' calls a voice, and Chiara turns her head, programmed to respond.

'No, not you. You're a grunt cleaner, remember.' Zoe's whisper hisses in Chiara's ear. 'Stop acting so guilty; someone's gonna notice. Come on - in here.'

Zoe waves her pass at the sensor beside a door marked *'Staff Only'* and the entrance to the stairwell clicks open.

THE STAIRWELL IS cool and dim; a tall, echoing space, with stairs spiralling all the way from the basement far below to the roof, another twenty-five floors up. The walls are bare breeze-block, the steps unadorned concrete. It's normally quiet in here, but today a clatter of running feet sounds from above them. Some-one's in a terrible hurry.

Zoe leans out into the scary gap in the middle of the stairs and cranes her neck to look. The noise grows fainter; whoever it is isn't heading this way. They're rushing at a tearing speed up beyond the Genesis Centre floors to the higher levels. An exercise fanatic maybe? Chiara exhales; not their problem.

The Neonatal wards are two floors above. When they reach the door numbered '47', Chiara holds her ID card over the sensor, but an amber light flickers and the lock gives a low, prohibitive buzz. She tries again, and Zoe tries her card too, but with the same result.

'Crap!' Zoe exclaims. 'Faulty lock, maybe? Shall we go down to Shiny-entity, or whatever poncey name they call it on forty-six?' So they try on the floor below, but that lock won't release either; maybe cleaners aren't supposed to use the stairs? Chiara fingers her itchy neck; it feels naked without her hair. They run back down to Expectancy, where they came in, but even that door won't let them out. They're trapped in the stairwell.

'Shall I bang on the door?' suggests Zoe. Chiara tries to protest, but Zoe starts knocking anyway while Chiara gnaws at her finger-ends. Of all the problems, she never expected something so stupid, so banal. What if someone comes and recognises her? What if they ask what they're doing in the stairwell? What if -?

A sound comes from overhead. Feet again. Chiara grabs at Zoe's arm.

'Shh, Zoe! Someone's coming!' The runner completing their exercise routine, perhaps? It sounds like a softer tread. Please let it be someone kind, or in a hurry, or simply not over-bothered with security. Maybe they'll let Zoe and Chiara through the door without checking their ID. Just a couple of cleaners.

A pair of trainers appear on the flight above, then the legs of a man in scrubs. Not the usual plain scrubs, but patterned ones, like they wear on the children's wards. Scrubs with cartoon animals - laughing ducks today. He's rubbing alcohol sanitiser into his hands.

Chiara pulls up her mask to shield her face, but it's too late. The doctor's floppy hair hangs lank around his face, which looks oddly lopsided. His beard is rough and unkempt. When he sees Chiara, he stops, one leg hanging almost comically in mid-air, and he has to clutch at the handrail to save himself from falling. He stares at her across the bottomless gap in the centre of the stairwell between them.

'CHIARA,' Salvador croaks. 'I thought I saw you on one of the monitors, down on Expectancy, but I wasn't sure. I was coming to check. What are you doing here?'

His voice sounds all wrong. His face is a patchwork of mauve and yellow bruises, with a healing cut under one eye. The eye is half-closed, with a bead of pus glistening at its corner. He isn't pretty any more.

Chiara presses her back against the wall.

'Leave us alone.' Today of all days, she can't deal with this - with him.

'Who is it?' Zoe narrows her eyes and whistles softly. 'Someone beat the crap out of him! You know this bloke, Chiara?'

Salvador descends to the turn of the stairs, gripping the rail like an old man. Chiara raises a hand to ward him off.

'Stay away from us. Haven't you done enough?'

Zoe gasps.

'Ah, I get it! He's your ex; that slimebag turned you and Liz in. You total shit!' She starts towards Salvador, fists raised, but Chiara holds her back.

'No, Zoe; it was my fault too.' My fault for trusting him. Bile rises to her mouth; is he going to turn them in and finish the job?

But Salvador stands at a distance, his arms held across his

chest. He angles his head away and Chiara has to strain to catch his words:

'I wanted to warn you - I tried, but they kept hurting me, and they said they knew about Mariana, my sister, and they'd do something to her. Perhaps they were lying, but I couldn't chance it. It was one of the pharmacists - he was police, under cover, all along. They caught me with a load of drugs. I'm sorry, Chiara.' Salvador hangs his head; with his dangling hair, he looks like a broken mop.

'What did they do to you?' He looks pathetic. Both sides of his neck are covered in bruises.

'You don't want to know. They're evil, Chiara, the people who run this country. They paid me, but I didn't do it for the money, I swear, on my sister's life. I sent it all home to Spain, for Mariana, so at least she's provided for, whatever happens to me. That sounds bad, doesn't it, but they kept beating me, and - other stuff.' He shudders.

'No, I know you love your sister.' *More than me*, she thinks, and instantly hates herself. 'And I shouldn't have called you from the boat; Liz always said not to, but I was worried -.'

'I know; I should never have told you I was sick - should've known you'd want to look after me. I panicked.' For the first time he meets her gaze, and she glimpses some of the old Salvador in his rueful half-smile. 'What are you doing here? When I heard you'd got away - that was the only good thing.'

Zoe rattles the door handle.

'He's wasting our time. We've got stuff to do. Hey, shitbag, can you let us out of these stairs?'

She marches up to Salvador and pokes him in the ribs with a determined forefinger. He flinches.

'Why are you here, Chiara?' he repeats.

'None of your business,' Zoe retorts. 'Anyway, what d'you care?'

'Please, Salvador,' Chiara begs. 'Could you let us out onto

the paediatric floor? That's all we need. No one would ever know it was you, I swear.'

He rubs at his forehead as if trying to solve a puzzle.

'I think I know why you're here, and you're very brave, both of you. But please, leave now while you still can. It's way too dangerous, especially with all this trouble today. I'll take you both down to the Atrium and see you out safely.'

'Chill, it's only a demo.' Zoe rolls her eyes, but Salvador replies in a low monotone:

'This is different. There's a big scandal about corruption in the Ministry of Health - hand-in glove with the mafia, they're saying. It's brought everything to a head. People are really angry. The police have announced an emergency curfew, but no one's taking any notice. So Chiara, please, go home, keep yourself safe and forget about the baby. You tried your best, we all did, but there's nothing more we can do.'

He shakes his head, but a white flare of fury ignites in Chiara's chest. How dare he? How dare he tell her to give up? Liz didn't give up; she jumped into the river so Chiara could escape and rescue Amani, or die trying. Midwives are warriors.

So she steps right up close to Salvador. He smells of fear and disinfectant.

'No, Salvador. No. Safe is not enough. If I keep myself safe while women live in terror and babies are murdered, I despise myself. The same way I despise you. Safe! All I ever hear in this country is *safe*. Where is the point in *safe* if you die inside yourself? How can you ever be safe, unless first you are free? Tell me!'

But Salvador edges away, turning his face to the wall. Chiara throws up her hands.

'You don't have an answer. Okay then, just let us out of these stairs! Come on, Zoe.' She seizes his silly scrubs - like a toddler's pyjamas - and points. 'We need to get onto the Neonatal floor, and we can't waste any more time.'

Salvador's shoulders slump.

'Okay.' He leads the way painfully slowly, step by step.

'Are you sure about this, Chiara?' he mumbles as they reach the forty-seventh floor. 'What about your friend?' He glances curiously at Zoe, but Chiara can't wait any longer.

'We're both sure. Midwives don't give up; we fight until our last breath.'

Salvador raises his ID card to the electronic lock. Chiara and Zoe step out onto the corridor without looking back. Not even a glance.

70

JENNY

They find a laundry cart in the sluice room. The big metal trolley is half-full with sacks of dirty linen. The wheels squeak as they pull it along. Chiara cringes at every screech and bump but they make it unchallenged all the way along the corridor and round the corner to Neonatal Two.

'Ready?' Zoe mouths. Chiara nods. She raises her card to the sensor beside the door - surely it won't work here, if it didn't on the stairs? But at the first attempt, the light flashes green. Chiara picks up one of the empty laundry sacks and enters the room.

The stink of nappies and stale formula milk engulfs her. The nursery nurse sits at her desk. She glances up, but she's straight back to her mobile phone when she sees it's only the cleaners.

'Dirty linen,' Zoe says. The nursery nurse doesn't respond. She's the one Chiara met here before: the sharp-tongued woman with a child and no partner to help pay the bills. Her acrylic nails are mauve today, and she looks as if she's gained a little weight.

Chiara walks past the row of cots towards the linen hamper

at the far end, her heart skipping several beats. All the cots are occupied; six babies lie pale and silent. Have they upped the morphine doses? The first three look plump enough, but the ones further along have sunken fontanelles and dry, creased skin - sure signs of dehydration. The sweet-sour smell makes her want to gag.

The baby in the end cot has a sallow tinge. Chiara has to look twice before she's certain, but the label above the cot confirms all her fears: *'Female neonate of Robson. NBM.'* Nil by mouth. Amani's long lashes are closed over pale cheeks. Her tiny chest rises and falls almost imperceptibly. A cannula protrudes from her bruised and swollen left hand. She's alive, but for how much longer?

They need to move quickly now. Chiara unzips her bag, finds what she needs, and checks the nursery nurse isn't watching before giving Zoe a quick thumbs-up. She dumps the laundry sack and strides towards the desk. The nursery nurse looks up, startled.

'What d'you want? Can't you see I'm busy?' she huffs. A nursery nurse outranks a cleaner by several pay grades.

Chiara lays Rava's diamond ring down on the desk. The enormous stone glints and winks, catching the light.

'What's this?' The nursery nurse's mouth drops open. She extends a hand, then snatches it back as if the gemstone might burn her. Sensing someone behind her, she spins to look over her shoulder, where Zoe stands, grinning and holding out a twisted cot sheet.

'Keep quiet.' Zoe's fingers make a zipping motion across her lips. 'This is your lucky day. Sit tight, don't scream or shout or nothing, and I won't need to shove this rag in your mouth. It came outta one of them soiled linen bags, so it's probably not the cleanest. We need one of your babies, that's all, in exchange for that little beauty.' She nods towards the ring on the desk. The nursery nurse reaches for it, but Chiara is too quick for her.

She grabs back the ring and holds it out between her finger and thumb.

'Is that real?' asks the nursery nurse. Then she narrows her eyes and squints at Chiara. 'Have I seen you in here before?'

Chiara nods.

'I used to work here,' she says. 'But I left, because this is a horrible place. I hated it. And you hate it too, don't you? You told me that last time. Yes, this diamond is real. It belongs to the mother of one of these babies, but I know she'd want you to have it, in exchange for her baby. You can sell the ring and leave this job; maybe then you'll be able to sleep at night.'

The nursery nurse's eyes widen. She gazes at the ring as if she's been hypnotised.

'D'you know how much it's worth?' she begins, but a sudden sound in the corridor makes her start.

'Wait a minute; this is a trap, isn't it? You've been sent by them arseholes in Security and Government, or whatever they call it, to catch me out. That's just some bit of plastic crap. You think I can afford to lose this job? I got a kid at home. I'm calling Security.'

She picks up the hospital phone on her desk and starts to dial. Chiara catches her breath; it's now or never.

'Here. Have a look for yourself.' She leans forward and places the precious ring right into the nursery nurse's palm. Will she pocket it and call for Security anyway? Will she mock their feeble attempt at bribery? Chiara can't be sure, but she doesn't think so; there's a hunger in the woman's face. As she said before, this isn't a marvellous job.

The nursery nurse turns the ring over and holds it up to the light. It really is dazzlingly bright. She licks her lips.

'This has gotta raise enough to pay off my credit cards, plus some left over.' She speaks carefully, as if she's doing calculations in her head. 'My littl'un's been sick, see, so I had to go into debt. Which baby you after?' She glances along the line of cots, then back at the diamond. 'It depends which one you want, see. If I can manage the paperwork, say the mortuary boys came quick -.'

Chiara surveys the row of babies. One of them is crying weakly now. Another stirs under its covers. Zoe points towards the end cot.

'That one at the end,' Zoe says.

But Chiara knows that's the wrong answer. She sees Liz standing here, forthright as ever, in no mood to bargain. She sees Jajja, refusing all payment for her hospitality, promising her prayers. She hears Nonna's cracked old voice: *'Du' su' i putenti.'* Be the second kind of powerful.

'All of them,' Chiara says. 'We need to take all the babies.'

The nursery nurse snorts. Zoe gasps; this wasn't what they planned.

'Oh, come on!' the nursery nurse scoffs. 'That would lose me my job. All them babies - you gotta be kidding me. What am I going to say, when the boss comes round? They all went out for a tea party? This ring might pay my bills for a few months, maybe, if it's not fake. And after that? Who's gonna want a nursery nurse who loses all her babies? I'd be scrubbing floors, and that's if I don't end up in prison. What's my little girl going to do then?'

Zoe's starts to say something, but they're out of options. Chiara pulls all the rest of Rava's jewellery out of her bag: the heavy gold necklaces, the ring with the rubies, the gold and diamond earrings, the bangles. It's all there except for Liz's locket; she left that in Jajja's safekeeping. Chiara dumps it all onto the desk.

'There,' she says. 'That's everything I've got. For all the babies. But we have to take them now.' Her heart is thumping, but deep inside she's calm. Steady. She's doing what has to be done.

The nursery nurse tilts her head, weighing everything up.

'What you gonna do with them all? Adopt them or some-thing? You must be outta your mind. Some of them got mothers here in the hospital, you know, down on Serenity, hoping to get them back. You gonna sell them on the black market? What's your plan?' She shakes her head, but keeps sifting through the heap of jewellery. 'Is that a real ruby?'

'Chiara, are you sure?' Zoe says. 'I don't want to leave them here either. If one of them was my Dembe, I'd kill to get her out of this shithole. But, how? There's six of them.'

Chiara says nothing; there's nothing else to be said. She doesn't know what comes next, but something's driving her from within: a quiet determination. It feels good. She waits, standing tall. One way or another, she won't leave a baby to die. Never again.

The gold shines and glistens. A baby wails. The nursery nurse shrugs.

'All right,' she says. 'If the bosses are all taking backhanders, I don't see why I should miss out. But I don't rate your chances.' She grabs her handbag from under the desk and scoops all the gold into it. 'I'll head down the break room now, just for fifteen minutes, mind. When I get back, I'm raising the alarm and reporting the babies stolen, so you'd best be quick.' She snaps her bag shut and heads for the door.

Zoe's shoulders drop with relief, but Chiara looks at the babies. Two of them are crying now. That strong voice from inside her speaks again:

'Listen,' she says. 'I know this is a lot to ask, but - would you help us?'

'You what? I am helping you, aren't I? Getting out of your way. What more d'you want?'

Chiara touches the nursery nurse's hand.

'We need to feed them,' she says, 'before we go. Otherwise they'll cry, and some of them - the ones that are starving - might not make it out alive. Would you help us feed them, please, before we go? You said before you try to keep them comfortable, and I know you want to be kind.'

The nursery nurse looks at the door, then down at her bag, then across at the line of babies. Zoe stares at Chiara with slack-jawed wonder. Slowly, the nursery nurse takes hold of Chiara's fingers.

'All right then,' she says. 'A quick feed, that's all mind - ten minutes. But I can't take them wrist bracelets off, before you ask. Only doctors got the codes for that, or ward sisters. So soon as you get to the main lifts, all them alarms gonna be screaming the place down. Don't say I didn't warn you. Dear God, I must be losing my mind!'

She opens the storage cupboard and starts passing out bottles of formula. 'Here. Better get a move on, hadn't we? My name's Jenny, by the way.'

71

A LOVING VOICE

'Amani, wake up,' Chiara whispers, but there's no response, not even the quiver of an eyelid. Chiara loosens the tape from the back of Amani's hand and eases out the cannula. Only a few drops of blood leak out, a sure sign of the baby's dehydrated state. She strokes the infant's cool cheek, but Amani scarcely moves. She is lost in a drugged sleep. Her chest flutters, her breaths shallow and uneven.

Chiara lowers her ear to the tiny chest and finds the heartbeat. Too slow. She teases the corner of the baby's mouth with the teat of the bottle, but the synthetic milk dribbles across Amani's chin.

'Come on, my love,' she tries again, tickling her feet. Amani twitches one leg feebly, as if to say, 'leave me alone.' But Chiara's not giving up.

She reaches into the cot, undresses Amani down to her dry nappy, and lifts her into her arms. Then she sits on the floor and nestles Amani under her tunic - thank the good Madonna these borrowed scrubs are so baggy! She holds the floppy baby against her own heart, warming her with the warmth of her body, like the new mothers do on the Rosie Lee.

'Skin to skin and a mother's loving voice,' - that's what Liz
always says. 'And no hurry. Nature's a wonderful thing, if we
give her time to do her work.' That's all very well, but they don't
have time to spare. Chiara tries to relax her shoulders and
steady her own breathing. Come on, Amani, wake up, please!

Zoe and Jenny are busy feeding all the other babies and
swaddling them in blankets. Zoe offers her own full breast to
one infant whilst holding the bottle for another.

'Thank God for that,' she says. 'S'been hours since I fed
Dembe; thought I was gonna burst. Hope she's taking her bottle
all right from Jajja. How's your one doing, Chiara?'

'I don't know,' Chiara says. 'Come on, *chica*. You can do it.'
She lifts the tunic and offers the chemical-smelling milk again.
It leaks away untasted, but Amani's breaths have settled to an
even rhythm, and the nape of her neck feels a little warmer.

'If anyone shows up, we're screwed,' Jenny, the nursery
nurse, interjects. 'All of us. Ten minutes, I said. It's been fifteen
already. You might have to give up on that one, sweetie; she's
been four days nil by mouth. Can't expect miracles.'

'Just bring her asleep, like she is,' Zoe suggests. 'We can try
to feed her again later. At least she's quiet.'

'She was brought in wearing this; it'll keep her warm at
least. But we need to get moving.' Jenny passes Chiara a small
hat knitted from purple yarn. It's the one Liz made that last day
on the Rosie Lee. Chiara pulls it over Amani's fragile head.

'Just a little longer,' Chiara pleads. A mother's loving voice,
she thinks. On the Rosie Lee that night, before everything went
wrong, Rava sang to her baby. It was something sweet and
soothing - a Persian lullaby, Rava said; something her own
mother used to sing to her. Chiara doesn't know any songs from
Persia, but she remembers Nonna's lullabies.

Lowering her mouth to the curl of Amani's ear, she begins
to sing, so softly it's a secret between herself and the tiny girl,
the same lullaby she used to sing to the babies on Liz's boat:

'Dormi riposa sutt'a 'na rosa
alla susuta ti dugnu na cosa
ti vogghiu beni, ti vogghiu beni
chiudi l'ucciḍḍi ca 'u sunnuzzu veni.

T'a cuitari, t'a cuitari
comu si cueta l'unna dû mari
comu agghi' a ddiri, comu agghia a ddiri
l'occhiu ti joca e a 'ucca t'arridi.'

Chiara sings the song again, and a third time. The other babies are all ready, fed and double-wrapped to keep them warm and quiet. Zoe's at the door, listening for sounds in the corridor outside. Jenny is settling the fifth baby into the capacious laundry trolley. Chiara comes to the end of her song.

It's no good. They'll just have to hope Amani's still breathing when they get out of here. If they can find a way out, that is.

'I'm coming,' she says. She sighs, listens, and there it is: a cry like a kitten, a tiny mew, asking to be fed. Amani's eyes are open, slate-grey and sleepy. She is sticking out her little pink tongue

'Zoe,' Chiara whispers. 'Come here. See if she'll take your breast milk.'

Zoe comes, and Chiara passes Amani to her. Amani turns her face from side to side against the curve of Zoe's breast, rooting. Then she opens her mouth, latches onto the nipple, and drinks.

72

MONITORS

'I need to see my daughter,' Rava says.

'Mrs Robson.' The nurse lets out a long-suffering sigh. Her name, according to the sign on her office door, is *Sister Ingrid Miller*.' 'Your husband has declined to sign the parental paperwork for the neonate in question. In the circumstances, it would be against the law for the Genesis Centre to release the infant into your care. My hands are tied.'

'I'm not going without my baby,' Rava insists. 'I don't know how you got this job, Miss Miller, but you're an evil woman, keeping mothers from their babies.' Rava leans in so close she can see the pores under Sister Miller's make-up and taste her perfume. The nurse stiffens.

'Considering what being said about your husband, you're scarcely in a position to take the moral high ground, my dear.' The nurse clicks her computer mouse and the screen on her desk switches to the news.

'The whereabouts of Martin Robson are currently unknown,' says the presenter.

'Oh dear, he has got himself in a mess!' Sister Miller sneers.

'Perhaps you should go home to comfort him, Mrs Robson? Stand by your man, and all that.'

Rava keeps her focus steady.

'Where is my daughter?'

She feels stronger now she's up and dressed - more like herself - the person she's always wanted to be. For years she's felt incomplete, as if something's missing. She's never quite belonged, never entirely fitted in, now matter how hard she's tried. But now she knows who she is: she's a mother, and she belongs with her baby.

'Mrs Robson, please take some advice from me. You have not yet been sterilised. Your account here has been settled, and you are free to leave. You still have the potential to incubate again, although of course your mental health record would be taken into account in considering any future licence. I strongly suggest you go quietly.'

The Sister's lips close over her small, white teeth. She turns back to her computer, opens a document, and starts to type.

Rava presses her hands together.

'We're done here,' Sister Miller says, not looking round, but Rava doesn't move. She sits and waits, forcing herself to stay calm. Weeping and pleading haven't worked, but there must be another way; there has to be! Amani's somewhere in this building and she needs to find her.

She scrutinises the screens on the wall opposite behind Sister Miller's back. They must be monitoring the security camera feeds from every corner of the ward. Mothers doze in their rooms, nurses bustle around, and babies sleep in the ward nursery. Could one of those babies be Amani? Rava screws up her eyes, trying to focus on each infant's fuzzy features. The Sister said Amani's upstairs, in another ward, but she might be lying.

One of the monitors shows a corridor and a lift door. The lift door slides open and three women emerge wheeling a big laundry trolley. The women wear surgical masks; cleaners, Rava assumes. Sister Miller keeps typing, her gaze fixed on her screen, fingers flying. One of the cleaners - she has short, cropped hair - keeps peering into the trolley as if there's something unusual inside.

'Please leave now,' Sister Miller says. The frilly white cap quivers on top of her head.

Rava doesn't reply. On another screen, a cleaner enters a patient's room. Instead of emptying the bin, like they usually do, the cleaner shakes the patient's shoulder to rouse her. Then she starts gesticulating and pointing. Rava frowns; Sister Miller types faster than ever. The woman on the monitor gets up from her bed, looking groggy and confused.

On the top left screen, the cleaner with the short hair enters another patient's room. This cleaner is holding some sort of bundle against her chest. It looks like -.'

Sister Miller huffs.

'Mrs Robson, I have work to do. Do I need to call Security to have you removed?' Her hand reaches for her desk phone, her golden Femband glinting on her wrist.

Rava bites her lip; a powerful instinct tells her to remain silent. Sister sighs and starts dialling. Rava keeps watching the screens.

Something odd is happening on the ward. That mother is leaving her room hand-in-hand with the cleaner, and she seems to be crying. The laundry trolley has disappeared from the corridor.

Sister holds the receiver to her ear, waits, frowns, and puts it down again. Something squeals nearby. The wheels on that trolley perhaps? Unless it's a baby crying? Rava's over-full breasts tingle.

Sister Miller stands up and takes a step towards the door, looking puzzled. No; she mustn't go out there. Not now! Before she quite knows what she's doing, Rava leaps up and stands in front of the blonde nurse, barring her way.

'You have to give me my baby!' Her voice rises to a shrill pitch. Sister narrows her eyes and purses her orange lips. She grasps Rava by both shoulders and shoves her back down onto the chair. For a petite woman, she is surprisingly strong.

'I don't have to do anything,' she spits. 'Right, stay there, you jumped-up little trophy-wife. I gave you a chance to walk out of here, but perhaps a spell on a secure ward at the People's Hospital will help you sort out your priorities. I don't think your esteemed husband will have time to bother about you for a while.'

'It can't be worse than in here!' Rava retorts.

Behind Sister's back, one of the monitor screens shows a pair of double doors at the end of the ward corridor. The sign above the doors says *'Education Room.'* The short-haired cleaner - who looks weirdly familiar - leads the crying mother inside, and the doors swing shut. There don't seem to be any cameras in that room, so far as Rava can make out.

Keeping her eyes fixed on Rava, Sister Miller unclips the walkie-talkie from her belt.

'Security to Serenity Ward. I have a client who needs escorting off the premises.'

Only a crackle comes in response. Sister Miller taps her foot impatiently and gives the device a little shake. On a screen, one of the cleaners is rounding the bend in the corridor, coming this way, with a bundle in her arms.

'Serenity Ward Sister for Security. Security please?' Another long crackle is followed by snatches of an inaudible, sputtering voice. Sister's gaze flicks upwards, and she smooths a single errant hair from her forehead. 'Don't move,' she commands Rava. 'I'm watching you.'

She keeps trying the walkie-talkie, with the same garbled result. Is there some problem with Security? Suddenly, that high-pitched sound comes again. It's much nearer now, not far from Sister Miller's door. And it's not a trolley squeaking. Rava's breasts flood with milk.

Sister Miller presses all the buttons on her walkie-talkie. The large mole on her cheek looks redder than usual. She picks up the phone.

'Head of Security please, immediately. There seems to be a malfunction on my walkie-talkie. Yes, of course it's urgent. What d'you mean, there's an incident? I have vulnerable patients in my care. I don't think you understand!'

Seizing her opportunity, Rava slips quietly into the corridor. The nurse is still talking crossly on the phone. Rava closes the door behind her.

The cleaner with the cropped hair - the one who looked so familiar on the monitor screens - is standing right outside. In her arms, she holds a small bundle, wrapped in a blanket and wearing a mauve knitted hat. The cleaner smiles under her mask, and the bundle cries. She is calling out for her mother.

'Rava!' The cleaner lowers her mask. 'It's me - Chiara. Thank God! We thought you'd left the Centre already. Look - I think she knows you.'

But Rava is already scooping Amani into her arms, holding her close to her heart, and covering her with mingled tears and kisses.

73

EMERGENCY

'Amani! I knew you were here. Oh praise be to God! Praise be!' Rava is sobbing, praying and laughing all at once, but Chiara knows they're still in danger.

'Quick, this way.' Chiara steers Rava away from Sister's office. They've found the mothers for three of the other Neonatal Two babies, though one was too heavily drugged to rouse. Have they increased the mothers' sedative doses again? Voices drift from the staff room as they pass the side-corridor: two nurses moaning about their shifts.

'They treat us like effing robots,' one of them complains.

Chiara hurries Rava past the half-open door and into the central lobby area, making for the Education Room where Zoe and Jenny are waiting with the other mothers and babies. Once they're all together, they need to get out of here, and fast. Chiara's neck prickles.

They never planned to leave with six infants and several mothers. Someone's bound to see them; Rava's bright turquoise dress is unmissable. And the babies' security bracelets will set off the alarms on the exits. Perhaps they can use a service lift, or the stairs? Or -.

'Mrs Robson? Where are you going? The exit is the other way.' Sister Miller's crisp voice rings out behind them. Chiara's stomach somersaults.

'Keep walking. Don't look round,' she hisses to Rava, tightening her grip on her arm.

'Let go of her! Cleaning staff aren't allowed to have contact with the patients.' Sister's heels click on the polished floor, approaching fast.

'This lady was lost, Sister,' Chiara says, trying to sound English, terrified her accent will betray her. 'She asked me to show her to the toilet.' She turns Rava in the direction of the visitors' washroom, but Sister isn't fooled.

'What have you got there, Mrs Robson?' she asks. 'You're carrying something.' The clicking heels accelerate, and then: 'Heavens above - you've stolen a baby! Well, I did try to warn you, Mrs Robson.'

Chiara hesitates - she can't help herself; Sister Miller's cut-glass vowels still tie her insides into knots. Sister Miller makes a grab for Amani, but Rava isn't letting go of her daughter again. With a fierce cry, she clutches her baby to her chest.

'You're not having her, you bitch!' Her spit lands on Sister's cheek, just above the mole. Sister wipes it away and reaches for her walkie-talkie.

'Serenity Sister. Urgent Security on Serenity Ward please. I repeat, Urgent. Over.' She glares at the walkie talkie as if it has personally offended her. 'Patients at risk,' she enunciates, 'Over.'

A long pause, lot of fizzing and cracking, and, finally, a voice:

'Major incident in the Atrium. All Security staff currently engaged in a major incident. Over and out.'

Sister frowns at Chiara. 'Do I know you?'

'Yes,' Chiara begins, and starts fumbling with her mask; a

distraction might give the others a chance to get out. But Sister shrugs and turns away - only a cleaner.

'First things first. Do I have to do everything myself?' She speaks into the walkie-talkie one last time: 'Immediate assistance on Serenity Ward. Emergency tranquillisation please.' Then she marches into the nearest patient room, reaches for the red emergency button, and pulls. Ear-splitting sirens howl across the ward and the beat of feet comes thundering.

74

ZUCLOPENTHIXOL ACETATE

'Who is it, Sister?'

Two nurses appear, red-faced and eyes popping, followed by a sturdily-built healthcare assistant. A few dazed mothers emerge onto the central lobby, hands over their ears.

'Is my baby all right?' one of them asks. Chiara casts a furtive glance towards the Education Room, then back at Rava, who is bent over Amani.

'It's her.' Sister Miller points at Rava. 'Psychotic - she's trying to steal that baby. She's got the whole ward in chaos. Restrain her, now!'

One of the nurses steps forward, but Chiara stands in her way.

'Move over,' shouts the nurse over the sirens. 'This is a medical emergency; we don't need the effing cleaners.'

Chiara doesn't budge. Out of the corner of her eye, she spots a slight figure rounding the bend in the corridor. No, Zoe, stay out of this!

'Where's the restraint team?' Sister Miller demands. 'What is wrong with this place today?' She grabs Chiara's wrist and twists viciously. 'Get off my ward, whoever you are; you're endangering the patients!'

'Let go of her,' Rava snarls.

Sister's grip is steely. Chiara's feet slip and slide on the polished floor.

'Run, Rava!' she mouths, but a nurse has Rava by the shoulders, pinned up against the wall. The healthcare assistant moves in to take Amani.

No!' Rava screams. Chiara closes her eyes; she can't bear to watch. Not this again, after everything.

'RAPID RESTRAINT? How can I help you, Sister?'

The doctor's voice is measured. The emergency bells fall silent. Chiara opens one eye. He's wearing scrubs with cartoon animals.

'Zuclopenthixol acetate, one hundred and fifty milligrams. This should do the trick, don't you think, Sister?' He holds up a syringe, bright and sharp. 'Let's get this over with.'

'Salvador - no!' He advances towards the women, beaming cheerfully. With his bruised face and blackened eye, he looks like a madman. The two nurses exchange glances. What's he doing?

'Careful, doctor! Sharps can be dangerous.' Sister Miller lets go of Chiara. Her tone is suddenly hoarse. 'This is the patient, here.' She indicates Rava, who is on her knees, sobbing and gesturing wordlessly towards the cot where Amani now lies.

Salvador shakes his head, still smiling.

'I don't think she's the one who's delusional. Power-crazed, you say in English, don't you?' He meets Chiara's gaze, and all at once she understands. 'Chiara? Zoe? Can you give me a hand?' He nods towards Sister Miller.

Zoe moves first. Quick as a street fighter, she aims a kick at Sister's slender calf. Sister's eyes bulge in shock. She staggers sideways, and Zoe grabs a handful of her blonde hair.

'Ouch! Who do you think -?' Sister splutters. She tries to twist round to see who attacked her, but Zoe's not letting go.

Salvador advances, needle held high.

'Put that down, doctor!' Sister squeaks.

'Don't worry - this is one of your favourites, Sister Miller,' Salvador says, giving the syringe a little tap. 'Keeps the women quiet like a treat, doesn't it? This dose'll put you out for three days, I reckon. You'll feel like crap afterwards - worst hangover ever - but it shouldn't do any lasting damage. Would you like to do the honours, Chiara?' He extends the syringe towards Chiara, carefully turning the unsheathed needle away from her as he hands it over.

'Zuclopenthixol acetate?' Chiara asks, ever the conscientious nurse. Never give a medication unless you know what it is.

'You got it!' Salvador grins, as Sister Miller pulls free, leaving Zoe holding a big hank of her shiny hair. She swipes at Salvador, but he dodges out of her way, and, before Chiara can see how he did it, he's standing behind Sister, pulling her arms back and up so she's forced to double over.

'Anyone else want to help?' he calls, hooking a foot around Sister's leg. He brings her down face first, and Zoe flings herself onto Sister's back, pinning her to the floor.

'Yeah, why not?' says Jenny, who seems to be having her best day at work ever. 'She was always a bitch to me.' She dives into the whirl of flailing limbs, adding her not-inconsiderable weight to the pile-on. Sister Miller kicks, screams and spews out a stream of expletives Chiara never imagined passing her elegant lips. She pitches her head from side to side, yelling for her nurses, for Security, for a proper effing doctor.

But the nurses only watch open-mouthed, not joining the attack, but doing nothing to help their boss either.

'Serves you right, you selfish cow,' one of them mutters.

The healthcare assistant hesitates for a moment, then joins the fray, flinging herself over Sister's twisting, bucking body.

'Quick. Here.' As Salvador fights the pummelling legs, Chiara raises the syringe and plunges it through the fabric of Sister's skirt into the firm muscle of her buttock. She presses the plunger home, withdraws the syringe, and throws it into the corner of the room. Sister screams and wails, rivalling the emergency bells, as her neat little shoes with their kitten heels beat frantically on the floor. Her lily perfume can't mask the stench as her sphincters relax under the influence of the drug.

'That trolley - look on the top shelf. She keeps the straps in there.' Salvador wrestles Sister's struggling shoulders. She snaps her teeth, and he just pulls his hand back in time. Chiara runs to the emergency trolley standing beside the desk and pulls out the coils of black padded straps. They unfurl across the floor like a tangle of snakes.

Limbs are everywhere: Sister's arms, Zoe's long legs, Salvador's hands. The radio crackles at Sister's belt, unregarded. Chiara's sure Security will be here any moment, but no one appears. Somehow, between them, they bind the straps around Sister Miller's wrists and ankles, pull them tight and secure them. Zoe takes a flying fist to her stomach, but she only swears and holds on tighter.

As the drug takes effect, the drumming of Sister's feet slows to a furious twitch. Her words start to break apart, and flecks of spittle appear at the corners of her mouth. Her orange lipstick smudges across her cheek. The frilly cap has fallen off her head. Her face takes on a look of gentle confusion, like the old ladies with dementia at the nursing home in Sicily.

While Chiara checks her breathing - sedatives can be

dangerous - Sister Miller blinks once, twice, three times. Her eyes struggle into focus.

'S'you,' she slurs drunkenly. 'Should've known ... pity really ... could've been good nurse -.'

She trails off. Her pupils roll back and her head slumps to one side.

Chiara leans across Sister's unconscious body towards Salvador. He's breathing hard, beads of sweat on his forehead.

'*Grazie,*' she tells him. 'Thank you.'

'Should've done it months ago. You're right, Chiara - freedom's better than safety. Come on, let's move her. Security'll be here any moment.'

They scramble to their feet. Salvador looks happier than she's seen him in weeks - perhaps in all the complicated time she's known him. He stands tall, as if a crippling burden has fallen from his back. Chiara reaches out to touch the purple bruises on his throat.

'Can we begin again?' she whispers. And very softly, so as not to hurt him, she kisses his damaged skin.

75

LEAVING

Chiara and Zoe help Salvador drag Sister into her office. She's heavy and smelly. None of the ward staff try to stop them. Sister Miller mutters and moans, drifting in and out of consciousness, so Salvador leaves the straps in place on her wrists and ankles. Chiara insists on lying her on her side in case she vomits. Salvador takes her walkie-talkie and the heavy keyring from her belt, and they lock her in.

When they emerge, the older of the two nurses is speaking agitatedly on the phone, saying something about doctors, and psychotic episodes, and where the hell is Security?

'Sod whatever's going on in the Atrium,' she exclaims. 'No, don't put me on hold!' She swears and slams down the receiver. The younger nurse wrings her hands and makes noises like a chicken laying an egg. Two mothers carrying swaddled babies tiptoe down the corridor from the Education Room.

'What's happening?' one of them asks, wide-eyed. 'Can we take our babies home now?'

Chiara scans the little group of mothers and babies gathering in the central lobby. Rava has reclaimed Amani and tied her to her chest with a sheet. The baby nestles inside, feeding hungrily at her breast. Chiara smiles. Women are strong; that's something Liz used to say: 'You'll never cease to wonder at the fierceness of a mother's love for her child.'

'Who wants to leave with us?' Chiara asks. 'Salvador, can you get the scanner to unlock the baby wristbands?' Her voice has the level authority Liz used to exude; she has found her 'midwife voice.'

'Now hang on. You can't take patients off the ward,' the healthcare assistant exclaims righteously. 'Mrs Hitler in there -.' She jerks her head towards Sister Miller's office. 'She had it coming. Treats us all like her ladies in effing waiting. And it would've been against policy for us to get involved in a struggle with sharps involved, wouldn't it? One of us might've got stuck with that needle, and then where would we be?' Both nurses nod vigorously. 'If there's an enquiry, we were all busy protecting the patients from you psychos.' The two nurses nod again. 'But if patients go missing, that's something else. We'd all be in the shit.'

'Yes. No one's leaving,' asserts the older nurse. Her face is bright pink. 'I'll try Security again. The operator said there's an incident. Can you get these women back to their rooms? And give me that walkie-talkie.'

Salvador shrugs and lays it down on the desk.

'Maybe you haven't heard,' he says, 'but there's a riot going on. Hundreds of people, thousands maybe, are out demon-strating against the Population Policy. That news about corrup-tion at the top of the MPH has finally lit the bonfire. Security's got bigger problems than Serenity Ward right now.' He turns the screen of his smartphone towards the nurse. Sounds of shouting interspersed with bangs and yells emanate from the device. The nurse turns pale.

'Get the trolley, Zoe,' Chiara says. It's now or never. Zoe and Jenny run to the Education Room and return pulling the big laundry trolley. The cat-like cry of a newborn rises from its depths.

'Oh my God!' says the healthcare assistant.

'What the hell?' The older nurse puts down the phone and goes to look, while her colleague flaps her hands helplessly. 'Those neonates belong in the hospital,' declares the senior nurse. 'They're still under medical supervision. None of them are signed off to go home.'

'Yeah, right.' Jenny steps up to confront her. Like Salvador, she seems to have grown several inches taller. 'These are my Neonatal Two babies, sweetheart. Medical supervision, my arse! All right then, I thought it might come to this.'

With a roll of her eyes, Jenny reaches into the trolley, finds her handbag, and pulls out a selection of Rava's jewellery. She throws it onto the desk with a flourish. 'Take your pick, girls!'

'If you think I'm going to turn a blind eye to bribery -,' begins the older nurse. But the healthcare assistant has already picked up a pair of diamond earrings and thrust them into her pocket. 'Hey, wait a minute, let me see that.' She makes a grab at her colleague's tunic. The younger nurse, awakened from her panicked trance, pushes the others aside for a better look.

'Well, this ring's mine.'

'Says who, you greedy cow? I'm senior, so I should get -.'

'Listen to yourself, none of this is legal. You'll lose your job, for starters.'

'Only if someone tells, and you can't, can you, not if you're taking the earrings?'

'The earrings! I need more than a pair of sodding earrings to cover for you, Adele.'

'Move over! Let me see that necklace.'

BEEP. Beep. Beep. Salvador points the scanner at each of the babies' wristbands. Each security band snaps open with a click. Rava and two other mothers carry their rescued infants, and Zoe has the fourth baby, whose mother they couldn't wake. They try shaking her and splashing water on her face, but nothing works. She's probably had a hefty dose of the same anti-psychotic drug they used on Sister Miller.

'Can we get her into a wheelchair?' Chiara wonders, but Salvador shakes his head.

'It's chaos down there; she'll be safer here. Quick, write her name and address on your hand; we'll take her baby. Otherwise he'll be straight back in Neonatal Two. You'll find a way later to get him back to her.'

'Okay, let's go,' Chiara says, glancing over her shoulder at the nurses still squabbling over Rava's jewellery. 'We've been much too long already.'

Chiara and Jenny pick up the two remaining babies from the trolley. Their mothers aren't here, Jenny says; one of them came to Neonatal Two from the People's Hospital, and the other was brought in by the police.

'But we can't leave the babies here,' Jenny adds. Her face shines with a new sense of purpose. Chiara can scarcely believe this is the same woman who sat scrolling while babies starved to death.

'Wait for us.'

To Chiara's surprise, two more mothers carrying babies join their little group hurrying towards the ward exit.

'We're coming too. Who knows what might happen to our babies if we stay here?'

THE CORRIDOR outside Serenity Ward is eerily quiet. Where are the porters wheeling beds, the hurrying nurses, the visitors? Chiara's footsteps echo on the floor; the motherless infant is heavy and warm in her arms. As they approach the lifts, Salvador comes alongside her.

'Let me speak with the guard,' he whispers. 'He will listen to a doctor, I hope. I'll tell him there's a medical reason to be moving these mothers to another floor.'

But the bank of lifts is silent and unattended. The security guard is missing. The back of Chiara's neck is ice cold. This is too easy.

One of the lifts stands open as if it's waiting for them. Chiara presses herself against the mirrored wall as they all crowd inside: five mothers, eight babies, Jenny, Zoe, Salvador and me. Rava bends her head over Amani, repeating prayers or words of endearment under her breath.

'Santa Maria, prega per noi.' Chiara presses the button marked Atrium. This is it, then. You pray too, Nonna, if you can hear me. She feels for the rosary beads in her pocket and closes her eyes. Warriors till our last breath.

76

WHITE MARBLE

It's snowing! That's Rava's first thought when the lift door slides open onto the Atrium. Her second is: *I can't take my baby out there.* Her nostrils flare, fighting to suck in air, but she tightens the sheet binding Amani to her. The air smells hot and metallic as if it's on fire, full of white flakes falling. There's no soothing music; only shouts, screams, and a heart-stopping roar of gunfire. The police are firing into the high ceiling. Firing to disperse the crowd.

Rava wants to cover her own ears, her face, but she won't let go of Amani. She can't trust the sheet to hold her; can't trust anything anymore. Her legs turn soft; all she can see is whiteness. She tries to press back, but there's no space, and she stumbles, almost falling onto the mother beside her.

'Try not to panic - I've got you.' A man's voice in her ear, and a hand on her arm to steady her. 'Wait here. I'll go out first.' It's that doctor, Chiara's friend. Rava draws a shaky breath and tries to makes sense of the scene confronting them.

A torrent of terrified people streams towards the exits under the triple archway, herded by bellowing, faceless figures in black. Abandoned protest signs and placards lie scattered across the floor. A man drags a child by its wrist. Someone shrieks, and Rava sees a policeman jab the muzzle of his gun into a woman's back, forcing her forward.

Two receptionists crouch on the floor behind their desks, their hands over their heads. An empty wheelchair lies on its side, wheels spinning. As Rava clutches Amani still closer - 'Make sure she can breathe,' someone says - there's another eruption of shooting, and an ugly crater appears in one of the marble carvings: a smiling family shattered to dust.

'Clear the area!' barks an angry voice.

'Are they rubber bullets?' someone asks.

A guard approaches their lift; he is wild-eyed and sweating.

'Out, all of you! Evacuation. Hurry!' He waves his weapon at the cowering huddle of women and babies. 'What've you got there? We've had reports of explosives.' He pokes the gun towards one of the bundled-up babies. Vomit rises to Rava's mouth. 'Move!' shouts the guard.

'I'm a doctor,' Chiara's friend says, stepping forward. 'These women are in my care.' He holds out his pass, but the guard takes no notice. One of the mothers starts screaming.

'Come on,' Chiara says, taking hold of Rava's arm. 'We need to get out of here. Let's stay together and head for the left arch - it looks a bit less crowded.'

Rava swallows down the vomit. The women start to shuffle forward.

'Hurry up!' says the guard. 'Terrorist incident.' He jerks his gun in the direction of the archway and the fleeing people.

'Terrorists,' one mother whimpers. 'Is there a bomb?'

'I want to go back,' says another. 'This isn't safe.' She shrinks into the corner of the lift, but the guard reaches in and yanks her out. The doctor puts an arm around her shoulders and draws her into their group.

Together, they cross the white marble floor. Rava covers Amani's face, trying to shield her from the dust, the noise, and the terror. They pass an old man edging painfully forward on crutches, and a pregnant woman leaning on her husband's shoulder. Spilled coffee drips from the edge of a cafe table. The high, animal scent of fear fills the air.

As they approach the scramble for the exits, Rava spots Martin's face grinning up at her from one of the broken placards on the floor. She catches her breath. 'Sewer Rat Robson,' proclaims the text. Is this all because of Martin? What will happen to him? Where did he go after he threw his phone out of the window and fled?

Another round of gunfire rings out. Amani wails. The archway yawns closer.

'Keep going,' Chiara says, 'we're almost there.'

How can she stay so calm in all this madness? Bodies push and shove. They're being squeezed through the arch, pressed in, forced from behind. Let me through; let my baby breathe. It's too close, too hot, too narrow.

All at once they're outside, standing at the top of the stone stairs. Beneath them, the Plaza is a heaving ocean of bodies. Dozens of police cars and riot vans are lined up around the square, but the police are vastly outnumbered by women, children, fathers and mothers - hundreds upon hundreds of them. They're all making a tremendous noise - shouting, chanting and waving banners.

'No more lies!'

'Birth rights are human rights!'

Rava gasps. The protestors have been driven out of the Atrium, but they haven't been silenced, not yet.

'Wow!' says Chiara at her side. 'That's amazing - but how can we get out of here?'

There's no space on the pavement beneath the steps. The

whole square is packed, and cordons of police with riot shields are forcing people up against the buildings, driving them into the narrow exit roads. They could all be crushed down there. Rava bends over Amani, trying to take courage from her innocent face. When she looks up again, faceless men in black are pouring out of vans on the far side of the Plaza.

'They've got tear gas!' someone shouts.

Screams of panic ring out as clouds of white smoke mushroom upwards. People push and shove in every direction, crying out for water, pushing past armed police to throw themselves into the fountains. An acrid smell of vinegar fills the air. The left side of the square, clear of gas for now, throngs with frantic people, desperate to escape. A few younger people stand their ground, throwing bricks and stones at the police, but everyone else is fighting for an exit.

'Quick, this way.' Chiara pulls Rava towards the left-hand end of the steps. 'There's a bit of a gap down there. I think we can get though.'

Rava looks. Yes, there's a little space on the pavement over on that side, and no gas that way. She takes a step down, then another, holding Amani close. But then she sees it, and her heart skips a beat. Right there, close up beside the building, stand three Government cars parked in a tidy line. And that first car is Martin's; she'd know it anywhere. It's his number-plate: *MPH 09,* and - oh God! - there's Daniel sitting at the wheel in his chauffeur's cap. They've come for her; come to swallow her up into the massive Mercedes, and take Amani away. No - not now, not after everything.

Rava's whole body goes rigid.

'This way,' says Chiara again, tugging at her arm, but Rava can't move; she can't take her eyes off the car. You can't see inside, but he's in there, watching her, waiting.

As she starts to tremble, the driver's door opens and Daniel gets out. He's seen her. Martin must have sent him. Daniel speaks to someone at the foot of the steps. Then he looks up, straight at her and Amani, and starts to ascend the stairs, threading his way through the people still descending. He's coming for her - for both of them.

77

A BLOSSOMING ROSE

Chiara spots Devorah. She's still standing at the bottom of the steps with her friends and family, still holding up her sign. *Grazie a Dio e alla Santa Madre!* Perhaps Devorah and her friends can help us get out of here. Chiara raises a hand to wave, letting go of Rava's arm. It's only then that she sees the man in the peaked cap climbing the steps towards them.

What's he doing? Everyone else is fleeing the opposite way. But before she can signal to him to turn around, three more smoke bombs explode, closer this time. Screams ring out as the protestors scatter.

'This way, quick!'

Hoisting the infant higher onto her shoulder, Chiara hurries her group of mothers and babies down the steps. Almost halfway now - they're going to make it. Is everyone still together? Chiara glances round to check: Zoe, Jenny, one, two, three mothers ... Wait!

A piercing shriek comes from above her head. Rava's still standing under the archway in her turquoise dress,. with Amani tied to her chest.

'Rava, this way!' Chiara shouts, but Rava isn't listening. She's staring, transfixed, at the man still ascending the stairway: the man in the peaked cap.

'No, you're not having her!' Her eyes are round with terror. The man's almost reached her. He gesticulates, tries to say something, but Rava edges away. Suddenly, she turns and runs under the arch and back into the Genesis Centre.

'Rava!' cries Chiara. She can't leave Rava behind. 'Wait, I'm coming.' She passes the baby she's carrying to Zoe. 'Get the others out of here.'

The top few steps are almost deserted now; Chiara's up and through the arch in no time, but Rava is already out of reach.

Hair flying out behind her, her dress bright as a flag, Rava hurtles across the snowy floor. The weight of her baby only seems to add to her momentum; she's almost flying. She rounds the cafe, passes the fallen wheelchair, keeps going. Perhaps someone calls out a warning, but Chiara doesn't hear it. Nor, it seems, does Rava; or if she hears she doesn't stop.

She keeps running as the gunfire rings out. They're still firing at the ceiling, aren't they? Oh, please God!

Chiara holds her breath. She should move, but her legs won't work; she should shout, but her throat is paralysed.

Rava swerves for a split-second; is she changing course? But no, she keeps going, heading for the lifts, where she maybe doesn't see, or doesn't care, there are three - no, four policemen with guns - real guns, not tasers - all trained on her.

They won't shoot. She's a mother, a patient. She's holding a baby. Unless - do they think it's a bomb? Surely, they can't, they won't?

Rava skids to a halt metres from the police. Her hands fling around Amani, bundled deep inside the sheet. They'll send her back out here, won't they?

But they haven't lowered their weapons; they're aiming right at her, all four of them.

'Drop whatever you're carrying and raise your hands above your head!'

They think she's a terrorist. Rava doesn't move, only stands there, head bowed, holding onto her child - a vivid, turquoise target.

Silence falls - a terrible, muffled quiet, as if the world has gone deaf. Thick, stifling dust fills the air.

CHIARA FEELS the movement before she sees it: somebody else is running. He's sprints straight towards the men and their guns, and he's fast. He runs like an athlete, cornering the over-turned cafe tables, dodging the wheelchair, tearing through the open barriers. As he nears Rava he dives headlong, like a goal-keeper making a save. She stumbles, but he sends her stag-gering sideways, towards the receptionists' desk and out of harm's way.

Rava crawls for cover, still clutching Amani. The man picks himself up; he's face to face with the police. He's trying to speak to them, but no one is listening.

Chiara rubs her eyes; the dust clears a little. The man - Salvador - starts to raise his hands. He's a doctor - they can't - they won't -. But all at once, flashes explode out of all the guns - bright scatters of pitiless light. They're not aiming at the ceiling this time; there's no more snowfall. The only thing falling is the man.

Salvador falls, hands flailing, knees buckling. His head hits the floor, and Chiara feels the crash, the quake of the earth, though she hasn't moved from the far side of the wide Atrium.

He lies face up. His limbs twitch and convulse. Chiara should get up; she should go to him, but two people are holding onto her and they won't let go. She should give him CPR, mouth-to-mouth; she should use her fists to stop that hole in his chest, hold the blood inside, hold him together. He always needed that. He was never strong, not really. Until today.

Slowly, Salvador's head rolls to one side, then the other, then stops. He lies still, not moving at all, while a blossoming rose of blood spills out of his heart and spreads across the floor.

PART VI

PART VI

78

PIECING IT TOGETHER

Rava doesn't remember who helped her and Amani out from under the reception desk. She has a fuzzy impression of being pushed along in a wheelchair with Amani crying in her lap. After that, the next thing she recalls is sitting in the back of Martin's Mercedes, but Martin isn't there. Instead, the car is crammed to bursting with women and babies.

Days later, she's still piecing it together. It was Daniel she'd got all wrong. Those mysterious visits to the apartment when Martin was out - she'd assumed he was spying on her. But all the time it was Martin he was watching: gathering evidence, planting listening devices in their apartment, preparing to expose him as a fraud.

'But I loved him; he was my husband,' Rava protests, when the Jewish lady called Devorah tries to explain. Devorah has blue-rimmed glasses and a quiet, bookish husband. Her baby, Isaac, has just started crawling. He sits on the rug in Devorah's mother's kitchen, chewing a toy giraffe.

'I'm so sorry,' Devorah says. 'We worried about you a lot. Daniel should've warned you sooner, but he was afraid you might tell Mr Robson. It was a dreadful mistake to scare you like that just as you were escaping from the Genesis Centre. Everything was crazy that day.'

Rava nods and settles Amani onto her other breast where she sucks away greedily. She's putting on weight already; it won't be too long before she fits into Mama's embroidered dress.

'I didn't want Daniel to do it,' Devorah says. 'Not at first - it was so dangerous. He'd been in that job for years - that's what made him ideal, of course - Mr Robson trusted him.'

Daniel, Rava now knows, is Devorah's cousin - part of a vast Jewish extended family.

'If you've got as many cousins as I have, one of them's going to be a Government driver, right? He got the job back before the whole yellow-band thing and somehow managed to keep his Jewishness quiet. He liked chauffeuring at first - good money, and Mr Robson was an okay boss to begin with. But once the population controls came in, and with Mr Robson heading up women's health -.' Devorah grimaces. 'Daniel was going to quit, until one of our Rabbis said maybe God had put him there for a reason - that he might be able to help our community.'

Rava's eyes widen.

'Help with what?'

'Information, mostly.' Devorah scoops up Isaac who has crawled to the back door and is making for the garden. 'Come here, you little rascal. Plans to extend the fertility restrictions, hospital closures, that sort of thing. We knew it was going to get tough, but at least we had an idea what was coming next. We were doing okay until they arrested both our midwives in the same week. That came as a massive shock - especially for me. I was seven-and-a-half months pregnant.'

Rava lowers her head. She's been so focused on her own problems, she's scarcely thought about the impact Martin's had on other people, other families.

'What did you do?' she murmurs.

'We found another midwife - an old lady on a boat.' She smiles at the memory.

Rava clasps a hand to her mouth.

'Liz,' she says. 'You mean Liz, don't you?'

IT TAKES a long time for the two mothers to share their stories. Rava is enthralled by Devorah's birth story. Devorah marvels that Liz is Amani's grandmother. They weep together over the feisty old midwife's death. They exclaim at Chiara's courage and wonder how she's coping now.

By the time they are done, both babies are fast asleep and the women are friends. When Devorah's mother, Naomi, serves dinner at the big table, Rava finds she has an appetite for the first time in many weeks. She accepts a second helping of chicken and roast potatoes. She's only here as a guest, until she and Amani can leave for Scotland, but she feels like part of a family. It's a feeling she hasn't known for a very long time.

OVER THE NEXT days and weeks, Rava sits for long hours in Naomi's kitchen, feeding and caring for Amani. Naomi won't let her help with any of the household tasks, insisting that a new mother must rest. Rava sleeps with Amani at her side and a Hebrew prayer of blessing on the wall above her bed. She tells Naomi she's Muslim, but the older woman only smiles and says God calls us to welcome the stranger.

Devorah shares more about Daniel and Martin. Daniel knew about what went on behind the scenes when midwives were raided. It was brutal, he said, and he worried that Martin was becoming obsessed with the hunt. The midwives had a lot of people protecting them, and Martin grew frustrated. He started meeting Mafia connections in empty car parks; he had a contact at his karate club.

Daniel had to drive Martin to some of the assignations, so he started taking photos and videos, mostly to cover himself at first, and one thing led to another. Soon he was building a portfolio of evidence, waiting for the right moment, hoping he could trust the Rabbi's media contact.

He was still hesitating, not sure if the time was right, when he drove Martin to see the boat where the old midwife drowned. This, Daniel realised, was where Devorah and several others of his relatives had given birth. A place of refuge had been invaded, and to top it all, the midwife was Martin's own mother. Knowingly or not, Martin had signed her death warrant to advance his own promotion prospects. Daniel was sickened.

The final blow fell when he realised Martin wasn't going to let Rava bring Amani home. Daniel knew what happened to babies whose fathers didn't want them. Regardless of the danger to himself, he couldn't wait any longer. He shared his information, and the riots erupted.

'So where's Daniel now?' Rava asks, dreading the reply. He risked everything for her and her baby. He was a husband and father. He was kind.

But Devorah smiles.

'He's a survivor, our Daniel. He's lying low for a while, well away from London, in case the gangs Martin was mixed up with put two and two together. But he'll be back; I can't see him quitting the fight. He'll grow his *peyot* - his side-locks - and his beard, and blend in nicely. To the Mafia, or the Government, all Jewish people look the same.

THEY FOUND Martin's body at the bottom of the stairwell in the Genesis Centre. He was trying to run away, but something went wrong. No one seems to know whether he jumped, or was pushed.

'The gang bosses have no mercy,' Devorah's father says gravely.

Did Martin deserve things to end as they did? Rava's still struggling to make sense of it all. She believes he meant well at first - he cared about saving the planet, and he wanted to protect her too, in his own way. But the Defender's system preyed on his hunger for adulation.

Losing his sister at an early age must have had an impact, and the estrangement from his mother made things worse. He saw women and girls as weak, and the chance to get political capital out of hounding midwives was too tempting. He thought it would salve the pain of his childhood, but it only made things worse.

Rava does her best to take each day as it comes, focusing on Amani and their plans to go home. Grieving for Martin will be a long, complicated process. Despite everything, she loved him. He was Liz's son and Amani's father.

'He wanted to be a good man,' she says, 'and he gave me my daughter.'

Devorah stares at Rava, puzzled, but Naomi takes her into her arms and holds her while she weeps.

79

EMPTY

'So are you coming back to Italy? There's not much space here, but we miss you.'

'I don't know, Gemma.'

Chiara can't find the words for her sister. Making any decision, even the simplest, is impossible right now. Mamma and Gemma heard about the riots on the news, so she gave them a sanitised version of what happened at the Genesis Centre: some protests got out of hand and she's lost her job, but she's fine - nothing to worry about.

She misses them too, but she still has no passport, and they're renting a cramped, one-bedroom flat in Milan. Gemma's working in a nail bar, but Mamma still can't find a job. Chiara would be a burden if she joined them.

'One day, I hope,' she says, feeling anything but hopeful. 'I'll call again next week, okay?'

Chiara hangs up and sits dry-eyed with her lips pressed together. Since Salvador died, there haven't been any tears. Just a big empty hole in the middle of her chest.

She's still staying with Jajja and Zoe, eating their food,

sleeping in their bed, and fixated on the news. The DBC reported four deaths and twenty-nine people injured in the demonstrations at the Genesis Centre. Other sources say there were many more.

The Government blames the disturbances on 'far-right terrorists and Jewish activists plotting to undermine our crucial healthcare systems.' Three houses burn to the ground in Stamford Hill in the following days, but thankfully no one is hurt. Devorah's family manages to reunite one of the rescued babies with its parents, and finds foster homes within the Jewish community for the two unclaimed infants. Rava and Amani are doing well; they'll be leaving for Scotland next week.

'Yay, we did it!' Zoe rejoices. Chiara knows she ought to be happy too, but the price was so high.

Oddly, Salvador's death is hailed with much hand-wringing by the authorities. *'Heroic doc saves mum from mob,'* and *'Gunned down by anarchists,'* the headlines lament. Salvador's face appears on everyone's screens for a day or two: his old, handsome face, with the floppy hair, and the boyish, blue-eyed smile. No blackened eye or bruised throat to be seen. Chiara saves all the pictures and spends hours looking at them, but the cold nothingness inside won't go away.

The mainstream media barely mentions Martin Robson; maybe the focus on Salvador is intended as a distraction. With almost indecent haste, a new Under-Secretary of State for Women's Health appears on the DBC bulletins. She's a thin, angular woman hastily recruited from a senior role in one of the big energy companies.

'Rest assured,' the Under-Secretary tells the cameras, 'I am committed to a fair and sustainable healthcare system, delivering quality fit for a modern nation. Our work continues to be research-based and fully aligned with the Government's future-facing population and health policies.'

'She'll fit in nicely,' Zoe comments wryly.

Chiara sighs. Has anything really changed? If the police are still looking for her - if they come to Jajja's home - she will hand herself in. She's too exhausted to run any more, and besides, what would be the point? But the days turn into weeks with no knock at the door and no mention of midwives in the Government media. Perhaps something has shifted after all?

The disappearance of six babies from the Genesis Centre goes unreported. Presumably, the new Under-Secretary is reluctant to publicise the existence and purpose of Neonatal Two. And no one ever hears about the forcible tranquillisation of a senior Sister; questions about heavy-duty sedatives on the postnatal ward could prove embarrassing for the Ministry of Population and Health. With Martin Robson gone, hunting down the last midwife doesn't seem to be anyone's priority.

The Defender still makes speeches about the importance of sterilisation for national security, and how a registered child is a happy child, but the focus shifts to the Peaceful Rest euthanasia programme. As a new inducement, the first-degree relatives of anyone over fifty-five can get housing upgrades when their family member signs up for Peaceful Rest. The advertisements show pictures of candles, roses, and lilies cutting to a happy young couple opening the door to a bright, modern apartment.

'Give the ultimate gift,' croons the narrator. 'Unlock their future.'

ONE AFTERNOON IN LATE OCTOBER, Zoe comes home with news.

'Guess what? The old boat's empty,' she says with an enthusiasm Chiara wishes she could share. 'The pigs are gone - took all their crime scene tape away - can't be bothered with it no more.'

Chiara nods, but doesn't speak. Her memories of the Rosie Lee are a minefield. She's still having flashbacks to the night of the raid; the smell of male sweat, blue lights, or sudden loud noises can all send her into a dizzying panic.

'So anyway.' Zoe fills the silence. 'The boat's just sat there. Not even squatters on it. It's a bit of a mess, but there's quite a bit of your and Liz's stuff still there. D'you want to come and see?'

CHIARA HAS A SLEEPLESS NIGHT, but by morning she knows she has to go back if she's not to be haunted forever. Besides, Liz wouldn't want her precious books and supplies left to rot.

They find the Rosie Lee still moored where she lay on that stormy night. The poor old boat looks forlorn. The tomato plants and marigolds in the roof boxes have collapsed into a tangle of rotting stalks. The chicken coop stands empty. Zoe knocks on the roof, but no sound comes from within.

'Hello? Ah, about time!' A stocky man calls across from the cruiser moored alongside. He's one of Liz's long-time boater friends. 'Am I glad to see you! What a business, but I always knew old Liz would go down fighting. If only I'd been there that night, them coppers would've known about it all right. Come in for a cuppa, both of you.'

Over a brew even stronger than Liz used to insist on, the man tells them he's been keeping an eye on things. He shares his opinions of the police in colourful detail.

'But they're gone now,' he concludes, 'and good effing riddance. I suppose they kept the squatters away, and most idiots seem to think it's cursed, what with all that rubbish about Liz being a witch.' He snorts. 'There's been a bit of looting - I can't be here to watch all the time - and a few kids have been in and out, but I've put the fear of God in them, don't you worry!'

Mugs drained and neighbour profusely thanked, Chiara and Zoe return to the Rosie Lee. A rough board covers the entrance where the door was smashed in. Together they lift it aside. A dank smell of mould and abandonment rises from the gloomy interior.

'Hello? Is anyone here?' Chiara tiptoes down the steps, wincing every time a board creaks under her feet.

'Hello?' Zoe echoes, but no one replies. In the kitchen, the stove is cold, and mouse droppings lie in little heaps across the surfaces, mingled with smashed glass and the dregs of spilled tinctures. Chiara sighs: so many months of collecting, drying, and infusing lost. *But you know the recipes by heart,* whispers a little voice in her head.

The bowls and cooking pots are all gone, taken by looters. The little fridge is missing, and most of Liz's hand-written note-books, but her midwifery library is untouched. The police must have decided all these old paper books weren't worth the trouble of carting away, and the thieves might have been afraid to take a witch's spell-books to burn as fuel.

Perhaps they thought Liz's hand-made patchwork quilt was enchanted too, because Chiara finds it scrunched up and shoved into a corner. As she picks it up, out tumbles the red enamel kettle. There's a new dent below the spout, but it looks as if it will still hold water. Chiara carries it into the galley and sets it on the stove where it belongs.

THEY RETURN next day with Jajja. Devorah has stayed in touch, repeatedly asking if there's anything she can do to help, so Chiara calls her now, and she comes to the Rosie Lee. Together they set to work, scrubbing and mending, bleaching and sweeping, lighting a fire in the stove and re-hanging the rosy pink curtains.

The man from the neighbouring boat brings fuel, tools, and fresh water.

'I've got a mate at Broxbourne boatyard can get you a new door,' he says. With the neighbour's help, and after several attempts, Chiara manages to start the engine. The Rosie Lee rumbles into life.

'What if the police come back?' Chiara worries.

'How about repainting her?' Devorah suggests. 'She could do with brightening up, and there are thousands of boats on the waterways. We'll give her a whole new identity.'

It takes several weeks and some repairs at the boatyard which Devorah insists on paying for, but at last the old narrowboat is reborn. They give her a new coat of fresh, green paint, decorating the sides with purple heartsease flowers and yellow daisies.

Chiara hesitates before painting over the *'Rosie Lee'* lettering, but she bites her lip and imagines Liz nodding calmly and saying, 'We do what has to be done. No need to fuss.'

So now the boat needs a new name. They debate back and forth, coming up with all sorts of suggestions - serious, sentimental, and silly - but nothing is quite right.

'No rush,' says Devorah. 'It'll come to you, Chiara.'

———

CHIARA's busy making everyone a well-earned mug of tea one afternoon when Devorah appears in the galley holding up a small knitted bag, rather grubby-looking.

'What's this?' she asks. 'It was on the roof, wedged under that old wheelbarrow. Something's inside, I think.'

Chiara loosens the drawstring and pulls out Liz's ancient pinard stethoscope. Somehow the police must have missed it, or maybe they simply ignored it as a useless piece of old tat, having no idea of its function. She rolls it against her cheek. It's smooth as silk, the warm wood aged to a deep mahogany brown.

'Thank you, Devorah,' she says. 'I'll be needing this.'

80

PRESENCE

A few days after moving back onto the boat, Chiara goes to visit Salvador's old apartment. It might be a crazy risk, but she can't stop herself. She still has his spare key and an aching sense of unfinished business.

The lift takes her up to his floor where everything looks and smells so familiar she half-believes he'll be waiting for her behind his front door. Perhaps his things will still be inside - his clothes, his football boots, the sofa where they used to snuggle up together. Perhaps she might feel less alone.

But the door opens onto a neutral, soulless space. The apartment is empty, cleared out ready for the next occupant. The walls have been freshly painted in an institutional cream with a reek of solvents. There's no clue that Salvador was ever here at all. Chiara puts the key down on the table, closes the door behind her, and leaves.

She returns to the river. Salvador wasn't in his apartment, but that afternoon, as Chiara walks the towpath, she senses his presence. For the first time in all these weeks, she can feel him walking beside her. She can hear his terrible jokes, recall his dark, floppy hair and beard, breathe in his clean-cotton scent. She imagines his hand, firm and warm in hers. She remembers his smile. Her eyes seem to be leaking, and she brushes at them with the back of her hand, but before long her whole face is wet. She lets the tears come.

She walks on, mile after mile, ignoring the glances of passers-by and the gradual fading of the light. By the time she reaches the boat, her t-shirt is damp and her face swollen, and still she weeps. Her sobs subside and begin again, coming in waves, like birth surges. She crawls under Liz's quilt and gives herself up to the process. Everything aches and breaks and howls, but it has to be gone through.

NEXT MORNING, Chiara wakes to the sound of high-pitched squeaks outside the porthole window. Not rats again? She rubs the mucus from the corners of her eyes; her face is stiff with dried tears and snot. Pulling back the curtain, she peers out to see a tiny, triangular face looking in at her. Not a rat after all, but a pink-nosed, furry-eared kitten.

She gasps, and the little creature scurries out of view. Moments later, Chiara stands outside in the dawn light, watching in wonder as not one, but two miniature kittens chase one another around the deck and across the roof of the boat. One is black with a white throat and paws; the other is ginger.

'Che bello!' she exclaims. How lovely! The black-and-white one scampers to hide under the seat, but the ginger kitten stands his ground, staring at Chiara with hungry blue eyes. So she goes to the kitchen and opens a tin of evaporated milk. Gaskin used to love it. She pours some into a saucer and carries it onto the deck. The kittens lap it up in no time, demanding more with fierce little mews.

When he can drink no more, the bold ginger kitten leads

his sister inside. Together they explore the old narrowboat from prow to stern before curling up in a furry heap in front of the stove. I'm going to have to find names for them, Chiara realises. After a little thought, she calls them Vitus and Apollonia, or Loni for short.

81

AMANI ELIZABETH

Dearest Chiara,

The locket and the photograph arrived yesterday. Thank you so much. How wonderful that you managed to find such a treasure tucked inside one of Liz's old books!

Amani really does look like poor little Emily - the same eyes and the shape of her chin. I can see why Liz was so struck by the resemblance.

I have put the picture of Liz and her twins on the wall above Amani's cot, and I will keep the locket to give her when she is older. I want her to know where she came from and how much her Grandmama loved her.

She has pictures of Martin too. He was not a perfect husband or father, but I tell myself he tried his best. Bitterness serves no purpose; God is forgiving and merciful, so we should also try to forgive.

Amani is crawling now, and pulling herself up to stand on the furniture. She's very cheeky and loves all her food. Aunt Nasreem's ghormeh sabzi - that's a Persian herb stew - is one of her favourites, though she makes such a mess eating it. Her cousins visit often and make a fuss of her. I'm know I'm biased, but she really is the sweetest little thing, and clever too. She can already say 'Mamma' and 'Gan-pappi,' which is what she calls Baba.

My Baba is receiving care from the hospice, but he's still at home with us. The nurses are wonderful - so kind and patient - they remind me of you, Chiara. It has been a most precious gift to spend this time with my dear Baba. He is fading now, but he still lights up every time he sees Amani. He calls her his little moon, and the crowning of his old age. Amani adores him and loves to sit in his lap - they are the best of friends.

The dress Jajja sent fits perfectly - please thank her for me! Amani looked like a little angel in it, until she got chocolate all over her face. I hope you like the pictures.

My job at the nursery school is going well. It's taken a while to get used to being around children all day, but I'm starting to enjoy it. Aunt Nasreem looks after Amani while I'm at work. She'll be seventy-nine next year, but she still seems to have boundless energy.

I do miss London sometimes, and Martin too, but not so much as I feared. Becoming a mother has changed me. I feel like a different person - less afraid, less worried about what others think. Nasreem and I clash at times - two women sharing a home has its challenges - and I'm not the perfect little Muslim girl - far from it! I still have plenty of questions, but I know that God is good, and he cares for us.

I'm so glad you bumped into Jenny again, and great to hear that she's found another job. If she ever wanted to move to Scotland - it's difficult, I know, but there are ways - we would give her a warm welcome here.

What great pictures of Louis! He looks as if he enjoys life on the river. Thank you for taking him in when Daniel's wife said they didn't have space for a dog. Give him a kiss from me.

Blessings on you, dear Chiara. Give our love to Devorah and Naomi, Daniel and all their family. Without all your help we could never have made it home.

Peace be upon you,

Rava and Amani Elizabeth

82

NONNA'S ARK

'Beautiful. You're nearly there. In a moment I'm going to tell you to pant, to breathe your baby's head out.'

Chiara has a warm compress on the mother's perineum. She watches intently, waiting for the next contraction.

'I can't, I can't -.'

'Yes, you can. You've nearly done it. Can you pass me a towel please, Zoe? Perfect. Okay, here comes the next surge.'

The mother squats on Liz's old birthing stool. Her bare feet are planted on the towels carpeting the boards of the ancient narrowboat. She opens her mouth wide and shouts her birthing cry:

'Oohhh!'

'Yes. Now pant, yes that's right, let the head slide out.' In a gush of waters, Chiara catches the purple, wet infant, slippery with vernix. It's a girl, sweet and plump, her skin velvety like apricots. Chiara passes her into her mother's arms. The woman sobs with joy and relief.

'I did it,' she cries. 'I did it myself. Hello, little one.'

This moment never loses its wonder. There's plenty more to do: a placenta to be birthed, a safe home to be found for another unregistered infant, but every birth reminds Chiara why she still does this.

ONCE THE NEW mother and her baby are tucked up together in the big bed, Chiara takes her cup of tea out onto the deck while Zoe tidies up inside. She still prefers her tea light and herbal - the thought of those brick-red brews Liz used to drink makes her pull a face - but the habit of drinking tea after a birth has stuck.

The ripples on the river sparkle in the sunshine, and the air smells of water and green things. Swallows dip and weave over-head in their endless quest for flies. Long grass edges the towpath, mingling with thistles and ox-eye daisies. Chiara spots a clump of orange calendula and makes a mental note to gather some later to make salve. It's her favourite soothing balm - you can never have too much. She should pick nettles too, and elderberries to make syrup. Late summer is a busy time.

But herb gathering will have to wait, because two of Chiara's favourite people are heading this way. Louis barks excitedly as he sees them coming. He's become an affectionate friend and a useful guard dog. Chiara worried at first that he might chase the kittens - now rapidly growing into cats - but in fact he's much more nervous of them than they are of him.

Jajja steers a battered pushchair along the path. Her glasses still make Chiara think of a benign old insect - a friendly grasshopper, perhaps? She's as thin as ever, but she must be made of steel because her energy is unstoppable.

From inside the pushchair, Dembe waves a chubby hand to greet her Auntie Chia. She kicks her feet and strains at the straps, wanting to climb out and walk herself. They celebrated Dembe's first birthday back in April with a cake baked in Liz's wood-burning stove.

A pair of mallards glides up to the water's edge with a family of seven fluffy ducklings in tow.

'Quack-quack,' calls Dembe, pointing with her plump little finger. 'Feed quack-quack.'

Chiara fills Liz's old *'Midwife at your Cervix'* mug with oats to feed the ducks. Good thing Dembe can't read yet, she thinks, although, with her mother as a midwife-in-training, Dembe is likely to grow up with a knowledge of the ways of birth far beyond her years.

'Zoe,' she calls, hoisting Dembe up onto the deck and reaching out a hand to steady Jajja as she climbs aboard, 'Jajja and Dembe are here.'

'Yay. What's polyhydrammy something?' Zoe emerges from under the low door with her nose in a midwifery textbook. For a girl who never attended secondary school, she's showing an impressive interest in Liz's library.

'I ain't stupid, you know,' she insists. 'Just never had much of a chance.'

Chiara doesn't need reminding. She wouldn't be able to do what she does without Zoe's determined, often outspoken assistance. Zoe is strong and scarcely seems to need sleep. She can stay up all night helping with a birth, then go home to spend the day playing with Dembe and helping Jajja with laundry. She still works a few cleaning shifts now and then, although not at the Genesis Centre.

Chiara has invited her and Jajja and Dembe to come and live on the narrowboat.

'I know space is tight, but we could make it work. It's cooler than that container; there's always a bit of a breeze on the river.' But Jajja won't leave her sewing machine, or her life-sized

Madonna statue, or the families at the camp who depend on her kindness.

'I'll be a frequent visitor,' she said, and that's working out fine.

Dembe flings handfuls of oats onto the water. Her hair is a mass of tumbling curls, her eyes are tawny gold. She's wearing colourful patchwork dungarees, hand-stitched by Jajja. She has Zoe's singleness of purpose and Jajja's sweet nature.

'Auntie Chia help!' Dembe commands, pointing to the ducks, who have been joined by a small and expectant flotilla of swans.

Chiara obeys. Dembe giggles as the birds gobble up their food.

'Greedy quack-quacks.'

When the ducks have been fed, and Dembe is snuggling under Zoe's t-shirt for a quick breastfeed, Chiara fetches her antenatal bag.

'Are you okay to stay here this afternoon?' she asks Zoe. 'Keep an eye on this mum and baby, and help her with the feeding if she needs it. Call me if you need anything. I've got clinic in Tottenham, and while I'm there I'll see about a safe house.'

Chiara jumps down onto the riverbank. She turns to look at the old boat with her leaf-green paint and the bright flowers all along the sides. Feathery carrot-tops sprout from the roof-boxes, and the tomatoes are ripening from green to scarlet. At the prow, the new name stands out in bold, lettering: *'Nonna's Ark.'*

THE HALL behind Our Lady and St Joseph's church is as damp and as clean as ever. Peggy Newton, Maureen, and their fellowhelpers are busy unfolding tables and making up food parcels when Chiara arrives. Five or six young mothers are already waiting to be seen, some of them with toddlers in tow, as well as the usual assortment of sick and elderly people.

'How are you, my dear?' Maureen asks. 'Custard cream?' She holds out the plate of biscuits. 'Go on - take two - it's going to be a long one today.'

Chiara thanks her and asks after Father John, the parish priest, who was taken in for questioning last week. The authorities wanted to know what activities go on in his church hall. He was released without charge after roundly insisting that nothing illegal happens parish premises, but the poor man was badly shaken. He's promised to protect Chiara, and she believes him, but this will have to be her last clinic at Our Lady and St Joseph's for now. Fortunately, the Jewish community in Stoke Newington have offered the use of one of their schools.

The landscape of birth is dangerous and constantly changing. Chiara is breaking several laws every time she cares for a pregnant woman. She hasn't been arrested yet, but a reliable contact today could be a betrayer tomorrow. The next mother she cares for might be a Government spy. But for now, Chiara gets on with her work. There is always so much to do.

She still has nightmares sometimes about everything that happened last year. But the dreams come less often these days, and she hopes they will fade until they are manageable fragments of memory, like broken shells on a beach.

'Is my baby all right?'

Chiara helps the first mother-to-be up onto the couch. Her warm hands palpate the woman's abdomen, locating the rounded bottom, the spine, the firm little head. She places Liz's pinard on exactly the right spot, lowers her ear, and tunes into the rapid, regular patter. The sound of new life. She squeezes the mother's hand.

'Your baby sounds wonderful,' she tells her. 'Thank you for letting me listen.'

IT's a long walk back to the mooring. Chiara's tired after last night's birth and the afternoon clinic, but she takes a detour through Abney Park cemetery with its tall trees and ivy-covered tombstones. Some of the paths are completely overgrown with brambles, but Chiara knows her way through the forest of green stone angels.

She climbs the crumbling steps of a war memorial and bends to pass under low branches to reach the ruined chapel at the centre. Here, where the trees part to let sunlight in, wild flowers grow in profusion. She gathers white campion and purple michaelmas daisies, leaving plenty to seed themselves for next year. Then it's back through the green tunnels to the eastern gates and the river.

The sun is low by the time she reaches the towpath. Boats line the banks, two or three deep, but she finds a gap under the trailing branches of a willow tree. Liz's body was never recovered, or at least never identified. Chiara thinks perhaps it's better this way. She likes to imagine Liz was swept all the way to the Thames and far out to sea. Unlikely perhaps, but who knows? Liz was always a free spirit.

'Amani's doing brilliantly.' Chiara speaks to the smooth, dark surface of the river. 'You must be very proud of her. She's learning to talk and walk, and she's healthy, strong, and beautiful. Rava's a wonderful mother, with a big family to support her.

And guess what? I heard from Jamila last week. She's been in hiding for ages, somewhere in Kent, but she said she wants to practice again, now things have eased up a bit. She asked if she could come over and borrow some of your books, and we're going to help each other when we can. So I'm not the last midwife, not yet anyway. We're still going - we'll never give up. Warriors, like you said, Liz. I think of you every day. Sleep well, my love!'

Chiara casts her bundle of flowers onto the river. The stems soon separate and drift away, floating downstream into the soft dazzle of evening light on the water.

EPILOGUE
WE NEED YOU!

New Opportunities in Peaceful Rest

Here at Eternal Rest Solutions Limited we're excited to be part of the Government's rollout of enhanced Euthanasia services across London and South-East England. Our Essex, Kent and Hertfordshire teams are recruiting at all levels NOW!

Join our caring and professional team as a Nurse specialising in Euthanasia Services. We are dedicated to providing dignified and humane care to individuals making the profoundly personal choice of euthanasia.

Key Responsibilities:

• Provide empathetic and respectful care to patients throughout the euthanasia process.

• Conduct thorough assessments to understand each patient's unique situation and needs.

• Collaborate with healthcare professionals to ensure a supportive and safe environment.

• Assist in educating patients and families about the euthanasia options available.

Qualifications:

• Valid nursing license with relevant certifications.

    • Exceptional communication skills and emotional strength.

    • A drive to excel and a commitment to continuous professional development.

    • A strong work ethic and the ability to thrive in a fast-paced environment.

    • An openness to new knowledge and techniques in the ever-evolving field of assisted death.

Why Join Us?

• Be part of a forward-thinking team that prioritises compassionate care.

    • Engage in ongoing professional development and training.

    • Work in a supportive atmosphere that values your contributions and insights.

    • Excellent remuneration and benefits package, including housing and healthcare credits.

    • If you are passionate about helping to implement cutting-edge care that makes a difference, we encourage you to apply!

How to Apply

If you are ready to take the next step in your career and join our prestigious team, we want to hear from you. Please send your CV and cover letter to recruitment@eternalrestsolutions.com

Join Eternal Rest Solutions Ltd and be a part of a team that is setting new standards in ending human lives. We look forward to welcoming you aboard!

ACKNOWLEDGMENTS

Writing 'The Last Midwife' has been a four-year journey. It would not have been possible without all the wonderful people who have encouraged and supported me along the way.

I want to thank my beloved husband, Adrian, and all my family members who have read parts of the book, suggested plot ideas, and generally cheered me on.

My friends have been amazing, and special thanks go to Susie, who was the first person to tell me I really must write this book.

My writing mentors include Helen Corner-Brown and Kathryn Price, the incredibly generous Sophie Hannah and her Dream Author programme, Sarah de Nordwall, and all my brilliant writing group friends who have provided invaluable feedback.

Huge thanks go to my amazing beta readers. Helga, Janita, Bonnie, Jacky, and others. I'm specially grateful to Natty, Maria, and Chava who provided invaluable insights into Sicilian, Islamic, and Jewish cultures, as well as checking the midwifery content.

Thank you all!

Karen

ABOUT THE AUTHOR

Karen Lawrence is a mother and grandmother, living in Billericay, Essex, UK. She has seven grown-up children and two grandchildren (so far!).

Karen previously trained and worked as a midwife in the NHS. After leaving this role she became a health visitor, pregnancy yoga teacher and antenatal instructor. She remains passionate about empowering women to have life-enhancing birth experiences.

Karen started writing during the Covid pandemic and hasn't stopped! Before publishing The Last Midwife, she wrote a book about finding calm, a memoir about having a child with Down syndrome, and an account of a walking pilgrimage. She is currently working on two new novels, as well as a book of poetry.

When she isn't writing, Karen loves walking, swimming in the sea, and relaxing at the family caravan in Suffolk. Karen has three degrees in English Literature, including a PhD on Religious Faith in the Victorian Novel.

Karen is a Catholic Christian, on a lifelong quest to discover beauty, truth and goodness. She is fascinated by medieval art, stories of faith, and ancient pilgrimage routes. She hopes one day to complete the Camino de Santiago from St Jean Pied de Port to Santiago de Compostela.

Karen's youngest daughter has Down Syndrome, and Karen is a keen advocate for people with disabilities and their families and carers. She has pledged to include at least one character with Down syndrome in every one of her novels.

You can visit Karen's website at:
https://karenlawrenceauthor.com/

instagram.com/karenlawrenceauthor
facebook.com/Karenlawrencewrites
tiktok.com/@karenlawrenceauthor

ALSO BY KAREN LAWRENCE

LETTING THE LIGHT IN:
HOW A CHILD WITH DOWN
SYNDROME CHANGED MY LIFE

How does it feel to discover that there is something wrong with your baby?

Karen thought she had the perfect family. But when her seventh child, Martha, was born with Down Syndrome, Karen's world was shaken to its core.

This memoir tells the story of Martha's early months and years. Karen shares her tears, her struggles, and her joy as she slowly came to accept the many unexpected gifts that Martha brought.

Karen's faith, her family, and her very sense of identity were all shaken by the arrival of her baby with Down Syndrome. Martha needed life-saving heart surgery in her first year. Karen questioned everything she had previously taken for granted. The journey was not easy. But it was life-changing.

Letting the Light In is available as a paperback and a Kindle ebook from Amazon. Audiobook coming soon.

Purchase your copy here

WALKING TO WALSINGHAM: MY PILGRIMAGE TO ENGLAND'S NAZARETH

Walsingham is a special place. A sleepy English village buried deep in the north Norfolk countryside, Walsingham hums with a spiritual resonance so gentle you might mistake it for the baa of the sheep in the fields or the burble of the little river. According to tradition, the Virgin Mary appeared here in the eleventh century. Walsingham became known as *'England's Nazareth'* - a place for miracles and answered prayers. Pilgrims have been coming here for centuries, but few people arrive on foot nowadays.

Karen had vaguely considered walking to Walsingham, but it seemed like an impossible dream. Then one day she saw a guidebook for a new *'Walsingham Camino'*. A plan began to form.

Over more than a year, Karen spent her free weekends walking from London to Walsingham. She followed rivers and ancient trails, traversing forests and exploring historic towns and villages. On the way she explored medieval churches, ruined abbeys and the largest turf labyrinth in the world.

This book is Karen's pilgrimage story. Join her as she slogs through mud, marvels at Anglo-Saxon art, and gets lost in a military training zone. Share her journey of discovery, encountering mad March hares, East Anglian saints, and bats in belfries. Learn about flint-knappers, Roman burial mounds, and Walsingham's two modern-day shrines. Discover the blessings of a slow walk through nature, history and faith.

Walking to Walsingham is available as a paperback and a Kindle ebook from Amazon:

FINDING YOUR CALM SPACE: THIRTY-ONE WAYS TO FIND CALM IN A CRAZY WORLD

Life is stressful. Especially these days. Mental health statistics are soaring. Inflammatory disease is on the increase. Everyone needs calm in a crazy world.

This book offers thirty-one simple ways to find calm for wellbeing, health, and happiness. It is designed to be read over one month, discovering a new calming practice each day. Most of the practices can be done in just ten minutes. Each one is explained in easy steps.

Karen Lawrence shares anecdotes from her wide experience of yoga teaching, reflexology, parenting, and midwifery as she introduces each calming practice. It's time to find your calm space.

Finding Your Calm Space is available as a paperback and a Kindle ebook from Amazon:

I USED TO BE A MIDWIFE: BIRTH STORIES AND POEMS

This little book is a collection of short stories and poems inspired by my experiences as a student midwife and a midwife.

Becoming a midwife was one of the most thrilling and challenging adventures I have ever undertaken. It took me to places few people are privileged to enter. I shared the intimacy of home births, learned the language of the labour ward, and even visited a remarkable birthing clinic in the Philippines.

Midwives undertake the awesome responsibility of welcoming numerous new lives into the world, answering the call to be 'with women' in some of their most intense and memorable moments.

I Used To Be A Midwife is available as a FREE download from my website:

https://karenlawrenceauthor.com/